PRAISE FOR
THE CAPE DOCTOR

"Historical fiction at its best…The story is a good one, but it is the exquisite writing and the portrayal of women in the first half of the nineteenth century that make *The Cape Doctor* such an intriguing book…In real life, Barry made significant contributions to medicine. *The Cape Doctor* is a literary contribution that will enthrall readers with clever writing and a sympathetic story."   —Sandra Dallas, *Denver Post*

"Though it's a compelling story of one particular transformation, this wise, emotionally resonant novel makes an intelligent, heartfelt plea for compassion as it sifts through the wrongheaded assumptions we make about identity…What's most striking about the novel is Levy's fearless depiction of Margaret/Jonathan, her authentic rendering of this voice, her fleshing out of a little known historical character full of complications."   —Connie Ogle, *Minneapolis Star Tribune*

"*The Cape Doctor* is a rare achievement: equal parts brains and heart, a page-turner and a deeply moving exploration of precisely what it means to be human. E. J. Levy breaks open what we think we know about gender, identity, and love and shines a light on the devastating limits of each. I can't stop thinking about this gorgeous, thoughtful, heartbreaking book."

—Lauren Fox, author of *Send for Me*

"How should Barry be considered? Trans? Male? Female? Levy opts for the last, adopting that perspective so her narrator can explore—sometimes painfully, sometimes wittily, always persuasively—the differences between a woman's experience of Georgian and Victorian society and the masculine freedom to be found when those social constrictions are eased."

—Alida Becker, *New York Times Book Review* (Editors' Choice)

"The Cape Doctor does what the best novels do. It invites us to put aside our own lives for a time in order to live someone else's. And it repays the moral imagination that requires with something like wisdom."

—Richard Russo, author of *Chances Are...*

"Levy has done an absolutely superb job of novelizing Barry's life while her realization of him as a character is flawless. He is brilliant, impetuous, unafraid (perhaps foolishly) of making enemies in a good cause, an ardent supporter of women's rights, and an equally ardent enemy of slavery…An unforgettable work of art." —*Booklist* (starred review)

"The Cape Doctor is one of those rare wonders of historical fiction: a novel that is so utterly transporting, so fully steeped in its time and place I kept looking up from the page and wondering where I was. And how did E. J. Levy do it? Was she there? The story of its hero, Dr. Perry, an Irish woman practicing medicine undercover as a man in nineteenth-century South Africa raises powerful contemporary questions about the nature of border crossings—of gender, of class, and ultimately of love." —Sarah Blake, author of *The Postmistress*

Also by E. J. Levy

Love, in Theory

THE
CAPE
DOCTOR

A Novel

E. J. Levy

BACK BAY BOOKS
LITTLE, BROWN AND COMPANY
NEW YORK   BOSTON   LONDON

Copyright © 2021 by E. J. Levy
Reading group guide copyright © 2022 by E. J. Levy and Little, Brown and Company

Hachette Book Group supports the right to free expression and the value of copyright. The purpose of copyright is to encourage writers and artists to produce the creative works that enrich our culture.

The scanning, uploading, and distribution of this book without permission is a theft of the author's intellectual property. If you would like permission to use material from the book (other than for review purposes), please contact permissions@hbgusa.com. Thank you for your support of the author's rights.

Back Bay Books / Little, Brown and Company
Hachette Book Group
1290 Avenue of the Americas, New York, NY 10104
littlebrown.com

Originally published in hardcover by Little, Brown and Company, June 2021
First Back Bay paperback edition, August 2022

Back Bay Books is an imprint of Little, Brown and Company, a division of Hachette Book Group, Inc. The Back Bay Books name and logo are trademarks of Hachette Book Group, Inc.

The publisher is not responsible for websites (or their content) that are not owned by the publisher.

The Hachette Speakers Bureau provides a wide range of authors for speaking events. To find out more, go to hachettespeakersbureau.com or call (866) 376-6591.

ISBN 9780316536585 (hc) / 9780316536592 (pb)
Library of Congress Control Number 2020931934

Printing 1, 2022

LSC-C

Printed in the United States of America

*For Margaret Anne Bulkley and James
Miranda Barry, by any name,
and for Leslee Becker (1945–2022)*

Ex Africa semper aliquid novi.
— Pliny the Elder, *Naturalis Historia*, VIII/42

If I were to write the story of my life, I would shock the world.
— Caterina Sforza

How long is this posthumous life of mine to last?
— John Keats

What follows is a work of imagination. *The Cape Doctor* is inspired by the life of Dr. James Miranda Barry (born Margaret Anne Bulkley circa 1795 in Cork, Ireland), one of the most eminent physicians of the nineteenth century. Dr. Barry's life has long inspired novelists and biographers, to whose efforts this book owes a debt (most especially the exhaustive 2016 biography, *Dr. James Barry: A Woman Ahead of Her Time*). I have changed the names of key figures for the purposes of fiction.

I have striven to accurately reflect the facts of Margaret Bulkley's and Dr. Barry's extraordinary life. Though they lived over 150 years ago, we know this: Margaret disguised herself as James Barry in 1809 to attend Edinburgh University, in order to pursue a medical education unavailable to women at the time. Having excelled in his studies, James Barry entered the military as an army surgeon, serving in Cape Town, Mauritius, and Jamaica, eventually rising to the rank of Inspector General. A dandy, a duelist, a flirt, Dr. Barry had a close bond with Lord Somerset—the powerful, charming, controversial, aristocratic Governor of the Cape Colony—which resulted in a sodomy scandal that rattled both the Cape Colony and London society. We know that Barry was the first to successfully perform a caesarian in Africa. And we know that the "layer out," who tended Barry after his death, reported that the doctor was "a perfect female," whose body showed evidence of having carried a child.

Barry did not leave a will, but he had left instructions (decades earlier when gravely ill) not to be undressed after death, without saying why. Biographers have speculated variously but inconclusively about this choice, but almost nothing remains of the intimate thoughts of Margaret or James. We are left to imagine.

THE CAPE DOCTOR

CHAPTER ONE

FORTUNATE SON

She died, so I might live. Margaret. I owe her my life. Not a day goes by when I don't think of it. Of her. As not a day goes by when I don't think of him.

She died, so I might live, but isn't that the lot of women? To sacrifice, as our Lord was said to have done. Few speak of Mary's sacrifice, of course; that, we are to assume, was unexceptional. To martyr oneself for others is the expected lot of mothers and daughters. It's rarer in sons, except in war. So naturally, given the choice, I chose to be a son. Given the choice, who would not?

There are so many things we do not know until it is too late. Among them, that it is never too late. The American ambassador Franklin said it best: "I want to live so I might see how it turns out." We do. I can see that from where I am now—wherever that is, in this almost afterlife of imagination or fact (who can say for sure which it is?)—I can see that my life will be a scandal, and an inspiration. Charles Dickens will write of me, and Twain, even Havelock Ellis; I will be a riddle that generations will try to answer. A riddle I am trying to answer now.

When I was a boy, I was told that when I began a story,

to begin at the beginning and continue to the end, so I shall. The question, of course, is where it all began. Where does any story start? Where did mine? The ending, alas, is always all too clear.

But to understand my beginning, you must understand her end, Margaret's.

Although it has been a very long time since I saw her—more than a lifetime, or several—I recall her vividly; though now she is more like an echo, an idea I once had, a dream. Yet for years when I looked in the mirror I saw her, looking back with my blue eyes. And somewhere in a parish church in Cork, there is a baptism recorded for the second child of Mary Ann and Jeremiah Brackley, who was christened one early April, our parents' eldest daughter, Margaret Brackley, an ungainly name for an unpromising start.

No one who had ever seen Margaret Brackley in her infancy would have supposed her born to be a heroine (or so Jane Austen might have written of her, had she been informed of Margaret's entrance into the world in 1795 or so). Her situation in life, her mother and father, her own person and disposition were all equally against her. Her father was a prosperous greengrocer in Cork, without being neglected, or poor, and a very respectable man, though his name was Jeremiah—and he had never been handsome. His eldest daughter, Margaret, had a thin awkward figure, sallow skin, unruly red-blond hair, and diminutive features, and not less unpropitious for heroism seemed her mind. She greatly preferred dogs to dolls; she had no taste for needlepoint or books, drawing or dances. There was nothing in the appearance of Margaret, in short, that would have suggested her as a likely heroine of this or any story. And she had what was considered to be in the late-18th century, as in too many centuries before and since, that most appalling defect at birth: she was born a girl.

My uncle, Jonathan Perry RA, was already a famous painter in London when I was born. (He went by Perry now, a name close to my mother's family name, but English; the name change necessary to pass among the powerful, to pose as one of them.) From our comfortable provincial parlor in Cork, my uncle's life seemed like a fairy tale, a myth or legend as remote as King Arthur and his knights. I did not know who Sir Joshua Reynolds was, or Edmund Burke, my uncle's friends, but I knew enough to be impressed by their names, to know these were important men from the way my mother spoke of them, as if they were our rich relations. When I first was told that my uncle was a member of the Royal Academy, I mistakenly thought this meant that he was royalty and that I might grow up to be a prince (although in those days I'd have hoped to be a princess).

Likely my uncle would have remained a mythological figure in my childhood bestiary—no more real to me than a satyr or the sphinx—had it not been for my brother's extravagant failure, which necessitated our journey to London to seek his help. It would have been more fitting for our father to make the trip to petition assistance from my eminent uncle on our behalf, but besieged by creditors, he could not leave the country without tempting the gaoler and debtors' prison. And though they'd long ago fallen out of touch, brother and sister had once been close, so my mother took up her pen and wrote to him. Or rather, since her hands shook at the thought of writing to ask for his help, I did, though I was only nine.

My uncle seemed to me in those days close kin to Ovid's

conjuring on those Sunday afternoons when my father sat with us at his desk, the windows thrown open to the walled garden outside, the lazy buzz of bees in the apple blossoms, the air musky with lilac, as we sat over his old Latin grammar and Roman texts, his idea of an antidote to my mother's Catholic Mass. The lessons were meant more for my older brother's benefit than mine, but my brother Tom had no head for books; he was given to gazing out the window and tossing twigs at rabbits in the underbrush, so we were all amazed when he announced his intention to pursue law as an apprentice in Dublin.

My parents were delighted—that a grocer's son might rise to become a solicitor or barrister, a man of property and name. When my brother's head was quickly turned from his studies by a young lady of good family—Miss Ward—my parents did not despair; they settled the better portion of their estate on him, so he might buy a farm and set up a home befitting the good marriage he had made. But my brother was unaccustomed to hard work. His considerable intelligence had been blunted by a lack of meaningful application, which bred in him arrogance and petty attachment to rank; he seemed to feel entitled and undeserving both, which made him cruel. When his affairs on the farm failed to prosper, he was quick to borrow against his land and fell quickly into debt. Soon the farm had liens against it and debt collectors were at his doors and ours, seeking to collect the £700 we did not have, and so, in that early spring of 1804, because of my unsuccessful sibling, I made the acquaintance of my successful uncle, whose help, in desperation, my mother sought.

I never knew exactly why they had fallen out of touch—my mother and her once-favorite brother, whom she had watched nightly as he sat up late to draw by candlelight, and who had read to her when they were children; I know only that they had once been very close and then for nearly 40 years they did not speak. He went off to Dublin, then to Paris, Rome, and London, where he made the acquaintance of great men—the philosopher Edmund Burke and the famous Dr. Johnson—and became one himself.

I suspected my father came between them; he considered the connection beneath my mother's station, which—like our own—he disastrously imagined superior to what it was; he considered my uncle an untoward influence, being both a painter *and* a radical. (Of the two, he considered the former far the worse.) My father considered it unseemly to have an artist in the family line, despite my uncle's renown; he looked on him as one might an opium addict or a madman, a failing for which he could not quite fault my mother but from which he felt it best to separate her.

My father was nearly forty when my parents met, a plump and grasping man, whiskered and well upholstered, though my mother described him as robust and (if not precisely hand-some) appealingly ambitious. I could see in my brother the young man my father must once have been—lively with an easy manner and a discerning eye, quick to see the value of a thing. My father had only to meet a horse to take its weight and worth; the same was true of land and ladies. In marry-ing my mother, an educated and attractive young woman of property, he had done well. He would see to it that his son did still better.

And although she never said it, I believe my mother imag-ined that in marrying my father, she was saving his Protestant soul. My mother was possessed of a keen intelligence, well tempered by curiosity and skepticism, a stalwart and steady woman for whom religion was her sole significant vice: she was strongheaded and clear-eyed save when it came to the church. She committed that singular sin of the devout: she flattered herself that she was in league with salvation. Her devotion to the church was, like her brother's love of painting, an aesthetic matter: as with the beauty of a good cross-stich or a well-turned hem, she liked to see a thing well done, irrespective of its end or aim. But her faith was tinctured too by melancholy, a genteel weakness for a lost cause.

I sometimes thought that if Catholics had ruled Ireland when she had come of age, instead of being besieged, she'd have dismissed the lot as so much superstition; it was precisely because Catholics were wronged that she was loyal; she was a woman who naturally gravitated to the losing side of any fight. Which perhaps explained her attraction to my father. Still, twenty years her senior, he must have seemed a man among boys. Watching him set out the fruits and vegetables in the wooden crates beneath the shop's awning, in barrels and in baskets, she had shivered in the sunlight to see his large bare hands smoothing dirt from the delicate ankle of a turnip, his thumb gently brushing the firm ripe skin of an apple.

She told me all this and more as we sailed to London together in that almost-summer of early June 1804—part bedtime story, part reminiscence, trying perhaps to instill in me an understanding of my father and something of the tenderness she'd felt for him then. Perhaps trying to revive such sentiments in herself.

My uncle had not answered our first letter, which we'd sent off two months earlier in April; we could not know if he had been in receipt of it, given that the address we had was of uncertain accuracy. So in June, at my father's behest, we'd set out for London to secure the assistance of my mother's famous brother. It had been my father's idea to contact my uncle and seek his help, but by the time we sailed for England, my mother had ideas of her own.

London—when we stepped onto the docks south of London Bridge that June—was a roar, a cacophonous jumble. Masts and boats and vessels of all sorts could be seen all along the broad green river, which reeked of sewage, dead fish, and rot. My mother pressed a kerchief to her nose against the stench, but it was the sound that buffeted my senses; a wall of sound that seemed a physical thing, like the dark green waves that broke at Ballycotton. Cart and carriage wheels and horses' hooves clacked over the cobbles; one could hear the *click* of women's pattens on the sidewalks, the cries of peddlers selling onions and rabbits, eggs and eels, dolls and books and rat poison, china; there were dogs barking and pennywhistles, and the mournful melodies of hurdy-gurdies.

As we rode away from the docks in a hired hackney coach, the stench of horseshit overtook that of the river and lent the crowded city the pleasant feel of a country stable, even as the streets swarmed with more people than I'd seen in all of Cork. In those days, London was a city of children; small persons of indeterminate sex and age darted in front of carts, dodging wheels, visible along the riverbanks like bugs working a dung pile—*mud larks*, I'd later learn—scavenging cloth and metal, a reminder of what might lie ahead for my sister and me if we were unsuccessful in our errand.

We had hardly settled into our lodgings when my mother sent me out again; she thought it best to get me to my uncle's home in Little Castle Street directly and unannounced, presumably so that my uncle could not evade the meeting. He was famously reclusive and infamously volatile. (She could not go herself, she said; if he recognized her, he might refuse to see us, but I suspected she was ashamed to beg. She was beautiful, clever, still proud then.)

Before we'd departed Cork, my mother had taken the precaution of having calling cards printed up and now she presented me with one, writing my name under hers in careful script, so I might present it to the servant at the door, should I find my uncle out, thus impressing upon him that we were gentle people familiar with morning calls and at-homes, that we were suitable company for society. It was a beautiful thing—the calling card, a heavy ivory paper with my mother's name impressed into it; I ran my thumb over it, held it to my nose. I wondered if this was where my mother's ring had gone. A family ring she'd worn on her forefinger. For bits of paper. Another loss among many. She cautioned me to look to my uncle's mantel for similar cards and to memorize the names. Armed only with necessity, a calling card, and blood kinship, which even at the age of nine I recognized as depreciating currency, I set out for Little Castle Street to meet my famous uncle.

Number 36 Little Castle Street appeared to be uninhabited when I arrived. The glass of the lower windows was broken, the shutters closed, and the door and walls spattered with mud. When I first turned down the street, a group of boys were collected outside the house; they shouted, pointing to the upper windows, until they were dispersed by a parish officer. When I enquired the cause of their outrage, I was told the house was occupied by an old wizard or a Jew (this point seemed unsettled), who lived there in "unholy solitude," the better to dedicate himself to unrighteous mysteries. Perhaps it was the wrong house; I hoped it was.

As I approached the door, I saw the yard itself was strewn with the skeletons of small animals, a dog's skull, marrowbones, wastepaper, fragments of boys' hoops and other playthings, and with various other missiles, which had been hurled against the premises. A dead cat lay upon the projecting stone of the parlor window, reeking a sickening sweet.

I hesitated on the doorstep before tapping on the door. It was mud spattered, with a feather plastered there, perhaps with dung. No one answered, so I rapped harder. I was startled when it opened, like a crypt from a gothic novel by Walpole or a maw.

"Is Mr. Perry expecting you, Miss?" The girl who answered the door was hardly older than I, but her skin was thin and loose, which lent her a fragile, anxious aspect, as if she were lacking more than food.

"I am his niece," I said, reciting what my mother had taught me to say.

She didn't offer to take a card. "I'll tell him you been round."

"Do you know where I might find him?" I set my gloved palm against the door, preventing its closing.

"He's gone out."

"The matter is one of considerable urgency."

The girl squinted at the street, and then at me. "You're his relation, you say?"

I nodded.

She seemed uncertain whether to let me in but disinclined

to argue, acquiescing to bullying, even a child's, as those beaten down will do. Or perhaps she took pity on me. She pulled back the door to let me by.

"Can't see the harm in your waiting in the parlor. You can wait, if it suits you."

"I will wait."

And so I did. I was delighted by his rooms, though chill and dim, smelling of dust and turpentine, and not as fine or comfortable as ours in Cork had once been, before father had sold the better things at auction; my uncle's parlor was filled with surprising objects—paintings were everywhere leaned in stacks and hung to the ceiling, dimly visible, and curiosities that invited touch: an animal's skull, a plaster cast of a horse head and of a human arm and leg, canvases on which he had begun to sketch in charcoal. The figures in his paintings had a twisting, tortured look, the way I had imagined the tormented in hell when my mother took us to church.

I waited perhaps a quarter hour, perhaps an hour or two; I must have dozed after the long travel, for I did not hear the charwoman depart and woke to a storm of sound.

He blew in like a northern gale, his voice booming from the foyer, resonant in the parlor, where I sat waiting.

"Damn it all to hell. Where is that catastrophe of a girl? *Sibyl!* Where in Christ's name has she put my things? Every time she cleans, she *hides* my things. Last week it took me two days to find a sketch I was on. Two *days.*"

I heard another voice, a rhythm I did not recognize, the words rounded and warm, like the farmers who spoke the old tongue in the villages outside Cork, though this sounded more like a sort of French, like the baker's wife, who'd come from Calais. "—true revolution is born not of a change in government but in the way men think and feel."

"You needn't lecture *me*; I've lectured at the academy on that very point. For all the good it did."

"It must have done some, surely. Lord Basken is eager to establish a subscription on your behalf."

"Is he? Well, he need be quick about it before I starve."

I had rehearsed on the journey to London the speech my mother would have me say by way of introduction, as none was there to make one for me. But when the two men entered the parlor, I was startled into silence. I recognized my uncle immediately from the self-portrait I had seen. He had my mother's face, my own.

It took them a moment to notice I was there, my uncle going through his letters. The taller man saw me first.

"A gift from your charwoman?" the tall man asked. His hair was thick and white; muttonchop sideburns framed a broad and pleasant face. He was dark, as were his eyes. Child that I was, even I could recognize that he was uncommonly handsome.

"How in Christ's name did that get in here?" my uncle said.

"Your maid, sir," I replied, standing.

"You are her relation?" he asked.

"No, sir. I am yours."

The handsome man laughed. Clapped my uncle on the shoulder. "Congratulations, Jonathan. You appear to be a father."

"I am no such thing. What are you?" my uncle demanded. "Explain yourself before I call the constable."

I forgot my speech almost entirely in my fear, stammering out that I'd come from Cork, hurriedly explaining who I was and how I'd come. I did not say why.

I was a slight thing then, a sprite of a child, undersized and pale.

"What wood nymph is this?" the tall man asked, stepping closer. "Have you brought us one of the famed little people of your land, Jonathan?"

"I am not a little person," I said, piqued by his condescension. "I am a child."

He smiled. "And how old are you, child?" The tall man squatted before me to look me in the eye.

"Ten."

He raised an eyebrow at this. My size must have suggested otherwise.

"Nine and a quarter," I admitted. (Later, historians will debate the point, of course, whether I was nine that afternoon in London or fourteen, whether I was born in 1790 or 1795. Does it matter? As Menander wrote, "Judge me not by my age but by the wisdom I display among you.")

"I am General Fernando de Mirandus," the man said, bowing his head. He spoke as if I should know the name, or as if he were pleased that it was his. "It is a great pleasure." He stood again.

"Wonderful," I said.

General Mirandus looked bemused. "A wonderful pleasure?"

"Your name," I said. "In Latin. *General Wonderful.*"

He laughed. "Do you know Latin, child?"

I knew only a little, what my father had taught us on Sunday afternoons, so what I said surprised us both: *"Homo sum, humani nihil a me alienum puto."*

I've no idea why the Roman playwright's words came to mind. Only that they did, and that the general appeared delighted. He laughed to hear me quote Terence: "I am a man, so nothing human is foreign to me."

"Why, she's a prodigy, Jonathan," he said, turning to my uncle. "Your little niece is a prodigy."

"*I* was a prodigy," my uncle said, turning to a cabinet behind him on a far wall. "Burke called me so himself. Will you have a glass of port?" My uncle filled two glasses.

"But she's a marvel," Mirandus said, looking me over as if I were indeed a fairy. I sensed he was not referring simply to my modest attainments in Latin.

"She has had a little learning. That is all. It's the rage to educate even girls."

"As it should be," Mirandus said.

My uncle drank off his glass, poured another.

Mirandus crouched down before me again. "What brings you here, child?"

My mother's words came back to me then: "I have come to speak with my uncle," I said. "In. Private."

"Speak," my uncle said, dropping into a chair, not offering me one. The general gallantly pulled up an ottoman for me, inclining his head to indicate that I might sit. I stood facing my uncle instead, preferring to meet him eye to eye. He propped his feet on the ottoman, so I faced his bootheels, the soles dirty from the street.

I had expected that a man concerned for and capable of producing such beauty would be beautiful himself; I was shocked to find him coarse, vain, belligerent, as if all the loveliness in him had been transferred to the canvases hung to the rafters, propped against the walls. Leaving him none.

But it made it easier. Had he been kind, I'd have felt obliged by his kindness; showing none, he liberated me to feel what I truly felt: dislike of him and my own need.

At the time I did not comprehend my uncle's distress and mistook it for dislike of me; I didn't know that he'd recently been dismissed from the Royal Academy—for criticizing the professors there, making "improper digressions" in his lectures, which is to say, picking fights with the powerful, which one rarely wins—the only Academy artist to whom this had ever happened (and the last to whom it would, for more than two hundred years).

More than his pride had been wounded. The academy had paid his salary and commissioned his murals for years. Now his income was in question. He was desperate for money, as we were. Harried by fear. But in that first interview I would learn an important lesson: that one could disguise vulnerability with arrogance and disdain. My mother's gentility had availed us little since my brother's calamity; my uncle offered another possibility, and a lesson: one might mask fear with belligerence. I might, too.

Perhaps my uncle would have answered my mother's letter if he'd been doing well, despite their decades-long estrangement, if only for the pleasure that siblings take in showing the other up; he might have been generous to us to underscore her need. But he couldn't afford such a slight. Like us, he was hungry. But unlike us, as a man, he had honorable means by which to make his way in the world.

Though I thought his townhouse grand, filled as it was with all manner of fascinating things, it lacked even the modest elegance of our home in Cork. I noticed now that the lamps and fire went unlit, and that a pane of glass was covered with a panel of oilcloth to mask a hole in the glass. I was not alone in noticing.

"What's this?" Mirandus asked, crossing to the oilcloth pane.

"One of the local urchins," my uncle said.

"Covered your window?"

"Broke the pane. Put a rock through it."

"They are Tories?" the general asked.

"They are monsters," my uncle said. "They take me for a necromancer. Loathsome things, children."

The general turned to me. "Present company excepted, of course."

My uncle took no further notice of me that day, once his initial fury had subsided. Though I would return to his home half a dozen times that summer, my uncle would take no more interest in me than he did on that first meeting. If anything, he grew less fond as the general appeared to grow more.

"Do let the girl dine with us, Jonathan," the general proposed toward the end of that first meeting. "The poor child looks half starved."

"Had I proposed we dine?" my uncle asked, absently. "I suppose we must. Why don't we go round to Wardour Street or Brook's?"

"That's no place for the child."

"Precisely," my uncle replied.

My uncle turned to me, as if perhaps I hadn't understood. "So good of you to pay a visit. But your mother must be quite beside herself with worry. I'm sure you really must be going."

I was conscious that he did not invite me to dine, conscious too of the ache of hunger in my stomach. Need is an ugly thing. Though I didn't realize it then, it had made my handsome uncle ugly, too.

I looked to the general, but he was paging through a book

on the table, careful not to interfere, as if noticing rudeness were a kind of rudeness in itself.

"Of course, *Uncle*," I said. I thought I saw him flinch. "I will not forget your courtesy." When I glanced over, the general was watching me with an expression I could not read.

"Let us call you a hackney coach," the general said.

"Thank you for the offer, sir, but I cannot afford it."

"Surely your mother would not object to your accepting such small courtesy," the general replied.

My uncle looked shocked. "Accepting? Who's offering?"

The general said coldly, "I am."

"The girl plainly walked here," my uncle said, nodding at my boots. "She can plainly walk back."

"My uncle is correct, sir," I said.

"The streets are no place for a child at this hour," said the general.

"The streets are over*run* with children at this hour," said my uncle.

"If she walks," the general said, "I shall accompany her."

Neither my uncle nor I had foreseen this: I could not imagine the mortification of being walked through the streets like an errant child.

"It's good of you to offer, sir, but unnecessary, truly…"

"Fine," my uncle said. "Fine." And off he went to find a coach.

Although in time my uncle would prove my greatest benefactor—giving me my name, my very life—that coach would be the only courtesy he would ever knowingly offer.

It's tempting to say that this was the moment that set me on my course to the Cape, to becoming a surgeon, a soldier, a scandal, to meeting Lord Somerton, to all that would follow. But is there ever such a moment? What makes a man, a life? How much is name and parentage, education or the accident of birth? How much is choice? How much of our lives' making is in our hands and how much is forged by fate, the intersection of trajectories as mysterious as electricity's conduction once seemed? It's easy to look back now and say, *That was the meeting that changed all that followed, that would end Margaret's life and give rise to Jonathan's.*

But I'm skeptical of retrospection, even as I indulge in it now; it seems poor policy, given that time itself does not run back and recollection is often self-flattering fantasy more than fact. I prefer a scientific method. Observation, hypothesis, evidence weighed. That is my aim now, to weigh the evidence.

That first summer in London, I had only one true conversation with my uncle. I don't recall the occasion, though no doubt it was occasioned—as they all were—by my mother's insistence that I petition him to sign over to *me* the deed to our home in Cork. The house had been left to my mother, but it was held by my uncle, since my mother—as a Catholic—could not own it herself. She wanted it safe from my father. So each week I went to my uncle, humiliated, to ask what he would not grant—that he sign the deed over to me. I remember the angle of light through the windows, the dust in the air fanning into faint bars like a lady's fan, a tannic haze; I was looking at a book of paintings open on his heaped table in the drawing room when my uncle came in. "What are you looking at?" he shouted. I stepped back, expecting to be reprimanded or struck, but instead he crossed to me and began to talk about the pictures. He did not explain as my mother might—

telling me about the Biblical tale depicted—he spoke of the artist's work. "Notice the muscles here, in Mary's forearm? How the light comes from the right? How it changes on the child?" He explained that the model for Mary had been a man, not a woman, possibly a corpse, stripped of its flesh. He might have been trying to shock me, but I was gripped. "See how he lingers," he said. He sounded almost tender as he spoke. My uncle with the beautiful searching eyes so like my mother's.

"Genius," he said at last, "is a long patience." It was then he told me what Michelangelo had told his student—a beautiful boy whom he drew again and again, immortalized, as my uncle hoped to be, by paint and canvas—"Work, Antonio, work, Antonio, work, Antonio, and don't waste time." He shut the book. As if the exhortation had been to himself. "You know your way out." He turned without a glance and went upstairs to his studio.

When my mother and I left London three months later, having run through all our funds, having failed to secure the deed to our house or any financial help, she insisted that we leave a calling card at my uncle's home on our way to the docks, as *le bon ton* would do, a card on which she had written *PPC* neatly on the back—an abbreviation, she explained, for *pour prendre congé (I'm leaving)*—as if my uncle were a gentleman, as if he would care.

It was on our return to Ireland that matters grew desperate, though at first it seemed the tide had turned in our favor.

My father was in uncommonly good spirits when we returned to Cork, and the reunion was surprisingly tender. To be met by my little sister, Juliana, and our father at the door of the cottage in Water Lane was a sweet thing after the months in London's stench, where rain came down black and turned white cloaks grey after a morning's stroll, and the very air burned in our nostrils.

After hurried embraces and a few inquiries about our travel and expressions of delight at our safe return, we stepped into the parlor; my father pressed my mother's hands in his and said, "We're saved."

"I fear not," my mother said, gently retracting her hands to loosen her traveling cloak. "Jonathan will not help us. Even the sight of his own poor, unprotected niece could not soften his hard heart." My mother set a hand on my shoulder. "The man is stone."

"It's no matter," my father said. "The answer is beneath our feet. All around us." He spread his palms as the parish priest did on Sundays, when he spoke of God's grace just before asking for alms.

For a moment I thought my father had got religion in our absence. Our world had been turned upside down; anything seemed possible. My mother looked at my father as if he'd lost his wits.

"You would sell the house?" she said. "The roof over our heads."

"Not sell, not sell, merely offer as collateral, until Tom regains his footing."

"He will not do it," my mother said, throwing down her gloves onto a table, leaving unclear if she referred to my brother or my uncle. "I will not do it."

My mother moved toward the fire, as if the conversation were done.

"I will write to him," my father continued, "or go to London myself. I can sign a promissory for the house over to the creditors before I leave, as security."

"The house is all we have," she said.

"Which is precisely why we must offer it against our debts." My father's voice was strange and soothing, petitioning, a voice I'd never heard him use before.

"I will not sacrifice my home to..."

"*Your* home?" My father's familiar tone returned, cudgel blunt.

"The house is in my brother's keeping," my mother said. "It was willed to me."

"Which makes it mine. Or have you forgotten you're my wife?"

"Have you forgotten that you have daughters as well as a son?"

"Our son will care for his sisters and us."

"Tom cares for nothing but himself and his own ease," my mother said. "He will squander everything, if you allow it; he will put his sisters in the street. And us."

I was standing just inside the parlor, beside my sister, close enough to see our father's jaw set hard, a muscle twitch in his cheek, as it did when he confronted a farmer who could not supply what had been promised.

"By God I'll put you there myself, if you defy me. It's a matter for men to decide."

"Tom has squandered all, and you would give him more?" My mother beckoned me over with impatient hands and began tugging at my cloak and cap.

"You will do as I say," my father said, stepping toward us. His tone raised hairs along my arms.

"I will do as my conscience bids," my mother said.

"I am your conscience."

"God is my conscience. You're just a man, and little enough of one at that."

I heard the blow before I felt my mother lurch against me. When I looked up, my father's palm was raised to strike again; I don't know if it was her expression or mine that stopped him. He dropped his hand, as if defeated, and pushing past my sister, he walked out.

In the months that followed, their arguments would grow common and cruel. My sister and I became accustomed to the sound of broken china and of blows, of chairs overturned. We lay in bed and listened to the storm below. Juliana was more yielding, more tender than I, sensible and patient; it was clear that she had our mother's keen intelligence and the desire to apply it well. She was forever inventing some more efficient means for maintaining our household, for improving its economy without diminishing its comforts. But even she could not calm our father's rage.

It turned out that in expectation of receiving the deed, my father had in our absence offered the house as collateral to the debt collectors. He pleaded with my mother to understand his position, claimed that if he went back on his word now he'd be made a liar and a fool. My mother said his premature offer of the house had made him both already.

My father talked of taking legal action against my uncle, of going to the West Indies to pay off the debt, but save for collectors rapping at the door there were few comings or goings. My brother moved in with his wife's family after he lost the farm, and shortly thereafter both bride and brother moved in with us, when her family refused support. My father lived among them like Lear visiting his daughters, solicitous and mild, while my sister and I played the part of maids. My mother banged pots and dropped platters, spilled soup at dinner, clumsy with rage, and in a fury one evening said she'd rather be dead than see her family home go to creditors.

By the following January, we were in the street—put out not by creditors but by my father, who had taken my brother's part and turned us out—my mother and me. My sister, Juliana, stayed behind to serve as maid. I hoped it might keep her safe. We stayed for a few weeks with Mr. Penrose, an attorney and childhood friend of my mother's; we wrote to my uncle but received no reply, so in late February 1806 we made our way once more to London.

I was loath to travel, to make the exhausting journey by ship and coach, which would take the rest of my mother's jewelry and all our courage. We had nowhere to stay; no friends there, no relations, save for my uncle Jonathan, who hardly qualified as either. But we could not remain in Cork, as I wished to do, for—as our mother explained—any labor we turned our hands to there would be our loss, our father's gain, since a wife's earnings belonged to her husband, by custom and law; we could starve, she said, and our labors benefit us nothing; the only course was to return to London. My mother and I would go alone to beg my uncle's help—if he might settle on me the house that had been willed to her, it would be safe from my father's creditors, saved; without the change in deed, that single piece of paper, we were lost.

We arrived in London after a difficult winter crossing by boat to find the city choked with fog, a suffocating yellow haze blotting out the dim winter sun. My mother seemed indifferent to the chill and the stench of sewage and stables. She hired a hackney coach directly from the docks to take us to my uncle's; we were jostled through the cluttered, reeking streets, past bookshops and glass-fronted stores with heavy signs, coffeehouses and ale houses and taverns, circulating libraries and small brick churches and open markets, and glistening above it all the great dome of St. Paul's Cathedral; sedan-chair men carried well-dressed passengers past gentlemen who might have been lawyers or doctors, past ballad sellers and beggars, while footmen clung to rattling carriages; the streets clogged with tradesmen of every sort—milk women and town criers, knife grinders and vendors who shouted out their wares, selling oysters, fish, and apples, until at last we reached the narrow door at Little Castle Street, on which a wreath tied with black ribbon hung and a simple handbill, confirming what my mother had most feared: my uncle was dead.

"We're saved," I said, thinking of the inheritance.

"We're ruined," my mother said, sinking down onto the trunk we'd carried from Cork, which contained all of what little we still owned.

Barred by both marriage and religion from ownership of land, her inheritance would pass to our father, she explained, leaving us destitute and now alone.

Had our family been Protestant, with a daughter even modestly dowered, my mother might have thought to marry her eldest girl to some young man of good prospects if not of actual fortune. But the prospects of a good marriage were not good at all. The most my mother could hope for her eldest daughter was a position as a governess to a respectable family, a post not lucrative but sufficiently genteel to reassure my mother and reasonably secure; Margaret might expect to earn a small income with which to support mother and sister, and in time perhaps make a modestly good marriage to a second son, a vicar, or possibly, with luck, even a rector or solicitor.

I was not keen on marriage and shared my uncle's dread of children—the first of many traits I would discover that we held in common—but the options for a young woman from Cork without a father or brother or fortune or faith to lend her value were limited. London's streets were proof of that, where thousands of prostitutes strolled the streets and solicited from doorways, a reminder of where poor prospects might take a country girl; what we might face.

Word of my uncle's death was sure to reach Cork soon and my father, and with it would come a petition for the sale of the house, leaving us nowhere to go, save back.

It would not take us long to realize that if we were to save ourselves, we must rid ourselves of Margaret. Which is to say, of me.

My mother rose and knocked at the door, hoping we might find the charwoman in and collect a few family mementos, perhaps spend the night, but we found my uncle's rooms beetled with men of indeterminate age and dark coats, who moved through the rooms like undertakers, unwilling or unable to offer my mother information or assistance. We were on the verge of leaving when I heard a familiar voice from the foyer, and turned to see General Mirandus in the doorway, consulting with the maid who had let us in. I could not tell from his expression if he was pleased or dismayed to see us. The past two years had been trying; perhaps we were unrecognizable.

My mother had been fastidious about her appearance in the past, ours and hers and that of her home. Now she wore a filthy dress and cloak without seeming to be aware of the mud or stains upon them. She no longer bothered to brush her boots or shoes. She often did not brush her hair or even sponge-wash the soot from her neck when she came in. I had observed the change without being aware of it.

"I was not aware you were in London, Mrs. Brackley," he said, crossing to my mother.

"We've only just arrived," my mother said.

"If I might know where you are staying, I will ask the solicitor to call on you. He is most eager of an interview."

"We have no money for lodgings," my mother said. "We had depended upon my brother's generosity in undertaking this trip. The journey has taken all we had." It was a humiliating admission. For the first time, I was ashamed of our circumstances and afraid. But my mother spoke calmly, without petition. She had been a charming, beautiful, self-satisfied woman; adversity had stripped her of social graces; she had grown plain and modest and admirable in adversity; I saw that now. Perhaps the general did, too.

It was getting late; the light in the room had noticeably dimmed, and the few lamps were being lit by a different charwoman from the one who had let me in two years before, a lifetime ago. Mirandus asked her to build up the fire, to set out supper; he handed her some coins, then excused himself to speak to one of the beetle-men and presently they departed. Finally, he returned to my mother.

"It will take some time to catalogue the contents of the estate," he told my mother. "Christie's men are here but a few hours each day. Why don't you and your daughter reside here for the time being?"

My mother's expression must have betrayed dismay at the

prospect of staying in my uncle's decrepit home. Kindness had disarmed her, left her vulnerable to wanting.

"It lacks charm," the general said. "But it has the great benefit of being without cost. And yours. You are the sole beneficiary of the estate, I believe. There was, I think, a brother."

"We have had no word of him in many years." My mother seemed to sway slightly, as if a breeze had caught her. "Perhaps we might sit down."

"Of course. Forgive me. You've had a long journey."

The general pulled up chairs before the fire, and soon after a tray was brought in. I heard the general telling my mother that my uncle had received a hero's burial, a grand funeral, laid to rest in St. Paul's beside his former friend Sir Joshua Reynolds. I took up my perch on the ottoman closest the fire, hearing but not attending to the adult conversation behind me, until I heard my mother laugh. A high, girlish laugh—a sound I had not heard in years.

When I turned, I saw my mother's hand resting on the general's arm. He smiled, did not withdraw it. I would learn in time that it was his particular gift to make whomever he spoke to feel like the singular focus of his attention, the most fascinating person in the room. Later I'd recognize this as the seducer's art, but at the time it seemed to me generous, a species of genius, this ability to illuminate others with attention, as women of necessity do.

It was there by the fire that evening a fortnight after my uncle's funeral that Margaret's death warrant was written, that her life began to end and mine begin. I see that now; this must have been the moment that changed our lives, though none of us recognized it then; instead my mother and the general spoke of an education. I listened as they decided my fate.

I felt the general watching me, as I sat by the fire on the ottoman my uncle had rested his boots on, my cheeks warmed by the fire, my face lit like one of the women in my uncle's paintings at the Royal Society. My muslin gown illuminated like a candlewick; a black satin ribbon beneath the bodice, an inadvertent nod to my uncle's death.

"Let the girl come to my home," he said.

My mother let her hand fall from his arm.

"She's too young," my mother said.

"Girls her age are married, Mrs. Brackley. They are mothers."

"She's only just eleven."

"She will be thirteen soon enough."

"She's still a child. It would not be seemly to…to…"

"Educate her…?"

"Is that what you call it? She needs another kind of education, sir."

The general seemed genuinely shocked. "I have a wife, Mrs. Brackley."

"You have a mistress," she said, finding her old courage. "It is said, sir, that you have many."

Looking back, it occurs to me that he might have laughed, pleased that word of his conquests had traveled so far, even to the wives of Cork. He didn't.

"You are speaking of the mother of my children," he said simply.

"And I am the mother of Margaret."

The general looked over at me.

"And as such, Mrs. Brackley, you have nothing to fear."

My mother was too genteel to protest further. To name what she most feared and had to. What, after all, was the alternative?

"Let the girl come study in my home in the mornings and afternoons; in the evenings she will come home to you. It will take some months to put your brother's affairs in order; you and your daughter might reside here while it's accomplished. I will inquire after more suitable lodgings."

I was delighted by the prospect, though my mother clearly was not. Neither by my uncle's rooms nor by what she would later refer to as my so-called education.

My mother spent the following days issuing warnings. I was relieved by her bossiness, even her irritation, which seemed to bespeak a return of spirit. She instructed me in how to speak in the general's home and when not to, urging me to be modest, self-effacing, obedient, silent. Never to ask for anything. No questions. No requests. I was to appear as a vase, a portmanteau ready to be filled with whatever they wished.

It was advice I would forget entirely as soon as I entered Mirandus's home; I was dazzled, seduced the moment I crossed the threshold.

The woman who answered the door at 27 Grafton Street three days later was striking: she had a long and slender face, more handsome than beautiful; her gaze was direct, not the unfocused harried glance I'd come to expect in adults, as if they were weary of looking at what they saw. Her hair was loose; her figure shapely beneath a man's linen shirt and breeches cinched with a belt, a boy of three hanging from one hand.

I can't pretend I was not shocked to meet her, Sarah Andrews; I was acquainted with a mother who was not a wife (this had been true of the baker's mistress in Cork). But I was shocked by the difference in class. The general was a man of considerable standing with a house in Grafton Street and the best library in London. It was rumored she had been his housekeeper. I was the child of a greengrocer and had the superstitious sense of propriety that is often a talisman of those in the ascent socially, eager to distinguish themselves.

"I have come to see the general."

"You must be Jonathan's niece. We've been expecting you." She took me by both hands and drew me into the bright foyer in an affectionate assault.

"I'm afraid Fernando has been called away, but do come in, come in—" Her Yorkshire accent wasn't delicate like his, but of another sort—like rivers rushing with words, a wild lushness. A sort of susurrus, as if a breeze blew through her phrases.

She introduced me to the children, Fernando and Leandro, and showed me over the house, telling me how she'd loved my uncle, how he was the best friend she'd ever had, the most sincere and disinterested of men; I wondered if we spoke of the same man. She introduced me to the maidservant and cook, whom she said I should ask if I required anything. "You are to be part of our family now."

I spent that first afternoon alone in the general's library, amidst his thousands of books, his maps of South America, looking over a volume of drawings I had found out on the desk, bound in the finest material I'd ever seen, leather smooth as river stones, with tortoiseshell paper from Italy (though I did not know it then), listening to the gentle reprimands of Sarah Andrews as she sat with her children in the small garden in back, warning them not to hurt their pet rabbit, but otherwise letting them run wild. They spoke a mix of French and Spanish and English, a delicious stew of words. But for all their lively chatter, I felt, even in his absence, Mirandus's presence in the house, as if the whole of it were under a spell, waiting for him to break it, as if we were all slightly holding our breath.

For a long while I sat in silence in a large chair beside the general's desk. Eventually I grew bored, then curious. I began to page through the book of drawings—its marbled boards the color of agate, its spine soft leather ornamented with gold—*Smellie's A Sett of Anatomical Tables, with Explanations, and an Abridgement, of the Practice of Midwifery*. The book was the size of a small traveling case, heavy as one full stone. It cost me much to lift it from the desk and shift it to where I might read it from the chair. Its cover looked like polished stone or like a pool of wind-rippled water, colors swirled on its surface. Opening it was like opening a door, a slight creak to the binding, a smell of age in the pages. The book was the size and proportion of a cabinet door, or a large coal chute, an opening I might fit myself through, enter, revealing another world—foreign, beautiful, terrifying, marvelous.

I was indifferent to the preface, in which the author set forth his purpose to aid the young practitioner of midwifery.

I turned to the first image: *The First Table—Front View the Bones of a Well Formed Pelvis*.

From the first I found it unaccountably unspeakably beautiful—the bones before me looked like a geologic feature, a stone cavern perhaps, a cave, the pelvis etched there seemed carved by water, like river boulders, the spine rising from it like a knobbed tree trunk; images of dragons could not have compelled me more; it seemed sublime, the shadow and light. It must have been an engraver's trick, but the bones seemed lit from behind or from within, or perhaps that was simply how I felt. Looking at them. Lit within.

I turned the page.

I turned another.

Then another.

Table Four—The Female Parts of Generation—showed a woman's fat thighs draped in cloth, her flesh dimpled and vivid as if she lay before me on the desk—sex exposed, as I'd never seen before, nor seen my own—not terrifying but exquisite, the labial folds like a river's eddy, pubic hair like a decorative filigree, the dark delicate star of the anus. Flesh of legs dimpled as Michelangelo might have drawn.

Two blank pages followed, then *Table Five*—

One might have wondered what had befallen those that they should find themselves displayed here for the observer's delectation, as I am now laid bare before you. It didn't occur to me then. I was gripped by the body's spell.

Seventh Table—Represents Abdomen of a woman opened in the sixth or seventh month of pregnancy. I found it beautiful. The plump ribbons of intestines festooning the uterine bulge, the glimpse of her full left breast, barely covered by cloth.

Eighth Table stopped my heart. A child, drawn from life, perfect in form and every feature, still in its shell of flesh.

Ninth Table—Uterus in 8th or 9th Month of Pregnancy (containing the foetus intangled in the Funis). Hair on its head, body plump and perfect as Michelangelo's babe in its round frame, its neck and upper arm snaked by dark umbilicus—the source and sustenance of its life, its undoing. It had strangled in the womb.

Tenth Table—Two infants lay cradled in the uterus. Two perfectly formed infants curled in the cave of their mother's womb, curved like the Chinese symbol for yin and yang; the child to the left raised its head toward the mother's heart, breach; the child to the right had its head facing down, its head pointed toward the cervical opening, preparing to enter the world of men, though neither would. Its right hand held up to its lips, as if to say *unspeakable*, or as if urging discretion. In eternal slumber, cords garlanding their limbs, strangled by the very thing that gave them life. Forever twinned, forever entwined, seemingly at peace. I thought of Romulus and Remus, stillborn.

I put the book aside. Leaned back against the sturdy leather of the chair. I could hear a clock tick on the mantel. Hear hoof falls in the street and the clatter of wheels on cobblestones.

When I returned to the book, I turned its pages like a dreamer reviewing a dream. The dream of the body.

When General Mirandus came in, just before evening, he shouted for Sarah, and she shouted back as she came out to embrace him, the children in her arms; there was none of the formality my parents had insisted upon, as if the forms could improve our fortunes. He kissed Sarah and she spoke to him quietly, and I saw him glance through the library door, where I sat at the desk watching them. I looked away.

He stepped into the library and for an instant I feared that he would be angry that I had taken up his costly book, but he smiled.

"You have good taste. There are only six dozen copies of Smellie's atlas, and I have one."

"It's wonderful," I said.

"Like me," he said.

Mirandus was an epidemic of a man. The handsome man from Caracas would later be known throughout the Americas as "Il Precursor," his ideas having inspired Bolívar's eventual liberation of those American colonies from Spain. But for me he was the precursor in another way, the first man I loved before I met the only man I would. His appeal among women was like contagion; no one was immune. Not even I, a girl of nine when we'd first met two years before. Catherine the Great, he once told me over dinner, had begged him to remain in St. Petersburg. He had declined. "Her bed was warm, but the winters too cold," he said, lifting his glass to inspect the claret's color in the light. The scandalous novelist Madame de Staël had been his lover as well.

Sarah would press her lips together tightly when he told these stories, which she said she'd heard too often ("I could recite them by heart, like a rosary"), and excused herself; she had made a certain peace with his charm, it seemed, but that did not mean she was immune to pain.

It was hard to tell in those first few months in London if I was falling in love with the general or with his library or with his life; the excitement that I felt each afternoon when I heard his feet on the boards outside the library, when he entered the room—my mouth dry, my stomach tight, my laugh too easy and high, as it would later be when I learned to drink champagne—confused and delighted me; certainly our afternoons closeted together for an hour before dinner were among the loveliest, most memorable hours I spent in London.

"Have you read all these books?" I asked that first afternoon.

He laughed. "The majority. There are one or two I've only skimmed."

"Then why keep them?"

"It is a pleasure to possess beautiful things," he said. "Is it not?"

I shrugged. "It must be marvelous to be a clever man," I said.

"Do you think so?"

I nodded, not taking my eyes off the books.

"And how is it to be a clever girl?"

"I've noticed that wit is rarely mistaken for virtue in a girl."

"Some mistake it."

I went back to walking the room, dragging my fingers idly along the spines.

"You are fond of reading?" he asked.

"I don't know," I said. "I've read little. Our father considers it a waste of time."

"To read?"

"To educate daughters."

"He taught you Latin."

"He taught our brother. I was merely present for the lesson."

"You are a quick study, then."

"You're the first to suggest it, sir." I sensed that I had disappointed him with my answers. I knew I must not disappoint; our lives depended on pleasing this man. "Our father had no objection to our reading books, provided they contained no useful knowledge at all."

He laughed. "Tell me about what you've read." He came over and sat on the edge of the desk.

I was embarrassed to have read so little by the advanced age of eleven. "Novels mostly," I said. I hadn't the courage to name them, such books as *The Monk* or Walpole's *The Castle of Otranto*, which I felt sure would not do me credit.

"And have you enjoyed them?"

"Stories are like dreams," I said. "They all but vanish from memory upon their ending."

"Not all," said the general. "I shall guide you."

True to his word, he set me a course of reading, which I'd follow over the next three years—Shakespeare's history plays and Petrarch's *Africa*, Milton's long poem and Rousseau's scandalous *Confessions*, Dante and Ariosto and the work of the general's friends Thomas Paine and Jeremy Bentham and the late Mrs. Wollstonecraft, as well as Euclid's *Elements* and Newton's *Principia*. On Saturdays we would read together Plato's accounts of his teacher, Socrates, and Aristotle's theories in Greek and would have continued the lesson on Sundays, had my mother's devotion to Mass not taken precedence.

Most days I would arrive early and have a cup of milky tea with Sarah and the children and then read in the library until the sun was low and the room dim, and he would come in and walk me home—discussing, as we went, what I had read that day.

It was a course of reading calculated less to provide an understanding of any particular field—his was not the pedant's predilection for linear progression—his selections seemed governed by another principle altogether, that of pleasure, both mine and his, selecting works that had inspired his curiosity and enthusiasm to see what might whet my own.

The general was utterly unlike my brother's tutors in mathematics and history who had visited our home, myopic men whose bodies seemed to have been diminished with their minds' increase—delicate men around whom the very air seemed dimmer. They had made education appear a poor prospect, unromantic in the extreme. But Mirandus, as his surname promised, was a marvel and made education the most intoxicating of adventures, as good or better than the travel he'd made in ships when he sailed to Madrid from Venezuela as a young man, the women he'd bedded, the prisons he'd escaped. Books picked the lock that opened everything—all the greatest minds of history—and which no one could ever take from us.

Waiting for execution in France after the Revolution (which he had supported until it turned against the vulnerable), he claimed to have recited from memory Voltaire's *Candide* and so charmed his gaolers that they had helped him escape—though I suspected bribes had inspired them as much as literature.

I often learned more in our discussions than in my reading. He brought out points I'd overlooked, details I had not noticed, and sometimes—to my delight—I would notice things that he had not. I would raise a point or make an observation that surprised him, and his surprise seemed to give us both great pleasure.

I remember most particularly one evening, strolling through Hyde Park—the light lingering as it does in late spring, as if loath to end the day as I was, the air a deep indigo—as I told him how the whole of Shakespeare's *Julius Caesar* was like Mark Antony's funeral oration, the author appearing to praise what he actually condemned.

He seemed puzzled. "Say more."

"Well, the men possess authority in the play, but he gives to women the command of wisdom, which men like Brutus and Caesar are too vain or foolish to heed. Had either man listened to his wife, they'd not have killed their king…"

"*Emperor,*" he corrected, gently.

"The point is, the play seems to be a peen—" I hesitated over the word. "A pain—"

"A paean," he said.

"Yes, right, a *paean* to a powerful ruler in the face of fractious mobs, but really you could see it as a challenge to the foolishness of men, even powerful men, who ignore the wisdom of their women."

"Mrs. Wollstonecraft would have delighted in you," he said, resting a hand on my shoulder with a gentle pressure, as if I were a cane.

"But don't you think it's curious?"

"It was written for a queen," he said.

"So artists are to be mere flatterers of those who pay their wages?"

"You sound like your uncle," he said. "He believed the artist should be supported by society in order to transform it, free of the taint of personal patronage." A flock of dandified young men strolled past, like peacocks. "What do you think?" he asked, pausing in our walk.

This was where my education began, in that single question, the expectation that through effort and sound reading—through the proper balance of sensibility and reason, founded on sound principle—I might forge an answer for myself; we *each* might. A democracy of thought.

"Perhaps my uncle was right," I said.

"Perhaps he was."

The ardor I discovered for learning that spring—and in the years that followed—was a kind of love I'd never known, and one a lesser man might easily have mistaken for another sort of passion. He could have ruined me, twisting my admiration into something smaller, more private. To his credit, he did not. Perhaps Sarah intervened on my behalf? Or perhaps fate did. Whatever the cause, I was left free to focus my ardor on the library. When Mirandus spoke of my joining him in Venezuela, one evening when I'd stayed to dinner, I sensed a proposal in his words, a veiled promise, but in his house I was treated only as a daughter—that is, until I became a son.

I was turning the pages of a novel by Richardson one afternoon that first spring when something fluttered to the desk in front of me. I feared I'd torn the page; I looked down at the blotter and saw nothing there, save for a single thread, a hair, pale as gold wire, the length of a joint on my finger, wavy as a river seen from a hill, a hair no head had ever worn. I recognized it instantly. I laughed to see it, at the incongruity.

How had such a hair found its way to the pages of a novel? I thought to ask Sarah about it, but thought better of it. If it were hers, it would seem I had been spying. If it weren't hers, it would be worse. I thought to leave it on the blotter, but I feared he might think I'd left it there. I didn't know if I should place it in the book, if that was indeed where it belonged.

I was pondering options for its disposal when I heard boot falls outside the door. I pinched the hair up and dropped it into the pocket of my dress.

Only later, when I discovered other hairs placed among the pages of other books—some blond, some black, one red—did I understand it was a collection, like a reliquary in the religion of desire, of the body. I thought of what he'd said the day I first arrived, how it was a pleasure to possess beautiful things. I looked for a pattern in their placement. I wanted to ask him whose they were. If he knew, if he recalled each woman by her hair. I never asked.

I feared the general would find me out that day, as he thumbed through the book on the desk; did I imagine it or did he look concerned, searching for what was missing? We conversed as usual about what I'd read, but when I left, I took the pocketed souvenir with me. For years I kept it sewn into the hem of a handkerchief like a charm; later I placed it in my own copy of *The Metamorphoses*. I thought the old Roman would have approved.

A few months after my studies began, the general sailed for America to gather support for his efforts to liberate Venezuela from Spain. He would meet with the American presidents Jefferson and Madison; en route he would design the Venezuelan flag. My mother seemed relieved to have him gone. While he was away for those eighteen months, I missed him—our conversations and his encouragement—but I felt more at ease, alone with Sarah and the children. My schedule remained unchanged. I liked to imagine my presence was a comfort to Sarah. Certainly we grew more intimate, as the weeks and months passed, alone together, as if we were our own small family. I knew she missed the general, as she called him; I wondered if she feared she might lose him.

"Do you not wish to marry the general?" I asked Sarah one afternoon in the garden as we took our tea.

"Why?" she laughed. "Do you?"

"What a question," I blushed. "I'm a child."

"And I am not," she said. "I am not chattel to be bought and sold by men. We do not need the state to ratify our affections." It sounded as if she were quoting someone.

"But it would make your life more secure, surely, and your children's."

"No life is secure, child; you know that. Did marriage protect your mother?"

She set down her teacup. "When people promise security, they are usually scheming to take something away."

Perhaps I looked alarmed, for she stretched out a hand and covered mine on the table. "The only security is to be found in yourself."

"What of love?"

"Ah, that's the least secure of all, but we can't live without it, can we?" She looked out over the garden, the doors swung open to let in the late-summer breeze. She rose and stepped into the light.

For a time, several happy years, our lives were stable again, lodged in a house just north of Fitzroy Square, not far from the general's, sustained by a generous subscription raised on our behalf by my uncle's friend Lord Basken. A loyal patron of my uncle's to the end, Lord Basken had proposed after my uncle's death to pull together a volume of his drawings and essays whose sale might support poor Perry's indigent relations—by which he meant us. My mother was aghast at the prospect, but we had few others. And it bought us time.

When the general returned from his travels on New Year's Day, 1808, a year and a half after he'd left, the house was often mobbed by guests. They came like crows. Noisy. Preening. Rancorous. Young Mr. Simón Bolívar. Mr. Jeremy Bentham, who looked like an egg with a wig. The rooms filled with heady talk of politics and revolution. General Mirandus let me linger and listen, or at least he did not put me out. I stretched out quietly behind a sofa or sat silent in a chair with a book, so I might overhear. I did not speak, but I grew accustomed to the arguments of men, words like cards thrown down in whist, the pleasures of debate, and of winning.

Mr. Bentham's visits were especially lively and loud, reaching a volume that made young Fernando cry but delighted me. Bentham was always invoking some principle he had invented, as when he railed against what he called "deep play"—when one risks greatly for uncertain gain. He believed it best to maximize pleasure in life. He and the general debated the point one evening over dinner, after Bentham had called for a prohibition on the "evils of deep play." The general claimed the theory was mistaken because it ignored the pleasure that comes of acting on principle, even for uncertain reward:

"The individual may fail," Mirandus said, "but the collective gain thereby, and human happiness thus be increased, not lessened."

But both men missed the mark, I thought. To risk everything for uncertain gain is a gamble women know well; mothers engage in it every day in the birthing of a child. To prohibit it would be to outlaw childbirth, and love itself, and every foolish necessary self-sacrifice in its name.

I said so. They stared at me, as if I were a talking dog, shocked that I'd spoken, before they broke into applause.

Mr. Bentham was the most thoughtful man about his own death that I ever met. When he told us that he intended to be publicly autopsied, the general cautioned he take care it not be *vivisection*, given all the enemies he'd acquired. Bentham gave his high-pitched laugh and waved away the threat, eager to tell us about his *latest* plan: he'd decided that his corpse should be taken apart for public study, then *reassembled for public display*, like a vase. He wanted to be mummified and rolled out at the university on special occasions. (He was.)

The idea of the body as an object of inquiry, impersonal, delighted him. And me.

The only visitor I did not like was the young Mr. Simón Bolívar, a frequent guest. Handsome and brilliant as Bolívar was, I did not trust his silence, his quiet voice, his watchful attention. I did not trust him. Perhaps it was rivalry; we were both Mirandus's protégés, after a fashion. He seemed to be calculating advantage in every exchange, tallying losses and wins in the room. Careful that he would win.

After the general's return from the Americas, I noticed another shift in the house. How the general's eyes lingered on me, how he gently rested his hand on mine as I translated from the Greek, how he wrapped my hand in the crook of his arm when we walked home each early evening. I noticed, too, that Sarah seemed less pleased to see me. She was irritable with Leandro, and stormed out one morning when the boys were fighting with no more explanation than "Jesus wept." And one morning when I arrived early, Sarah did not greet me at all but the maid, so I slipped into the library and took my seat only to hear a fearful *thud* upstairs and shouting.

I quickly forgot the incident, absorbed as I was in my studies. Each day I discovered new words and new ideas and new capacities, as if the mind were a house of many rooms, through which I wandered, discovering new doors each day. I learned the pleasures of mathematics reading the *Principia*, the delight of musical compositions; I pored over anatomy texts. I discovered with delight that whatever I read lingered, so that I had only to read a page of Socrates's final words after his trial to see them clearly before me, when conversing with the general, as if the book were held open in my hands. I had only to begin speaking of a text to know what I thought about it, which I had not known before I spoke. It came so easily, if not without effort, each day revealing to me new capacities, as if they were not my own. And the pleasure in learning was matched by the pleasure in seeing the general amazed.

Emboldened by the men's combative talk—and by my own success after three years' study—I made the mistake of asking the general one evening over dinner why he was in London, if his nation needed him, if its liberation was his goal. "Would it not be better to be there among your people, there to lead them, than to be discussing ideals over dinner half a world away?"

I knew instantly that I'd gone too far.

Mirandus said nothing, only turned the stem of his wineglass on the table. Sarah stared at me before she rose from her chair, hurriedly excusing herself to bundle the children off to bed.

"An idealist acts without sufficient thought for strategy," the general said finally, as if he'd said it many times before. "A strategist without sufficient thought for ideals."

"And which are you?"

He did not answer. When I left soon after, no one saw me out.

"He is both," Sarah would tell me later, clearly pleased to school me in the man we loved. "That rarest thing: an idealistic strategist."

I believed that the general was pleased with my progress and fond of me, so I was dismayed when he said—shortly after that dinner, in the autumn of 1809—that he would need to speak with my mother. I feared that the argument I'd overhead or perhaps my comment at dinner had damaged his enthusiasm for my presence in their house. I knew how quickly domestic calm could be undone.

"What have you done?" my mother asked when I related his request.

"Nothing," I said.

"You've done nothing? All this time in the library has availed you nothing?"

"Nothing out of the ordinary, Mother; I have done as I always have—I've read, and reported to the general on my reading." I was exhausted by her suspicion, which felt petty, beneath me now. Perhaps she sensed my dismissal, like my father's before me.

"Heaven help us if that good man turns against us now."

"He's not turned against us," I said, though in truth I wasn't sure. I'd not told my mother of the row I'd overheard. I'd hardly told myself.

As the days passed, I came to dread the coming meeting. I prayed for some disaster to avert it—hoping I might be struck by a cart or fall ill with some conveniently brief fever, lasting just long enough to garner sympathy and a postponement of the conference. But the day arrived. We sat beside the fire in the parlor with a tea tray and a portion of seed cake, a favorite of mine for which I had no appetite.

At first they spoke of other matters, of his sons, the weather, until the general swung round to his point.

"Your daughter is quite extraordinary, Mrs. Brackley. She has a mind like Mrs. Wollstonecraft's. It would have been a pleasure to make an introduction."

It was clear from my mother's blank expression that she did not know the name, or what it represented, which was to my advantage, as she'd likely have refused to allow me to study further had she better understood his praise.

"She has the potential to do great things," he said.

"She has always been clever," my mother allowed.

"She is more than clever."

"Then you will help her find a position as a governess?" my mother asked.

"I will do more than that," he said. "She is prodigiously gifted."

My mother looked at me with what seemed alarm, as if she'd just been told I had two heads, a failing that she'd failed to notice.

"She has expressed a desire to study medicine and literature," General Mirandus said. "It is my hope that she shall."

"We cannot afford to pay for training as a midwife."

"A doctor, Mrs. Brackley. A surgeon."

"Would they let her in?"

"They would let *him* in."

My mother stared at the general, as did I.

"They would admit Jonathan Perry's nephew."

"My son, Tom?" It was the first time in months she'd mentioned my brother's name.

"Your daughter, Margaret." The general turned to me. "Your nephew."

I was too shocked to speak. It seemed an impossible plan. A joke.

If my mother's sense of propriety was offended by the idea of passing off her eldest daughter as a son, practicality eventually won out. While they stayed up late by the fire, discussing my future, I slept to the murmur of their voices. By morning, it was settled. I felt a thrill of dread at the news: I would become a boy, at age fourteen. I was to play the part of Jonathan Perry's unfortunate nephew, and enroll in medical school in Edinburgh that autumn.

It was my idea to add a middle name in honor of my patron. So we saw the last of Margaret and the immaculate birth of a fortunate son: Jonathan Mirandus Perry.

While the general arranged for a tailor to visit, saying that I was the precise size of an absent nephew for whom the clothes were to be cut, it fell to my mother to sew my linens—half a dozen shirts and cravats. If she resented playing the part of tailor to a newly christened son, she made no mention. (Or perhaps I conveniently forgot her complaints, my debt. It's convenient to forget what's painful to recall.) There were bold striped silks of emerald green and a double-breasted red waistcoat with a monstrously high horse collar. In addition to a single pair of breeches, reserved for formal occasions, I was outfitted with a pair of skin-tight pantaloons that came to mid-calf and tied with ribbons, showing off my slender legs with Hessians that came to my knee.

For a fortnight, while clothes were arranged, I practiced before the mirror. Elbows in, then out, wide swaggering steps, chin down as if deep in thought; I knew our lives depended upon my striking the right calculus of character and imper-sonation. As a girl, no one would admit me to university. And the generous support of my uncle's friends was as unreliable as memory—who knew how long they would think of us? Jonathan Perry's poor relations.

It was Sarah Andrews's idea to cut off my long hair. My sole faint claim to beauty. When she took the scissors in her hands, a cloth across my shoulders, my red-gold hair braided down my back, I sensed that it was not simply for the sake of my education that she took up the shearing. I felt the scissors against the curtain of my hair; the pressure tugged my head back.

"Hold still," she said, tilting my chin down.

My scalp tingled and then I heard a tearing as of cloth being rent and a weight lifted from me. My head felt strangely buoyant, too light.

She might have left my hair long, to the shoulders, as General Mirandus's was, but she opted for the French style *à la victime*—first worn in defiance of the Revolution, but now reduced to mere fashion and called the Titus coiffure—with the nape cut close and the top and sides combed forward into a tousled fringe, as on a head straight from the guillotine. My mother was aghast when she saw me—"Your hair," she exclaimed, her eyes moist. "Your beautiful hair." She had not wept to lose her home or eldest daughter, but she wept now, holding my braid in her hands like a corpse.

That night, as I lay my head against the pillowcase, I reveled in the altogether new and startling sensations, the direct contact of skin and scalp with linen and air.

But despite the haircut and new clothes, I remained unconvincingly male. My mother took me to Hyde Park to watch the dandies on parade, to no avail. I spent weeks practicing manliness and failing, until I began to despair of ever mastering the lesson.

One afternoon as I stood in the window overlooking Charles Street, despairing of ever playing the part well, I watched a coach arrive and saw a gentleman step down, then turn to help a lady to the curb. I imitated the gestures, and in impersonating that small courtesy there in my room, I felt something happen in my spine, faint as the tap of teeth together, or a key in a lock, or knuckles cracking. I felt the shift—how I settled back into my body as one might into a comfortable chair. Condescension was the key. Authority like a scarf settled on my shoulders. I felt the confidence I'd had as a child running the green hills of Cork. I knew I could play my part.

After a solid month's preparation, practicing in our rooms, my mother sent me on an errand one morning early. Pressing a coin into my palm, she proposed I go buy sausages in a neighboring street. When a night-soil cart nearly ran me down, I was shocked, then delighted—not for the splash of muck on my breeches and boots, but for the epithet hurled at my head: "Boy, have you no sense? Get out of the street!" For the first time I knew that we are what we say; that people see what we tell them to. *We are our own canvases,* as my uncle said.

Nevertheless, I walked a good ways from the shops we knew, to a district we had not frequented before; I steeled myself and stepped into a shop.

"Help you, lad?" the butcher asked.

I glanced over my shoulder, looking for the boy he addressed.

"What'll it be, boy?"

My voice sounded faint and far away, entirely too high as I asked for the length of sausage for my mother, but if the butcher noticed, he didn't show it.

And that was what amazed me: no one noticed. Later, when I was accustomed to being addressed as *sir* or *Doctor,* I'd realize it was not sartorial sleight of hand that changed my fate that day, as I'd imagined. Diminutive as my stature might be, I carried myself as free men do, as if I belonged in the world, or rather as if the world belonged to me. It was not my clothes that convinced them, it was my carriage: I walked as if my body were mine. I walked as if the world were my inheritance, as if I were a fortunate son.

I had not realized before how I'd held myself back when in the street or entering a shop, shrinking from attention—having been handled on occasion by a merchant in Cork who pretended to steady a sack of oats in my arms or by a carriage man helping me down from a seat and taking hold of other parts; even my brother had pressed himself on me before he'd left for Dublin, claiming the education would do me good. "You don't want your husband to find you ignorant, do you? Keep quiet, and I won't tell our father what you've done." It was unthinkable that I should speak of it, he knew—knowing the shame would be mine alone.

After that first voyage out, matters progressed rapidly. School was organized, and lodging, instruments, and books. General Mirandus arranged for our financial support through a friend he trusted to be discreet, a Dr. Fryer. As I prepared to enter the university at Edinburgh in December 1809 at age fourteen—five years after I'd first made my uncle's acquaintance, three years since his death—life seemed a present waiting to be opened; briefly my future seemed clear: I would train as a doctor for three years, and if I excelled I would go on to serve as a Medical Dresser in London, then travel on to Venezuela, where I would join General Mirandus as his physician and with luck take charge of health policy for the new revolutionary government he intended to establish there. It was a prospect I considered with an admixture of dread and joy.

Mirandus and his family accompanied my mother and me to the docks south of London Bridge on the late-November morning we set out from Wapping on the Thames. He had arranged for the five-day passage on one of the Leith smacks bound for Edinburgh, having secured me a place in the medical school there through the offices of his friend Lord Basken, whom I was to visit later that year. I did not know it would be the last time I would see the general, that my mother would not last three years; I did not know that my education would equip me to save my patients and bring new lives into the world, even as it would take from me everyone I loved. I would gain an education but lose everyone I loved.

Mirandus bent over my hand, only to stop himself. He straightened and pulled me into a manly embrace, then released me.

"The hour of departure has arrived, and we go our ways," Mirandus said.

"You would quote Socrates?" I said, recognizing the philosopher's parting words to his protégé after being condemned to death.

"I would quote anyone who suits this sad occasion," he smiled. "But don't worry, I do not go to my death. I go to Venezuela. Where I will await you."

"It is Venezuela that awaits you, General."

"Let us hope I prove worth waiting for," he said.

"I've no doubt of it." I looked up to see Sarah watching me, and I blushed, before she looked away, over the green-brown water.

"Ah," Mirandus said. "I'd almost forgotten." He lifted from Sarah's arms a package wrapped in paper and twine and placed it in my hands. "For your library."

He knew that I had none, as I knew he cared for his books as if they were children. A gift from his library would be like parting with a child. I fingered the corners, enjoying the weight in my hands.

"From yours?" I asked.

He inclined his head in assent.

"You're too generous," I said.

"I am," he said. "You can return it to me when you come to Caracas."

It's possible that the general had other plans for me in Venezuela—he had plans for everyone, above all for his beloved country, which he hoped to free from the bootheel of Spain; it's possible that he thought to make a mistress of me or to marry me to some brilliant young man; I would have followed whatever direction he had given. I owed him my life, my very name.

He had shown me what my parents could not—that a life can be forged by will, that we can invent ourselves and our histories and shape history itself to our vision. Most everyone else I knew seemed a sleepwalker by comparison. I was not the only one to discern his virtues—the Emperor Napoleon himself called Mirandus "a Don Quixote with the difference that he is not mad." But unlike Napoleon, Mirandus did not live for power alone; he was thoroughly democratic, honoring equally politics and pleasure.

On board the ship, settled out of the icy wind, I unwrapped the package and saw that it was Smellie's atlas, of which only some few dozen had been printed—I fingered the gilt spine, the marbled boards, the Italian paper like tortoiseshell, turning over the pages heavy with copper engraved plates depicting images of a fetus in utero, the delicate cavity smooth as a carved bowl, in which lay a perfect infant curled like a rabbit in its den, an image that might have been an image of myself, beneath my boy's clothes, a portrait of a new life at its start.

CHAPTER TWO

AN EDUCATION

Edinburgh was gloomy and wet when my mother and I arrived there in December 1809. A cold drizzle fell perpetually under what seemed perpetually dark skies. The rooms we rented in Old Town at 6 Lothian Street were modest but comfortable, without being in the least bit delightful, a short walk from the Royal Infirmary and the neoclassical colonnades and massive portals of the university's New College. Our building was one of many such tenements along the street, tall and narrow, inhabited by intellectuals and aspiring artists, drawn by the glamour of what was widely held to be the seat of Scottish genius, where just half a century before, David Hume and Adam Smith and Robert Burns had walked the cobbled streets, as now the greatest minds of medicine did.

My first day at university, I walked along the corridors, aware of those who had walked here before—now I, among them; I could hear the voices of students ringing out along the hallways, the sound of a door closed, another opened. The chill of the stone archways seemed like time distilled, stopped; I paused beneath an arch and leaned my back against a dark stone column simply to observe the place, amazed by what men are capable of. What I was. When I heard bootheels against the stone of the corridor, I hurried on to class.

The medical school at Edinburgh was almost 85 years old by the time I enrolled there and was renowned throughout the English-speaking world. Our classmates came from all corners of the globe—India and the West Indies, North America, and throughout the British Isles. We were the younger sons of landed gentry, the children of squires and prosperous merchants, the sort of men my brother might have been had he applied himself, cared to learn.

Our decision to move to Scotland was not purely intellectual. I could not attend Oxford or Cambridge nor hold public office given the Test Act, which barred Catholics from all those things, restricting such privileges to members of the Church of England—a standard that happily did not apply here.

In Edinburgh, our religion was intellection.

I arrived at the university timid and awkward, despite the general's careful preparations. I realized quickly that my language was unsuitable, too grave, too cultured, too careful; the cultivated talk of dinner tables and drawing-room debates that I had developed in my conversations with General Mirandus was out of place here among boys my own age, absurd. Whatever the subject under discussion—a body part, a brothel, beer—I seemed to strike the wrong note. Pedantic. Humorless. Elderly. Still I forced myself to join the knots of young men who gathered outside the lecture halls, to insert myself into their company, struggling to belong.

Eager to distinguish myself, I did not evade notice, as I

should have sought to do. In my anxiety to appear friendly, I interrupted conversations, held forth irrelevantly on matters unrelated to me; I was overly familiar where formality was required, formal where intimacy was called for. Eventually I settled on being distant but polite.

I spent my first weeks in the lecture halls in a state of barely contained panic, heart pounding, hands shaking as I struggled to take notes, afraid of being noticed, terrified of going undistinguished. I yearned to be home with my mother in the little apartment in Lothian Street, free of observation and of the chest bindings that chafed and made it hard to breathe, the wet air making the bandages moist and irritating against my skin, raising red welts that festered, peeled white, and smelled sour; I observed other boys, a few like myself, who sought to ingratiate themselves into the ranks of the more at ease. I noted above all how those timid boys laughed when others laughed at them, as if they didn't mind.

A few weeks into the term, an enormous boy from Canada, Chesterton, as he was called, drew in his elbows to his waist, as I did mine, and let forth a flurry of words in a high-pitched voice in obvious parody of me, as a group of us stood talking in the hallway before lecture. I knew that I should laugh, make light of the insult as others did, accept my low rung in the hierarchy of boys becoming men, but something in me rebelled against the injustice, perhaps the same muscle that twitched in my contumacious uncle; the casual humiliation of the vulnerable by the powerful struck me as monstrous, an outrage, as if it were emblem of all that learning, study, civilization, and revolution were meant to eradicate and which I must in turn stamp out wherever I found it, and so I surprised myself and my tormentor when instead of laughing at the joke, I raised my fist like a cudgel and hit him squarely in the face. I insisted he apologize at once.

Silence fell and it occurred to me to run. The boy I'd hit was much larger than I; almost everyone was. If he struck me, he might kill me without even intending to, given his preposterous size. But I resisted the impulse. He touched his nose and frowned. "Bloody hell," he said. Blood had begun to leak from his nostril.

"*Apologize,*" a voice said, and I wondered if I had spoken again; I had wondered at my courage to speak at all, as if some other self had stepped forward. But it wasn't me. All eyes had shifted to someone behind me.

It was an elegantly dressed student, whom I'd seen in the lecture hall.

"You owe him an apology," he said. "Apologize."

"*He* hit *me*, Jobson."

"*You* insulted him."

"For Christ's sake, Chester, just apologize; we'll be late to Monro's lecture."

"It's *not* my *fault,*" the Canadian protested. He lurched toward me, and I stepped back in fear, but he only cuffed me on the arm.

"Apologies," he said.

"Accepted," I said.

And we all went in. I walked far down the stairs to find a seat near the front of the hall, a place I never sat; I knew better than to sit so close, given students' penchant for pelting Dr. Monro with peas and rotten fruit in protest of his incompetence, but I wanted to be alone, to calm myself.

Monro's anatomy lectures were soporific as chloroform and his cadavers were always long past their prime and of truly appalling smell; his excavations of the body bordered on the criminal and the comic, both. Everyone had heard the stories. Once, while seeking to display a uterus, he'd hauled out the bladder instead and a length of fetid intestine that slid to the floor with a terrible wet sound, prompting jeers and an exodus of students from the lecture hall. He was said to have wrenched off a finger once while trying to dissect a hand, and I myself would later witness him rummaging about in search of a gall bladder, like a man desperately seeking a sock in a cluttered drawer. "It's in here somewhere," he kept repeating, as if we might find the words encouraging.

So I was surprised when the well-dressed boy who'd spoken up for me took a seat beside me.

"He'd have killed you, y'know," the boy said, slipping into his seat. "Why in the world did you hit him like that?

"He had insulted my honor," I said. I struggled to keep my voice deep.

"I know *why* you hit him, but why like *that*, with your hand like a mallet? Have you never thrown a punch before?"

In fact, I hadn't.

He took it upon himself to try to teach me in the weeks that followed, to show me how a sharp jab from the chest could land a blow, but I didn't practice as he urged. We both knew that I had better avoid such altercations in future. Or risk being killed.

John Jobson—the boy who rescued me that day—was a good-natured and unimaginative fellow, with the easy manners

and generous heart of one whose wishes have ever been indulged, for whom privation is as remote as their own demise,
a second son whose chief qualifications for the practice of
medicine appeared to be a strong stomach and a father with
£10,000 a year in Wales. He displayed an Olympian lack of
curiosity when it came to the body's intricate structures—the
fretwork of musculature and tendons, veins and nerves, the
magnificent clockwork parts—and a majestic indifference to
smell. He possessed what I'd later learn from Lord Somerton
are the virtues of a good hound: loyal, attentive to whatever he pursued, oblivious of the rest. My first boyhood
friend.

It was precisely Jobson's lack of imagination that secured
our friendship. Whereas other students quickly took note of
my voice—squeaky and high—and my too-smooth cheek,
Jobson was generously oblivious of such details. He seemed to
see only a frail Irish boy, rather younger than the rest, whose
protection he sought to secure as he might have done for a
wounded starling, a squirrel, or a rabbit.

He had, in short, a tender heart and—though hardly
taller than I—an athlete's powerful build and the sportsman's
unencumbered view of life: that of quarry and hunter. The
landscape he traversed in the pursuit was of only incidental
interest. He had grown up in the country with an open and
gentle nature, his face more freckle than skin, his hair a
disheveled mop of pale brown, the sort of kindly boy whom
others naturally tormented, although he was so good-natured
and robust that he won respect in place of contempt.

After our lectures, Jobson joined the others to drink in
public houses and whore, and pursue the pranks that were the
medical student's first attempt to make his name, as doctors

must. He did his best to instruct me in the manly arts of beer guzzling and belching, bare-fist boxing and brothels, but I was more Beau Brummell than Jem Belcher. I preferred to return to my rooms to read and study Latin.

In truth, there was little to distract me from my studies, although Jobson made a herculean effort. He was naturally kind, and exceedingly generous. He often stood me and other students for a drink or a meal when we hadn't time between lectures to return home, and he seemed sincerely grieved when I failed to join them in the evening.

I knew that I was considered aloof and eccentric by the other students, unduly reticent. But the convivial fraternity of my fellow students was not one I was eager to join; their raucous parties featured ample beer and pranks—wrenching knockers off doors and painting anatomical details on local sculptures (a practice that Jobson maintained had reputable classical origins: "Alcibiades knocked the pricks off priapic sculptures for sport," he said. "It's good fun").

It wasn't snobbery that kept me apart, but fear. Fear of exposure and of failure both—I studied every waking moment when I was not at university lectures or at Barclay's or Fyfe's for tutorials in dissection. Unlike Jobson and the others, I could not depend on family wealth should I fail my exams in three years' time, as many did on the first try. My mother and sister depended on me to pass, so we might leave this purgatory of penury and social isolation and enter a more secure condition abroad in Caracas with the general, where I might throw off my disguise and practice medicine openly, where our origins would not be closely considered, where we'd be well beyond the reach of my father and brother.

Not knowing how much would be required to pass our

exams, which a fair portion of the students failed each spring, I studied with fierce self-discipline; I made myself sick staying up late and alone to memorize Latin and anatomy.

Ours was to be a three-year course, covering a range of practical and theoretical studies: anatomy, natural and moral philosophy, medical jurisprudence, and Greek; chemistry, botany, *materia medica* (pharmacy), and the theory and practice of medicine. In addition to attending lectures and wards at the Royal Infirmary, I would undertake an oral examination and written exams on the whole of my studies, culminating in a defense of my dissertation in Latin conducted by a panel of professors.

Classes were held in the surgical amphitheater, the lecture room, and bedside, and—if one had the money, which thanks to Lord Basken's generosity I did—in private tutorials in dissection, where the most valuable lessons might be learned. The leading surgeon of the day, Sir Astley Cooper, was known to exhort his students in London to look to *themselves* to learn their profession: "Never mind what others may say," he said. "No opinion or theories can interfere with information acquired from dissection." I would attend Barclay's and Fyfe's private dissection lectures for all three years—1810 to 1812— inspired by his words.

A grim snow fell as Jobson and I made our way to Dr. Fyfe's for our first private dissection that evening in January 1810— a few weeks into the term; our shoulders fell together companionably as we walked the uneven cobblestones. Despite the brooding cold, I found Edinburgh more thrilling than anywhere I'd ever been, save perhaps for Mirandus's library in London. Still, the weather oppressed me.

"If Edinburgh is truly the Athens of the North," I told Jobson, as we walked, "it's no wonder Socrates killed himself." I missed Mirandus and his little family. I missed the stinking agate-green Thames and the little garden and our walks through the wide green expanses of Hyde Park.

"It's not so bad," Jobson said. "After a few pints. Join us tonight, why don't you?"

I shook my head. "I've reading to do for Hamilton, and Monro."

"You can't be serious," Jobson said. "You *study* for Monro? The only study required for his lectures is how to stay awake."

"The man's dullness is so extreme," I said, "it's almost an attainment."

Monro's incompetence was one reason we were there that night to attend the dissection tutorial at Dr. Fyfe's home in Horse Wynd, as later we'd study with the famous Dr. Barclay, whose school in Surgeon's Square was in such high demand that even with six tutors Barclay often had to lecture twice each day to keep up.

"If Barclay ever runs short of corpses," Jobson said, "perhaps he might look into retrieving the bodies of students *bored* to death by Monro."

I laughed.

We joked, in part, to dispel the fear we felt; we'd all heard stories of these tutorials: of a man's head cleaved open on a table, an arm discarded on the floor, fingers and hands tugged on by rats and fought over by hungry birds in the corners of the room. How students fled their first dissection, sick from the smells or the sights.

But our true dread was of contagion, or should have been.

Despite the Murder Act—which had legalized autopsy 60 years before, providing medical men with the corpses of those hanged for murder—there were never enough bodies to go around. We took what we could get. It was understood that our tutors bought corpses where they could; if consumption had been the cause of untimely death, the Resurrectionists who provided them didn't know it. Nor did we.

The Murder Act had made autopsy possible by providing medical men with legal corpses, but the taint lingered like the scent of rot, giving our work a criminal air. It didn't help our reputation that the church still considered human dissection a sacrilege, and there were always too few bodies available, despite the flourishing state of homicide, so our work had all the glamour of grave robbing. The effort to dress up our suppliers in religious rhetoric did not improve the matter: call them Resurrectionists as we might, they remained grave robbers and body snatchers in the popular imagination, a breath away from murderers themselves.

When we reached Fyfe's home, we were let into the front hall by a servant who led us back to a chill, dim room at the rear of the house, a room illuminated faintly by candlelight; it took a moment for my eyes to adjust, distracted by the appalling smell. That was my first impression: a scent solid as sound, like the streets of Cork after the autumn slaughter when offal rotted in the lanes. The reek of mortality is sweet and fetid, emetic. The stench of three-days-dead, the putrid sweetness of decay and rotting flesh.

Jobson appeared to take no notice—he strode straight up to the corpse on the table as if to introduce himself, as if approaching the host of a party or a bar in a public house, as if he expected the cadaver to sit up and address him by name.

I pressed a kerchief to my nose to stifle a gag as I made my way slowly to the center of the room, where the body lay, undisturbed as yet, upon the table surrounded by tall stools. I was conscious of the scent of wine and smoked meat, which I'd later learn were sometimes used to preserve corpses; across the room lay another body on another table, the floor slick with fat and flesh; cast-off digits jerked as rats gnawed the bones. It was like stumbling into someone else's nightmare.

The body laid out on the dissecting table was grey as marble in the low light, skin mottled with dark spots; it was surprisingly hard when I touched it, and cold; the skin of the face and chest had contracted like stretched canvas, making it difficult to discern whether this had once been man or woman. A cloth draped its waist; an unusual gesture, I'd learn; I wondered who'd put it there. Why. Despite the reek of rot, I did not feel the horror I'd prepared for. I searched in vain for the revulsion I'd expected and found only an uneasy excitement, like that I'd later glimpse in the faces of my fellow students in brothels.

When Dr. Fyfe joined us some minutes later, dressed in a bloodied smock, we arranged ourselves around the table. Fyfe commenced that first session with an exhortation, borrowed from the English surgeon Thomas Chevalier: "Gentlemen, you must know the magnificent machinery of the body as precisely as the great artist knows its outline to translate it to paint or stone."

My uncle would have been delighted.

"Pompous ass," Jobson whispered to me.

I nodded, but in truth I was entranced. I loved the bombast

and the secretive nature of our proceedings, these solemn rites, which felt ancient and vaguely religious, though I had scant belief in theology, which seemed—from what I'd observed— more an impediment than a spur to understanding in our age. This seemed a truer religion than the one I'd got from the priests in Cork. The sacrament of body. I longed to be among the initiated, to enter into its mysteries.

Having gathered us around the corpse, Fyfe drew a blade from his cutting kit and made the first incision, starting at the throat and bisecting the cadaver down the sternum, then below the clavicle before he lifted with forceps the mottled grey-blue skin to reveal grey flesh and pale bone within; blood black as coal seeped out at the seam where he cut. I saw Chesterton turn away.

Fyfe continued to cut, as if skin were dense fabric, naming what he encountered as he went, splaying the skin, taking a saw to the sternum and ribs, cracking open the chest to reveal the fleshy pulp of heart and lungs. He yanked out a grey lung like a useless wing before continuing the autopsy in detail to the waist, where he removed the cloth that had concealed the sex. An aged woman, not an aged man, the distinctions few in death.

At the end of that first evening's session, Fyfe—perhaps conscious of the high fees we were paying for the privilege— offered each of his six pupils the opportunity to claim a memento. I thought it ghoulish, but Jobson clucked with delight.

"I'll take an ear," he said cheerfully, politely, as if it were a cut of meat at dinner.

Someone else beside me proposed to take the tail, which got a laugh.

Chesterton took a nipple.

I declined.

It was one thing to disregard the superstitious fear of sacrilege with which the religious condemned dissection, fearing that we might be stealing souls, desecrating God's handiwork; it was quite another to reduce the body to a trinket, a mere commodity to be trafficked. When we left the dissection room, I felt light-headed and stepped away from the others and bent over into the street behind a lamppost, and was—for the first and only time there—sick.

In da Vinci's day, it had been a scandal to look on women's living bodies, so Michelangelo painted men, my uncle Jonathan had told me, pushing the picture book toward me, one of the few times he'd deigned to speak to me the summer that we met. "Look," he'd said. "His Mary Magdalene has the arms of a stable hand." Now when I looked on the Renaissance madonna, I would see those arms and think of the names of the muscles along the shoulder, the upper arm. Names I could recite like lines of a poem by Dryden or Cowper, and which seemed as beautiful to me.

I could not help but wonder, then as now, *When we look at a man or a woman, what is it that we see?* We make too much of the difference: having been both, I can say the distinctions are both greater and less than they appear. As a surgeon, I can attest that once the skin is peeled back, the distinctions are few; save for the reproductive organs, one cannot tell man from woman—one cannot say, *This is a woman's brain or lungs, a man's heart.* They think and beat just the same.

But there were, of course, a few irrefutable differences,

which imposed themselves each month, reminding me of my past, my secret, of the need to conceal both.

Occasionally a fellow student would fall ill and not return to class and we would hear that he'd been taken by consumption, which was rumored to be the source of the steady stream of corpses whose company we enjoyed.

But arrogant with youth and its delusion that age, infirmity, and death are things that happen to other people—to one's parents, say, who have foolishly failed to retain the youth and health that we possess—we imagined that, like death itself, contagion could not touch us.

Nonetheless, I was fastidious in my ablutions—carefully bathing my hands in hot water and in wine after our sessions, an eccentricity that my fellow students mocked.

"Poor Perry doesn't know where to put the wine."

"Who knows what other anatomy lessons he's got wrong?"

"Get the boy to a bawdy house, before it's too late."

But I failed to consider what I should most have feared: the danger I posed to others.

As the weeks passed, I grew increasingly confident in my attire, even cocky. As I began to excel in my studies and impress the faculty, I noticed less the bindings that wrapped my chest, the discipline of deepening my voice; speaking with authority became reflex. Masked as I was, I felt seen, as if I wore my true face in the world. That of Jonathan Mirandus Perry.

My masquerade proved adequate in the self-regarding company of boys and men, but I feared I might be discovered in the close company of more observant women, so I avoided them. I felt lucky that the century—with its wars—had divided the sexes, separating men from their womenfolk and protecting me from too-close inspection by the fairer sex, safeguarding my secret.

So I was uneasy when I received the invitation from Lord Basken, our patron, to dine at his home in George Street to celebrate the New Year. There would be no avoiding women at the dinner. It was one thing to present myself in classrooms, to pass myself off among boys and merchants, but quite another to impersonate a young gentleman, a university student among those accustomed to speaking with same. I considered pleading illness, perhaps injury—a limb broken just enough to prevent me from lifting a fork? My mother was excited on my behalf. I knew I could not evade it. We owed him our lives.

That first dinner at Lord Basken's would be a test, one I knew I must pass.

Preparing for the dinner took much of the day. My mother oversaw my attire: she insisted that I wear an emerald striped jacket, a vest of embroidered maroon silk, a starched yellow muslin cravat; the shoulders of my coat were padded, its plush cuffs ornamented with buttons; she could not persuade me to relinquish my long surtout in favor of a more fashionable shooting coat.

I held my elbows in to keep my chest bindings steady. I stood before the cheval glass, brushing my hair forward, plucking my collar up between my fingers, settling my face into the bored, disinterested expression of men. And thus prepared I went out into the cold, wet evening to have dinner with the eleventh Earl of Basken, the patron we'd never met.

The uneasy glances directed my way when I first entered the drawing room, where guests had gathered before dinner, told me that I was younger than I hoped to appear, or less fashionable. Or less convincing. My long surtout was a regular subject of fun among my fellow students. My mother had insisted that I improve my dress, but I drew the line there.

I heard a woman's voice say, "Why, he is a child."

My patron replied, "He is a relation of Jonathan Perry, the painter—you know of him, of course."

"Of course. But is he . . ." She lowered her voice.

"They *say* he is a nephew."

I had studied what I could from my few formal dinners with General Mirandus, had been coached by my mother; this was to be my exam. *Could I play whist? Would I remember to remain when the women retired to the drawing room? How to toast? Would I remember which fork was for salad, which for fish, for meat? To keep my voice low and calm? Would I think to tip the soup plate away from me to bring up the last spoonful of turtle soup? Would I know how to speak of nothing at length?*

Saying nothing is an art. My dinner companions appeared to have mastered it.

Lord Basken led me around the room, making introductions to people whose names I forgot instantly, despite my mother's warnings. They spoke of hunting and of balls and occasionally of books. Wanting to impress, awkward with small talk, I defaulted to debate. Doubting my capacity to charm, I would be memorable, admired. So I challenged premises reflexively.

"Surely you can't believe that?"

"And what should I believe instead?"

Lord Basken roared with laughter. "You truly are your uncle's—" he paused.

"Nephew, sir. I am indeed." Where we do not find love, it's easy to seek its poor surrogates—admiration, envy. I understood my uncle better now; I was perhaps like him.

When dinner was announced, we proceeded to the dining room and I had to suppress an urge to ogle the silver, which glowed with a high polish, to inspect the Spode china, the bright crystal goblets for water, wine, port. Even in the soft dim candlelight, the room and the table dazzled. Candlelight lent it all a pink, fleshy cast.

I hardly recall the food; I hardly ate, so focused on the utensils, the patter of chat.

When we were served a dessert of cake—a confection of pastry and coconut and whipped cream that resembled millinery more than pastry—I wished I might sketch it for my mother. There was a chocolate cream and an elderflower ice, then an enormous silver bowl of fruit of every kind was brought around: small green apples and small red ones, oranges and fat purple figs, grapes and even a pineapple, and strawberries—sent, it was said, from Lord Basken's greenhouse at Dryburgh Abbey, where impossibly they were said to grow throughout the year.

"You must come stay with us during your vacation, Master Perry."

"I would like nothing more," I said, wondering how I might arrange to have my sister join us, my aunt.

A woman on my right described to me the ruins there, the haunted beauty of the place, until we were interrupted by a debate over the education of women, which Lord Basken was vehemently in support of.

"Am I not right, Master Perry?"

I wondered what he knew of me.

"I am all in favor of the education of women," I replied. "There's nothing I should like to see more, except perhaps the ruins at Dryburgh Abbey."

It did not seem to me base flattery that I practiced, but social grace or alchemy. Like an experiment performed in chemistry—mixing vinegar and baking soda—I sought a combination that would produce the most pleasing result, the approbation of my host.

After dinner I won at whist while appearing to lose, so charmingly, so ineptly, inviting the help of female advisers that my victory was cheered by all except one young man, who threw down his cards in disgust. A matron beside me set a hand on mine, and said that I simply must come for an at-home when her niece from London was next in town. She had come out the prior spring.

I was a great success.

It was almost a week before I found time to sit at the table by the window and report to General Mirandus on the dinner, to share these small triumphs and see in his response their value, their weight in the world, giving them a reality they seemed to lack; I wanted to prove him right; I wanted him to know he'd not been wrong about me. I wanted to assure myself. I longed for news of him, and of Sarah and their sons. No one else— save for my mother—knew the thing I'd done, the worth of it, the cost.

It was while I was a student in Edinburgh that I began to keep my little book of quotations and definitions, *bons mots* and words that I didn't know or whose etymology interested me. Terms and stray phrases from the books that I read and liked. I favored *Honi soit qui mal y pense; Shamed be he who thinks evil of it*, the Order of the Garter's motto, that Anglo-Norman maxim. Often they were simple words. Familiar words whose etymology made them seem new. Strange and delightful. As the body now seemed.

Manifest had particular charm. It still does. Like an incantation, as if to say it were to bring one's will to pass. As I sought daily to do.

Manifest.

A *manifest* was originally a document that detailed the contents of a ship, its passengers and cargo and crew, from the mid-century Italian *manifesto*, from the Latin *manifestare* (to make public), from the Latin *manifestus* (caught in the act).

But that is not its only meaning. As an adjective it refers to that which is obvious, clear to the eye (*the hospital's manifest failings*); as a verb it means *to display or make evident, to demonstrate* (as in, *I manifest the virtues of a man*); it can refer to that which becomes apparent through symptoms, such as an ailment (*a disorder that manifests in middle age*), or to the appearance of a ghost or a spirit (*a deity manifested as a bird*). The Americans, in that still-new century, would come to believe their *destiny* was manifest, obvious, as I believed mine was then—they believed in westward expansion; I believed I would rise. And I did. Quickly. My skill manifest to all.

But it was not without cost, my rise.

My mother was a strong woman, but she drew her strength from customary surrounds and comforts, her pillows and needlepoint, a familiar hearth and streets she'd walked as a child. Whereas I took heart from the new world revealed to me in Edinburgh and in my lectures on literature and medicine, my mother seemed daily drained. When news came from Mr. Penrose, a family friend, that my father was in debtor's prison in Dublin, she was not comforted by the news, as I was. Perhaps she missed him, for all his faults. Certainly she missed the only home she'd ever known—Cork with its familiar streets, its defining rivers and bridges, her parish priest. Everything that bore witness to who she had been and was.

I took her waning as a sign of sorrow, did not read in it, as I should have done, that she was weakened by her cloistral days inside the four rooms of our tenement home, spacious as it was. The long cold days, the damp mornings that became damp afternoons.

Perhaps I should have been ashamed to have my mother laboring on my behalf, but I was not; I was too absorbed by my studies. I was gratified to have her bustling around me as I worked at the kitchen table, or endeavoring to be quiet, to leave me undisturbed as I studied by the fire. I felt important that I could command such silence, such effort, on my behalf. I told myself I would repay the debt with a home of her own.

We spent many pleasant evenings discussing the house that we would set up for my mother, sister, and me—once I was a doctor. My mother was keen on settling in Rome or Madrid, for the weather *and* the faith. She dreaded the prospect of the Americas, which she was convinced (thanks to Royall Tyler's novel *The Algerine Captive*) were overrun by rabid Protestants, savages, and brutish colonists, whose inhumanity was proved by their refusal to relinquish the barbarous practice of slavery (though that trade had only recently been abolished on English soil). She was certain all Americans lived in log cabins and wore animal skins. Only the promise of settling in the capital city of Caracas in a Catholic nation on a Catholic continent could soothe her doubts and briefly reconcile her to life in the New World.

We spoke of the house we might have—each in turn imagining an addition she would like: a pond with colorful fish for my sister (when she joined us), a Roman-style atrium for me, a vegetable garden and orchard for my mother; I imagined a stable with a brace of grey horses and a bright red carriage. I read up on the plants and animals and soil, the sugar plantations and cacao.

Imagining our future became a consolation, our principal entertainment. We talked about what we would buy, what we would wear, what we would eat once we were rich. I spoke of books I would acquire, paintings; my mother spoke of food. Each night we devoured an imaginary banquet: oysters, turtle soup, partridges, fish, beef and lamb and blood sausages, strawberries with cream, pineapple, Orange Fool, chocolate cake and cream pastries, walnuts, biscuits filled with jam.

"We can plant lemon trees," my mother said.

"Better," I said. "We can grow bananas."

"What's a banana?"

"I'm not entirely sure, but it is said to be a fruit both soft and sweet, with a heavy skin, and shaped rather like a cutlass."

"Sounds dreadful," she said.

"It does, doesn't it? We can grow oranges instead."

We contemplated growing our own cacao—though neither of us was quite sure what that might entail, or even what the valuable seeds looked like—but we relished the idea of having hot drinking chocolate every morning, rich with cinnamon and cardamom. We passed that first dark, rainy winter in

Edinburgh in happy reverie: inventing a life for ourselves, sunny and bright and free of the past, combining familiar comforts and companions with the promise of adventure in a new world.

Delighted as I was by the progress I was making in my studies, I was only truly at ease and content in my mother's company, forthright, gruff, but affectionate. We would read to one another in the evening and talk of our future, which seemed certain to be brighter than the past.

When my studies were complete, we would bring my sister with us to Venezuela. I could imagine the delight her presence would cause among the general's acquaintance in Caracas, among those capable of discerning superior qualities despite obscure birth. And I allowed myself the vanity of imaging that I might, with application and the general's patronage, rise to a level of prominence that might secure my sister's own. For surely if nature were the measure of merit, she would stand far above the rest. And so together we passed bright days despite the brutal grey cold of that first Scottish winter.

Despite the miserable weather and the stench of corpses that lingered on my hands and in my nose, I was happy where we were, there in Edinburgh. Each day I felt more at ease, more the person I had always been, privately, when as a child I'd closed my eyes in the dark. I was discovering among men that winter a freedom of movement that I'd never known before, even as a girl, but I learned quickly that this was not the same as liberty: I'd thought a man's life would grant me freedom, but my movements were simply constrained in novel ways. I could reveal to no one, save my mother, the body that was mine, whose proportions I learned to disguise with the corseting another generation had reserved for women but now esteemed in men.

When the other students visited a bawdy house, or came to blows, I was careful to steer clear to preserve my secret, which gained me a reputation for being delicate. I missed the physical freedom I'd known as a child in Cork, where my sister and I were allowed to wander the fields around town, gathering flowers to press among pages of newsprint or bits of cloth, picnicking in muslin gowns loose and light as leaves, secure in the liberty conferred by disregard.

To counter the effect of my growing reputation for delicacy, I took to imitating our teachers' belligerent intellectualism. I learned to be caustic, arrogant, indifferent to prevailing opinion. The only unforgivable sin in our ardent age was to be bland, to be without fervor in a sentimental era. We felt ourselves to be living in a great time, on the verge of something extraordinary—an age of new discoveries in science and medicine and politics that thrilled those of us ready to embrace new understandings.

Our faculty were a cavalcade of eccentricities, from the majestic Dr. Gregory, who taught us physic and wore a hat cocked over his brow throughout lectures and was given to rages that rivaled my uncle's, to the stately Dr. Hamilton and the soporific Alexander Monro. Our teachers were flamboyant and contentious, given to extravagant fits of opinion and temper. It was rumored that several had come to blows.

"Did you know Gregory bludgeoned Dr. Hamilton with his walking stick?" Jobson asked, as we waited in the lecture hall one February morning for Dr. Gregory to begin; we watched him sift through his notes at the podium.

"Doesn't seem to have damaged Hamilton's wit," I said. "Or improved his looks."

Jobson gave his polite patrician laugh, which sounded like a cough.

"Damaged Gregory's purse," he said. "They say he paid a hundred pounds in damages."

"A sure spur to contrition," I replied.

"Not at all. Gregory claims the pleasure of beating Hamilton was worth every penny."

I laughed and drew the glare of Dr. Gregory, who raised his walking stick at me in warning. I covered my mouth with a fist and pretended to be mid-cough. We'd heard he was given to beating students as well, so were careful not to provide occasion to witness it.

Of all our faculty, only Dr. Gregory seemed to disapprove of me, to grow more hostile as my answers in class that spring term grew more keen, precise. I was accustomed to winning praise from my teachers, so I was dismayed to find I inspired rage in Gregory instead. I endeavored not to care. I'd heard he was competitive with his students. Given to fits of pique. I chose to take it as a badge of honor. In lectures I tried not to delight in others' failure, which amplified my own success.

Of all the thrilling discoveries of those years at university, the most magnificent was my discovery of that greatest liberty of men: not to have to please. To be able to indulge bad temper and dislike, to feel whatever I might. Without apology. I shrugged off sweet disposition like a cloak.

My favorite lectures were those of Dr. Alexander Hamilton, who taught Midwifery. Hamilton's lectures followed his father's famous text, *Outlines of the Theory and Practice of Midwifery*, beginning with Anatomy and Physiology, then Pathology, then Labours (those requiring Hands alone and those Necessitating Instrumental Delivery)—including the monstrous Caesarian section, an operation reviled by our teachers and texts. Extreme narrowness of pelvis or extraordinary bulk of the child were considered the only justification for recourse to the "horrid operation," which I had observed only in autopsy. As Hamilton said, "Some positively deny that a woman can survive the daring attempt." Sir Fielding Ould called it "a detestable, barbarous, and illegal piece of inhumanity." I noted it.

The life of the mother was paramount in our minds, as in any sound physician's. It was understood that we were charged with delivering *her*, the mother, of the child. I learned from Hamilton that the physician's work is to facilitate the body's method, to assist nature, be her midwife. It was an unusual doctrine, almost heresy in our age of increasing intervention among *accoucheurs*, often at the patient's expense.

That first year, one book above all impressed me: William Harvey's *de Motu Cordis, On the Motion of the Heart and Blood in Animals*, which revolutionized our understanding of the blood's circulation, which men had mistaken for over a thousand years. I studied Harvey's work—and his life—eager for a model for my own.

I first heard of Harvey in a lecture by Dr. Hamilton. "It has often been said," Hamilton began, "that the world knows little of its greatest men, and in the case of William Harvey the statement is strikingly true." *It knows less of its greatest women,* I thought.

We studied Dr. Harvey, of course, because he'd discovered

the circulation of the blood two centuries earlier and revealed the true function of the heart. Before him—thanks to the Greek physician Galen—the pulse was thought to be a kind of *respiration*, air sucked into arteries, with vessels acting as bellows. There was *imaginary* respiration all over the body. That blood *moved* was known, but Harvey was first to see that it moved in a *circle*—and that respiration and circulation had distinct aims. For 1,500 years before Harvey, Galen's fictional body was taken for a fact.

We treated imaginary bodies. We still do; to some extent, the body is a figment of the imagination of its time.

William Harvey was Physician to the King when his book was published; it destroyed his reputation, even though he was correct. His revelation that Galen was wrong—and thus prevailing medical practice founded on a fantasy—enraged his readers. He was dismissed as mad, "crackbrained"; his fellow physicians turned on him. When he died thirty years later, he'd lost friends, reputation, even the power of speech.

At home that night in Lothian Street, I told my mother about Harvey's discoveries and his scandalous claim that "the *heart* of animals is the foundation of their life, the sovereign of everything within them." Usually she'd nod complacently when I spoke of my studies, but this time she enthusiastically agreed; Harvey's gospel of the heart's supremacy confirmed what she held most dear—sentiment our salvation. *Is it the heart that moves us, or the mind?* My mother had no doubt. She was sure my uncle would have helped us had *he* had a better heart; my father would not have turned us out had his been good.

But I argued it is the thoughts of men that guide them, and govern their actions—and should. Sentiment, the heart, is a fickle master, unreliable as a mob and as unpredictable; it can turn hard and ugly quickly.

Harvey's discoveries were the result of dissection, observation, induction, as I hoped my own would be. I thrilled to see such rigorous logic applied to the body and that most important mystery, the heart.

The body was not, as my mother feared, profaned by examination, as if one were cross-examining God, but honored by attention. Love, all love, is attention. To be seen truly is the greatest gift.

Throughout that first winter, I studied Harvey's text and others, aware each day of the slightly longer light, still burdened by the velvet darkness that arrived with the cold and the wet early each winter afternoon; looking out the window onto a woolen-grey sky, the steep shingled rooftops of the facing buildings, the dirty black chimney pots and facades with windows blank as dead eyes, the sounds coming up from the street below, voices in the hallway, the chill ahead of me, the fire by which my mother sat warm at my back.

Gradually, increasingly, when I joined my mother by the fire, she did not speak, except to ask if she might perform some service—did I want another pillow? She no longer called me by my given name, Margaret. As if her daughter were truly dead. I ached to embrace her, to talk as we had, but she rejected every attempt; when I held her, she stood stiffly, as if it were improper, unseemly, then stepped away, saying she had work to do.

One evening when I put on a nightgown to sit by the fire, without my usual chest bindings, as the bandages had left my

chest chafed and sore, she shouted at me, asked what I thought
I was doing. I didn't understand. "What if a neighbor saw you,
dressed like that?" I knew she meant with my chest unbound.
You could, I realize, see the outline of my body beneath the
thin fabric against the fire. I felt ashamed. Lonely. We no
longer spoke of the future in Caracas.

As the months passed and we settled into Edinburgh, I
missed the general more, not less, as my relations with my
mother cooled. In the past, my mother had depended on me,
confided in me; no longer. At night, while she sat by the
fire mending and sewing, I sat at a desk by the window and
read, alone.

In London, I had told her of Mirandus's home, of the room
of books and hot chocolate and the pet rabbit. Now, when I
described the eccentric faculty or some new bit of knowledge,
she smiled politely, listened attentively, but the old warmth
between us was gone, replaced by a respectful formality. As if
the chill of Edinburgh had cooled our hearts.

Only when we were out on the street did I feel my mother
draw near to me; she would take my arm as we walked, I
nearer the curb to protect her from any mud that might splash
up from passing carriages and carts; I helped her into carriages
and out, took off her cloak and returned it to her shoulders.
It was when we entered a shop and she deferred to me that
I felt the bond between us most keenly again. "My son will
take care of it," she'd say, with unmistakable pride, confident
in my abilities, and I would. I would search out small things
to delight her—ginger biscuits and hot chocolate to drink,
corned beef and cabbage, butter, cream—hoping to spark the
affection we'd once shared.

When my mother slipped and called me "Tom," mistaking me for my brother, I tried not to mind. I failed to see it as a sign, a warning.

I slipped up only once that first year, when I ventured to invite Jobson home with me for tea that winter.

"Jobson, may I present my mother, Mrs. Brackley."

He bowed. "It's a pleasure, Mrs. Brackley."

"I'm gratified someone takes pleasure in it, I'm sure," my mother said, looking put out to have to pause in her tasks. "You'll be wanting some tea, I imagine."

I did not realize that her irritation was over my grave error.

"That would be delightful," I said. "Thank you."

"Your *mother*?" Jobson asked me later, as we sat alone together awaiting tea in the tiny parlor overlooking Lothian Street.

"Did I say *mother*?" I smoothed a crease on my breeches. "She is *like* a mother to me, I suppose. I meant, of course, *my aunt*."

Later my mother scolded me, anxiety making her shrill: it was the first time I noticed how thin she had grown, how worn out by the masquerade. In contrast to my own liberty, my mother lived in isolation to protect our secret. While I flourished in the role of a bright young man, my mother played the part of the widowed aunt, and our roles seeped into our skins like the constant damp of Edinburgh.

Despite the rift his first visit occasioned, Jobson visited our home often after that. He was a great admirer of the bare-knuckle boxer Belcher and made much of the calculation required in the sport, whose distinction from mere fisticuffs or street brawling he claimed was evident in the fact that it was governed by rules. Often, as we sat studying together in the endlessly cold dark afternoons in the lodgings in Lothian Street, quizzing each other on Latin texts and the Hippocratic Corpus, he would grow restless, rise and stretch, his arms over his head, his vest straining across his broad chest, then he'd clap me on the ear and raise his balled fists, legs braced apart in the pose of combat.

"Let's do battle with our books, Jobson, not one another, shall we?"

"Up," he'd insist. "Get up. Do you good. Can't be salubrious to sit all day in a chair."

"We've only been at it an hour, Jobson."

"Time for a break, then. Up you go."

And I would patiently stand with my arms folded over my chest while he tossed punches in my general direction, bouncing on the balls of his feet, his arms twisting to deliver what he narrated as now an undercut, now a left to the jaw. When he was feeling particularly sporty, I'd hold my forearms over my chest and cover my face with my fists to buffer the blows.

"Are you quite done?" I'd ask from behind my hands.

"Almost," he'd say, panting.

He insisted on calling boxing "a gentleman's sport," and claimed it was part of an ancient tradition of combat, such as the Greeks and Romans had engaged in to test men's mettle and to bond, appealing to what he knew to be my classical interests. Boxing, he claimed, was close kin to the ancient Olympic games of *pankration*—a wrestling match whose sole constraint on its participants appeared to have been to disallow the gouging out of eyes.

But despite his prodding, he could not make an athlete of me. And I came to suspect it was not for me that he exhibited his pugilistic prowess, but for my mother, whose presence made him gallant and almost witty, quick to recount stories of our teachers and of dances he had attended in London, a glamour that she seemed delighted to admire. She lingered over the tea things when she brought them in, served us and sometimes laughed, as she never did now when we were alone.

I learned quickly that first year in Edinburgh that man's measure is woman. As dark was defined by night, so we were to be defined by our relations with the fairer sex. It was then I grasped that the dismissal of women was not contempt, but contained fear—mixed with the rage that attends unsatisfied longing.

"That's a fine Scottish filly," Jobson remarked as an open carriage drew past our group with a familiar local beauty, its red-haired mistress, seated inside.

"Be a pleasure to ride her," said Bertram, a spotty youth from the American wilderness of Massachusetts.

"I'd take her bareback," Chesterton said. "You feel the sweat against your thighs."

I colored to hear him, embarrassed less by the rough remark—than by memory. I knew what sort of experience such boys had. I'd had enough hands on me in Cork to know; a palm shoved between my legs in a crowd, down the bodice of a loose dress; shoved against a wall out of sight of others; age was no obstacle.

"Have we offended your delicate sensibility, Perry?" Chesterton asked.

"Not at all."

"But you're blushing like an English maid."

"I was only wondering," I said. "Have you much experience of horses, Chesterton?"

"I've mounted a filly or two." The others laughed.

"Do you ride them hard?"

"I've had my pleasure."

"Ah, that's the easy bit, no? Question is, have you given any? Or are they the sort of old nags one pays for the pleasure of mounting, stabled by others for the purpose?"

Chesterton pushed forward and shoved me in the chest before Jobson stepped between us, calling it enough.

"Let him alone, Chest," Jobson said, holding him off. "Perry's just having his fun."

"At my expense."

"Less expensive than an old nag," I said.

"Enough," Jobson said. "Enough."

I knew the sort of experience that Chesterton must have had, the sort he bragged on now, as if it were an honor he had earned, the sort my own brother could have claimed; I'd heard maids speak of being forced by boys like him, had once even seen my brother take a servant girl into the potting shed, her eyes wide with fear. I could not forgive myself that I had not stopped him; I had turned away, refused to meet her eyes, refusing the connection, the vulnerability we shared. From his ostentatious brag, I sensed that Chesterton's interest lay elsewhere, not with girls at all, but with Jobson perhaps, whom he adored. Though it would have cost him his life to admit it.

The argument would have been unmemorable if it hadn't led me to a bawdy house that night, an invitation that Jobson said, under the circumstances, I really could not decline. So I joined the others that evening and entered the sad, dim parlor where girls no older than myself were offered to my friends and me. When the time came to choose, I picked the youngest, saddest of them—a girl of thirteen or fourteen— and followed her up narrow stairs and into a room hardly big enough to hold the narrow bed where she dropped her peignoir and, thus stripped, lay back down on the bed, arms over her head. There was nothing erotic in such abjection. I turned away, embarrassed for her, but mine was a delicacy she seemed more to resent than appreciate.

"Just my luck," she said.

"I beg your pardon?" I said.

"You a poof, then?" she asked.

"I beg your pardon?" I repeated, turning to her.

"You know—like boys more than girls?"

I must have colored at the inquiry, shocked that she spoke of such things openly. It was known there were clubs, societies where such things took place, but sodomy was also known to be a crime, punishable by death. She seemed to mistake my blush for confession.

"Just my luck. Don't get paid unless we do it."

"I'm not a poof," I said.

"You sound like a poof."

"Well, I'm not."

"What's wrong with your voice?" she said, sitting up on her elbows.

"Nothing," I said. Then, in a deeper tone, "Nothing."

"Well, then," she said, "that's more like it. Why don't you join me," she patted the handsbreadth of bed beside her.

"Look," I said. "I'm only come because my friends insisted,

but it's not my...habit...to pay for this sort of—for female attentions."

She let out a long breath and leaned back onto the bed again. "Poof," she said again.

"Look here," I said again. "I'll pay you *extra* if you simply tell the others that it was wonderful, that I was wonderful, but you must never let anyone know that we did nothing."

"You pay me for nothing," she said.

"I'll pay you extra," I said. "For the story."

She seemed uncertain about whether to accept the offer until I pulled out a half crown and set it on the bed beside her. It was twice a laborer's daily wages; it could buy a whole chicken in London, well more than that here. I promised I'd not tell the mistress of the house. It was for her alone. She rolled onto her side and reached out for the coin, but I covered it with my hand before she'd touched it.

"But if I hear that you've breathed a word of this to anyone, ever, I will come and cut you stem to stern, clavicle to cunt. I will cut out your heart. Do you understand?"

She stared at me and nodded, saying not a word. Whether it was the money or the threat, she appeared to warm to me after that, and we spent the allotted time in quiet, easy conversation. I told her about dissection and was surprised to find her interested; her questions about the heart and circulation of the blood were keener than most of my fellow students'. I told her things that Mirandus had told me, of how women were left longing for him, desperate when he left.

"What do you suppose he did to them?"

"Told them stories," I said.

"Women don't fall in love with men for their stories."

I shrugged. I thought perhaps I had.

When we left the room, she was blushing, holding my hand. She kissed me tenderly at the foot of the stairs, in front of the others, entreated me to hurry back; Chesterton never spoke of the matter again.

By the end of our second term, we'd lost a number of our acquaintances to illness, to marriage, to family obligations in the West Indies, and Jobson and I became closer for our narrowed circle, though in truth he won friends with an ease I could only admire, never emulate. He remained a favorite among the students and faculty, who often invited him to their clubs or to dine at their homes. Given his popularity, I was left more and more alone—to myself, to my mother's company— but I did not mind.

Anatomy remained my favorite subject, despite the absurdity of Monro's lectures, and I often lingered long after our private tutorial at Barclay's or at Fyfe's to go over what we'd examined that day. I took to bringing a pasty or some cold meat for supper, since our sessions often ran late into the night. One evening, my mother arrived at Barclay's and I startled to see her there in the doorway. I rose and went to her.

"Is everything all right?" I asked, fearing for her.

She nodded. "I just thought you might want supper." She gestured to the basket she carried, covered in a cloth. "What an awful smell. What *are* you doing, Nephew?"

I thought she spoke this last word with undue irony.

"Morbid anatomy," I said.

"*Morbid* indeed. Is it gory?" she craned her neck to see around my shoulder to the body splayed on the table below.

"Butchering a chicken's worse," I said. "At least here when

you cut into the neck, the body doesn't run about. And you get enduring knowledge for your trouble."

"I'd rather have supper," she said.

"As would I, right now," I nodded to the covered plate. "But I'll eat when I get home. Thank you."

"Think nothing of it."

I suspected she had reasons of her own for the visit, beyond a generous heart. I knew that she was lonely, eager for company. She had only me. It was not enough. But company could be costly. Exposing us all too much.

When my mother fell ill with fever in late April, I sat by her bed whenever I was home, but she insisted that I continue to attend my lectures unimpeded. I returned from class one evening to find her pale, lips tinting blue, barely able to stand as she oversaw the cooking of a stew. I insisted she stay in bed. Each day when I returned from class, I cooked meat broth, spooned it into her mouth, aware that what she needed was sleep, rest, a warmer sun.

I consulted Dr. Hamilton, who urged a sojourn in warmer climes, Italy or Spain. When I explained that we hadn't the funds, he considered the matter gravely, then proposed what he said he rarely urged: "Sell capital." I thanked him and left, closing the door quietly behind me.

My mother asked to see a priest, but I dismissed it as an unhealthy submission to despair.

"You will recover your strength," I said. "You need only rest for a month or two, somewhere warm and dry, where I will join you come summer."

I wrote to Dr. Fryer, who had helped General Mirandus arrange funding for my education, and asked to borrow money to send my mother to Italy for the remainder of the term. Dr. Fryer was the only one besides the general who knew my secret. He reluctantly agreed, but she refused to go without me. We both knew she hadn't the strength to travel alone, and I had not the option to interrupt my studies. We agreed to wait out the term, then travel together.

At night I attended her as any dutiful daughter would— brewing tea, making bone broth, serving both in bed by lamplight, the shadows in the rooms deepened by the light, but glad to be in her company, to be together in the night. It rained, the sound beating the roof tiles and the windowpanes like buckshot, as I held my mother's hand, her skin soft as calfskin but chilled; inside we were warm, dry, but my mother complained of the chill, even under heavy blankets and her feather-down quilt, brought from Cork.

My studies slipped. In anatomy class I misidentified the gastrocnemius and soleus; once in a physic lecture, I fell asleep and woke to Dr. Gregory's cane striking between my shoulders. I shouted in pain. The hall erupted in a roar of laughter that even Jobson could not suppress. The laughter echoed in the vaulted ceiling, off the tall glass windows that framed the lecture hall.

My mother's condition worsened. I knew that she would not last the spring here. When I received the advance against the legacy from Dr. Fryer, I packed her trunks; I took a carriage to Leith and walked to the docks and bought passage on a Leith smack set to sail direct to Barcelona in a week's time. Dr. Fryer had friends there, who would house her until I arrived. For the first time, I cut classes so that I might launder clothes and pack her trunk to prepare her to sail for Spain, where the heat might return color to her cheeks, warm her blood again.

On the night before the voyage, I stayed up late reading and listening to my mother cough; when the sound ceased I was relieved, until I felt an absence, as if she'd already left, and fearing for her ran to her room, only to hear the awful coughing resume, and I put out the candle for bed. When I woke, the silence in the house was peaceful, the stillness after snow, a promising pearl sky, and I stepped into her room to rouse her. When I touched my mother's shoulder it was stiff and cold, her cheek was grey; she was gone. Like a candle snuffed out. I fell to my knees and leaned my forehead on my mother's hand, my cheek against the quilt she'd brought all the way from Ireland.

I had never believed in my mother's God, never shared her faith, but in the wake of her death I longed for the parish priest who'd seen us through other losses, who'd have known the proper way to say goodbye and mourn. Who might have given her last rites.

My mother had dreaded burial among Protestants more than she'd feared death itself. I thought to send the body back to Cork for burial, but I knew that no one must discover who we were or where. All we'd planned for would be undone if her identity was discovered, and with it mine. My mother's death would raise too many questions, alert my father to my whereabouts, and bring his creditors down upon the modest legacy that my mother had labored so hard to arrange.

It was clear that she must be buried here in Edinburgh, at whatever plot I might find, and that no one must suspect our identities. Inquiry into her family would reveal my own. So I told no one, save for Jobson, of my loss, and to others said only that my aunt had returned to Ireland, so I'd be seeking other lodgings soon, should they know of any.

I moved through my classes like a somnambulist, rotely taking notes, conscious of all that was said but numb, given to bouts of sudden rage and piercing longing, unable to speak to anyone of either, save for Jobson. Jobson felt keenly my loss and said so, gently setting a hand on my shoulder to commiserate, saying how very sorry he was for the death of my dear aunt. He accompanied me to the churchyard, where she was interred and blessed by a local priest, who prayed for her soul and wished her what she had for so long lacked—rest and peace.

I would have neither.

CHAPTER THREE

PASSING

It was Lord Basken, my late uncle's friend, who arranged that I should move into Dr. Anderson's home in town as a lodger, shortly after my mother's death in the late summer of 1810. Under other circumstances the move would have been a happy one, promising as it did connection and stimulating conversation of the sort I craved more than any meat; Dr. Anderson was an editor of *Edinburgh Magazine*, a renowned biographer and scholar, whose home was a center of fashionable literary society. His fourteen-volume edition of the poets of Great Britain had made him an intellectual celebrity, and his home hosted many ambitious literary young men. But I was indifferent to society's charms.

I was relieved to have an excuse to close myself off from company and the sentiments that importuned when I found myself not alone. Misery does not love company; it loves rigor, absorption in something inhumanly abstract, in anything other than fellow feeling. I understood in an instant the drunkard's logic—not to surround oneself with others when in despair, but to drink them out of existence, to drown them like sorrow itself. Never having acquired the taste for spirits, I drowned my sorrows in my work and took comfort there.

* * *

The taste of ambition is metallic, like a bit in the mouth or blood, strong as love but of another order, a feeling fierce and ancient, a drive as powerful as desire but colder, steelier; in its possession or perhaps in possession of it, I felt urgent as lust, still as the eye of a storm. It was potent as strong drink; made me feel invulnerable, indifferent to everything save for *success*. I was confident I knew what that was then.

It became my custom at Dr. Anderson's to hide my dirty monthly linens in an empty chamber pot in my armoire, until I could wash or dispose of them in the fireplace of my bedroom. If there was a scent of burning meat late at night, or of blood, it would offend no senses but my own. It was an age of eccentricity, a romantic time when idiosyncrasy was honored and everyone had their passions and the only true vice was a lack of strong sentiment. Convention was the crutch of lesser men. The greatest could do without it.

So it was easier than it might otherwise have been to disguise base necessity as charming whim and pass off my need for solitude as an excess of fastidiousness. I refused a valet, insisting on dressing myself, even when later a guest at Lord Basken's Dryburgh Abbey, and I laundered my most private linens in my own basin, regularly refusing maids access to my room. I justified all this as attention to sanitation, but I knew that in truth I feared the keen observations and inquisitiveness of those who serve.

Sometimes I would wake in the night to the sound of my mother's voice or my sister's, only to find it was some servant in the corridor. I was frightened by how quickly I had lost them—in the wealth of new acquaintance. (I missed my sister, but I could not write to her for fear of being found out; she was as dead to me as my mother was.) My past seemed more and more remote from the life I lived now, the young man of fashion I was rapidly becoming. Inattentive, lost in a fog of grief and routine, I grew careless.

I had been at Dr. Anderson's a month or two in the autumn of 1810 when I arrived at the morning's lecture without my notebook and was forced to return home to collect it. I took the stairs two at a time and burst into my room, where I startled a maid, mid-cleaning, despite my instructions that none was to enter my rooms. When I walked in, it was hard to say who was more surprised. At her feet were piled the bloodied rags that I had stored that morning beneath my bed in an empty chamber pot to burn that night.

She turned to me, her face confused, embarrassed as I.

"Sir?" She seemed to be asking whether I was one.

"Who gave you permission to enter these rooms?" I shouted, and understood in an instant why men used rage to cover vulnerability: the advantage was immediately mine.

"I'm . . . I'm beg your pardon, sir. I was sent to clean up."

"You appear to have accomplished quite the opposite," I said, ignoring what lay between us, as if it were her doing.

"I'm sorry, sir."

"Get out," I said. "Now." As she passed, I grabbed her arm. Our eyes met briefly, but we said nothing before I let her go.

It was the first and last time that I would be thus unprepared. When on occasion I bled onto the sheets after that, I took pains to cut myself to explain the stain. When the necessity arose, I would enlist a female friend to provide an alibi. I developed quite a reputation for deflowering local girls. I learned to bring my own linens wherever I traveled, and bleach. I maintained this was an article of sanitation. As a surgeon, few questioned when the water in my washing basin was bloodied.

Still the bellow of iron each month would remain hard to explain, the stench impossible to cover, so when the time drew near each month, I was careful to leave out my cutting kit by the washing table, to rinse the bloodied tools in the basin each night. Leaving the polluted water there for a curious maid to see, should any inquire. If the household staff suspected anything, no one spoke of it. Later, in the barracks at Plymouth and Chelsea and aboard ships, the general stench of unbathed men and overflowing chamber pots, rotted fish and flatulence overwhelmed any concern for my monthly reek of blood. On the battlefield and in the barracks, the pong of blood was nothing new.

I wrote a single letter to Mirandus that year, after the New Year's dinner at Lord Basken's, but I had not heard back. It seemed likely that he was traveling, or too absorbed in obligations on his arrival in Caracas to reply. Still, I waited eagerly, whenever a rider came to the door; ready to frank the letter. But none arrived.

I was comforted by the thought of a reunion with the general and with his family, a family that at times had seemed as much mine as my own kin. Now gone. I had no other friend or relation to confide in, no one else who knew my past, no one to work for, save the dream my mother and I had shared those evenings by the fire. Every plan we'd had was gone, like fog. I moved through a shadow-scape of former plans and ambitions, pursuing the course we'd laid out together.

Though I continued to study with fierce self-discipline, I

could not shake off my grief. I lived in a state of agitation and languour, in which disbelief replaced mourning; I lived in anxious anticipation, as if awaiting my mother's return. As if— were I to perform my duties well, study hard, pass my exams— she might come back, casting off death like fancy dress. I vacillated between sorrow and longing, as if I carried a storm gale within me. I was acutely self-conscious, then full of rage. I longed for company and in company longed to be alone again. It was as if my skin itself no longer suited me, no longer fit, always too tight, too thin, aching.

During the long summer vacation of 1811, a year after my mother's death, I was invited to stay at Dryburgh Abbey, the country estate of Lord Basken. The eleventh Earl of Basken had been a great friend of my late uncle's, and ours, though I'd met him only once, at New Year's dinner in St. Andrew's Square eighteen months ago.

Lord Basken was an ebullient man on whom the concept of a private pleasure was wholly lost—for him, the phrase was an oxymoron: all pleasures for him were public, shared. He had only to happen on a person reading a book to be inspired to interrupt them with a query, or an ejaculation about the beauty of the day or a quote from Hume, or to ask whether it was an absorbing work you were reading, hmmm?

He took a lively and proprietary interest in the arts and intellectual fashions of the day, and his library rivaled that of General Mirandus's, which for me was recommendation enough, as was his selfless kindness to my family.

I had been shown into the library shortly after I'd arrived, while waiting to be received by Lord Basken, and there happened on Smellie's atlas.

I startled as if glimpsing an old acquaintance in a crowd.

I was flooded with the memories of London, those long languorous lit afternoons of solitary reading; the taste of warm chocolate and milky coffee; the radiant rose-red innards of a rabbit disemboweled against the grass, revealing fetal young. I took it down from the shelf.

"Smellie," Lord Basken said, coming up beside me. "Magnificent volume. Have you encountered it before?"

"I own one," I said, turning to greet him.

Lord Basken raised his brows.

"I have it on loan from General Mirandus."

"I understood he never parted with his books." He looked skeptical for a moment, as if perhaps I'd pinched it.

"He gave it me as a going-away gift, with a promise of its safe return."

He looked at me as if taking my measure anew. "He set great store by you," Lord Basken said.

"I endeavor to prove worthy of his esteem."

"I never knew a better judge of character," he said, before continuing his perusal of the books. He pointed to a volume of Charles Lamb's and pulled it from the shelf to offer me. "I never knew a subtler mind," he said portentously, as if judgment of art were itself a kind of artistry. "Though I met his sister once—a most peculiar woman. She seemed quite witless; she startled at our arrival as if she'd seen the dead. You'd think a clever man would choose clever companions."

"I have noticed men choose female companions for many reasons. Rarely for their wit."

He laughed. "Do not let Lady Margaret hear you say it," he said, referring to his wife. "I like my company clever."

"I must be grateful that elegance is not the measure here. I'd not measure up."

"You'll fare well enough with our young ladies," he said. "They're simpler than the fashionable young women of London. I'll be delighted to make introductions."

It hadn't occurred to me that I would be in the company of young women here; Lord Basken was known to be devoted to the study of antiquities; he'd bought Dryburgh Abbey in order to preserve the twelfth-century ruin there. I'd not thought contemporary company would much interest him, a fact that had recommended this retreat for the long vacation.

"I'm sure that I will be much obliged," I said, though what I felt was panic.

Lord Basken was possessed of a generous, exuberant spirit; his one fault was that he required an audience for his wealth in order to enjoy it. He kept his house full of guests throughout the long vacations, a revolving set of artists, intellectuals, a mix of landed gentry and intellectual aristocrats. Unlike General Mirandus's, Lord Basken's circle of acquaintance exceeded his own attainments, leaving a gap which he filled with elaborate hyperbole, referring to George Washington as "my dear cousin," as he did the King, his family tree bent low with such claimed cousinage. But true to his words, his dinners were never dull nor was the house.

At Dryburgh Abbey, I attended balls and parties, recitals and picnics and readings; we took boats onto the River Tweed and strolled through the picturesque stone ruins of the abbey under radiant blue skies and scudding clouds. I developed a passion for whist and amateur theatricals, hats and dancing.

To an observer, our diversions must have seemed idle pleasure, but for me they were simply another classroom, where I learned the manners of those I would now live among—aristocrats, politicians, writers, radicals, painters, progressives, and sundry *flâneurs*. Conversation was lively—from the Venezuelan independence declared in July to Lamarck's *Philosophie Zoologique* with its novel concept of animal evolution, from the merits of Pleyel versus Haydn to the promise of steam-power locomotives and the stain of slavery. We stood self-conscious on the threshold of great discoveries, new possibilities, revolution, machines that seemed capable of making men more than they had ever been before, new capacities that stood in stark contrast to the barbarity we countenanced—slavery, sickness, starvation, poverty, war.

But as soon as decorum allowed, I made my way back to the privacy of the library to read. Occasionally a guest would intrude upon my studies, but Lord Basken kindly kept them at bay, stood guard over my solitude, save for when he wished to interrupt it himself.

He had a most annoying habit of coming in to read beside me in the large and splendid library, only to erupt a moment or two after he'd settled to exclaim over some passage in his book. "Listen to this," he'd say, and proceed to distract me utterly from the lesson I was on. "Fascinating," I would reply, while he returned to his reading without a comment, as if *I* had interrupted *him*. "Oh, by Jove," he'd say again. And if I failed to respond, he'd simply carry on as if I had: "This is really most extraordinary," he might say. "Do listen to what Plutarch (or Burke or Mrs. Wollstonecraft or Mr. Lamb) has to say about X or Y." I found myself bracing for his entrance, sneaking upstairs to my room with a volume tucked under my arm at the sound of his voice in the corridor.

I passed most days in the library, and after the evening's diversions I retired there to study further. Lord Basken seemed to approve my sedulousness; we both knew that I would have to write and defend my dissertation within the space of a year. I knew, if he did not, that my life depended on passing the exams.

I was governed by a singular desire: to become a man of consequence, a brilliant physician like those I studied under, my mentors, to possess a name as great and honored as my past was obscure. It became my life raft—what I clung to when every other support fell away in the storm of days. Love did not last, those we loved did not last; honor might. I could not let affection distract me nor allow the temptation of security to weaken my resolve. There is no security. We can only be courageous.

I had been at Dryburgh Abbey a fortnight when she arrived with a party from London. I noticed her first at dinner. A lovely brunette with the subtle expressions that are too easily overlooked in more effortful, showy company. While other guests preened at table, striving to outdo one another in their wit and acquaintance, she observed them in what appeared to be a thoughtful silence. You could not call her *pretty*. But she had an open, handsome face, across which emotion moved like shadows over summer hills; her eyes were grey, her neck long and delicate as a calla lily.

I had hidden myself away to avoid flirtations, which were as regular a part of our recreation as whist, and I noticed that she seemed to shy from these as well. The next morning, I came on her reading in the shade of the garden while the others were off boating or gossiping in the drawing room over needlepoint. I was loath to disturb her, given my own dread of interruption, but as I began to withdraw, she spoke. Or rather she seemed to speak, although in truth she merely glanced up, saying nothing. Nor did I. I bowed and withdrew.

I was startled that evening to find that we were to be seated together at dinner.

Lord Basken commenced to introduce us when my companion said, "We have met."

I raised an eyebrow at this. "I cannot imagine that I would forget our meeting."

"In the garden. Do you not recall? We were introduced by the flowers. But Mr. Perry declined their entreaties; he seemed thoroughly immune to their charms."

"But not yours, surely," Lord Basken interjected.

"Surely not," I said.

"You are the young Mr. Perry, am I correct?" she asked.

I bowed. She was introduced as Miss Erskine, the niece of Lord Basken.

"It is a pleasure," I said, leaning over and kissing her hand.

"Why, your hands are as delicate as a girl's, sir," she said.

"Perhaps a girl's are as strong as a man's?"

"Do you suppose that women possess the strength of men?"

"I am confident they possess the wit."

"And what, may I ask, inspires such confidence? Have you sisters?"

"One. And I know from experience that a woman's intellect can be every bit the equal of a man's, even greater."

"Then how do you explain our lack of equal attainments?" she asked.

"It's obvious, is it not? How can women equal men if they lack access to higher learning? There is not a woman known has studied in Edinburgh's great medical school or dissection theaters."

"Surely no woman would seek to do so. Women are interested in life, not death."

"Would Lady Macbeth not argue to the contrary?"

"But she's a fiction."

"But Lucrezia Borgia is not, nor Queen Elizabeth, or Anne Boleyn. May not the fiction be women's gentler nature? In Ireland, I recall seeing a peasant woman behead a chicken with an ax; she seemed utterly unencumbered by the gentle reputation of her sex."

"And would I make a more fascinating figure with an ax in hand rather than a book?"

"I cannot conceive of anything that could make you more fascinating than you are."

She smiled and blushed, averting her gaze, when dinner was announced and we went in.

It was thrilling to have such attention paid to me by a woman of rank, even as it terrified. I had feared women's greater acumen, but discovered that, like men, they were blinded by vanity, if of another sort; women endeavored to treat every gentleman's statements as wit, to refashion—with their laughter or a gentle touch of fingers on the sleeve—a comment about the weather into some astronomical insight or romantic double entendre.

And I understood for the first time the arrogance of men, the sense of self-importance that had blinded my brother to the possibility of failure and his own ignorance—it was a gift conferred by feminine attentions, the flattering admiration of women, who sought to see in men the mythic authority they pretended to possess.

I discovered that women of rank did not see through me, as I'd feared; even well-born women were so habituated to seek the attentions of men that they appeared hardly to notice those whose attentions they sought. Women flirted the way men sparred, to win prestige and secure their standing. As in hunting or a duel, the target was often largely irrelevant. What mattered was taking the shot.

"Is it true that you are a military man, Mr. Perry?" one of our company asked from across the table, a fashionable young man whose name I did not know.

"It is Mr. Perry's intention to be an army surgeon," replied Lord Basken.

"I would not have taken you for a soldier," my graceful dinner companion said.

"Seems more likely to play the part of a poet," said the nameless young man.

"I allow that I am taken by wanderlust. I should like to see Caracas, now that Venezuela is independent of Spain." In truth, a military career would enable me to travel—allowing for a rapid rise in the more fluid society of the colonies—which I hoped might help me avoid detection. Even my stays at Dryburgh Abbey and at Dr. Anderson's caused me concern; I felt too readily observed.

"And where is your home?" Miss Erskine asked.

I hesitated. It was a question that pained me, despite a practiced answer. A question I'd learned to dread, and not yet learned to answer easily. But looking into the expectant face of my interlocutor, I found a reply readily at hand:

"Whenever I am in the company of a beautiful woman," I said, "I am perfectly at home."

This brought a laugh and a change of conversation to the next day's weather and the prospect of a shooting party.

* * *

Miss Erskine remained at Dryburgh Abbey, despite the return of her companions to London to prepare for the autumn season, despite their entreaties to return to town with them, and gradually we fell in together more and more on our walks through the melancholy ruins of the abbey or reading in the library in the afternoon. Between us, friendship grew like the roses in the conservatory greenhouse: out-of-season blossoms, lovelier for their unexpectedness.

"You do not like company," I observed.

"I can find no fault in our company," she replied.

"And yet you are often alone."

She explained that she refreshed herself in solitude as others did in company, hearing their opinions echoed in another's, whereas she needed silence in which to recognize her own.

Friendship arose between us gradually, simply, steadily, and I found with time that I could confide in her, if partially, my plans for the future, if not my past. In time we formed the habit of coming down to breakfast at the same hour and walking out after taking tea. We did not discuss these plans but seemed to arrive at them together, as often our minds ran on the same track, unbidden. "At dinner last night, you mentioned Sterne…" "I was just on the point of mentioning that myself…" We laughed at the coincidence. "I've been thinking…"

The more pleasant the days, the more unsettled my mind. I could not seek to attach her, but attachment seemed a thing inclined to happen of its own accord, like the changing of seasons, autumn giving way to the first cold hints of winter. When the winter term began, I welcomed the excuse to absent myself from Dryburgh Abbey, while Lord Basken's niece was present, but when I heard that she had been called away to London, I was gripped by despair that I might not see her again. When I spoke to Jobson of my dilemma, he failed to see the problem in attracting the attentions of a beautiful woman with £5,000 a year. I could not say more. Receiving no word from Mirandus, I sank into gloom—which even Jobson's relentless good cheer could not disperse.

Despite my social success, I felt the gap. I had become cultured, even learned, without ever attaining the ease that others possessed; I labored to achieve what remained out of reach, a sense of belonging, of a right to these rooms. I returned to my own room ill-tempered and studied harder to alleviate my discomfort, to calm my mind. If others mistook this effort for prodigious gifts, I did not correct them.

I discerned in my companions at Dryburgh Abbey, as in my classmates, something more important than wealth or formal education; I had the proper shirts, a fine coat and vest of green silk, beautiful shoes with buckles, books of my own to read by candlelight, but I lacked some more essential ingredient— authority, the sense of belonging not just there but anywhere in the world.

I understood then that this was what those conversations with General Mirandus had been about. Those questions that seemed pointless at the time, speculative games at best, were all for this one end; in soliciting my opinion on books and art, on politics and history, he was *not* trying to ensure that I had been diligent in my reading, as I'd thought then.

He was teaching me to *have* opinions, or rather he was teaching me what my companions possessed without thought or conscious awareness of it, *entitlement*: he was teaching me to believe that my opinions *mattered*, that something—law or policy—might come of what I thought, that my arguments counted, that I could, that I would, like him, shape history. Girl that I was.

When I returned to Dryburgh Abbey the following spring to complete my dissertation, I was disappointed to find Miss Erskine absent—and I was relieved. I gave myself over to my studies, an impersonal refuge of the mind. I was hard at work by then on my thesis, "De merocele, vel hernia crurali," a dissertation of femoral hernia, which I had begun at Dryburgh Abbey the prior autumn.

I walked out to clear my thoughts after a morning's study, when I came on Miss Erskine returning from her own stroll among the ruins and eager to join in mine, having just that hour arrived. The next morning at breakfast, we seemed inevitably seated together.

I was delighted by her return, and we resumed our friendship as if no interruption had occurred. I was too glad of her company to be unsettled by our growing intimacy, which I should have recognized would be misconstrued. A fear quickly confirmed when one evening after dinner, Lord Basken approached me, as Miss Erskine played "Für Elise" for us, Beethoven's recent composition, and said into my ear, "A man may not marry a woman for her wit, but one might do well to marry where there is both wit and beauty."

And fortune, I thought, though neither of us said it.

In the days that followed, I grew concerned that Lord Basken might make inquiries into my background in expectation of an impending engagement to his niece and might thereby get word of what no one but General Mirandus and Dr. Fryer knew: my true name and nature.

When Lord Basken closeted me for a private conference a few days later, his uncharacteristic gravity gave me pause. He sat behind his desk, appearing pinched with concern, seemingly at a loss for how to begin.

"I have had a letter," he said. "From Dr. Fryer."

I felt my skin go cold.

"Indeed," I said, feeling my face warm. "I trust the doctor is well."

He nodded gravely. Studied his manicured hands. "His letter had but one subject: you."

I felt sweat break out beneath my horse collar, pricking at the edges of my brow, where curls fell forward. "I cannot imagine that I am worthy of such attention."

I had not repaid the money that I owed him, which I'd borrowed to send my mother abroad; I had no means to do so.

"It was a most urgent letter," Lord Basken said.

"Indeed," I said. "And may I know its content?"

Lord Basken looked up at me for the first time, nodded. "Look to your Latiny," he said.

"I beg your pardon."

"If you are to pass your exams, you must look to your Latiny, sir."

"Ah," I coughed in relief. "Yes. I will do so, thank you."

My relief was so acute that I fairly stumbled into the foyer and out the doors into the open air with a joy I had not felt in months, not since before my mother's death, and in my delight I unthinkingly embraced Miss Erskine, when I met her on the path, embraced her as I would have done my sister had she been there, only too late realizing my mistake.

"Mr. Perry," she said, stepping back.

"Miss Erskine," I said. "Forgive me. I forgot myself. You remind me of my sister."

"Of whom you were fond?"

"Quite," I said. "Quite fond."

"Then I am glad to be a pleasant reminder. And where is your sister now?"

Her words recalled me to myself, dispelling the veil of giddy relief. "She is in Ireland," I said, too frankly.

"You must miss her," she said.

"I do," I said. "Very much."

I knew that I would miss Miss Erskine, too—miss our conversations and our silent walks—but I also knew that I could not return to Dryburgh Abbey after this visit. I could not risk affection.

Back in Edinburgh, as the time for the degree examination drew near, I closed myself off from all company, save for Jobson's. Together with our fellow students, we applied to the University Senate for permission to sit for the examination. And then together we embarked on our frenzied, half-ecstatic preparations, the orgy of intellectual self-absorption that is among the chief pleasures of academic training; like athletes poised to run a race at Olympia, we primed ourselves to hold forth in an ancient tongue on the many ailments that might assail a human body.

We stayed up nights in a row in his rooms or mine, chewing charcoal biscuits and drinking coffee to keep our minds sharp, reading and rereading our notes and case studies and practicing our Latin. I had achieved that delicate state of suspension when I was composed almost entirely of others' words, what I had studied, an almost ecstatic, quasi-religious state of self-transcendence brought on by lack of food and lack of sleep and almost constant study, when I got word that I would *not* after all be allowed to sit for the examination.

"There must be some mistake," I protested to Jobson, when I received the letter refusing my request on account of my "extreme youth." But no effort to petition our examiners seemed capable of altering their decision, and without the exam I was without a degree, without a vocation, without a profession, just a girl in young man's garb, with a knowledge no one would allow me to apply. I'd have called on General Mirandus to assist me, but he was half a world away, inaccessible in some American tropic, so I turned to the only other source of help, fearing that I had forsaken his assistance in quitting his home so decisively: Lord Basken.

I waited in dread for his letter, or its lack. But within two days I had his answer, and better, I had him in person at Dr. Anderson's door, with an offer to intervene on my behalf. He left for the university immediately and before nightfall had given a personal deposition to the senate, in which he argued that the university's regulations had in fact no age requirement for degree candidates; by evening, he returned with word that I would be allowed to sit for the exam. After a celebratory dinner, I sat down and added an epigraph to my thesis, quoting the Greek dramatist Menander: "Do not consider whether what I say is a young man speaking, but whether my discussion with you is that of a man of understanding." I hoped they'd like the joke.

When the day of the examination arrived, the faculty who would examine me assembled in the library of Dr. Monro's home—Doctors Monro, Hamilton, and Gregory. I tried to focus my attention on the room itself, the titles on the bookshelves, but my eyes blurred, failing to focus on the words; my eyelid twitched; I held my hands knotted behind my back in an attempt to still (or at least hide) their trembling; I looked at my teachers, my examiners, and knew who stood with me, who against, a reflexive tally, as if I were weighing beans or butter in the grocery in Cork. It was too close to call.

When the examination began, I was asked to interpret two quotes from Hippocrates, then diagnose a case before I was to defend my thesis. As I rose from my seat, a strange sense of floating overtook me, as when I had stood on the cliffs over the sea at Ballycotton.

I heard someone clear his throat; then Monro blew his nose, and—as if it were the signal I'd awaited, the starter's gun in a horse race—I began.

I spoke first of my gratitude for their consideration of my thesis on femoral hernia and of my credentials, then moved on to quote Menander, all of which I had practiced in case nothing more should come to mind. I feared that I would forget all I had learned. And for a moment my mind *was* blank, my ears rang. The sound of my own voice—assured, commanding, if perhaps too loud—came to me from far off and surprised me, as if it were not my own. But hearing my voice, unwavering, I felt possessed of a curious authority, an overwhelming sense of well-being, as if General Mirandus were there and posing his questions affably, rather than the skeptical faculty. The words—in Latin—came to me as if whispered in my ear, as if I were merely the instrument through which others spoke. I seemed not to think at all, as I quoted Ovid and Galen, Astley Cooper's studies, my professors', and my own. The arguments came easily and well.

When I was done, a silence fell over the room and I feared that I had misjudged the situation; in my voluble ease, had I said too much? Had I been too critical, too hard on the work of some of those assembled? Had intended homage tipped into criticism, given offense?

The silence grew longer and I felt a blush rise along my neck, sweat between my bound breasts. The silence deepened before Dr. Hamilton stood and said, "Bravo." Dr. Monro followed suit. I had expected disputation of my arguments, some questions. Perhaps some praise. Instead Dr. Hamilton came and stood beside me; he clapped me on the shoulder and complimented my cravat and shoes.

The message was clear: I was one of them now; we could relax into the trivial. He confirmed what I'd suspected for some time: that ours was an art of performance, a confidence game, a trick, in which looking the part was as essential as— perhaps more important than—knowledge.

Only Dr. Gregory sat silent in the aftermath of the examination, his cane held between his spread knees, hands clutching its top, as he leaned on it. I suspected that he had had some hand in the conspiracy against me, angered by my laughter and ready answers in the lecture hall. He seemed still angrier now that I had acquitted myself well on the exam, as if failure might have endeared me better to him. I failed to endear myself. Not for the first time, or last.

I passed with notable excellence.

I was not yet eighteen, and I had obtained a degree in medicine from the foremost medical school in the world with the highest possible mark. My father was in debtor's prison, my mother was dead, my siblings lost to me; no woman in the history of the world had done what I had; few men had acquitted themselves half as well. I had made myself a surgeon, almost a gentleman. It had been a most remarkable journey.

I returned to my friend's rooms triumphant, eager to share my news with Jobson and to celebrate together, confident of his success, but I found him nowhere. I searched our usual haunts—the tavern, the club, the library—until finally I returned home, chilled but still elated. Lord Basken had heard of my triumph, and he had sent a note inviting mc to dine with him. I bathed and readied myself for the dinner and was on the verge of heading out when Jobson arrived at my rooms, reeking of acrid vomit and ale; I stripped his clothes and helped him into a chair beneath a blanket. He did not need to tell me he had failed, where I had succeeded.

I had measured myself against my peers relentlessly the last three years, and when I prevailed, as I almost always did, I reveled in it, feeling the sting of their envy like a kiss, a strange inverted bond, as if such measurement could draw us close, make me matter more than I did to anyone now or thought I ever would. I lived in such triumphs, besting those I knew. I thought they would admire me for it, or at least envy me—that poor proxy of affection. A frisson of feeling that approximated love.

But I did not relish my friend's failure that day; I had relied on our succeeding together, even if I hoped to be the more brilliant of us, the more praised. It hadn't occurred to me that he could fail.

I took no pleasure in his loss. It was my loss, too. For a moment, poking the fire to raise its flames, it seemed too much to bear, to leave my friend. We had planned to go together to London to be dressers to the famous Sir Astley Cooper; we had planned to share rooms. Now I would go on alone.

By the time my friend woke, I had brewed tea, brought fresh currant buns from the baker's, a rare flash of blue in the sky, despite the cold coming through the pane.

"The majority fail the exams on the first try," I said. "There's no shame in it."

"Shame not to be together," he said.

"I will still be in London when you come next year," I said. "Perhaps by then I will have learned to box."

"I very much doubt that," he said.

I told him I'd be back from dinner early, would not linger.

"Take your time. I'm not going anywhere."

Stepping out the door to go to dinner at Lord Basken's, I pulled my coat tighter against the cold, but the chill reached me anyway.

There was much to hold me in Scotland. My mother was buried in its ground. My only friend was there; my patron, Lord Basken, was nearby. But I could not stay. It would never be safe to linger in any place, which is why I would be a military surgeon, once I finished training. My only consolation was the prospect of a reunion with General Mirandus and his family.

Having applied and been accepted as a pupil dresser at Guy's and St. Thomas' Hospital, assigned to Sir Astley Cooper for the coming year, I returned to London in the autumn of 1812. When I got off the boat in London, I arranged my lodgings first, then went straightaway to Laundy's, the premier manufacturer of surgical instruments, to get a proper cutting kit.

Then I went directly to General Mirandus's home in Grafton Street, passing through streets I'd walked so many times just a few years ago. It was eight years since I'd first visited that city, six since I'd been invited into Mirandus's library, three since I'd been rechristened Jonathan. It seemed a lifetime. When I presented myself at General Mirandus's familiar door, I was overcome with a sense of elation and relief; I had made it. I had arrived.

When I knocked, an unfamiliar servant answered and informed me that the general and his family no longer resided there. *Where had they gone?* He could not tell me. I thanked him. He closed the door. And with that I closed the door in my heart that they had opened years before onto that unexpected garden, and prepared myself for the life before me, the days ahead, in which none would know me, not even—I feared— myself.

I will be dead less than a month when the debates will begin over my body, partisans taking sides as if I were a bill in Parliament, a horse on which to wager. Dr. Bradford, with whom I worked in the West Indies, will write in the *Medical Times and Gazette* to gallantly insist that I was a man through and through, if "devoid of all the outward signs of manly virility," while the *Manchester Guardian* will assert with equal certitude that I was a woman all along. There are those who will claim (erroneously) that my body bore evidence of multiple children, others that it was marked with a caesarean scar. Still others that I had no sex at all, like an angel, or rather that I was in possession of both, a Colossus straddling worlds.

In a way, I suppose I was.

There are those who insist I was intersex, hermaphrodite. They claim to have studied my "case"—speaking of me as if I were a patient to be cured—declaring with proprietary authority that I was "an imperfectly developed man," a man in a female body. How else to explain my success? They debate my corpse as if it were a question, a riddle.

Does it matter? Why can't we get over the body? Give it a rest? We are measured by our works in the world, for better or for worse; the honor we do out-lasts and outlives us, weighs in the scales of time far more heavily than do our bones, so why weight the body so? What matter if I were a woman or a man?

Rather, ask what I did with my time. Ask only did I reach, did I go beyond what was easily within my grasp, did I excel, triumph, amaze? Did I live up to my imagining? Is there any other measure?

They're right, of course, who say that I was not a woman pretending to be a man: I was something far more shocking—a person no longer pretending to be other than that, a person simply being a person, the equal of any—simply being who I was: witty, difficult, charming, obstinate, brilliant, angry, no longer pretending *not* to be that person. That is the scandal, the real shocker, even now. That I, born a woman, might be a distinguished surgeon, a charmer, a great flirt, a greater success, a legend, a scandal.

These anatomists of my past seem incredulous, outraged, baffled by the possibility that I might successfully assume the name and attire of a man to make my way in the world, succeed; shocked still more that I'd retain both after my retirement from medicine and the military, as if my good name were mere fancy dress, a masquerade, and not after all my truest self.

Who among us is undisguised, after all? Which of us reveals himself truly to the world? My name was borrowed, yes, a kind of mask, but I was the doctor, I was the lover, I was the scandal and the hero, I was Jonathan Mirandus Perry. There was no one else.

CHAPTER FOUR

THE CAPE DOCTOR

There is a spring wind that blows on the southern Cape of Africa, southeasterly up from the Antarctic, that breaks ships against the rocks and blows clear the skies over the settlement of Cape Town, clearing away the soot and fumes, the stench of sewage and men's sweat, like a great broom sweeping clean the air, carrying the dust and heat and pestilence out to the Cape Flats, leaving the air fresh for those who live to breathe it. It wraps itself around Table Bay and pollinates the silvertrees, swirling through the colony, like a gorgeous Malay twirling at a Rainbow Ball. Fierce and terrible, unsettling and healing, the wind was affectionately known by the Dutch locals as *die Kaapse dokter*; the English, in the dozen years I lived there long ago, knew it as the Cape Doctor. As I was known.

I arrived in Cape Town in August 1816. In October, *die Kaapse dokter* did.

It's hard to describe the effect of Cape Town. The exuberance of it. A riot of life. After the cloistral student years in Edinburgh and London, the cold and clammy damp, Cape Town was like throwing open a window after a long, arduous winter—the kind of winter you find only in the north Atlantic, wet and dank and smoky from fires. Everywhere you turned in

Cape Town, your eye was met with marvels, as if in reward for having made the dangerous crossing. The sea was a glistening blue-green, palest jade to lapis lazuli, the steep green mountains rose sharply above bone-white beaches, and presiding over all of it, the grey cliffs of Table Mountain, across which fog rolled each evening like a cloth and withdrew again each morning, like a woman dropping her dress. The mountains surrounding the bay were wreathed with strange, unearthly flowers—the prehistoric *protea*, which resembled pine cones in brilliant orange and yellow and red; flowering stalks of candelabra lily; trees strange and skeletal and knobbed as a human spine; and brilliant pink Watsonia flowers—made more radiant by the pale blue sky and bluer sea, the shore a marvel of surf-rounded monoliths as if Stonehenge had been arranged by nature here.

The Cape of Good Hope—which I'd later see with Lord Somerton—was like a jewel, a mountain carved out of emerald, a tent of green, color of County Cork; tall as a Salisbury Cathedral draped in green silk, cascading to the gem-blue sea. Steep as the cliffs of Cornwall.

As a girl, I'd heard young women in Cork sing ballads of true love and read novels that made romance sound like meeting one's destiny. I'd felt that only once before in my life—looking into the landscape of the body in Fyfe's dissection theater. But I felt it again on arriving in Cape Town. Here was my home, so far from it. I did not feel, as so many Europeans mistakenly would claim to, that this was *my* land, but rather that I was *its*—I belonged to this place, without having known it existed.

The journey from London had been long and tedious and full of tiresome subterfuge, as I fought to maintain privacy on board ship—tossing out my cabin mate each morning that I might dress—so I was relieved to set foot on firm ground again (the bustling, fish-reeking docks at Table Bay) even as my legs were unsteady and my lodgings unpromising in the extreme. I was to be quartered at the Castle, where all military men were sent, a damp, dim, stone structure in port, whose chill dark corridors could not entirely extinguish the exuberant light of those days. I took comfort in the thought that Mirandus had spent time in a similar circumstance in prison in France. I vowed, as he had, that I'd not linger.

I had failed to find General Mirandus in London, had not heard back from him after my last letter, so when I completed my studies with Sir Astley Cooper, I entered the army as a military surgeon. I had accepted a first post at Plymouth, then Chelsea, now in Cape Town, hoping that I might hear from the general any day with an invitation to join him and his family in Caracas. But I received no word, no news. Except for the little that I read in the press.

It was odd to have no word of him, but I did not flatter myself that I could weigh heavily in his thoughts, when so much else demanded his attention. Still, I scoured the papers for items about him, had asked on board ship whenever we took on new crew, what they might have heard.

The ship's captain had been full of news, collecting word of other men as some collect coin, as if it were a kind of wealth. From him I'd learned that the Cape Governor, Lord Somerton, was a difficult man—arrogant and autocratic, given to extravagant loyalty and enmity both. Like me, the governor was recently arrived from England, having come two years before with a young family. It was said Lord Somerton had once been an uncommonly handsome man and as vain as a woman about his looks, and was sensitive about his age, now that he had passed two-score and five. I wondered that a man could keep his vanity in so rough a place, so far from fashionable society, but he was said to keep abreast of fashion and to covet the latest news from Paris. He was rumored—though surely this was a joke—to have persuaded the captain of the ship that had borne Napoleon to St. Helenas the previous year to pause in Cape Town to give a thorough accounting of the latest Paris fashions to Somerton's wife and daughters. This was considered especially funny, since his sympathies were entirely against Republicanism, and he was rumored to have lost family to the guillotine in France.

He sounded like the model of everything I loathed. A man whose name alone, not merit, had carned him rank, contrary to the meritocratic impulse of the age. Hearing him described aboard ship, I recalled Mirandus's quip: *A gentleman should always be wary of rank, given the word's rancid concomitant, "decay."*

We were unlikely ever to be friends, Lord Somerton and I, if only by virtue of unequal birth. But he governed the Cape colony in more than politics; I'd heard he was its social arbiter as well, and if I was to successfully enter this society, it was through him that I must do it. Lord Basken had instructed me to introduce myself as soon as possible, and had supplied me with a letter of commendation to that end; he had called it my "ticket to soup," pleased to know the common idiom, assuring me it would grant me an invitation to dinner at the very least. I'd planned to call on the governor as soon as I was settled, only to find that before I could, I was summoned—the very morning I arrived—to Tunhuys (or Government House, as the

English called it), the governor's palatial residence, to tend to his daughter, who'd fallen ill.

I went at once, taking time only to change my coat.

I declined the offer of a carriage, preferring to walk after the weeks aboard ship, despite unsteady legs. I walked quickly through the dusty streets, dodging wagons and men on horseback, and dark-skinned men in chains, through the bustle of a major port, which Cape Town had recently become with Napoleon in residence nearby. (I'd heard the traffic in claret alone sustained the Cape economy.) I walked through the shade cast by the Groote Kerk before I reached the pleasant walkways of the Company's Garden, much discussed on the voyage over for its abundant produce and leaf-shaded paths.

The governor's residence seemed all the more stately in the midst of the raw colonial town. Its walls were crocus yellow, the columns and portico a brilliant starched white. I had heard that Lord Somerton had spent a king's ransom on the renovation of the ballroom, an extravagance that secured my dislike of the man I had yet to meet. A fortune on a *library* I could understand, but redecoration of a ballroom seemed to signify a trivial mind. What I'd heard of him on ship had inclined me to this view. He was a man whose reputation preceded him, as did that of the beauty of his daughters and of his late wife.

I don't know how I looked to him the day we met, but I can guess. There is a portrait of me from the time, painted on ivory when I was in the barracks in Chelsea, in which I have the long, sad face of Botticelli's *Venus*; aristocratic cheekbones, high and prominent; and fine, small ears beneath a cap of golden ringlets. My nose is my best feature—long and slender—setting off my dark eyes, my pencil-thin brows; if my mouth is too small, it is a minor fault. It suits well the delicate curve of my chin. I look every inch the young poet, the serious young man, my gaze a contradiction—at once direct and far off; I seem fixed on some distant goal, some great thought. Every inch the Romantic hero; Young Werther himself.

In the final famous photograph taken of me in Kingston, Jamaica, 20 years later, I retain the posture of the dandy I once was, if not the hair. My hair and face are a ruin, as my heart was. Desolate. Despite my turned-up collar, my neat tie, my highly polished boots and well-cut coat, I am a wraith in that final famous image, flanked by the manservant Dantzen and Psyche, the dog. I look altogether too much like a poodle; the dog and I share a face, in fact. My right hand rests gently on her head. My left thumb tucked into my pocket on my vest. My long Ciceronian nose, still my best feature, too large against my shrunken face. My jaw grown long and bony, my mouth a small dark frown; my earlobes hang, framing eyes that seem to squint. As if trying to see what's coming, what lies ahead. We never do. For better and for worse. I didn't know what was coming.

When I first saw him standing in his offices at Tunhuys, the governor's back was turned to me, hands clasped behind him, gazing out over the gardens; he struck me as a monumental man by virtue of his height and dress. But when he turned to greet me, the impression changed: I thought he was too pretty to be a man. His features were too delicate, like a young woman's. There was something self-consciously manly about him, as if he were slightly straining for the effect. Though later I would think that he was straining to cover grief, to offset an impression of melancholy, of which he was conscious and by which he was embarrassed.

"Doctor Perry, good of you to come." Lord Somerton was polite but curt, his courtesy born of breeding not inclination, bespeaking condescension if not slight, making clear he was indulging in a pretense of social equality where there was none, and that my rank did not merit in his eyes. He could not disguise his dislike of my profession.

He offered me a chair and I sat, noting that he did not. Instead, he began to pace. Like a man whose energies are too little engaged by his work, who would rather be out hunting, riding, shooting things, a man for whom these rooms were too small, too tight a fit.

I'd heard that he was given to guns and dogs and horses, which interested me not at all. But if he was to be my patient, I came prepared to be patient with him. Having heard about Her Ladyship's death from fever the year before, I had expected to find a man chastened by loss, but on him even grief wore the face of glamour.

"Your uncle commended you most highly," he said, as if he rather doubted the letter I'd borne with me on my journey, which I'd had the good sense to send ahead with the servant who had summoned me. He held the letter out to me. I took it. My passport to this new world.

"Lord Basken has been most generous," I said. "Although we are not kin, we are as close as affection can make men; he has graciously treated me as if we were."

"Your kin are..."

"Far from here, Your Lordship," I replied, perhaps too quickly, steering him clear of that which I dreaded to discuss, the rocky shoals of personal history. "But yours, I understand, are near at hand and in some distress. Which is why I have come. I am at your service." I stood. "Might I see the patient?"

Another man of his station might have been affronted by my obvious refusal to reply to a reasonable inquiry—after all, if I was to attend his daughter, he had reason to want to be assured of my quality. But the assurance he sought was not any I could give. I had only my character and skill and Lord Basken's letter to speak for me.

He stopped his pacing and turned to face me, his hands folded behind his back.

"You're rather..." He seemed to be grasping for the term as he looked me over. I feared he might say *impertinent*. "...*young* for your position, are you not, Dr. Perry?"

"Surely we can agree that *age* is not the measure of a man," I said.

He raised his chin, as if trying to discern insolence in my remark.

"Given primogeniture, one's age often makes and unmakes men," he said.

"Indeed," I said. "I am an only child."

"What then would you say measures a man?"

"Surely that depends on who is taking it: a tailor or an undertaker, a lover or a patient. In the last case, a man's measure must be his ability to heal." I quoted again the dramatist, as if it were an incantation conjuring me: *"Ne hoc consideres, se junior loquar, Sed si viri prudentir sermones apud te habeo."* I could see that he understood the phrase at once: *Do not judge me on my youth but on my knowledge as a man.*

My mother had maintained that land was the source of security, a faith my brother had proved woefully unwarranted. General Mirandus had counseled knowledge as the only lasting treasure. Once more I found that Latin was the key in the lock that opened society to me.

"Then let us take *your* measure, doctor," Lord Somerton said. "The patient, my daughter Georgiana, is upstairs."

Sir Astley Cooper at Guy's in London had taught me that the performance of decisiveness is itself often decisive in the treatment of a patient. As I mounted the stairs beside the governor, I felt his trepidation rise and my courage fail. I held the banister to steady my hand's shaking. We did not speak as we mounted the staircase to the private rooms above; when we came to the door we were to enter, I stopped him with a hand.

"You may wait here," I directed His Lordship at the door. It was a dangerous gambit to give orders to a vain and aristocratic governor, but I sensed that my confidence would encourage his own. He did not protest. I opened the door, stepped in alone.

Inside the drapes were drawn against the midday sun, the massive sash windows to the balcony fastened closed. All was oppressive heat and the sour smell of sweat and illness. When I approached the bed, a maid I had not noticed stood up from the far corner, curtsied briefly.

"How is she?" I asked. I'd learned that those overlooked often observed more keenly than those looked to for their observations.

"Poorly, sir," the girl replied. "She hardly moves at all, except in pain."

The girl in the bed was flushed and seemed unconscious of my entrance; using the Parisian Laennec's recent invention, I rolled a tube of paper to form what he called a *stethoscope* and placed one end to her chest, which revealed—as I feared it would—a rattle there; her heartbeat slow. He condition was far worse than I'd imagined.

"How long's she been like this?"

"She's had the fever for more 'an a day now, two."

"And the treatment?"

"Why, none, sir. None's seen her afore you."

"She has had no treatment at all?" I was incredulous. This was not a debtor's prison, yet the patient lay as neglected as any there.

"His Lordship dislikes doctors," she said. "Begging your pardon, sir. After all that happened with Her Ladyship."

"Of course, of course," I said. I was not interested in personal details. I raised the girl's wrist and felt her faint and erratic pulse. The room's conditions were perfect to induce the illness that she fought. I strode to the window and yanked back the curtains, raising the large sash windows so that a cool breeze blew in.

"Won't she catch her death, Sir?"

"With luck, she will catch her life," I said. "Here's what you will do…"

I ordered her to run a bath, as hot as could be withstood, and to fill it with herbs from the Company's Garden—ginger, eucalyptus, peppermint, camphor, if they had it—so that it steamed the room, and to bathe Miss Somerton there twice daily to clear her lungs and raise her blood. She was to scrub the room with bleach to clear contagion; I ordered clean linens and fresh air. Prescribed hot beef broth with garlic hourly and warmed wine to induce a sweat and break the fever. *The truth of principles must be confirmed by observation*, Sir Astley Cooper had said; the best I could do was prescribe from sound principles and observe the consequences, then adjust.

I was jotting down instructions when I noticed a bottle of tonic on the bedside table; I took it up and read the label, though I hardly needed to—here as in London, apothecaries made fortunes poisoning patients. I knew what it contained.

"And throw this out, for God's sake. She's to have no more of it, or any like it—is that clear?"

I told the girl to send for me as soon as Miss Somerton woke. When I stepped out of the room, I spoke to the governor only briefly to say that his daughter was quite ill but would recover with proper treatment as I'd prescribed.

"No need to see me out," I said. Then I descended the stairs alone. As I departed through the gleaming monumental columns, I hoped that what I'd promised the governor proved true.

I spent the rest of that afternoon seeking new lodgings and quickly secured rooms in the Heerengracht, a fashionable and trafficked thoroughfare despite the open sewer that ran down its center. Cafés, shops, and trees lined the street, and each morning it would become my habit to walk to the bakery run by Mrs. Saunders for Dutch coffee and sugar buns, to sit and read the news from here and abroad to the delightful crunch of cane sugar between my teeth, delighted to have word of the larger world, even if it was months old.

In Edinburgh, I had read with joy of the liberation of Venezuela from Spain, which Mirandus had long dreamed of and fought for; in London I had read with fear of the terrible earthquake in March that had killed thousands in Caracas and given ammunition to those who questioned the new revolutionary government's justice in the eyes of god. Now I searched the pages for any mention of my friend. Found few. None that told me what I longed to know: how he was.

The following day, Miss Somerton awakened from her stupor (which confirmed my suspicion that it was not induced by fever but by the laudanum-laced "medicine" she'd been prescribed). I visited daily during her convalescence, which happily was brief—far briefer than I'd thought possible. Attending to the governor's family, I was excused from my duties as a medical assistant at the hospital. Soon enough she was well enough to descend to dine with her family, and I was invited to dine with them as well.

The dining room at Government House was of pleasing proportions, the floors polished to a high shine, the walls a pale hue that lent warmth to the pleasantly cool chamber, a balance of elegance and simplicity. Candelabras down the table illuminated the family's faces in a soft glow. At table were His Lordship, his two daughters, and his youngest son, as well as the local bishop. I was not surprised to learn that the governor himself had commissioned the room's redecoration in addition to the renovation of the ballroom. He was a man who clearly enjoyed worldly pleasures. Which made it odder still to find that the bishop dined regularly with them. At first I thought this a sign of piety, then of respect for his late wife; only later, when I knew them better, would I understand that the bishop was present to provide a figure of fun.

Showing me over the house before dinner, the governor had told me of how he had added wings for a ballroom, updated it to its sleek Georgian style; he told me the house had originally been a storage shed, and hardly better than that by the time they'd arrived two years before, "not fit for hounds." I'd heard on board ship as we'd sailed here that he was extravagant, self-indulgent. Perhaps he didn't care to govern well. The Cape, after all, was said to be a place where reputations came to die; I intended to be sure mine did not.

Now as we sat down to dine, Lord Somerton announced, "The doctor approves of our ballroom." In point of fact, I didn't—but I appreciated that he spoke as if my opinion might matter.

"It is impressive," I said.

"More than you might guess," Lord Somerton said. "The house was hardly better than a dog's kennel when we arrived."

"Lucky dogs," I said.

Bishop Burnett smiled at me from across the table with gorgeous teeth, and I felt myself recoil. Beautiful dentures were to be seen all around London before I'd sailed for the Cape—the Waterloo ivory, as it was called, plucked from corpses on the battlefield. In truth most came from common graves, from bodies disinterred for sale. Seeing such ivory in the mouths of men in the Strand or Piccadilly, my nostrils filled with the sick-sweet stench of battle and the dissection theater—rotted flesh, gunpowder, offal, mud.

"That suited the hounds, of course," Lord Somerton said, "but not us, so we've made improvements."

It was hard to tell if the governor was praising or mocking me when he spoke of my miraculous powers. "You're a magician, Doctor," he said. "We suspect you of alchemy."

"I'd hate to think that reason is so rare in these parts as to seem supernatural."

"How did you do it?" He reached for Georgiana's hand, seated to his right, covered hers with his and then raised it to his lips, kissed it. I disliked his politics, but it was hard not to admire the man's tenderness toward his family.

"Medicine is often a matter of optimizing the body's ability to heal. As with a ship, one must avoid overburdening it." I feared I was dull, pedantic; I must charm. "As in life, success often depends on the judicious application of wine."

"I will quote you on that," said the governor. He signaled a servant to fill our glasses. "Doctor's orders."

It was clear that he was trying to win me over, a fact that disconcerted me. He had no need of my good opinion, although I was relieved to have stumbled on his. Still, I was wary, watchful.

What I noticed that night was how Lord Somerton seemed transformed in the presence of his family, with the constraints of office cut, leaving him to gentle, mocking exchanges of admirable tenderness and wit. He treated his children as equals, although only Georgiana had reached an age—at 23, two years my senior—that might qualify as adult; he indulged them with most tender affection. Conversation was like a sporting match, each in turn offering a topic that was struck about like a badminton shuttlecock. They discussed local fashion, hunting prospects, the antics of their pets—among which numbered two lizards, four dogs, two monkeys, and a snake.

We were halfway through the soup course when a monstrous creature, scaly and pale with small shining eyes, rose up from behind the soup tureen and began to make its way down the long oak table, striding like a boxer entering a ring, head down, shoulders raised, occasionally stopping to lift and lower its head like a Mohammedan at prayer, prompting the bishop to drop his spoon into his dish, which caused a clatter and a mess, before His Lordship directed the man at table to serve the lizard its dinner elsewhere, which delighted the youngest girl, Charlotte, no end.

"Do use the Wedgwood," she whispered to the manservant as he left.

"As you wish, Miss," he replied.

The child looked at me earnestly, without a trace of mirth, and said, confidingly, "He won't eat from anything else."

"Ah," I said. "Nor would I. He has good taste. And has he a name?"

The child looked at me as if I were daft. "But of course."

Georgiana came to my rescue, "She calls him *Mr. Franklin.*"

I nearly spit my soup. "For the American ambassador?"

"Because he has an enormous appetite, a bit of a belly, poor eyesight, and appears to want nothing more than his own liberty."

"I hadn't realized one named lizards," I said.

"One names one's dogs," Miss Georgiana said, as if that explained it.

"Didn't Napoleon have a dachshund named *Grenouille?*" asked the bishop.

"The American president John Adams is said to have a hound named *Satan,*" said Lord Somerton.

"*Cerberus* would be more fitting," Miss Somerton replied.

"Not all the colonies are Hell," I said.

"Not all the colonies are colonies," said Lord Somerton. "The Americans have seen to that. And now, God help us, the South Americans have taken it up."

"It will be their undoing," said the bishop. "Mark my words."

"Or their making," said I. "I understand that Adams also has a horse named *Cleopatra.* But perhaps that's more understandable—what man would not want to mount Cleopatra?"

The bishop stared at me and the table was silent. I was

accustomed to dining with soldiers and sailors and fashionable London society, for whom wit might take any subject. I feared I'd overstepped the bounds, given the presence of young ladies, but Miss Somerton smiled and Lord Somerton laughed.

"By God, I'll name my next mare that," he said.

Night had settled over the bay, and through the windows came the scent of the salt water, the breeze fragrant with jasmine, the lazy hum of flies and bees and birdcalls, and in the distance the sound of drums or surf. Candlelight twitched in the breeze.

It was Georgiana who turned the conversation from Cleopatra to Shakespeare's plays.

"Aren't they mounting Cleopatra at the African Theater next month?" she said, smiling.

"Now that's a performance I'd be glad to observe," I said.

The bishop cleared his throat. "I fear you may be disappointed, Dr. Perry, coming from London. Our theatricals are in a sorry state."

"Indeed?" I had seen the glorious African Theater, was surprised to hear it was in disrepair.

"It is most regrettable," Bishop Burnett said. "The enlisted men are in great need of salubrious recreations."

Miss Georgiana coughed into her napkin, evidently to cover a laugh.

The bishop was a man who would always choose an obscure term over a modest one, not for precision's sake but vanity's; he tortured his phrases on the rack of egoism. I'd later learn Miss Georgiana took great pleasure in imitating him behind his back; hearing the bishop speak, I was seized with the absurd sense that he was parodying obfuscation instead of indulging it.

From our first meeting, I disliked him. The bishop combined

the worst aspects of religion: false piety and true pomposity, which in my experience were lethal for both good conversation and good sense. He was a man who took great pains to dictate liberality to others, as if to balance the little generosity he himself possessed. He was thoroughly benevolent in word, if not in deed. He complained bitterly of the local matrons, who refused to give alms to the poor and the lepers, but when asked of his work among them, sniffed and said that of course he *wished* he had the luxury of time for such pursuits but that his official obligations prevented him. I thought I noticed Miss Georgiana smile at this—as I did.

"I only wish I could be more useful, Doctor; I am not one of those who spare their own trouble. My sole desire is to be of use to His Lordship and all Cape Christians....Regrettably, my health and spirits put travel to Robben Island quite out of the question."

It did not appear to impede his theatergoing. He held forth on the splendors of Shakespeare and the African Theater and rapturously described having seen an absolutely marvelous production of *The Tempest* the previous year.

"Quite apt for our circumstance," he said, "stranded as we are."

I thought the bishop seemed rather worldly for his post.

"You see, doctor, there is a paucity of soldiers to perform the female roles. Our soldiers are not amenable to having female parts."

I could not help quipping, "As a physician, I must say it would be most distressing to discover that the soldiers here had female parts."

Lord Somerton laughed his curious laugh—"Ah, ah!"—as if breathing in joy.

The bishop looked distressed, gave his pursed little disapproving smile. "I meant, of course, female roles."

"Ah."

The bishop continued, warming to his subject. "At first I had found it rather alarming to see soldiers dressed as women, but I understand it was the tradition in Shakespeare's time."

"Women weren't allowed on stage." I tried to keep any hint of bitterness from my voice.

"And what of Viola?" Georgiana asked of the heroine of *Twelfth Night*.

"An interesting case: Viola was of course played by a man, pretending to be a woman pretending to be a man."

"How very confusing," Georgiana said.

"Impersonation often is," I said.

"Of course, the reverse is not true," said the bishop. "It's an absolute delight to see a female perform in a male role, but it is far too rare. Women make such fine men."

"Of course," I said. "No impersonation is required." An edge in my voice.

"What can you mean?" the bishop asked.

"Only that women needn't impersonate men; they need simply cease impersonating women."

"That's quite true, Doctor," Georgiana said. "But you're the first man I've heard own it."

"The doctor is a rare man," Lord Somerton said, looking at me over his raised glass.

"His sort of man is rare indeed," the bishop said, with what I sensed was not admiration.

"In an age of taxonomy, you'd think our classifications would be more meaningful," I said, encouraged by the governor's evident approval. "We make too much of the distinction between men and women; the differences are less than they appear."

"The differences are obvious, surely," Lord Somerton smiled at his daughters. He seemed to enjoy an argument, as if we were pursuing a fox through brush, chasing clarity.

"It's not obvious at all to me why a daughter should be denied a son's education," I said.

"This claim of rights for women would wrong the women it claims to aid," Lord Somerton said, as if settling the matter. "It would deny them their privileged status, make them no better than men."

"Is it a privilege to be denied an education, to be denied the liberty to walk freely in the street, to earn one's way? Is it a privilege that denies them vote and rights?"

"I'd not have taken you for an enfranchiser, Dr. Perry," said the bishop.

"I'd rather that than be taken for a fool. We disguise all manner of harm in the name of protection—it's always someone else's best interests we're looking out for, when we are looking to our own. The English 'protected' the Irish out of their lands. They are doing the same here."

A silence fell over the table. It was clear I had gone too far.

The Governor cleared his throat, signaled with a graceful hand to the footman to clear the plates. "It is late, Dr. Perry. We mustn't detain you any longer."

I thought I saw the bishop smile.

I was miserable that night, walking home and later tossing in my bed in the Heerengracht, writing and rewriting in my mind a letter of apology that I would send to the governor at dawn, knowing I could send none. There was no undoing such words; as if my words had been an incantation, I had worked a spell that cast me out of their charmed circle. He was a Tory, an aristocrat, a defender of everything Mirandus and I stood against. There was nothing I might say to change that. It would be changing history itself.

I did not hear from the governor and did not expect to. I spent the next few weeks in the errands that constituted the better part of my job as an assistant staff surgeon. Dressing wounds. Taking histories. Writing reports. Scrubbing down examination rooms whose filth had most likely done more harm to patients than the physician had done good.

I consoled myself that I was not here to court the good opinion of an aristocratic governor but to cure, or try to. It was a tall order. The military hospital, where I reported the next day, was a catastrophe. The rooms were filthy and overrun with animals of every sort, the windows broken. Birds flew in and flitted among the rafters, dropping their shit. Pigeons roosted in the examining rooms and chickens and pigs ambled down the halls; the hospital wards were ample, but they had been commandeered by a few officers for their private use as apartments, leaving the ill to lie on narrow cots in overcrowded corridors and in a few smaller rooms, shoulder to shoulder in the filth.

A stench of manure and human waste and festering wounds permeated the place, relieved only by the fresh breeze that blew through the broken windowpanes. Flies covered patients too ill to bat them away. To compare it to a stable would be to insult the stable. When I inquired of an orderly where the local people were treated, as this was reserved for the military, I was told they were housed mostly in the *tronk*—

the local jail. I had expected challenging conditions, but I had not anticipated cruelty, bald indifference to the suffering of those in need. A boy of four—a soldier's son, I assume—died of a diarrheal illness as I stood by his cot. When the surgeon in charge asked what he'd died of, I told him frankly, "Indifference and poverty."

I wrote to the governor daily with my concerns about the conditions at the hospital. I did not hear back.

I woke one night to the wind howling outside my window overlooking the Heerengracht, the rain like pebbles tossed against the glass, then a pounding on the door, and my landlady's voice, "Dr. Perry, someone's come for you!" I opened the door expecting a summons, a gaoler. For a moment, I thought I'd been found out. But it was a boy, saying a ship had sunk. I was needed at Camps Bay.

The call came early, as they always would, urgent as nightmare. Something awful, the boy said, hundreds of bodies on the beach. I pulled on my boots, took my pistol and medical kit, descended the stairs, and together we rode down to the water's edge, to the beach where they lay heaped like lumber or like seals sunning themselves, the bodies of more than a hundred men, among them women, children, infants. The stench of excrement and decay, bitter rot and brine like a choking fog.

I didn't need to ask what sort of ship had gone down; only one kind has a human cargo. Word of a slaver rounding the Cape was always news, as the bounty offered on the illegal ships had become nearly as valuable as the sale of the enslaved once was.

It was rare to have the bodies wash ashore; when the slavers went down in storms, chains usually pulled their human cargo down, the crime swallowed by the sea. Not now. I walked among them, picking my way carefully over the corpses, turning them gently to see if any hint of life or breath remained. If any might be saved.

Most were swollen; some few appeared sleeping save for a skin of sand over their own, which they did not bother to wipe away, proof of their state. There was no knowing what had happened aboard ship that they were free of chains when the vessel sank, but I guessed the captain had freed them, hoping to save some lives for later sale. Here was the body of a child not more than five, hair fanned out like Caribbean coral or a lady's silk fan. I bent down to brush the sand from her cheek, raised her thin wrist in my pale fingers, felt for a pulse, found none.

The following day, the town would talk of it in a pantomime of compassion, which was really just an excuse to revel in the death that was not yet one's own. I was gripped by a hatred of the frontier town, of its people, the merchants and landowners, the slaveholders and petty bureaucrats, the sailors and soldiers; they seemed an infestation, an overgrowth or tumor upon the skin of Africa, a lesion, suppurating us.

It was while walking through the Company's Garden my first day in Cape Town that the idea came to me to take notes on local flora. I'd make a study of Cape plants and their possible medicinal uses. It seemed only sensible, given the remarkable richness that arose here in the margin of the world, where the unexpected and unlike collide—mountains and sea, two oceans. Nature itself seemed denser here, richer, more vivid, where life in all its variety mixed.

I disliked the English habit of turning every place into England; I preferred to consider where I was. Although I had little time to explore the hills outside town, I took notes on the native plants in town where I found them, making small sketches, inquiring of locals about the uses to which they put each. My landlady noticed my interest and recommended that I speak with a pharmacist she knew, a Mr. Poleman. An amateur botanist.

It was a week before I managed to find time to pay a visit to his shop, one afternoon after I had finished my hospital rounds. I found him unassuming to the point of near invisibility. Rumpled, pale haired, though hardly older than myself, he had a touching wariness, a modesty and anxiety that one rarely found in men here or anywhere; his eyes avoided mine, seemed fearful when ours met; it made me feel almost gallant, but it was the shop that most impressed me; it was spotless, orderly in appearance as the man was not. He seemed absent of vanity. I liked him immediately.

He was more like a bird than a man. Later I would realize what seemed curious and comforting about him: he was a man seemingly without sex. Mild, slender, he had almost no physicality. He smelled of bleach and lavender.

I asked about the source of his remedies, whether all were imported, which, if any, were from local plants. He answered with a completeness uncharacteristic of local merchants— he did not boast of the quality of his products, but spoke of the unreliable shipping, the damage done in transit, the loss of efficacy due to cold or heat, of the excessive reliance on opium and mercury, both of which he considered to be more poison than tonic.

"Often what kills can cure, if administered in a proper dosage," I said.

"That is the principle," he said. "But dosage is often wrong."

That was true.

We spoke of local plants and their possible uses.

"Are you a botanist, Dr. Perry?"

I wasn't, I said, but I was eager to learn. Especially here where there was so much to study. When he invited me to come out for a collecting trip the following Saturday, when an assistant could watch the shop, I was delighted to accept. He proposed we gather samples from Table Mountain to evaluate later in the small lab he kept for his private use behind the shop.

There was a kind of greed in me for learning, a passion that seemed to have taken the place of the erotic desire others claimed to feel. At night I would lie in bed and see before me the leaves I'd collected, recall the scent of a fresh-picked stalk and the taste, imagining what might be compounded, what cures might be discerned. The green fug, the bitter leaf. Curiosity has its sexual side.

The following Saturday morning, Mr. Poleman and I hiked out into the hills at the base of Table Mountain, gathering samples, especially plants that local peoples used in cures. As we walked, he spoke with reverence of the "sacred beauty" of the place.

"Nature is a mystery, Mr. Poleman," I said, "not a psalm."

"Can't it be both, Dr. Perry?"

"No," I said. "Reverence is fatal to understanding. We don't question what we revere." Men always spoke of land and women thus.

I filled a satchel for later examination in his lab; when we returned to town we deposited our samples there, then parted, agreeing to meet in an hour to dine and discuss the day's collection. I would join him for dinner at his home, where he promised a stew seasoned with some of what we'd gathered; he admonished me to come promptly at six.

An hour later, having washed up and changed, I was standing outside the door of Mr. Poleman's house, a few minutes before the hour, when a horse galloped toward me at an alarming rate and pulled up short, before the governor swung down from it.

"A word, Dr. Perry."

I feared that my insistent correspondence had incurred the governor's wrath, which was a topic of local discussion (he was said to have broken a cane over someone in a dispute). But to my surprise he was courteous, if not cordial. He said that he had read my reports with interest and wished to clarify several points. He might have summoned me to Government House for a discussion, of course, but I imagined I was not welcome there.

So I stood in the dusty street and explained what I had made perfectly clear in my reports. I appreciated his interest, despite the redundancy; nonetheless, I was relieved when Poleman came to the door and opened it impatiently—"Perry, where *have* you been; you're late"—only to see the governor. "Your Excellency," he said. "I did not mean to interrupt." He began to withdraw into his home, like a hermit crab, but I stopped him and made an introduction. The governor said, "It is I who is interrupting, Mr. Poleman. I'll detain you no further, Dr. Perry. Thank you for your report. Good evening, *gentlemen*," he said, though clearly we were not.

When a letter arrived the following morning as I took coffee in Mrs. Saunders's café, I thought it was at last word from my friend in Venezuela, summoning me. I longed for news of

Mirandus; I longed for London and my few friends. I turned the envelope over and saw the governor's seal; my heart sank. I opened it and read:

Forgive me, Doctor, although I cannot forgive myself, from having kept you from your dinner. You were too polite to tell me it was cooling as I kept you gossiping beside the door, so please do me the courtesy of joining my family for what I promise will be a thoroughly hot meal.

I was charmed despite myself. Not simply by the promise of a good dinner, but by the governor's self-deprecation. It is a rare man who wears his power lightly. I was startled by how the invitation pleased me. To be welcomed again into their charmed circle. But I knew better than to trust him, or anyone.

That evening at Government House was enchanting, as were the many evenings that followed there, or at least *I* was enchanted. I delighted in the governor and his children, not yet grown, save for Miss Georgiana; they possessed an unaffected grace and curiosity, high spirits combined with gentleness and natural manners. They seemed—the word that came to mind surprised me—*uncorrupted*. Something from another age, before the fall.

It was Georgiana who proposed—one evening after dinner—that Lord Somerton teach me to ride.

"Don't be absurd, the good doctor knows well enough how to hold his mount."

The truth was, I didn't. Nor could I shoot straight. I had managed in my brief time as an army doctor always to ride in the supply wagon, never needing to keep my own mount. It was both more economical, since I needn't pay for the purchase and upkeep of a horse, and avoided the awkwardness that would surely follow should I fall and require examination on the field.

"In fact," I admitted. "I do not."

"Good God," said Lord Somerton. "You call yourself a soldier?"

"I call myself many things, Your Lordship. I am called still more by others."

The governor smiled; he appreciated a joke, as long as it was not at his expense.

"Oh, do let us teach him," Georgiana spoke in the same tone I'd heard her apply to her pet monkey, when petitioning that it be allowed to sit at table or join a game of whist.

"I warn you," I said. "I may fall more than ride. You cannot judge a doctor by his grace in the saddle."

"We'll arrange a hunt," said Lord Somerton.

"You've imported foxes, as well as hounds?" I was amazed at how far a sportsman's devotion could go.

"An African hunt," he said. "On the Cape Flats, a jackal's as good as a fox."

"From the fox's perspective, considerably better, I'm sure," I said. I had always pitied the fox, another reason I'd declined to ride out with the others at Dryburgh Abbey. "Perhaps we might arrange something a bit less vigorous?"

After some considerable discussion, I managed to persuade Lord Somerton to commence our lesson with something less arduous than a hunt; I proposed a trip to Table Mountain, a small hunting party of two, having heard from Miss Georgiana how he loved to hunt up there.

On the appointed day, Lord Somerton met me at his stables near Roundhouse above Camps Bay; he proposed to match me to a majestic monster, a splendid beast of seventeen hands, a dappled Andalusian named Zeus, easily twice my height, but Georgiana came to my rescue and drew forth from the dark barn stalls a charming little roan filly hardly taller than myself. She stepped drowsily into the light, her coat gleaming, her eyes half-open.

"You can't be serious," Lord Somerton said to his daughter. "The doctor needs a proper horse, not a child's pony."

Miss Georgiana ignored her father, affectionately stroking the horse's neck. "She's very docile," she said. "But she's not afraid of anything. She won't rear at a snake, or a leopard."

It hadn't occurred to me that we might encounter either, but I did not say this.

Evidently weary of delay, Lord Somerton swung up onto his mount, a stallion of magnificent proportions. It was instantly clear why Somerton bred horses; he was a man who seemed more at ease on a horse than off one. As if he were a centaur— half man, half beast. When I'd arrived at Roundhouse that morning, he'd toured me through his stables as another man might display his gardens or his pictures. Many covet wealth, but few—it seemed to me—truly enjoyed it. Somerton clearly did. He relished beautiful things, unapologetically: beautiful horses, beautiful guns, ballrooms and houses and clothes. Wealth bought him beauty; it gave him pleasure and time to enjoy it.

He seemed to take the delight that animals take in life. I could not imagine him in London. For all his studied social graces, he had a wild heart. A lonely or perhaps solitary spirit. Standing between us in the morning cool, he stood apart. He was utterly unlike the general. Not simply because he was more delicate, an aesthete rather than a commander of men. The general belonged to Venezuela; Somerton seemed to belong nowhere. He seemed a man between worlds, which is perhaps what had brought him here, as it had me. Strange creatures suited to no place but here, like the king protea, the sugarbird, the silver trees. Strange and peculiar fauna and flora of the Cape.

Despite my dread of horses, I was surprised to find myself at ease in the saddle beside (or more accurately *below*) Lord Somerton and his enormous mount. Although my horse was tiny by comparison, I seemed to tower over the fynbos as we rode up into the hills, my heels skimming the tops of the sugarbushes as we rode higher, as the blue expanse of the Atlantic Ocean spread out below us.

The morning was cool and windless and bright, and we rode without speaking for what seemed hours. Occasionally steenbok burst from the bushes or a bontebok raised its masked face and twisted horns. I was relieved that Somerton left his rifle in its saddle holster. We paused for lunch near the top of Table Mountain. In the distance a small herd of zebra scattered at the sound of our voices—

"Do you often hunt, Doctor Perry?" the governor asked.

"Only for a good book at night," I replied.

He was not amused.

"When you take a shot," Lord Somerton told me, watching them, "remember, heart first, then head."

"What makes you think I'll take a shot?"

Somerton laughed.

The hound that had accompanied us shivered, straining against the leash that held it, silent as its master, until Somerton released it and it shot forward as if sprung from a trap.

When the dog returned he was carrying a small soft body in his mouth, which he dutifully dropped before us. The caracal kitten lay there, limp, paws stretched forward on the ground as if it were in mid-pounce. Its ears large as its head, no longer than two phalanges of my first finger. An ache overtook me that never did when human corpses were involved. I felt ill and stood. Then I leaned over and was sick beside a silver tree.

"Can't be moved by every death, doctor."

"What have we become, if we're not?"

"Men," he said.

"God protect me against that."

It was midday when we reached the top of Table Mountain. The sun was strong, shadows almost absent. The light was blindingly bright. The views of the Cape Flats to the east and the bay to the west were breathtaking, though a rising wind cautioned us not to linger too long. Storms could come up quickly in the afternoon and cloak the mountain in cold rain, washing out the trail. Hunters had been known not to return from a simple morning's hunt.

We sat on a ledge of grey stone, horses tied in the trees below the ridge, our legs dangling over the abyss, where hundreds of feet below us trees stood like tiny weeds. I heard the high-pitched keen of an eagle, and the shadow of enormous wings passed overhead.

"That's what he's after," Somerton said, nodding to a mountain hyrax not more than two yards from us. The creature on the rock outcropping before us was plump as a loaf of brown bread, its dark eye keen as my own, with a disconcerting glint that might easily be construed as intelligence. We wouldn't have believed it, had we been told then, that its closest relation was the elephant.

"I do believe it's regarding us with disdain, Lord Somerton."

He laughed and raised a pistol, but I set my hand on his

arm—the first time we'd touched beyond a handshake. I felt the shock. I felt him hesitate. He did not often hesitate. He looked at me, and for a moment it seemed that he saw what everyone had been overlooking for years. Who I was.

"Mercy," I said, withdrawing my hand, then running it through my hair, hoping to steady myself, but he seemed to think I meant the hyrax.

"Mercy's a mad policy in a wild place." He raised his pistol once more. But the hyrax had evidently heard us and clambered off, leaving the rock bare. Somerton put aside his gun. "Sentiment will be your undoing, Dr. Perry."

I looked out over the curve of the bay, the pale disk of Robben Island like an unblinking eye. For once I had nothing to say.

As we rode down the steep trail back toward Roundhouse, Somerton shouted back to me, "You can't spare every life, doctor. You'd starve in a place like this."

"What's the point in killing, when my vocation is to heal?"

"Surely you're no match for death?"

"Perhaps not, but I won't assist him in his labors any more than I would the bishop."

He laughed and said no more of it. We made no more mention of what we had seen on Table Mountain, what life had been saved or spared.

CHAPTER FIVE

THE AFRICAN KING

Had it not been for the African king, I might never have come to love Lord Somerton. For a long time, I'd not have called it that. Love. We use the word too easily; to mean too many things: tenderness, need, desire, ambition. I admired him, was flattered by his friendship, required his backing if I was to reform medicine in the Cape. But I know now that love's the wound we don't recover from. I was not yet wounded.

As I drank my morning coffee beside the bustling Heerengracht, dust gilding the air beyond the rippled storefront glass, the clatter of cart wheels and horse hooves coming in through the intermittently opened door, I read about myself in the Cape *Courant* and saw I was a scandal. Cape society was shocked by how quickly I had become an intimate of the governor's circle in the few months since my arrival. I was no less surprised.

I was regularly invited to dine with Lord Somerton and his children and their myriad pets; to attend the theater and dances together; learning to ride, if not to hunt. We rode out together often when affairs of state allowed, and often when they did not. Increasingly my meals were taken at Government House, save for breakfast, which was enjoyed in a Heerengracht café with

Mrs. Saunders's sugar buns, a bowl of Dutch coffee, and what passed for the newspaper. Occasionally after a day's ride we dined together at Roundhouse, his hunting lodge overlooking Camps Bay, or at Newlands, his Palladian villa at the eastern base of Table Mountain. I was absorbed into the governor's circle like a fish drawn into a net or like one of the peculiar pets they collected; I became part of the household menagerie.

I told myself these frequent visits were an opportunity to sound him out on various medical reforms, but I was not indifferent to the charms of luxury and power. To a thirty-year-old Chateau Margaux and intelligent conversation. If I neglected my duties as medical assistant at the hospital, no one dared to reprimand the governor's favorite physician. And our intimacy afforded me an opportunity to discuss the abysmal conditions at the military hospital, to discuss the urgent need for a public one, the appalling treatment of lepers, women, slaves.

As my intimacy with the Somerton family grew, I noticed that Miss Georgiana seemed increasingly to single me out for attention—we were inevitably seated together at the theater, at dinner, frequently invitations from Government House came in her hand. And I began to feel a familiar anxiety, that which had ruined my acquaintance with Miss Erskine five years before.

Despite my lesser rank, I was a rare commodity in the Cape colony—a gentleman bachelor. And I knew Lord Somerton favored such romantic unions, matches that defied society in favor of love. At twenty, he had scandalized society by eloping with the penniless sixteen-year-old daughter of an impoverished English lord. The match had been a happy one, lasting twenty-seven years before her death from fever soon after their arrival in the Cape the autumn before. Our social inequality might even recommend the match in his eyes, proving its sincerity. I could not quit their company, as I had quit Dryburgh Abbey, nor did I wish to do so, but something must be done.

Had I been in a position to marry a woman, Georgiana would have been an ideal mate—clever and well-educated, she was equally accomplished in those less-common attainments of good sense, generosity, humility, and self-knowledge. She had her father's delicate features, as they must have appeared in youth—though deepened by recent sorrow, given gravity by grief—and the gentleness of an excellent nature. She was self-contained, even as she was lively and quick to be amused. One felt she could bear almost anything. She was clearly her father's strength, as her mother once had been. One wanted her approval, or I at least did. But I knew I was in no position to court her good opinion.

So it was both from curiosity and to tarnish my too-sterling reputation with her that I began to frequent the Rainbow Balls those first months in Cape Town. That, and the rumors I'd heard, drew me there. I loved dances of any kind—relished the opportunity to display my body even as I disguised it. I had heard of them at the Castle my first day there, had heard their music in the night across the Heerengracht, the infamous dances where the city came together in taverns in the harbor, stripped of station—Malay and slave, soldier and freedman, women and men and those between. I relished the chance to wear my pea-green satin vest beneath a red coat, my black boots with their red heels, polished high; to dance and flirt.

I still refused to be attended by women in my chambers, but delighted in their company socially. I did not have to pretend to admire the beauty of the women at the Rainbow Balls. They were exquisite. The Dutch and the Malay, the African and the English. It would be like being taught to admire the beauty of a sunrise. They caught your breath, or at least they caught mine. No one needs to learn this, the beauty of women.

At that first Rainbow Ball I stood in the tavern doorway, watching the dancers move around the broad, rough-hewn building, its high wooden beams brightly lit by torches and candlelight, its mud walls seeming to undulate in the unstable light. I leaned in and smelled the appealing musk—sweat and leather, rum and smoke, curry and clove—and laughed at the pleasure of it. Before I stepped in.

Against one wall, behind a balustrade, sat a small orchestra of remarkably skilled musicians, playing tunes I'd rarely heard played as well in London. Violinists, a pianoforte, flutes, an oboe, and English horn played reels and waltzes, jigs and chanteys. They played from ear or memory, no written music before them. They wore shirtsleeves and vests, not coats, and they gulped beer between tunes, but otherwise it might have been a ball at Almack's—save for the fact that all but one were black men. I'd later learn it was a point of pride, among local Dutch and English, to have an accomplished orchestra of slaves and hired freedmen. Occasionally a local stringed instrument or drum was introduced to general delight.

That first evening I stood inside the doorway, scanning the room as if I might discern the person I sought by dress or face. When a small, very beautiful woman with magnificent teeth approached me and set a hand on my chest—"Are you looking for me?"—I laughed. "I should have been," I said. In fact I was looking for a local slave, called Sanna, who was rumored to be both woman and man. I had never met such a person, though I had read of hermaphrodites, even autopsied one; the subject fascinated. What was it to stand between worlds—what sort of creature could endure that? I told myself mine was a clinical interest.

Aristotle believed the heat of the heart, not genitalia, determined a person's sex; men were thought to be warmer than women. Each of us took our place along the spectrum: masculine women being warmer, feminine men cooler. Hermaphrodites were simply more balanced than most, a *blend*, as the term itself is a blend of the names *Hermes* and *Aphrodite*, who—according to myth—gave birth to Hermaphroditus, their child, a perfect copy of them both in one body. Galen dismissed this sexual spectrum, of course, maintaining that women were merely an inferior copy of men, our sexual organs being the same, but inverted—a poor imitation.

The hermaphrodite's renown had reached me my first weeks in the Cape, the way news of an exotic plant or animal might, but I'd not yet made her acquaintance. I did not delude myself into thinking that we might be kindred spirits or even friends, but the case—as a physician—was of great interest to me. And the stories of her mistreatment by her enslaver moved me to pity. It was said she was lent out to friends for their delectation, a rare pleasure for all but her. I did not have the courage to ask if Somerton knew of her. I did not want to know.

I asked the woman with wonderful teeth if she knew the person I sought, might point her out. She misunderstood my intention. "He is not here," she said. "Will I do?" I told her she'd do well. I was glad to be seen leaving in her company, quieting the voices that had begun to question my own— which was still too high and shrill, a source of fun and, I feared, of suspicion.

* * *

It became my habit after that to spend a night with one of the local women—always a freedwoman, never a slave, never a woman who could not choose for herself, decline to spend the night with me. At first it was for show—to avoid raising questions among the soldiers—but soon, later, it was for myself. Like anyone, I needed from time to time a laying on of hands. I was not the only one who came to them who preferred to remain clothed in their naked arms, to lay my head upon their breasts, to make love to them without baring myself. We would kiss and stroke and I learned my way around their pleasure the way I'd learned anatomy, listening for my tutor's approving sighs, her moans, her pleasure giving rise to my own.

I would come to them like Cupid, by darkness. But I stayed the night with only that one, the woman I met that first night. Liz. Her freedom had been purchased by a man who'd loved her and hoped to marry her, only to be killed in a barroom brawl shortly after her manumission. She had no trade, no education, no skills save for love. So she had turned to that most enduring and profitable work of women—comforting men.

I craved the comfort of human touch, yearned for it. By the time I arrived in Cape Town, I had been alone so long my body ached; the bandages that bound my chest were the closest I had come to an embrace in years. I'd sworn off brothels while garrisoned in Chelsea—save to treat the rampant disease there—but here I had my reputation to consider and protect.

I would not love. I could see the harm affection had done my mother; I had taken the lesson to heart. I would work. For me the heart would be just another organ. Sentiment and society became like a cadaver—a thing to be anatomized, dissected, taken apart, understood in its constituent elements, an intellectual matter rather than an emotional one. And as with a corpse, I inspected sentiment, but it could not touch me. Or so I believed.

It is an arduous matter to cross the terrain of life alone. I was not sure that I was equal to it. I had thought invulnerability to affection a kind of strength, but I was beginning to have my doubts, conscious of its burdens now.

When I mentioned at dinner having attended the Rainbow Ball, it was clear from Georgiana's inquiries about the sort of women there—their clothes and the music and hour—that she assumed I was seeking feminine companionship. I did not disabuse her of the misconception.

I knew that I would miss Georgiana, miss our conversations and our walks, but I knew that after this I must distance myself from her. I might be criticized, dismissed as a flirt, but no real harm would have been done, as it would be if I raised further expectations of what I could not pursue: intimacy with a like mind, which I longed for but could not have. Medicine and the army would be my family.

Miss Georgiana was not present at dinner the December night at Roundhouse when I first heard about the trouble on the eastern border of the Cape colony, along the Fish River, some 500 miles east of where we were. In general the governor avoided politics at table, but that evening he was agitated by recent news. There were armed forts along the river's western bank, but despite their presence, raids on settlers' cattle had grown more frequent and the settlers were increasingly wary.

There was talk of desertions among soldiers and Khoikhoi farm laborers as well as among slaves, who fled to the Xhosa—where they were granted wives and land in exchange for guns and information.

Some years before, Lord Somerton explained, an agreement had been struck between colonial authorities and the Xhosa king, Ngqika, to respect the settlements and protect them against attack, but the king was rumored to be among the chief benefactors of the raids. The situation had to be stabilized or settlers would pull up stakes, leaving the eastern frontier unprotected.

"Ngqika must be made fully responsible," Somerton said.

"But what if he's not?" I asked. I was not seeking to be perverse, but practical.

"Not what?"

"Responsible," I said. "What if he cannot command his people?" It seemed to me possible that the Xhosa chief might not have the authority to speak for his tribe. But men in power do not like to admit the limits of authority, or perhaps his was greater cunning than I knew then.

"Then we shall make him command them, or command them ourselves."

I knew better than to argue the point. It is the privilege and pitfall of power that it allows us to pretend our wishes are shared, that what is done for our own good is done for the good of others.

"I would like to have you with us, Doctor. If the hospital can spare you." This last was irony. I rarely went, absorbed as I was in my unofficial duties as the Somerton mascot.

It was a sensitive mission—part diplomacy, part martial display—and I knew that I should consider it an honor to be named among those few invited to join the expedition, but all I felt was dread. Dread of the three months of travel in exposed country, dread of discovery.

But the governor was as stubborn as he was charming. His invitation was not to be declined. When he proposed to include Miss Somerton in the expedition as far as the estate of Knysna, where she would serve as hostess, I could not refuse to ride along to ensure her safe return.

That night at Roundhouse, I woke in a cold sweat, panic rising. I lay awake listening to the booming surf like distant cannon fire and the susurrus of wind in the trees outside my bedroom window. Roundhouse itself was quiet. Occasionally I heard a cough or a servant's footfall in the hall. I spent hours trying to imagine some way to graciously bow out, refuse, but any obstacle I might imagine was one the governor might as easily remove: duties at the hospital, obligations at the Castle.

It was hopeless; I would have to make the three-month ride across open plains without a place to hide my monthly linens, with hardly any hope of solitude, except late at night within my tent. Even a tent could not offer much relief or privacy, given our shared resting and rising and meals, given how close they would be pitched together to protect against lions and rhinos.

We would move as one body across the land; it was hard to imagine I could successfully continue to disguise my own in such a circumstance.

A week before we were to embark on our long journey east to meet the African king, I was called to the Castle to tend to Emmanuel de Las Cases, Napoleon's trusted adviser—and I thought I'd escaped the noose. It was mid-January, early summer. I dressed carefully for the occasion, polishing my boots and wearing my red wig, as if dressing for a ball. I was honored to be attending him. I was not often overawed by men, but Napoleon's name would last a thousand years; he was almost a god and here was his counselor and confidant. But I also hoped that treating de Las Cases might provide an excuse to avoid the journey east.

When I was shown to his cell in the Castle, the chill was bone-deep despite the summer heat. De Las Cases was bent over a small wooden desk in a room hardly larger than an oxcart; a cot with a mattress of hay and a thin sheet was shoved against one wall. The stench of night soil and spoiled food thickened the air. Not wishing to give offense, I resisted the instinct to cover my nose with a handkerchief.

When de Las Cases looked up at the sound of the door opening, he seemed for a moment confused. He looked to me, then the guard, then back.

"Doctor's here to see you," the guard said.

De Las Cases stood with evident effort, bracing a hand on the desk. "*You* are the doctor?"

"I am," I said, stepping into the cell. "It's an honor to meet you, sir."

He smiled. "The pleasure is mine. But I'd have taken you for the governor's niece, not his doctor. Forgive me."

A chill rose along my neck. I had been disguised so long—seven years—that I had almost forgotten the mask I wore. Now, it slipped.

"Youth can be misleading," I said.

I sent the guard away and we sat together, conversing in French—I on the pitiful cot, he on his narrow chair. Had I not found his conditions so appalling, my sympathies would have been with him nonetheless, for all he had done in the service of liberty. I told him of my friendship with General Mirandus, and we spoke of him and of the past and of de Las Cases's present circumstance, which I promised to have remedied immediately.

"The governor would be appalled to know of your treatment," I said. "I assure you, he will see it corrected." I rose to leave.

"Such a pity about General Mirandus," de Las Cases said, to himself as much as to me. "I liked him, even if he did seduce my mistress. Such a good dancer, so charming, especially to the women…"

The floor tilted beneath me. I sat again on the cot, chilled to the core.

"Oh, dear," de Las Cases said, "you had not known of it…I am so sorry."

"He is dead," I said. "How did he die?"

De Las Cases did not know the details, only that Mirandus had been betrayed into Spanish hands in 1812, after the successful revolt in Venezuela; he'd languished in prison in Cádiz, where he had died on 14 July 1816, just weeks before I'd arrived here on the Cape. It was said that Simón Bolívar had betrayed him.

It took effort to rise from the cot, but I was eager to be out of the place.

"You need not fear a similar fate," I said, as I stood. "The governor will see to it."

"You were close?" he asked me.

"He treated me as a son," I said.

"I have a son," de las Cases said. "I would be most grateful if you might look in on him, Doctor. While you are here."

His 15-year-old son was held in an adjoining cell and broke

my heart when I saw him. Prison is no place for a child. The boy, when I went to him, was pale and thin and near collapse from the combination of constraint, unsanitary conditions, and nervous exhaustion from his indefinite confinement and the daily effort to transcribe his father's notes on the emperor. I examined him and found his skin and breath had an unhealthy sour smell, his breathing shallow and too quick. I shouted for the gaoler and inquired about their rations, sanitation, and exercise. I found the conditions shockingly remiss.

"Have you been charged with *detaining* these prisoners," I asked, "or *killing* them? You are quite close to accomplishing the latter with dispatch."

I ordered a change in diet, including a ration of good red wine and daily meat and vegetables from the Company's Garden, fresh linens weekly, hot baths, and blankets, as well as access to the yard for daily exercise. If these conditions were not improved immediately, the governor—I said—would hear of it.

He did. I reported to Government House directly after to confer with Lord Somerton, who was as outraged as I by the prisoners' conditions; he proposed to have them moved to rooms at Newlands, his Palladian villa in the mountains, where they might recover their health in the fresh air. Guards could be posted there, but they would be comfortable. I suggested that perhaps I should stay on at Newlands as well, to look after them in the coming weeks, but the governor only smiled and insisted that he could not spare me; I was needed, he said—*he* needed me—on the journey east. There was no escaping it.

When I returned to the Castle the following day, I found father and son much improved, as were their chambers—now clean and well lit, with ample blankets and wine. De Las Cases was overjoyed by the governor's proposal to relocate them to the mountain villa outside town. But the boy's spirits still seemed dangerously low. Unlike his father, he was not cheered by the ongoing effort to document Napoleon's life but was weighed down by the tedious task and lack of company.

He had a young man's impatient sense of time, which is especially burdensome in difficulty, when one cannot imagine that circumstances will ever alter from what they are. So before my next visit I arranged to borrow a carriage from His Lordship's stable; after arriving in the young man's cell and asking about his health, I urged him to look down from his window to the street below, where friends of mine were eager to make his acquaintance; as he bent over the stone sill, the two lovely Miss Somertons were there to send up their greeting. When the young man drew his head back into the chamber, his cheeks were pink with health. It was better medicine than any other I might have prescribed. For all of us.

Miss Georgiana's inquiries afterward into the handsome youth's health cheered me. I endeavored to interest her in the case, hoping he might engage her heart as I could not. But even my care of Napoleon's adviser could not provide an excuse for me to avoid the eastward trek, now firmly set to begin on January 27, 1817.

If this were a novel, our journey to the Xhosa king should consume a sprawling chapter, replete with romantic adventure— but in truth the journey was dusty, hot, and exhausting, despite the magnificence of the terrain we traversed.

The day of our departure dawned and we set out from Newlands at the head of a vast army of trackers, servants, soldiers, porters, and guides. Georgiana had taken great pains to ensure our party's comfort—there would be china, crystal goblets, silver, linens, silk rugs, abundant parasols, an armada of porters and servants bearing wicker baskets of fresh herbs, greens, fruits, and wines. It was only with great exertion that we managed to argue her out of transporting a four-poster bed and canopy, which she felt was an absolute necessity for a good night's rest.

I was grateful for her excesses, which made my own appear less extreme: Lord Somerton balked at my proposal to bring along my pet goat for the milk that was a staple of my diet, until I assured him we could eat her, if necessity required. In truth, I'd have let them eat me first.

I was not a man for early rising, a fact I regretted whenever I had occasion to rise early and see the world wake; everything seemed softer by first light, tender, more alive; the sky to the east was a radiant rose behind an archipelago of slate-blue clouds. I remembered the sailor's rhyme: *Red sky at morning, sailor take warning.* But it looked like a benediction, not a warning. We took breakfast silently, then mounted our horses—or in the case of Miss Georgiana, stepped up into an ox-wagon seat—to begin the long journey over what Georgiana would later call "more rock than road."

We rode east first, toward verdant farmlands, beyond which rose the daunting Hottentots Holland mountains, then moved southeast where False Bay gleamed, the water like a field of shattered jewels—sapphire, emerald, palest jade, tourmaline, and lapis lazuli. Glittering. The land we crossed recalled the landscape I had left—the gorse and lichen-colored rocks of Scotland, the verdant green-topped cliffs of Ireland that fell away abruptly to the sea. But instead of the falcons and foxes, rabbits and deer familiar from those northern places, here antelope and white-faced bontebok (with their curious outcurved horns and incurving ears) and mountain zebra confronted us, broke from cover at the sound of our wagons.

As we rode I remarked on the beautiful bontebok, which burst up, balletic, from the brush; Lord Somerton noted, as our trackers had, how few there were relative to years past. Overhunting, he thought. "You could protect them, surely," I said. "So I can," he replied. He said that he would and did, dictating that evening a proclamation to his secretary. A man whose word could change the world.

For the first few days we had traveled as if on holiday, or as if out for a picnic, eager to sit together in the evening and dine on the wine and cured meats and fresh fruits and vegetables brought from the Company's Garden and to talk over the things we'd seen that day—the shifting terrain, the lush beauty of Constantia's vineyards, the light on the mountains, the birds and beasts and unfamiliar flowers. We ate speared fish and fire-roasted crayfish, salted and buttered or oiled. Springbok. Then we turned toward the only viable pass to the east, the notorious Hottentots Holland Kloof, and began our ascent into those forbidding mountains, over the hard earth of the Roode Hoogte, as the road rose and narrowed into the perilous mountain pass that must be surmounted—as so many other perils would have to be—to reach the Fish River.

By the end of the first week we spoke little in the evenings, exhausted by each day's long ride, knowing many more lay ahead. We settled into a more intimate silence by the fire, while guards stood armed and ready to fire on hyenas or lions drawn by the smell of roasting meat. Occasionally we fell to the old arguments, the differences between men and women, the European and the African. I tried to engage the governor on the question of strategy, concerned that he placed too much faith in the African king's ability to command his people. Where once I had held that men and women were less different than they appeared, here I argued the opposite: that British military order might well not obtain among tribesmen.

Hierarchies that he took for granted, I maintained, were not a fact of nature but an artifact of culture. A point he was not eager to concede.

Like all men, Lord Somerton liked the sound of his own voice. He held forth even by a campfire. One of the principal pleasures of living as a man is not having to listen to men mutely. Rare is the man who likes the sound of another's opinion as much as his own; I did not hesitate to offer mine.

One evening as we argued about the rights of women, he said, "By God, Perry, next you'll be saying they should have the vote."

"Should they not?"

"Their emotions would unsuit them," he said, tossing a twig onto the fire.

"More than a man's?"

"Of course."

"Emotion did not unsuit Elizabeth to be queen."

"She was a son in daughter's clothing."

"Aren't all daughters thus?"

Somerton looked at me with an expression between incredulity and amusement.

"You're that most dangerous sort of person, Doctor: an idealist."

"Surely the most dangerous is the ambitious man *without* ideals?"

"There you are mistaken: an idealist's fervor burns first in his own breast but ends by scorching others."

"The strategist is no less pyromaniacal, surely," I said. "Just with less good cause."

"Spoken like an idealist," Lord Somerton said.

I suspected that his cynicism was only skin-deep—the habit of *hauteur*, rank, and grief. I knew that he'd issued a proclamation the previous year to halt the spread of slavery in the Cape. He could not abolish the loathsome practice, but he did the next best thing: created a registry of all enslaved persons, so that none who were free or freed or had bought their freedom could ever be enslaved again, as many sought to do. And he created a school to educate enslaved children and free them when their studies were done. He was a man of principle, however much he sought to disguise it.

I thought I knew the sort of man he was: one who believed that the protection of the vulnerable was an obligation of the powerful, too often neglected. *Noblesse oblige.* He thought arguments for enfranchisement would cause harm where they claimed to help; that women, children, natives, the enslaved required assistance and protection, not the burden of rights they were ill-prepared to shoulder; that they'd be harmed by those who wished to help them. Just as I knew that he was wrong. I was the proof. *Quod erat demonstrandum. QED.*

By day I rode alongside the governor and his aide-de-camp at the front of the group. We spoke less and less, lulled by the routine and the heat; I found myself increasingly aware of the bodies around me—their weight and scent, the horseflesh and the human. Time lengthened and eddied.

The February sun high and scalding overhead, shadows

pooled beneath us, the horizon a ripple of heat; lulled by the rhythm of the horse's slow steps, my mind sought the shade of other times and other places. An early morning, stocking the shelves of my father's shop in Cork, where dust motes caught the sunlight and the cool damp of the wooden stockroom was as lovely as a walled garden in its privacy; reading supine upon a leather couch in Lord Basken's library, a cool July breeze coming in through open windows. Increasingly my thoughts turned to Lord Somerton himself; things he'd said, how his back arched over a basin as he bathed; how he swung up onto his horse in the morning, calves taut.

To avoid such thoughts, I began to walk a portion each day, to collect botanical samples for study. Soon I fell behind the others, as my interest overtook my caution. I felt an almost gluttonous desire to know and identify the local plants and understand their qualities—the way others seemed eager for acquaintance.

Lord Somerton joked that I couldn't keep my mount. The guides seemed amused by my interest, but soon they began to confide.

The naming of things was a passion for me then—as I had rechristened myself and in so doing been remade. Names had an incantatory quality, seemed a species of magic. Only later, much later, would I recognize the horror of this, how names can fix and contain, diminish and delimit: call a person a *woman* or a *man* and we think we know what we are seeing, but do we? Name the boundary of a land—put the terms in a treaty—and what pretends to make peace becomes occasion for seizure and war.

A new name had given me my life, but a name had obscured me as well. Hidden the truth. Cost me. I had not yet grasped the truth of the warning: as soon as we can call it paradise, it is lost to us. As soon as we give it a name, we are separate, apart from that which we once were. When later I learned of a tribal tradition of delaying the naming of a child until it had reached its first year, it seemed wise—not simply because an infant might die and naming is a kind of claiming, making it harder to let go, but because, unnamed, a child remains part of us, inseparable.

I asked the porters many questions and took still more notes. "Don't touch," they might say of a thorned or toxic plant, or "Good for fever, and tea." Eventually they seemed to lose interest in my presence altogether, ignoring me as one of their own. A blissful obscurity.

But Lord Somerton did not grow accustomed to my delays. He grew irritated by my obsessive collecting and cataloguing en route. He took to harassing me with questions, riding up beside me, raising a choking cloud of dust, as I walked behind the entourage.

"What in the world are you looking for, Doctor? Have you become a gardener now?"

"Medicinal plants could be invaluable in treating the local population," I replied, not looking up from the specimens of leaves and roots I was collecting. "The tropical climes are a veritable pharmacopoeia."

He suggested that if I wanted to know about local plants, I'd do better to consult with a local farmer. "They know all there is to know about the local plants and their uses. Perhaps you would prefer to consult a witch doctor?"

He tried to disguise his irritation as amusement, his chiding as a joke, but he resented the disorder, rebellion, the refusal to fall into line.

I smiled, refusing to be baited into argument. "I've found it best not to credit others' opinions, but to form my own," I said, repeating Sir Astley Cooper's phrase. "The truth of principles must be confirmed by observation," my watchword.

"And what opinion have you formed of me?" he asked.

"It's a very complicated case. I'm still deliberating."

He laughed. "Let me know when you arrive at a diagnosis." He spurred his horse, cantered ahead despite the uneven ground.

Gradually I fell in with a young Khoikhoi boy, who was charged with leading an ox by its tether to ensure it kept pace. The child could not have been more than six, but he had an unnervingly adult expression, large, thoughtful eyes, which watched me with a disconcerting attentiveness that I sought to deflect with questions about the plants we passed.

"Why you want know?" he asked.

"Some may prove helpful," I said.

"They help already."

"Will you show me?"

The child did not answer, but as we walked he would nod to plants and seemed amused to see me hurrying to gather a sample. "Cures fever." "Good tea." "Stops heat." "Brings up stomach."

Later when we had stopped, I brought goat's milk and dried fruit to the boy, wine for his father who was a porter; we talked by the porters' fire of my pet goat, of London, of medicine. I showed them my sword; they laughed at my high red bootheels.

The child—whose name I learned was Pearl—reached up to touch my cheek, said something in a language I did not understand.

"He says, 'You have no beard,'" the father translated.

"It is fashionable to have a smooth cheek," I said.

The father translated.

The boy squinted at me, skeptically, and said something else. No one translated that, and I didn't inquire.

At night in my tent, I loosened my bindings. A sour smell arose from my skin. The skin around my ribs and breasts was painful to the touch—bloody, blistered, slick with pus where the bandages rubbed. In the past I'd felt my chest bindings to be almost an embrace, a securing, as if I were lashed to the world or my good name as Odysseus was to the mast, but in the tropical heat of that three-month journey, my bindings became stifling. I developed open sores where my bindings chafed as we rode, a bloody line of demarcation across my sternum and beneath my ribs. At least the horses' girths were removed at night; mine rarely were. I could not be sure when I might be called into the cold night, discovered by lamplight.

I tried binding tighter to prevent the bandages from shifting as I rode or walked, but the result was blinding headaches, a permanent ache in my chest and neck; I feared that I might faint. I added another layer in hope that the blood would not stain my shirt, seep through the fabric to the surface.

Throughout the day, I watched Lord Somerton's mood like weather, vigilant for signs of change. As our progress slowed and the summer heat intensified, I feared the governor's bad mood would worsen and all of us pay the price. We were already behind schedule, his aide-de-camp Josias de Cloete warned, endangering our meeting with the Xhosa king.

We had been traveling several weeks when one of the oxcarts rolled back down a dry riverbank and broke its axle, halting our already slow progress under the relentless summer sun. Lord Somerton insisted that we pause to repair it rather than load down the porters further in the murderous heat. While men set to repairing the wagon that we could not afford to abandon—piled as it was with supplies—heat shimmered off the horizon.

And in that single day's respite from travel, Lord Somerton's black mood lifted. He seemed immeasurably cheered by the opportunity to hunt, which provided both diversion and needed food for our massive retinue. He invited me to join the hunting party, but I declined.

Instead the child agreed to walk the perimeter of camp with me and gather plants.

I had never wanted children, had seen too much of women's suffering in birth, but I liked the boy who almost made me doubt my conviction. He was like a miniature man, earnest and grave. When I mentioned the child to Lord Somerton that evening, he frowned, not having remarked him. But I felt a tug whenever I saw the boy, especially when he struggled with the ox across the stones; I felt an urge to protect him, to help. Even as I knew I could not help, that it might jeopardize his father's position, his own, to appear a liability rather than an aid to our progress.

I had to remind myself that no one in the world was mine, or ever could be.

As I lay awake in my tent at night, I listened for footfalls—the crunch of gravel beneath a boot or paw—and my skin would go cold as I reached for my gun, knowing I could not shoot well; sometimes I would see a shadow pass between the fire and my tent. I began to sleep outdoors, where I felt safer; if trouble came, at least I would see its face. I was afraid not of men or lions or even death, but of being caught unawares.

That night I had left my tent behind, pulling my cot into the evening air, despite the bright full moon, which bathed the cot's blanket in silver light, when I heard sounds nearby and sat up to find Somerton at the end of my cot.

I was glad I'd not bothered to remove my shirt, my chest binding, or my breeches.

"Out for a stroll?" I asked.

"Poor night for sleeping," he said. The moon was full and bright.

I knew better than to ask if he was worried about the expedition. He would tell me what he wished in his own time.

"Perfect night for a fox hunt," he looked out over the silvery landscape. "Every creature will be out tonight seeking dinner."

"Lucky for them, you're not."

"Unlucky for me."

I had expected to find him more at ease in the saddle, riding out across the open landscape. But these open spaces were not soothing without a gun in his hand. Without a target in his sights. I understood then that it was not confinement that made Lord Somerton pace his offices, it was lack of quarry. Still, he seemed happier here than I'd ever seen him, more at ease.

"D'you know, the porters say you are a witch, Doctor Perry?"

"That's better press than the Cape *Courant* gives me."

"My family are said to be descended from the devil, on my father's side," he said.

"Melusine," I said, "the devil's daughter."

"You know the story?"

"Every schoolboy in England knows the story, Your Lordship."

"Do you credit it?"

"Men are capable of devilishness enough on their own. Don't you think?"

Much as I resisted its glamour, Somerton's family name was famous, the last of the Plantagenet line that had once ruled England, last of the "warrior kings" descended from Count Geoffrey of Anjou, who married the sole surviving child of Henry I (though it was said he had bedded the devil's daughter, Melusine). The governor's forebear had been saved from slaughter at Tudor hands after the War of the Roses by the happy fact of his illegitimacy. His ancestor was a natural son, a bastard; that alone had saved him. Somerton had a healthy openness to the outsider, the displaced, the illegitimate. But that did not temper his arrogance.

"What of your family, Doctor? You do not speak of them."

"There's little cause. Mine is not an illustrious line."

"The Cape matrons say you're a natural son of the Prince Regent."

A chill ran through my belly. I had not known that my origins were a subject of discussion here. Had hoped, absurdly, to have left all that behind.

I did not reply.

"Don't worry, Doctor. I like bastards. Our family was—"

There is hardly any sound as unsettling as a death wail in the night. The sound that ended our conversation that night was no animal's cry, but eerily human. The shots that followed confirmed it.

By the time we reached the site of the commotion, the boy was in his father's arms, a ruin of blood and dust, a massive lioness bleeding by his side. We heard in the jumbled half-phrases of the men's reports how the child had wandered off to check on my pet goat, how the lioness was on him before the dogs even caught its scent, how a single shot had taken the cat while the boy still was in its jaws. Only his arms drawn across his chest and face had saved him to suffer this long. A blow to the head had rendered him unconscious, which was a mercy. His arms were pierced like Saint Sebastian's, his face bruised and bloodied from being struck against the ground, but to my amazement the child lived. Breathed.

There was no knowing how long he might yet. If he would recover. The puncture wounds could be treated, but internal damage would reveal itself only in time; there was nothing to be done for it but wait.

"He must not be moved," I said.

Lord Somerton ordered a fire built on the spot, blankets, guards posted.

While two guards built a fire, the boy's father crouched with his son on a blanket. He seemed catatonic with grief. Staring, not making a sound. I feared he might not release the child from his arms, even as his embrace might be doing harm at that very moment. I was loath to separate them. The boy might last the night, I thought, but not the next day's journey over uneven ground. I knew our mission could not wait on a child. I administered a vial of laudanum to minimize the pain. The child's eyes were open; I did not dare to close them, as if the imitation of death would invite it.

"How is he?" Lord Somerton asked.

"Hard to know." I had treated the obvious wounds, the lacerated arms and head. It was impossible to know what internal injuries he had sustained.

"Movement now could kill him," I said. Rest was required. But I knew the mission could not afford further delay.

"We shall remain here, then," Lord Somerton said.

I was too shocked to speak.

Cloete was not: "Your Lordship, we are already well behind schedule—"

"We will remain," Lord Somerton said. "Until the boy recovers."

We all knew it might be its opposite that we awaited. I was grateful that he did not say so. For the father's sake, for the child's, for my own.

All men are hypocrites, the powerful simply more obviously so. But Somerton's hypocrisy was of the better sort: he betrayed his *hauteur* with unexpected tenderness. For all his *froideur*, he was a man of deep feeling. Men are praised for their reserves of strength, but I admired his reserves of feeling, the governor's capacity to be moved by the suffering of others— and changed by it. His enemies considered him high-handed and self-indulgent for his love of luxury, horses, races, and hunting, but he felt deeply, was unashamed of it. That woman's strength and saints'. He was moved and grieved that night, when there was no benefit in it for him, and I allowed myself the risk of liking him for it.

When the boy was settled, I returned to the main camp and its larger fire to allow the father privacy with his son; I would sit up in case I was needed. I was grateful when the governor joined me. Grateful he did not ask the boy's chances of surviving the night.

Instead Lord Somerton spoke of his childhood at Badminton.

The daily dinners for two hundred guests. The foxhunts his family held there.

"They say your family invented the sport," I said.

He frowned, declining the flattery. "We merely popularized it."

We fell silent, each in his own thoughts, until the moon began to set, waiting for a change in the boy's condition.

"Do you never think of marriage, Doctor Perry?" he asked toward dawn.

The question unsettled me. Surely he knew I'd be a poor match for his daughter. "Of course," I said. "Everyone thinks of marriage. I have the good sense not to act on it." He did not laugh.

"Are you not lonely?"

"What man is not? Marriage rarely seems a cure for loneliness from what I've seen," I said.

"If one marries well, it can be."

I did not reply.

"We eloped, Elizabeth and I. She was sixteen; I was not yet twenty. Terrible scandal. It was the best decision I ever made."

"You must miss her terribly."

"The hardest thing is to cure oneself of hope. I imagine sometimes that if I am simply patient enough, she will return. As if this were a test. The hardest part is the fact that she will never return. Have you ever lost anyone, Doctor?"

I wanted to tell him the truth, wanted to tell someone, ached with all that went unsaid; it swelled my skin, straining as my flesh strained against the bandages with which I bound my chest each morning.

"No," I said.

He nodded. "Georgiana's so like her. Sometimes I turn and see her and think it's my Elizabeth. But then I realize, of course, it's not. You can love like that only once in a life."

"Most never know such love."

"And you?"

"I've spent more time opening bodies than embracing them."

"By choice."

"And necessity."

"Surely a man needs both work—and someone to work *for*?"

"There was someone, once," I said, thinking of General Mirandus, of my mother and sister. "But. I'm hardly an easy man to live with."

"Few men are. Women seem to manage."

"So they do."

He set his hand on my shoulder and I felt again a charge pass between us, subtle as scent; for a moment I thought again that he knew. But he merely patted my back before he stood.

"Get some rest," he said. "Or you'll fall out of the saddle when we ride again. You are aware, Doctor, that the porters have a wager on when you'll drop."

"Have you put money on it?"

"I'm a betting man," he said. "I never miss a sure thing."

Looking back, it seems that was the night I began to love Somerton. It was not the love of ballads or novels, but something less common, more particular to that place. Like the plants I gathered. There is a love greater than that of physical desire, not that of monks or saints, but tender and extreme in its restraint. I loved him as if he were my father, or my brother. My almost only friend.

I loved in him that rarest quality between men, rarer still

between men and women—equality. He treated me, despite the difference in rank, as a confidant, with the open, frank, uncalculating manner with which he hunted. Buoyant and direct, he allowed me to be so as well. I had loved Mirandus, but he possessed the hard arrogance of a man who knew he was meant to shape history to his will; *everything* for him was calculation—every conversation, every kindness was part of a larger strategy. Even my education had been; I knew that now; perhaps I'd known it even then. I was to be his instrument. I had been lucky to escape that fate, although losing his company was the first great loss of my life. My first great grief.

But with Somerton there was no calculation; he was a great man, the way mountains are, or surf—it was a natural grace, born to be a force without willing it so. He would shape history not from personal ambition but because it was a pleasure to be in the world and of it. Perhaps title could not matter overmuch, because he was a second son. But I think it was something else. He was the rare man of title who judged men by their quality, by their character, not by their rank or stature or reputation or wealth or what use they might be to him.

He could be cutting, dismissive, casually cruel to those he deemed unworthy of courtesy. He was a terrible snob. I had seen him dispatch fools and flatterers. And he was vain. A gossip. Clung overlong to stupid opinions because he'd held them dear, or because someone he'd respected had. But he loved his children, his horses and dogs, his friends. And he had a natural authority, a sense of himself in history, as part of a human chain reaching back and going forward, aware of his own mortality as few men—even soldiers—are. In short he was a man worthy of the name. And for a time we were friends. Until the world came between us.

* * *

For two nights I did not sleep; I sat up with the Khoikhoi boy and his father, waiting for a change in his condition. To my amazement and no credit of my own, Pearl recovered his senses at the end of the second day; he was able to walk in three. Badly bruised, he showed no sign of the internal rupture of organs I had feared—he neither coughed blood nor passed it. The guard's quick action and keen shooting had saved the child's life. After four days' rest, we resumed our trek eastward. Now the boy rode in a wagon, the ox and goat tethered behind. I walked slowly behind them.

The relief we felt on reaching Knysna moved like a fresh sea breeze through our group, after the five-week ride. One could hear laughter among the porters, singing; even Lord Somerton's mood seemed to lift. Riding down into Knysna toward the lagoon, I had the strange impression once again that I was in an English countryside—the ivy-green hills and indigo water might have belonged to some Cornish seaside village.

Below us, as we descended to George Rex's estate where we would rest before undertaking the second half of our journey east, the lagoon was encircled by gentle slopes, richly forested, which gently curved around the water like arms in an embrace—two sandstone cliffs guarded the entrance to the Indian Ocean. I thought I'd never seen anything as lovely.

George Rex was the sort of man who goes to a remote place to reinvent himself. A man rather too much like me. And I disliked him. Even as we enjoyed his hospitality. Rumor had it he was an illegitimate son of King George III, a rumor that I suspected he encouraged in his ambition to acquire a kingly estate. He claimed to have made his fortune in timber, but I sensed there was truth in the stories that held he was among those who still profited by the recently outlawed trade in human beings. Nonetheless, we luxuriated in long hot baths and later in cool drinks on the veranda, overlooking the bay. Dined on fresh fruit and game and fish and cheeses imported—some said pilfered—from France. A braggart, a liar, and a thief, Rex's sole aim was to win, his only concern his own wealth. He was a man devoid of principle, a small piece of a person pretending to be a whole man. Shocking, repulsive, fascinating.

As we smoked after dinner, figures seemed to flit through the trees overhead, and when I looked up, I saw a Vervet monkey staring down at me, his thoughtful eyes unsettling, its dark face crowned by a corona of grey fur. He tossed a twig at me, leapt to another branch. I turned back to the conversation when I heard a shriek; Miss Somerton was batting at her hair and looking up into the tree that a moment before she had been leaning against.

"The thief," she said. "The little thief."

"What happened?" shouted her father. He stood and drew his pistol.

"The beastly monkey stole my grapes!"

George Rex gave a generous laugh. "There are plenty more," he said. He clapped hands for a servant.

I wondered if Rex identified with the thieving monkey. I disliked him, but it was impossible not to watch him. He had the generosity of one accustomed to losing heavily on the way to a still-greater win, a gambler's showy extravagance. It was hard to like such a man, even harder to trust him. The feeling, I suspected, was mutual.

"And you, Dr. Perry. What brings a man like you to the Cape? You seem more suited to..."

"*I* did," said Somerton. Ending the speculation. "I cannot do without him."

I was surprised by the declaration, touched.

"Indeed," Rex leaned back in his chair. "I have heard you have miraculous powers."

"Sound reason is hardly deemed miraculous in civilized parts of the world," I said.

He laughed at the obvious insult. "You must find us remarkably rustic."

"Rather unremarkably," I said. "No more so than the barracks at Chelsea."

I appeared to be the only one who disliked Rex. Lord Somerton seemed delighted to learn that evening that there were five kinds of antelope and bush pigs to hunt on the massive estate, as well as cheetah. Georgiana was taken by the forest elephants.

Having seen strange and magnificent birds on the ride in (including one that was an iridescent blue with a green chest and crest and head, red rings around its eyes, and a beak bright as my bootheels), I looked forward to exploring the forest the next day—until Rex told me there were more than twenty varieties of snake out there as well. My expression must have betrayed my dismay.

"Don't worry, Doctor," Rex said, speaking as he chewed a cigar. "Only five or six are venomous." He winked at Miss Georgiana; I thought I saw her blush in the lamplight.

When Rex proposed to show her the garden the next day, or to row her out to the cliffs for a picnic, I was not sure if he was seeking to seduce her or nettle me.

Rex offered to show her the planets that night, leading her by the arm to a telescope mounted on a wooden platform built for the purpose. I could hear them speaking quietly, saw Rex circle Miss Somerton in his arms to steady the scope before her, direct its gaze. I hoped Lord Somerton might object, but he seemed becalmed in the thickening darkness, lingering over eighteen-year-old whiskey, which tasted to me of the sea and smoke, like a sodden cigar.

When Georgiana exclaimed, it was with joy. "You can see the rings," she said when they returned. "And the red pox on Jupiter."

Much as I might wish to object, I would only be misunderstood, thought a jealous suitor. I held my tongue and hated the man silently. I hoped Georgiana noticed, as I did, the woman Rex retired to bed with that night, as he would each subsequent evening—a young and comely dark-skinned house slave. Only later in the afterlife, when all is known but nothing can be done, will I learn that Rex would later sleep with that same slave's daughter, the one who was already growing in her belly that very night. Siring his own daughter's child.

Of the meeting with the African king, a month later, there is little to say: like so much of life, the ostensible focus was mere footnote to what truly mattered. The public spectacle paled in comparison with the small private matters—a cup of tea, the smell of smoke, the myriad perceptions in a single day, the rise of love and antipathy among us, that weighty cargo.

The Persian rugs we had brought east were unfurled upon the ground and chairs erected in a semicircle, facing the river on its western bank. Around us, soldiers armed and ready stood at attention as we reposed, waiting for King Ngqika to come to us. Of course, he did not. Imagining ours was a trap, which in a way it was, though I didn't see it then. A trap of courtesy.

Eventually the king was persuaded to make the crossing, join us. He was given trinkets for his trouble—shawls, shoes, buttons, a looking glass, an excellent grey horse. A translator made the case we'd come to make—the petition for a treaty guaranteeing the safety of the settlers here. I thought the Xhosa king seemed uncomfortable, nodding his head when asked to affirm his commitment to protect settlers against raids, but always concluding with a flurry of words that seemed to contest his agreement.

The translator, a Xhosa man, tried to explain the flurry of speech, but perhaps he lacked sufficient command of English or feared providing a disagreeable translation. Only later would one of the porters, who spoke a little of the tribal tongue, clarify for me: the king would protect the settlers, but he could not command the others, as the English do their peoples. He was one king among many. It was not his to command, as it was not ours to demand it.

But demand we did. We asked what he could not provide. He accepted our gifts as a courtesy, a sign of good intentions, not a guarantee. I understood this but suspected Lord Somerton had not. When I spoke to him of it, when we arrived back at Knysna weeks later, he seemed unconcerned. He had secured the promise. That was all that mattered. That was what he'd come for: the king's word. Only later, when that brief meeting became the justification for a border war and seizure of Xhosa lands, would I understand it was not the king's word we'd come for at all. It was the pretense of an agreement that could thus provide the occasion for its breach and a justification for imposing English might. As Lord Somerton would a few years later. The first of many such assaults, which would become the basis for the nation-state.

* * *

It was hard to leave Knysna—its lush beauty, its many comforts—for the long hard journey ahead. But I worried for Georgiana there, and what increasingly appeared to be Rex's effort to attach her affections, despite his obvious attachments elsewhere. If one judged a man by his wealth, he might have seemed a reasonable match, and I was in no position to argue to the contrary. So I was eager to set out, but on the eve of our planned departure, Rex insisted that we linger one more day. He proposed to take us to a nearby canyon, where he said "were things the doctor should see," before our journey home. No one but I seemed inclined to decline.

So the day before we were to leave to begin the weeks-long journey home, Georgiana, Rex, Somerton, and I rode out with a tracker to a canyon northwest of Knysna, a morning's ride distant. Our Xhosa tracker had evidently grown fond of me in the course of our journey east from Cape Town (or at least of the goat cheese I had shared), and as we rode to the canyon that morning, he tried to cheer me with names of plants we passed. But my spirit was oppressed by the sound of flirtatious, silly conversation between Georgiana and Rex.

The canyon we rode into was radiant in the late-morning light, the sandstone walls tinting gold. Ahead of us, visible above the cliffs, were the high peaks of mountains. At a signal from the tracker, we dismounted and tethered the horses and walked a few dozen yards farther on until the tracker led us beneath a stone outcropping, which jutted out from a cave wall like a long low roof, barely high enough to accommodate Lord Somerton. The dim light beneath the outcropping left me dazzled while my eyes adjusted to the shadow there, and then, as my vision cleared, to my amazement the wall before me shifted from gold to red, from a solid to something liquid, moving, a pulsating skin of dappled color—for a moment I did not understand what I was seeing. And then, it came clear: human handprints, red as blood, covered the wall in front of us and the ceiling above. I shivered at the sight of it. Although none of us spoke, I felt a rising hum in my ears, as if the palm prints covering the stone wall before us were not images but sounds, each a voice, a note, speaking from some time out of time. As if we had slipped inside a living body here, its thundering heart before us.

When we stepped out into the sun again, the heat was a comfort, and we began to talk rapidly of the beauty of the petroglyphs; Rex held forth on who might have made them and why. The sun was high overhead now, and we agreed to take lunch before riding back. Georgiana saw to laying out a cloth on a large flat rock, around which we each took a seat to dine on smoked meats and fruits and fresh baked rolls and wine.

We were lingering in a delicious haze of gustatory contentment when I heard Georgiana exclaim in what sounded like delight.

I opened my eyes to see on the rocks above us a half dozen tiny tawny-colored deer, small as dogs, much smaller than Lord Somerton's hounds. Each one was no taller than my knee, with tiny horns, enormous black eyes and lips, standing on the tips of their hooves, like ungulate ballerinas.

"What darlings!" she whispered.

"Klipspringer," said Rex with a yawn, lying back against the rock.

The tracker smiled. "Umvundla," he said to Georgiana,

nodding to the creatures. He waved his hands over his head to indicate the ears of a rabbit. And laughed.

"The Xhosa call them rabbits," Rex explained, not deigning to open his eyes again.

"Oh, Father, might we take one home?" Georgiana said. "Please?"

"Of course," said Rex, answering before Lord Somerton could. "A beautiful woman should have everything she desires."

Georgiana smiled at the blatant flattery.

"I don't see why not," Lord Somerton said.

I thought the tracker looked unsettled by the proposal, but he said nothing. There was talk of how we might capture the tiny antelope and transport it back with us, until I inquired of the tracker what mode he thought best and he explained that the animal wouldn't last the journey.

"It would break the heart to separate them," he said. "They mate for life and once."

Rex was undaunted. "Then we'll capture two."

"And how will you know which two are mated?" I asked. "Or are you indifferent to questions of fidelity?"

Rex opened one eye and looked at me. "What of you, Doctor? Have you a little wife hidden away somewhere?"

"I'm not a man to marry," I said.

"Surely if you found a suitable match…"

"No woman would suit a man like me," I said. "Some men are unsuited for marriage."

Rex glanced at Georgiana, whose eyes were downcast and whose hands shook as she packed up our luncheon. "I'm not sure every woman would agree."

"If she knew me well," I said. "She would."

* * *

That night at Knysna, as we sat up late on the veranda after dinner, talking and watching stars, I heard a mournful singing through the forest, an unearthly sound, as if the trees themselves were lamenting.

"What in God's name is that?" Lord Somerton asked.

"The field slaves sing," Rex said, as if it were a tribute, a performance given for his delight. "No one can convince me slaves suffer when they sing so well and often."

"It sounds like a dirge," I said.

"So do Gregorian chants," Rex replied.

A woman's shriek from the house brought me to my feet. I ran toward the sound, ignoring Rex's voice behind me ("It's nothing, Doctor!"). I was not brave, as Georgiana would say later; I simply feared what I might face were I slow to act. I had heard stories of domestic catastrophes that attended these estates: a toddler fallen into a vast pot of soup, scalded beyond recovery; a cleaver-wielding cook who lost a digit to the blade or worse.

When I reached the house I pushed through the wooden door from beyond which the shouts came, and froze on the threshold of the kitchen. It was an unearthly sight: A woman suspended in midair, dark against the darker dim-lit room, hung from a rafter beam, her wrists bound by rope, shoulders wet where a lash had cut her.

"What in God's name?!" I shouted, though it was clearly another master served.

The man standing below her paused in his exertions, turned, saw me, then spoke, almost under his breath: "None of your concern, sir." I heard a child's sob and saw by the stove a small boy of no more than three crouched there. The man appeared not to hear or to be indifferent to the sound. He raised the lash again, drawing it back across the packed dirt floor, slithering toward me, until it came within a handsbreadth of my red bootheel. I stood on it, preventing him from raising it again. His stalled arm pulled him round to face me.

Perhaps I should have been afraid for myself then, for the man moved toward me with a speed and violence in the set of his shoulders that was truly frightening. But I was distracted from my fear by his face.

You would expect a violent man to have a violent face, to appear a monster. But he was not, and it shocked me to see him: handsome, young, unshaven, light-eyed and fair-haired, a hero out of a storybook. I was so distracted by his uncanny appearance that I didn't move. He crossed to me and shoved me in the chest, then jerked the whip from under my foot, sending me to the floor. I watched him snap back the lash and strike the woman again. Heard her shout, and then another woman's scream behind me. I turned to the doorway to see Miss Somerton.

No doubt the poor woman's assailant would have killed her there in plain view of her own child and me had not Georgiana arrived just then, and after her, Rex. Had not her plain horror forced his hand, counseled a pretense of humanity, forcing Rex to remedy the situation.

"Cut her down," Rex said, as if it were a horse to be untied. The brute began to explain the situation—something about a loaf of bread—but was cut short. "Now," Rex said.

Rex turned to Miss Georgiana to offer his apology but she pushed away, holding up her hand as if against a blow. I offered to accompany her to her room but she shook her head, and her maid said, "I'll see to her, sir." Then I went to see to the wounds of the young woman, who sat curled now in the middle of the floor. The child's hand on her shoulder.

When we returned to the veranda half an hour later, Rex spoke as if nothing unusual had happened. Perhaps nothing unusual had.

"Everything all right?" Lord Charles asked when we resumed our seats.

"Perfectly," Rex said.

"An overseer was beating a female slave," I explained. "To death, from the looks of it, had we not interrupted."

"Ah," Somerton said. I wondered at his equanimity, how he had remained seated here despite the commotion. I hated him then for his calm, his discretion, as if questioning his host were more unseemly than countenancing murder.

I asked if this was a common occurrence.

Rex's cigar ember glowed in the dark then died, then glowed red again. "Discipline is essential to the safe operation of a large estate," he said.

"You mean to the holding of slaves," I said.

"I have six hundred men working for me here," he said.

"Enslaved men," I said.

"They would not work if they did not fear the consequences."

"There are other ways to inspire men to labor."

"Spare me your speeches, Doctor. Morality is an easy pastime for a man whose life does not depend on the land. Pardon me for being blunt, but you don't know what you're talking about."

"I know that it's immoral to hold a man as property."

"Life is an immoral business, Doctor. Morality is a superstition." He paused, then added, "You benefit from slaves, as I do. You just have the luxury to pretend you don't."

He was right in one way. My morality *was* a luxury—one the woman I'd hoped to help that night could not afford. My intervention comforted me that night, but likely not her. To humiliate the man who would humiliate her must only have increased his rage, her punishment. The rage of the overseer would only grow for having been interrupted, corrected; in private, later, once we left, when there was nothing to be done, he would have his way—as men did with women— in private. It was the way of the world and on estates like this, where power was unchecked by justice, by shame, by rule of law. Then as now there were those who suffered daily so that people half a world away might be comfortable—and comfortably ignore them.

There was slavery in Cape Town, of course, brutality its handmaiden. But there at least slaveholders took some pride in the condition of the persons they enslaved. A contented family, a healthy servant, was the mark of a gentleman. As significant, as meaningful as a well-curried horse, a fine carriage, a large and well-kept house. It was part of the domestic tableau. In the city, men took personally the condition of their slaves and women and dogs.

As we began our long ride home to Cape Town the next morning, Georgiana kept her distance, riding ahead of us in a cart with the guide, silent now.

Somerton rode up beside me, so close that our knees nearly touched. "She's young," he said. "She'll recover. Remarkably, we do."

I hoped that he was right—that we would all of us recover from this.

CHAPTER SIX

THE LADY WITH
THE PET DOG

After our return from the Fish River, Lord Somerton and I grew inseparable; we were together every day, save for when he sent me to attend his friends or their families. He seemed inclined to make me out to be some sort of alchemist or magician, my reputation for incomparable skill augmenting his own. He would have the best horses, the best rifles, the most beautiful women and balls, the best physician. I was glad to play my part. To have any part at all.

The governor took pains to show his favor toward me; he made me a gift of the horse I'd first ridden to Table Mountain and a carriage, and put at my disposal the services of a manumitted slave named Dantzen, whom he provided with a livery matching my own distinctive dress, down to the red parasol and cardinal-red coat and red bootheels. He issued proclamations protecting bontebok, establishing a leper colony at Hemel-en-Aarde, and provided land for a hospital for the public. He made me the physician to his household, with an increase in pay and an offer of an apartment at Government House, where his family resided, which I declined for obvious reasons. He appointed me Vaccinating Physician to the Vaccine Institution, which carried a salary as well. I was gratified. But even this did not quell my fears and jealousy in regard to the governor. Favor among the powerful is a precarious perch.

Pleasure though his constant companionship was, it was painful at times, when I had to witness his intimacies with others, which I feared might someday rival our own. Lord Somerton shone at the balls that Miss Georgina arranged for his amusement, but to watch him clap another man on the shoulder or waltz with some local beauty in his arms gave me a most acute pain, even as I was gaining notoriety as a flirt and a favorite among local ladies, prompting more than one young blade to storm out with his intended dragged behind. It was not Lord Somerton's romantic interest that I coveted, but his attention. Above all, his love. In that I brooked no rivals, beyond those to whom greater love was owed by bond of blood.

So I was both sorry and relieved to lose his company when he set out for a week's foxhunting at Roundhouse; I set off for the Castle to attend to my neglected duties there, which the hospital administrator noted had been unduly ignored of late. Even the governor's protection could not protect me from that charge. I set to work at once—first seeing to the soldiers' complaints, then attending to a few private patients, writing up instructions for the proper care of the ill at home, taking notes on what might be improved.

Toward the end of our week's separation, I visited Simon's Town to tend to a ship's captain who had anchored there and come down with an inflammation of the eyes, which he had managed to severely aggravate by application of what passed for medicine in these parts; by the time I reached him he was all but blinded, a state that happily was not permanent. I prescribed a saline rinse and cleansing regimen, the suspension of all prior treatment, and good Cape wine to calm his nerves and pass the time; in return, I asked only traveling expenses back to Cape Town. He seemed so grateful I feared he might offer me a swordfish to bear home.

On the long ride back to Cape Town, the exhaustion of the last few days settled into my bones and I felt the ache to sleep, despite the exquisite scenery that I rode through—the green mountains, the shimmering blue-green bay, the polished stone monoliths; I thought to stop at Roundhouse to visit with the governor, but when I arrived near sunset, I learned that he had already returned to town, so I rode on, despite exhaustion.

I arrived back in the Heerengracht late that night deeply weary, so I eschewed my usual precautions; failing to bolt my bedroom door, I disrobed, unbound my chest, and slipped on a nightshirt. No sooner had I put head to pillow than I slept, only to wake in a confusion shortly after when there came a knock on my bedroom door and my landlady entered, followed by a frightened servant familiar to me from Government House but whose name I did not know, and whose face I would ever after remember as one who bore the message from Miss Georgiana that the governor had taken ill and was not expected to last the week. Would I come quickly, please?

I begged a moment to dress, just enough time to pull on breeches and boots and a coat over my nightshirt, which I tucked into the pants and without delay or thought before I hurried forth into the night.

When I arrived at Tunhuys, the house was lit as for a party and filled with voices, which carried onto the veranda as I crossed it, passing horses and carriages held at the door. The foyer, when I entered, was crowded with local functionaries—among them I recognized the bishop; Somerton's aide-de-camp; the Colonial Medical Inspector; and Lieutenant Colonel Christopher Bird, the Deputy Colonial Secretary.

"Dr. Perry," one called out to me as I began to ascend the stairs. "A word with you."

Miss Georgiana nodded her assent, so I crossed to the assembled men. I learned quickly that I would not be the first to see the governor, who had arrived home earlier that day in a fever; in my absence he had been attended by the director of hospital, who had declared his case foregone. Colonel Bird held in his hands a letter, which he was prepared to send forth to London, to notify Lord Bathurst of the governor's dire condition, so the authorities might prepare for his replacement, should that prove necessary. They awaited my corroboration as a formality.

The Deputy Secretary held out the letter to me. I refused to touch it, only scanned its few lines as if I were reading a warrant for my own death. My skin went cold. I knew the power of such official documents—that once the paper was signed, the news of his imminent demise dispatched to England, it would be as fact. My own life had been transformed by so simple and miraculous an act—I could not allow the letter to be sent. He would die of the news, I thought, by its reporting.

"Gentlemen," I said, defying them to contradict me. "He will live."

"Your sentiment is admirable, Doctor, but your optimism seems unwarranted. You've yet to see the patient..."

"I will see to the patient as soon as your departure allows it, but I must have your word that no mention will be made of this until I have made a determination in the case."

"I'm afraid his fate has been determined already," said the bishop. "By higher authority than ours."

"He will live," I said again. "Unless you condemn him to death with your words."

The men glanced at one another, understanding the threat I intended this to be. If the governor lived, their letter would serve as warrant for their own political demise.

"How much time do you need?" the medical inspector asked.

"A week," I said. "Perhaps two, depending on how I find him."

"You have two days," Colonel Bird said.

"That's hardly time enough to determine a cause, let alone provide cure."

"Two days, Doctor. That is all. Then we must notify the authorities or be remiss in our duty."

"Not a word of this until then," I said, knowing I would do no better, no matter the soundness of my argument; reason is no match for cowardice. "I have your word, gentlemen."

They looked to each other, then to me; they nodded. I did not wait to see them go; I took the stairs two at a time and found Georgiana waiting on the landing above. I asked her how he was and what had happened, and she told me of how the fever had come on shortly after they'd arrived at Round-house, after he'd returned from inspecting the local prison, but her father had ignored it—ridden out anyway.

When I asked after his symptoms, fearing he might be beyond giving a clear account of same, she spoke of headache, high fever, a rash on his chest that was spreading; when he'd grown intolerant of the bright sunlight that flooded Round-house and began to ask after his dead wife, they had returned home at once, hoping to find me.

She gestured to a room at the end of the hall. "He's in there."

I stepped toward the door, when she took my arm. "He

may not recognize you, Doctor. He has not recognized me today."

I entered the room and found what I'd most feared—the stench of typhus unmistakable as a stable's or the sea's. A reek of urine and grain. Not Behier's odor of blood but a mouselike scent, quite unlike the smell of death; it is closer to that of baked bread, attracting flies before the dying are even dead. I knew it instantly.

The light was dim, despite an oil lamp lit beside the bed—the smell flooded my senses. On his face, the sheen of sweat and glow of fever. Red spots were visible on his arms and where his gown lay open on his chest.

I had heard how typhus wiped out whole armies on the field before battle ever began; I'd heard much about the disease but never treated it, nor heard of it successfully cured. The cure, it seemed, was death.

I sank into a chair beside the bed and took his hand in mine, feeling for the pulse. He groaned and turned toward me, but his eyes had the moist brightness of delirium. When I reached for a cloth—from a basin beside the bed—to sponge his brow, his teeth chattered from the chill, despite the room's oppressive heat, the blanket-heaped bed. He grasped my hand and held it, pressed it to his lips, and for a moment I thought he knew me.

"Don't go," he said.

I was startled by his voice. "I won't."

"My love," he said.

I hesitated before bending to the edge of his bed, my head leaned close to his.

"Yes," I said. "What is it?"

"Elizabeth." His late wife's name.

I told myself it didn't matter if he mistook me for someone else; everyone did; everyone believed I was someone I was not.

Curiously, the error recalled me to myself; I stood and went to the door, ordered hot wine brought, garlic, gauze, scalding water, fresh linens, the house awakened as if it were midday.

Although this was my first case of typhus, it was a disease that I knew well by reputation; it had ravaged soldiers, laid waste whole regiments. I was afraid both for the governor and for myself in its presence, but I knew no one must sense my fear. Above all, I wondered, *What to do?* I recalled first principles, as a child recalling catechism. His body was fighting the fever; there was little to do against the disease itself, save for help him in the fight. So I set to cleaning the sores, ordered the bedding changed and linens burned, the governor stripped; I dabbed each open wound, each new red spot, with wine and hot water to lessen the contagion. To lend him strength I fed him spoonfuls of hot beef broth with crushed garlic, applied milk poultices to draw the fever, warm wine to strengthen the blood.

We had two days to prove the others wrong, to prove history itself wrong. It was true that a few men survived typhus, but the reasons were not clear—such survival seemed miraculous. I could not plan a miracle. Instead we sat together that first night shuttered in the room, which reeked now of bleach and garlic and hot wine, the curtains pulled closed against the coming morning light, which disease made painful to him; it was as if we shared a perpetual night, lengthened just for us. There was no treatment known for typhus; I knew it to be a painful and an undignified way to die, swaddled, oozing pus and shit, and though I'd long ago given up on gods, I prayed to whatever principle of life that there might be to save this man I loved, my friend.

When at dawn that first morning Colonel Bird returned to check on the governor's progress, I threw him out; I sent away even Lord Somerton's daughters.

"He is our father," Georgiana said. "It's only right that we be with him."

"And I am his physician, and I tell you that if you want to help him—and help me save him—you will get out. This is no place for women."

When there was a knock on the door a few moments later, I couldn't help it—I shouted. "What now, in God's name? This is a sickroom, not a society ball."

I flung open the door and found my servant Dantzen there, elegant as always in his red coat, cut exactly as my own. "I thought you might like some refreshment, sir," he said. He held out a pitcher of goat's milk, and a glass, upon his tray.

I could not see if it was wit or pity in his eyes. "I would, I would indeed. Thank you."

"Shall I set it down?" he started to enter the room.

"No," I said. "Safer not to. I'll take it. Could you ask them to send up more hot wine?"

As that first dawn waned into day, Lord Charles grew weaker, his teeth chattering despite the feather coverlet and blankets heaped on the bed, his face pale, slick with sweat, his fingers raking the sores that appeared on his arms and chest. Despite the gloves I had placed on his hands to lessen the damage done by his feverish scratching, his skin opened where he rubbed. I should have had him tied down, but I could not bear to have him restrained like Gulliver among the Lilliputians.

I did not sleep for two nights; I watched him as he wrestled with the devil of disease, invisible as spirits. Grateful that he had been and was a robust man, temperate in his habits, except when it came to women and horses and dogs.

As that first full day wore on into darkness, he stilled, grew quiet, his inactivity more chilling than his feverish movements had previously been the night before. I knew then that I would lose him; that he would die. And I knew that I loved him more than I had known, more than I had loved anyone. More than Mirandus. Perhaps even more than my mother and sister. And that his loss would matter more to me than even their loss had. It would be like losing myself. The prospect of life without my friend was as black and featureless as the moonless night outside.

I made a child's bargain with the night: that if I staved off sleep, Lord Somerton would live. I paced the room, as he'd have done; I read, watched him sleep, wiped his brow. Sometime toward daybreak I must have taken a seat in the chair beside the bed again and slept, for I woke there with a start, heart pounding. Alarmed. Sure that I would find him, as I had my mother, dead at dawn.

The room was dark; I heard no sound from the bed, no breath, no movement. I could not bear to light another lamp. Instead I sat beside him, waiting. As dawn came on that second morning, the light slowly filled the room, grey as water rising around us; I looked to the bed and saw the gentle rise and fall of the coverlet. He had survived the night. Might yet live. It was my last thought before I fell asleep again, exhausted.

A few hours before the colonel and his entourage were to arrive to make their final determination, I threw open the curtains on the now fading day and saw familiar stars—

Canopus, Sirius—rising in the east, the same stars we'd lain under together months before, when I thought them lucky. I loosened my shirt, tugged open the collar, discarded my coat, raised the window to air out the stench of sour sweat and loose bowels.

When I heard a sound from the bed, a moan, I turned and went to him. I leaned over him, the soft cloth of my shirt falling forward, loose to graze his chest.

I looked into his tired eyes, clear now of fever, clasped his hand; he smiled as he met my eyes, recognizing me at last, then he looked down and his expression changed. Like wind shifting on a sea or lake. First troubled, then amused. I reached up my hand to close my collar, but it was too late. I'd revealed what I had spent a dozen years disguising.

"It's not as it appears," I said, straightening, one hand on the bed to steady me.

"Evidently," he said.

"I can explain," I began.

"I believe, Doctor, you could explain away anything." He set his hand on mine. "But the truth of principles must be confirmed by observation."

And then he laughed—a crushed, croaking version of his usual laugh. And I knew that he would live. I didn't know if I'd survive all he knew. And all I did.

For a few days after Lord Somerton's recovery I stayed in town with Liz, the woman I'd met at the Rainbow Ball, avoiding my rooms in the Heerengracht, so as to dodge the governor's messengers, who came daily—my landlady said—most probably to summon me to Tunhuys. I took the occasion to make the long journey to Caledon to oversee vaccinations there. I visited the prison at Rondebosch to do the same. I visited my private patients, and the soldiers at the hospital and sailors at Simon's Town, claiming I'd been too much absent from these, remiss in my duty, but in truth I was afraid.

He had been amused, even tender, it's true, when he'd made the discovery, but he was still quite ill then, I knew. Having recovered his strength, his masculine egoism, the authority of his office and its prejudices, he might respond in ways I could not guess. I knew that he was a gossip, and on a whim might undo me. He was fond of jokes, but not when they were played on him.

So I busied myself with work. In Rondebosch I tried to get the warden to answer my questions on the prisoners' conditions—diet, exercise, ventilation—but I was met with silence and claims that no such records were kept. So I asked to see the prisoners themselves to inquire of them; their memories seemed far better than the warden's, who objected to the interviews.

"Why ask blacks, while Christians are present to answer?" the warden bellowed.

"Given the prisoners' conditions, sir, I'd hardly call you a Christian. Now, if you'll allow me to finish my interviews, we'll both be eager of my departure, I'm sure."

I sent a detailed report with my recommendations regarding improvement of sanitation, exercise, and diet, as well as the immediate replacement of the warden, to the governor's office. I did not go myself. I labored both to fill the hours and to find pretext to be far from Cape Town, but also to prove my worth as a physician, should Lord Somerton have occasion now to doubt it.

My fate was quite literally in his hands. If he chose to reveal my secret, it would mean more than public embarrassment, more than scandal, more than the loss of my position as the governor's physician. It would mean infamy, penury, court-martial, jail, very possibly death. At the very least, it would mean the loss of what I held most dear: my position as an officer and gentleman, my friendship with Lord Somerton, and Africa. I had made enemies enough in Cape Town to birth an eager audience to see me hanged.

It was our longest separation since we'd journeyed east to see King Ngqika, and I missed my friend, but I kept myself busy with the crises an outpost hospital will present. The wind blew hot and dusty in the day. Cool nights followed, littered with stars.

Twice, in the month after his recovery, Lord Somerton had summoned me to Government House, and twice I had declined on account of medical commitments. The third request threatened to send the next by armed guard. The notes he sent came in his hand and were curt, absent the warmth of his usual correspondence. He proposed that we meet at Roundhouse, where—though he was not yet fit to hunt—he intended to spend a few days convalescing, free of the cares of state and the dust and stench of town. Roundhouse was en route to Simon's Town, where I'd gone to attend to sailors; I could stop on my way back to town, he noted; it would not delay me in my duties to spare an hour there for luncheon. His daughters, he said, would have to remain in town for a ball; we would be alone, undisturbed, save for servants. Whatever was said, we would be the only ones to hear it.

I had no choice but to accept. So after early-morning rounds among the patients, I rode out for the hunting lodge where Somerton had taught me to shoot and ride a year before.

When I arrived at Roundhouse approaching noon, an unfamiliar servant showed me into the library, which overlooked the garden and the sea below.

"His Lordship will be with you presently," he said and left me there alone.

Beyond the window, the ocean boomed like a cannon. The strange monoliths arrayed like Stonehenge made me miss England. The sky was radiant aquamarine, the sea indigo, like a sheet of sapphire. The beauty of the day was in stark contrast to the darkness in my spirit. My mind raced. I imagined him enraged; I pictured him contemptuous and distant. I could not imagine how we might go forward from here.

Despite my trepidation, when he entered and I turned to see him there, I was flooded with relief to see my friend so well, restored to health, although his face was thin, clearly lighter by a full stone. He was followed by a manservant who bore a wicker hamper, such as we had used on our trip to the Xhosa king. For a moment I wondered if he intended for us to dine in the garden al fresco, as we had then, or if he had come to buy me off and send me packing.

His face was unreadable, a formal friendliness. Quite unlike the last time we'd met.

I hardened my face too, glad to have worn my dress uniform, my thigh-high boots with the polished red heels; if I was to be dismissed, I would receive the news in style. I touched the hilt of my sword.

"I am gratified to see Your Lordship looking so well."

"It is thanks to your ministrations, Dr. Perry." He turned to the servant. "You may leave the case there. We do not wish to be disturbed."

"As you wish, my Lord."

The doors clicked shut, leaving us alone.

"It's good of you to have come," he said.

"I was unaware that I had a choice."

"You didn't," he said. "But I'm nonetheless delighted to see you." I noticed that he did not pace. His stillness made me uneasy.

"I'd have thought you'd seen altogether too much of me," I said.

He laughed.

I blushed. "I did not mean," I began. "I meant, with your illness. You've seen too much of doctors."

"You're far more to me than that," he said. "I could never see too much of you."

I listened for irony, for dismissal, heard none.

"I owe you my life," he said.

"In this, then, we are equals," I said.

He frowned, as if considering the remark. He was vain of rank. I feared I had offended.

"You say you owe me your life," I continued. "You hold mine equally in your hands."

"I had no idea that I held such power."

"You may be the most powerful man in Africa," I said. "And you are the only man living who knows my secret."

"Then you have nothing to fear," he said.

"A secret can be very hard to bear alone," I replied.

"Which is why you shouldn't have to," he said. He walked over to the wicker basket set beside the green-silk settee and unfastened the latch. When he drew it back, a small white tuft of fur was visible inside it, like a tiny cloud or a miniature lamb. For a moment I feared he'd bought me an ermine wrap, some horrible feminine fetish.

"I've brought you a present," he said.

"What in God's name—"

"It has a god's name, in fact," he said, "or rather a goddess's. Meet Psyche."

He bent and lifted a small fluffy ball of white fur out of the basket. I could see it shivering in his arms, but it did not make a sound. Somerton crossed the room in three long strides until he stood close enough to embrace me; he set it in my arms. For a moment we cradled the creature together; I could feel his breath warm against my hair.

"*Psyche?*" I could not bring myself to look up into his face, so I looked at the dog.

"Surely a man of your learning knows the story." His voice was quiet.

"Of Cupid's wife?" My uncle had painted the image.

"The most beautiful woman in the world," he said.

"The world is full of beautiful women, in my experience." I was thinking of the balls at Government House. "There is a superfluity."

"This woman," he said, relinquishing the dog to my arms. "Was exceptional."

Psyche's story was as familiar to me as my own: Cupid had been sent by his mother, Venus, to poison Psyche, whose mortal beauty rivaled the goddess's own. But Cupid was so taken by Psyche's loveliness that he wished to marry her instead. The gods granted his request on one condition: Psyche must never know his true identity. Psyche agreed, and they were wed, and soon after she was pregnant. But her sisters encouraged her to learn her husband's identity before she bore a monstrous child, so one night as he lay beside her she lit a lamp, raised it to his face as he slept, saw he was no monster but a god, and lost him. Their love could survive only as long as his identity remained a secret.

I'd not had a dog since I was a child in Cork. My eyes filled. "She's beautiful," I said.

"Yes," he said. "She is."

An hour later we sat down to luncheon, what for years would seem in memory the best luncheon I had ever eaten. Knowing I would not eat animal flesh, he had seen to it that the feast was of the freshest available from the sea and Company's Garden. There were crayfish broiled in fresh butter, thick white hake seared to the golden crispness of flan, plump pink grilled tiger shrimp big as a Malay woman's bracelet, wine-poached scallops bigger than the buttons on my coat, and all manner of vegetables from the garden, roasted in salty butter. We finished off two bottles of cold crisp champagne; the breeze off the sea was deliciously cool in the heat of the day, like a cool cloth held to a feverish head. The sun warm as butter.

When I agreed to stay the night rather than ride back to Simon's Bay, I found rooms had already been prepared for me, anticipating what I had not: when he came to me that night, it was by darkness; we did not speak; we lit no lamps.

CHAPTER SEVEN

CONSTANTIA AT DAWN

I have often considered that—with the notable exception of humanity—the male of a species has the showier plumage on account of its lesser appeal; the female is naturally appealing and requires no ornamentation to attract a mate. So it is with certain women and men.

After my death, some will speculate that my reputation for extravagant flirtation had been born of an effort to disguise my true nature, but in truth I simply had an eye for the ladies. But after that first evening together at Roundhouse, it was absurd how Somerton absorbed me.

The next morning we rode out together, down to the sea at Camps Bay, and bathed there, in the frigid salty waters and waves, hidden from view among the stone monoliths that crowded the water's edge like giant prehistoric eggs, or sentinels.

At night, dining quietly together without servants in attendance, he held my hand as we sat beside each other at table, drinking wine, the sound of the surf coming in the window.

He told me of how, after Elizabeth's death, he had considered taking his own life, but had not for the sake of the children. He told me, as we lay in the darkness at night, how in my arms he felt he had "come home." Embarrassed by the declaration (*Why is it women are always compared to things they are not?*), I nonetheless understood what he meant, for I felt it as well. *At home.* He said there was nothing I could not say to him, that we could not say to each other. In darkness, in light.

As if Roundhouse were like Prospero's island, where another logic governed, another air, a different gravity, we lived for those few days without thought of the larger world beyond.

He spoke easily, but I could not. It was not reticence, exactly. I wanted to confide, but I could not. The habit of silence is hard to break, had become a way of life; the words and stories stuck in my throat as I sought to form them. It seemed a lie, that life, a phantom, a ghost story. As if my life were a spell that I might undo by speaking, saying the words. How I came to be who I was, all the lonely years during which I'd tried to forge myself into a useful instrument, a blade without feeling. Like Psyche with Cupid, I could love only as long as I did not examine too closely the body, the past.

I told him what I could: of my training in Edinburgh, of Dryburgh Abbey and Lord Basken's interventions on my behalf, of my training with Sir Astley Cooper, and of General Mirandus, whom he knew by reputation but had not met. I could not say more.

Save for with my sister and mother, I had never known such pleasure and comfort in the company of another person, company that did not seem to rob me of my solitude but confirmed and enhanced it. I seemed with him more myself, as if he were a mirror in which I appeared more clearly, in both fault and virtue; amplified, as our voices had been in the canyons near Knysna—which returned to us larger, bolder, yet still our own.

I was loath to resume life in Cape Town, afraid of what trouble we might encounter there in the course of our official duties. As Governor Somerton and Doctor Perry. But he assured me nothing would change.

What do I remember of that time? Moments. Our first morning together at Roundhouse, when he pulled back the sheet and looked at me and said, "How beautiful you are," and laughed when I grabbed at the blanket to cover myself. Later, as I was stepping from the bath, he held a towel open for me, but out of my hands. "No, wait," he said. "Let me look at you." I felt a shiver pass through me to be washed in admiration, revealed, released, as I had felt when we rode down through the morning heat to the cold salt waters of Camps Bay or rode out together in the heat rising off the Cape Flats, and I felt it loosening my muscles, lending me a suppleness I had not known before, an ease and confidence and pleasure in my body undisguised. Everyone wants to be seen.

I was surprised by the delight I took in my new role of lover and the power that attended it, one that girls are said to have even when young, but which I hadn't, although I had faintly sensed the possibility when I saw how General Mirandus watched Sarah Andrews or very occasionally when we sat conversing in his library, a whiff of sensuality faintly discernible between us, as foreign and intriguing as the unexpected flavors of his homeland prepared for dinner in the room below—meat roasted with salt, not boiled; garlic and onions and limes and tomatoes and a frilly green plant called *cilantro* that he had cultivated from seed.

I had been unsettled by Mirandus's appreciative glance when

he watched me, smiling, as I reported on what I had read or studied or discovered in his library that day or week or month. He smiled at me as he might over a particularly delicious champagne, a connoisseur's admiration. It was a look that I would later observe in Lord Somerton, when he considered a particularly promising horse—a calculating and appreciative gaze, half pride, half delight, an admixture of pleasure and cold assessment about what might be made of this, how far the beast might go with training and encouragement.

Somerton's regard for me was different than the general's, which had often made me feel curiously diminished, less than I was, slighter. This was the opposite: I felt multiplied.

Still, it was ambivalent pleasure to be thought beautiful, an appreciation I'd never known nor sought. Women's admiration of me had always been solicitous, self-regarding. It was not my looks they noticed when they flirted with me, but their own they wished to have admired, and I did—how could I not? They were lovely. Desiring women—and their desire to be desired—made me feel powerful, expanded, like heated gas. But to be the object of a man's fierce desire felt intoxicating, bracing and wounding all at once. A power most women know from girlhood, but which I never had, having become a boy before I ever became a woman.

But such pleasure had another face, like Janus. Which I discovered quickly on our return to Cape Town. For a time, all was as it had been between us at Roundhouse, save that we met far less frequently, barred from intimacy by the presence of family and servants and my landlady. But longing has its own savor, and our intimacy together, while rare, was more intense for our having been parted.

Gradually I came to notice a change, like a shift in the direction of the wind. When I strode into his office at Government House after having been away overseeing vaccines at Caledon or attending private patients near Newlands— ignoring Cloete, the officious aide-de-camp who wished to announce me—I increasingly found him distracted by papers ("Oh, it's you; I was expecting someone else," he might say) and I felt ashamed, as if my measure were his to take, and I had been found wanting.

At such times I felt humiliated and said curtly, "I won't detain you, then," turned on my heel and walked out, hoping to wound, but he did not appear to notice. Stepping out into the Company's Garden after one such encounter, some six months after our first night at Camps Bay, the heat raking the trees, the scent of frangipani and lemons, I thought better of my pique and turned back again. We had been apart for some weeks, as I'd had medical matters to attend to and he colonial affairs, and I had missed him. As I entered the cool marble foyer, I heard a rustle of fabric and saw on the landing above a blue silk skirt slip past the wooden door of His Lordship's office. I assumed it must be Miss Georgiana or her sister, although the perfume—heavy scent of cape jasmine and musk—should have told me otherwise. I knew it well.

When I reached his office door, I found it barred by Cloete.

"I wouldn't go in there if I were you," the Dutchman said, stretching out an arm to prevent me.

"Don't be absurd." I reached for the door.

"His Lordship is *not* alone."

The man's tone irritated me.

"He is with..." he hesitated, then smiled. "A lady."

I remembered the woman I'd seen on the landing, her figure as out of place as a field of sea pink or violets would be in the Company's Garden, an unseasonable bloom.

I let my hand fall from the doorknob; crossed my arms over the chest of my red coat.

"Well," I said, returning the man's smirk. "That's a fine Dutch filly he's got hold of."

The man straightened. "That's a bloody ugly thing to say," said Cloete.

"Truth is often ugly," I replied. I knew the kind of man Josias de Cloete was—wellborn, narrowly educated, insecure about his position, sensitive to insult, easily provoked; I was not surprised when he insisted on satisfaction. I'd hoped he would. I agreed to a duel at Constantia the next day at dawn.

I felt in that moment that I wanted to die; I wanted to kill the ache in my chest, this humiliating longing; I knew, as I descended the stairs and stepped out into the Company's Garden, that I might not survive the encounter. I was a terrible shot, but I wanted to strike something; I wanted to hurt a man, even if this wasn't the man I had in mind.

The ride to Constantia the next morning was dark and cold; Dantzen accompanied me to bear Psyche and my pistols, and—though we didn't speak of it—to report news of my death, if necessary. Dantzen had tried to dissuade me, even gallantly proposed to serve as my second; I had declined. The fight was mine, not his.

The cold morning air caught in my throat, burning like smoke as we rode. I could hear the blood pound in my ears as the horse moved beneath me, my mouth dry, the sky a heartbreaking violet blue, as it had been on our journey to the Xhosa king almost two years earlier; above the hulking dark of Table Mountain, the Southern Cross; a scent of grass and horse sweat; somewhere far off the cry of a rooster tolled the morning's first hour.

When we stopped and dismounted, Psyche barked once, then fell silent. Cloete was already there, waiting.

As the sun began to rise over Alphen estate, we chose our weapons, paced off our positions, then turned at our marker stones to face each other across the field. Cloete and I lowered our pistols to the height of one another's chests; I felt a curious detachment. For an instant my death became palpable, possible, as it had not been before; time slowed, grew thick as honey, before the signal handkerchief fell.

The barrel of my gun trembled as I started to pull back on the trigger, when I heard the shot and felt something hot—like an ember—across my left arm and saw the Dutchman's hat fly off like a startled gull.

"By God!" the Dutchman shouted, though the distance between us was not great. "You're a marksman after all! I'd heard you were a miserable shot."

"Opinion must always be confirmed by observation," I shouted back. "Next time I'll aim for a less-vulnerable part of your anatomy—your heart." But I knew that I had not aimed at all. I had not even pulled the trigger.

Cloete laughed. "Fair enough." He stooped to retrieve his injured hat.

"Are you all right, sir?" Dantzen said, appearing at my side. I smelled the faint but unmistakable odor of sulphur on him. "You're bleeding." He touched my arm.

"Thank you," I said with feeling. I reached up and felt the

burn at my left shoulder, the sticky warmth that I recognized as blood. "I'm wounded," I said, "but I'll recover."

When news of the duel reached Lord Somerton later that morning, his concern was gratifying. He insisted that I present myself at his office immediately and shouted in rage for some minutes before forbidding me all duels in future, though we both knew he had no power to prevent them. Duels were illegal already—a law that soldiers and gentlemen routinely ignored. I was challenged often by local men, enraged by the attention their women paid me.

"You could have been killed," Lord Somerton said.

"I was not," I said.

"Evidently," he said. He took a seat behind his desk. "It would be difficult to replace the governor's physician."

"You need not seek a replacement," I said.

"I'm glad of it."

"Is that all?" I asked.

"It is."

I left his offices, satisfied.

I did change certain of my habits in the months that followed. I was careful not to travel far from Cape Town or stay away too long, so as to be sure Lord Somerton and I had opportunity to meet most evenings. The curtains pulled against the night, the house asleep, no one to disturb us in his library or office, we resumed our happy privacy.

We maintained an unspoken agreement to reveal ourselves only in darkness, like Psyche and Cupid, in case a servant should pass by.

We continued to address one another by our formal titles— *Lord Somerton, Doctor Perry*—a poignant practice that delighted us, given that we were often naked as we spoke. But we could not afford pet names; we could not afford to forget ourselves.

There were rumors nonetheless. Occasionally a soldier would comment on my womanly figure as I rode (and would find himself summarily reassigned to a regiment at the remote eastern border), but I was unconcerned. I ignored them.

There are always rumors. I felt above them now. As if Lord Somerton's family crest shielded me as well: *Mutare vel timere sperno. I scorn to change or fear.* Their armorial motto.

For the first time in years, I let myself feel safe. That was my mistake.

We got away to Roundhouse and Newlands as often as we could, a retreat from town that I prescribed and justified as necessary for his health. It was. He was markedly improved there, hunting, fucking, even bathing in the sea, which I persuaded him to do eventually.

When I'd first proposed the bathing machine, he'd been appalled. Actually shocked. No one bathed in the sea who could afford a bath, he insisted. I extolled the healthful bene-fits of swimming and of salt water. But he refused, adamant. I suspected he was too vain to don a bathing costume. I told him a bathing machine would allow him to swim nude, if he'd prefer, unseen. Lord Charles was resistant to the idea, said it was unseemly for a governor to be seen frolicking naked as a babe, romping in the bay.

Only the prospect of including a team of his horses in the scheme—they would be necessary to haul the bathing machine into the surf and then out again—won him over. Like everything else, it became an occasion for our intimate meetings, while the horses stood hock deep in the surf.

As we entwined ourselves and fucked in the afternoons at Newlands or at night late in his office at Tunhuys, the poem of the body moved through my mind: *scapula, clavicle, coracobrachialis, gluteus maximus,* etc. I knew better than to say so, but my thoughts wandered. I thought of the names of the body's parts as ours were joined. Men must be adored, I'd learned, or it is unbearable. The love of men demands admiration and indulgence both. I was ill-suited to it. Still I loved him.

The morning sky was gaudy with seashell-pink clouds against a radiant aquamarine sky, a painting by Tintoretto or a minor Italian painter. The air was fresh and cool, a breeze coming off the sea. Psyche trotted beside me as we made our way up the Heerengracht to Mrs. Saunders's coffee shop. The street was already busy—the cheerful clatter of cart wheels against cobblestones, the call of the ragman and the clanging of the tin collector. Mr. Poleman was opening his apothecary shop, unlocking the gate with a rattling sound, the sun a gentle glow through the morning haze, turning the air to gold. It was my favorite hour, even if I rarely rose for it. The click of my bootheels added to the cheerful morning din, a satisfying report. A bell over the door rang, announcing our arrival, and we stepped into the warm bakery.

"Early today, Dr. Perry," Mrs. Saunders said. "I'll have your coffee ready in a moment."

I thanked her and took a seat by the window, where I settled Psyche in my lap before opening the paper. Mrs. Saunders set a plate of two plump sugar buns on the table before me before hurrying off to the counter to prepare my drink. Psyche shook gently beneath my hand, shivering with anticipation. She whined. She was a greedy dog. I lifted one bun to my lips and took a bite, sinking my teeth through the coating of granular sugar—like biting down on sweet sand—into the warm, sweet bread. Satisfied that it was not too hot for Psyche, I prepared her plate, tearing the roll into pieces no larger than a teaspoon, setting them out on the napkin, then setting that onto the table, where she might lift each piece from the cloth and take her breakfast. She looked up at me with gratitude, sugar dusting her lips and fur.

"You spoil that dog," Mrs. Saunders said, but her tone indicated approval.

"She spoils me," I said.

"Someone should," Mrs. Saunders replied.

She was always looking to matchmake. She was the sort of woman others called *good-natured*, when in fact she was many things but not that. She was steady, dependable, canny, judgmental, observant, an inveterate gossip. She was one of those women vital to the functioning of small communities, on whom others rely to settle feuds and tend the weak, to minister and mend. But it was not from Christian feeling that she did these things, rather from a sense of condescension, practical and impatient. If God was too busy with other matters, she would do her part.

I snapped open the *Moniteur Officiel*—the news from France long out-of-date but of interest still—when I saw that a woman had been arrested for impersonating a man aboard a naval ship. The item reported that "Madame de Freycinet, who had accompanied her husband to the port of embarkation in Toulon in September, had disappeared thereafter and, dressed as a man, had gone on board the ship that same night, despite the ordinances that prohibit the presence of women in state vessels, without official authorization...."

It was illegal, of course, to be female on a Navy vessel. It was illegal to be female in so many circumstances—a doctor, a soldier, a university student. Judging by the law, it would seem the female sex was monstrously powerful, in danger of overtaking men at every turn, posing a dire threat—a fearsome force, to necessitate such constraints. One might have thought we were a greater danger to the civic good than opium or gunpowder or the Enclosure Acts combined.

There was "indignation in official circles," according to the press.

I set the paper down, hoping to disguise the trembling of my hand.

"Is everything all right, Doctor?" Mrs. Saunders asked.

"Perfectly," I said. But I was restless. I didn't need the paper to remind me of the risks I ran: impersonating an officer was a crime, as was traveling on military ships, and impersonating a physician. In the possession of a woman, my medical degree would be worthless, my good name a scandal—worse, a joke.

I was rising to leave when my friend Tom Pringle, a poet and publisher, rapped on the glass, having seen me through it, and came in.

He proposed to join me for coffee, but I was just leaving for Government House, I explained.

"How can you stand that autocrat?" he asked.

I smiled. "He has his charms."

"Charm's a dangerous thing," he said. He knocked on the table in farewell.

I stopped into Mr. Poleman's shop on my way past to inquire about using his laboratory to experiment with the Plat Doom plant, which a local woman had suggested might have value for treating syphilis. Then was off.

* * *

Government House was in a flurry of preparations that morning when I arrived, still agitated from what I'd read in the paper. Hearing a commotion from the ballroom, I glanced in as I crossed the foyer and saw it was filled with what looked to be bags of cloth, but which in an instant I recognized as maids, curled on the floor like turtles on the beach, rounded backs, heads drawn into their necks, vigorously rubbing beeswax into the floorboards, bringing the wood to the high shine that boots would destroy that night. One was crouched down beside me in the foyer; I stepped around her as she tilted a beeswax candle over the parquet floor to drip wax before she rubbed the spot; I headed into the governor's office.

I had forgotten entirely about that evening's ball.

I went to wait for Lord Somerton more for the pleasure of his company than from any necessity. I would see him tonight at the ball, after all, but I would have to share him then, and I enjoyed being able to claim his company when I chose. To command his attention.

I was seated, waiting for Lord Charles in his office, reviewing my proposal for reforms to the local leper colony, when my dueling partner Cloete stormed in, waving something in his hand in a fury, insisting that *the blackguards should be hanged.*

"That's a bit *extreme,* don't you think?" I said, lifting the broadsheet from his hand to read it. It was another bit of doggerel about Lord Charles and me, lampooning my devotion. The sort of thing we saw often posted around town of late.

With courteous devotion inspired
Dr. Perry went to the temple of prayer
But turned on his heel and retired
When he saw that HIS Lord was not there.

"Perhaps the blackguards might be *inked* instead," I said. I handed it back.

"It's the most infernal insult," Cloete continued.

"Far worse is said in those regions, surely," I said, returning to my papers.

"How can you be so blithe, Dr. Perry?" he asked.

"It's only words."

"At your expense," he said. "And the governor's."

It occurred to me to destroy the thing before Lord Charles had a chance to see it, not simply to avoid causing him anxiety but to curb his impulse to stifle the press. He was a man who loved a good joke, but not at his expense.

When Lord Charles came in and read the quatrain, he paled, pursed his lips, and dropped the sheet onto his desk, turning from it as from an unclean thing.

"It's doggerel," I said.

"The implication is clear, Dr. Perry," he said. "Men don't deserve a free press who don't have the good sense to use it wisely."

"Who's to say what's worth saying—"

"I am," he said.

I did not argue the point.

I left with the excuse that I must dress for the evening's festivities. Everyone knew I was the best-dressed young man—a dandy—now that I was the governor's physician. Now that I could afford to be.

* * *

One of the chief charms of the very rich is that they needn't concern themselves with money, as others must, at least not overtly, as a daily matter. They can afford to pretend it doesn't matter, that its contemplation and discussion are a failing—moral, social, aesthetic. It was as if the table had been set by fairies, the art provided by the gods, a heady and Olympian indifference that made it easy to forgive the great crimes on which our comfort rested, from which it derived. Slavery, theft. Or worse, not to forgive but to forget all about them, those crimes. I'm ashamed to say I did, with the Somertons.

In their company such considerations seemed base, as if I'd dragged in something dead and fetid as I entered their glistening rooms. The ugliness seemed to adhere to he who noticed it; it was a relief—in their company—to pretend that I did not. I became, in a word, comfortable.

Money was like air, or like water to fish—a medium so pervasive, so essential to life that we could hardly perceive it; like time itself, we recognized it only by its passing. So with wealth. It did not occur to Lord Charles that his wealth was unearned, unmerited; it simply was. As he was. But its absence had taught me that nothing was as important—not self-possession, not wit, not even name.

Money absolved all failings: it purchased forgiveness, indulgence, love, friendship, beauty, forgetfulness. The only thing it could not buy off was death itself, at least not yet, though perhaps some future medicine would make it so. I could hardly argue against it: it was only possible to consider larger matters—liberty, justice, love—if one had the leisure that money bought.

I felt I should disapprove, but like General Mirandus I didn't. I loved this world—superficial, gaudy, petty, insular, extravagant. I understood why Mirandus had delayed his departure from London, his return to Venezuela. This. This was the reason—the social equivalent of tea cakes. The inessential marvelous.

The governor had made me his personal physician (as well as vaccine inspector) after his recovery from typhus, appointments that came with my own apartment at Newlands and a salary of 1,800 rix-dollars. I was at ease among his circle, now that I had money.

When I returned to Government House for the ball that evening, I went upstairs to leave Psyche in the care of a maid; I recall descending the familiar staircase, when I looked out across the guests gathered for the ball, spilling out into the foyer—in their wigs, their satin and jewels, the servants dressed in their best livery, the lamps lit and crystal dappling all of it with brightness. I felt my spirit rise and expand, felt what another man less self-scrutinizing might have mistaken for happiness, though in truth it was relief; I had arrived, had entered the enchanted circle to which it seemed no harm could come. Harm happened to others, outside our rooms, beyond this bright, illumined company. After years of struggling for a foothold, for the rung of security my mother had given her life for, I was here.

I reached out for the banister and went down to join the others.

I made my way to Lord Charles and his younger daughter, Miss Charlotte.

"Who is that tin soldier pestering Miss Georgiana?" I asked, noting the focus of their gaze.

"Captain Stirling Freeman Glover," Lord Charles said,

"but the rank's inapt. The man can hardly captain himself. Can't ride, can't shoot. Appalling at cards. Giggles when he's drunk."

"Monstrous," I said. "Shall I rescue the damsel in distress?"

"Oh, don't; do stop, Doctor," Charlotte said. "She's very fond of him—quite fond, I think. It's been a long time since she has been fond of anyone new."

We all knew that she referred to my arrival two years earlier.

In truth I had worried for Georgiana since our return from the Fish River a year ago; since then she had become solemn, devoted to good works. That vice.

"*The heart has its reasons, which reason knows nothing of,* isn't that right, Doctor?" Miss Charlotte said, repeating my line from a previous dinner.

"Damn the heart," I said. "My stomach has its reasons, and I am convinced by them."

I wondered if what I felt was jealousy; I was possessive of the family but of Georgiana and Somerton most of all. Irrationally, I felt they were mine.

As I made my way through the crowd toward the banquet room, I scanned the room. I frowned to see Bishop Burnett chatting with George Greig, the publisher. Among the many gathered were the hateful merchants who passed themselves off as medical men with their poisonous patent medicines; they were the true impostors here. I could be hanged for my disguise, but theirs was the true imposture, the greater lie. People died for it.

"You disapprove of the extravagance, Dr. Perry?" said a woman I recognized from other balls, the fiancée of an officer, as I recall, misreading my expression.

"How could anyone disapprove of anything so delightful?"

"And yet you disdain those in possession of it."

"I disdain good instruments turned to bad ends."

"Is beauty not an end in itself?"

"For many."

"But not for you."

"I admire beauty, and enjoy it, but I cannot help thinking of the stain."

"Admit it. You are a man of good works, Doctor."

"You make it sound like an affliction," I said.

"You must admit, there's hardly anyone duller than those devoted to the vice of good works. God preserve me from good men."

I wondered if this was a way to sound out my feelings on Miss Georgiana, who'd become conspicuously devoted to good works since our return from the Eastern Cape.

"You would keep bad company?" I smiled. It was dangerous to flirt with another man's fiancée, but it was hard to avoid, here where flirtation was as popular as whist.

"I would keep interesting company," she said.

"Ah, well. Then I won't keep you," I said.

The line got a laugh, as I hoped it would; I bowed and moved off into the crowd.

I was crossing the foyer on my way to the banquet hall when I heard my name and looked up, thinking I'd been called. A small knot of men stood at the base of the staircase, evidently discussing me.

"Is there anything the doctor doesn't inspect?"

There was a reply I couldn't hear and a laugh. I paused beside a column to listen.

"It's *said* he's the natural son of the Earl of Basken..." one said.

"Or Lord Somerton," another added.

"Certainly, the doctor appears *young* enough to be His Lordship's son."

"No one knows."

"He's like Athena, sprung from the head of Zeus."

"Perhaps he's like Athena in more ways than one?"

"His brilliance?"

"He is an uncommonly *delicate* man."

"Gentlemen," I said, as I stepped out from the column and passed near their circle. I was alarmed to realize that I recognized only one of them. My reputation extended beyond my ken; I was widely known and evidently envied.

I left the ball soon after, claiming that a medical emergency called me away. In truth I had lost my taste for the intrigues of society. I had begun to hate public dances, where I had to share my friend. I was jealous, fearful, a distasteful possessiveness had taken possession of me, visiting me in dreams of betrayal, dreams of being mocked by my love.

When there was nothing to lose, I had feared nothing. But now Lord Somerton's friendship, the esteem of his family, our intimate dinners and the sunlit apartment at Newlands, my brace of grey horses and a red carriage, my good name—it was a lot to lose. And it should have made me cautious, but it made me belligerent instead in the face of any threat, quick to parry danger. The lesson learned too well in youth: to overcome an adversary, seize the offensive. I had not yet learned the limits of this. Though I would.

What is it men see in a fuck out of doors? Something agricultural in the whole affair. I understand a preference for open windows, the scent of the sea, the sound of the surf coming through; fearful as I was of observation, that was a pleasure. Flesh on flesh in the cool of the evening. The sound of rain against the flagstones or steps.

But I never understood his predilection for a fuck outside; Lord Charles showed a decided preference for it. I did not. As I lay on my back looking up into the treetops silhouetted against the cloudless sky, I recall saying (politely, I thought), "Could you finish," breathless. He grunted in reply. Back aching as he pressed me against the ground, back and forth, up and down against the packed earth until I burst out laughing, begging him to stop, finding the whole too hilarious for words, and he stood, straightened, yanked up his breeches. It was a while before he wanted to have sex again. Nevertheless we met daily, spoke late into the night. Our days and nights settling into sweet routine. Indifferent to the consequences, to the possibility we might be observed.

It was many months—perhaps a year—before he summoned me to Government House one afternoon, calling me away from my hospital rounds; I found him in his office, agitated, pacing.

"I've had a letter," Somerton said, holding out to me a page that I did not take. "From the colonial administrator in London."

"Bad news," I said. It had not occurred to me he might be offered a commission elsewhere.

He turned toward the window, his back to me, and said, "He urges me to marry."

I felt the air go out of me. I reached out a hand to steady myself against a chair. "I see. And will you?"

"I told him it's impossible."

I was embarrassed by my relief. "Is it?"

"There's only one woman I could marry."

"Elizabeth," I said. Absurdly, I felt wounded, even as I knew his statement was just.

"Only one woman living." He turned to me.

It seemed an unkind joke. "Do you mock me?" I asked.

"I would marry you."

"Ask anything but that."

"I am offering you my love," he said. I noticed he did not pace. He did not move from the window. His stillness unnerved me.

"I believed I was already in possession of it," I said.

"Then," he smiled, "I am offering you my good name."

"It's a very good name, but it would be a poor bargain for me, surely."

"Must you speak of marriage as if it were a trade in horseflesh?"

"Why must you pretend it's not? When a man marries, he gains a wife and her estate. From his perspective, it naturally appears a romantic proposition. A woman loses her name and her property. I'd lose far more than that."

"I'm not afraid of talk," he said.

"I'd be a scandal," I said.

"You'd be a sensation."

"I'd be a spectacle."

"You'd be my wife."

"I would not be a doctor. I could not practice medicine."

I could see that Somerton did not understand, and it pained me. I hardly understood myself the dread I felt.

"I love you," he said. As if it were irrefutable argument, drawing that weapon so often used against women, to yoke them to impossible lives; *I love you*, that bludgeon.

"There are more important things than love," I said.

"No," he said. "There are not."

"I could be court-martialed for what I've done," I said.

He knew as well as I that impersonating an officer was a crime.

"It did not harm d'Eon's reputation," he said, recalling the late French diplomat, "when he was discovered to be a man in women's clothes."

"He was French," I said, as if that explained the matter. "And an aristocrat, and his secret wasn't discovered until he was dead. Which I do not intend to be any time soon." I smiled. He did not. He turned away to look out over the gardens.

"When I married Elizabeth, everyone was against us. We didn't care."

"You were young—and youngest children. You had less to lose."

"I don't want to lose you," he said. I could not tell if it was anger or sorrow in his voice.

"You won't. I'm here. Dr. Perry, at your service." I bowed to his back.

His hand struck the wall with a bang and I stepped back, startled by the sound.

"By God, you're stubborn," Lord Somerton said.

I felt light, unmoored.

"I would not be here if I were not," I said.

Cloete hurried in. "Everything all right, sir?"

"Perfectly," Lord Somerton said. "We're done. Thank you, Doctor. That is all."

I could not explain to him my reasoning. I barely understood myself, why I could not marry the only man I had ever loved or ever would. I could not explain—perhaps I did not grasp myself—that I had to give up the *second*-greatest love of my life, Lord Charles, to preserve the first: not medicine, but the liberty of my own mind. The right to think and speak and move as I chose, not as others bade me. To experience life on my own terms. The only liberty worth the name. Even if it came at a terrible price. As it would.

It wasn't money that tempted me to continue in my profession, or even honor. Certainly not comfort or wealth; I knew I'd have had a great deal more of both as Lady Somerton. It was something less tangible, far more valuable. Something akin to the way I'd felt when we rode out onto the Cape Flats together or on our long journey to the Xhosa, or when I'd first put on the clothes of a young boy—free to see with my own eyes, to meet life on my terms. Though my actions might be circumscribed by principle and exigency, by military orders, I was no longer beholden to anyone to dictate my perceptions. Although my life was predicated on a lie, a masquerade, it made possible an honest life: I might have to lie to others, but I did not have to lie to myself. Never to myself.

When I fell ill a few days later, it seemed as if my own spirit had turned against me, doubting my decision. I felt sodden with grief, heavy and ill at ease. My feet swelled in my boots, my breasts and joints ached. The least foul smell— of which there were many in the Heerengracht—left me light-headed and sick to the stomach. When my symptoms worsened, I took to bed for a few days. Which gave me time to think. To consider Somerton's proposal and my symptoms. To realize what was wrong. To realize what ailed me: I was pregnant.

I wanted to tell Somerton. But I knew I couldn't. Instead I

imagined sending a message asking him to meet at Newlands. How we would meet on the veranda there, in the warm evening, listen to the wind in the trees like distant surf.

I imagined our conversation so often that I began to believe it had transpired. Perhaps it did. Perhaps I only wish it had.

"I'm to have a child," I might begin.

"Are you quite certain?"

"I *am* a doctor. It's not a difficult diagnosis."

"My God." He'd walk to the balustrade, brace his arms, look out over the country he governed. He could command troops, stifle a free press, but he could not stop biology.

"What will you do?"

"I can't have it here, obviously. No one must know."

"Is there anything to be…done?"

"It's too late."

"So there's only one thing for it—"

"Yes," I said. "I'll go away and—"

"We shall marry, after all." Perhaps he'd smile.

"Don't be absurd."

"I eloped with Elizabeth. We were happy for twenty-seven years."

"The governor cannot elope with his doctor. His *male* doctor."

"But you're not male."

"Your powers of observation are dazzling. *QED*."

"Do not take that tone with me," he said.

"Forgive me. I take that tone with everyone *but* you."

"What will you do?" he said again.

"What women in my condition have done for centuries."

"I trust there has never been a woman in your condition."

"Perhaps not. I will…make arrangements."

"You don't intend to keep it, then."

"I don't appear able to keep anything I love."

The conversation, when it occurred, did not go as I had imagined. The night I went to see him, nothing went as planned.

To understand that night, it's important to understand this: a few weeks earlier, I'd been called to treat the wounds of Sanna, the hermaphrodite whose freedom I had purchased the year before. I'd thought to free her from the traffic in flesh that the Dutch slaveholder had put her to, lending her out to local landowners as one might a sow, for the pleasure of the rare experience of her. But my gift had proved a curse. Freedom is useless—worse than useless—where one is merely free to starve. When I was called to treat her wounds, I learned that she'd been beaten by a sailor who'd bought her time at a local tavern in the port, only to be outraged when he found she was not fitted to the form he had expected. Her face was bruised, a rib broken, but she'd survive. I was ashamed to have bought her freedom only to find I'd shackled her in another way.

I'd hoped to help. But freedom is not a virtue if you lack the money to make your way. *Freedom* was a dirty word for what I'd really offered.

I was grateful when Georgiana agreed to look in on Sanna when I was called away to Hemel-en-Aarde, to consult on the new leper hospital being built there. I worried for Sanna, even though she assured me that selling herself was an improvement over being sold. She would return to work eventually, I knew, but for a time at least she might rest from her labors. That endless labor of women: comforting men.

* * *

I was on my way back from Hemel-en-Aarde a week later when I stopped by Newlands to speak with Lord Charles, to tell him the news—that I was pregnant. I had sent word ahead that I would visit, but I could not be sure he'd be free, or even there; I almost hoped he wouldn't be.

What did I hope he'd say? It was ridiculous. A myth, like that of Cupid and Psyche, that love could overcome all obstacles. I knew better. All around was evidence to the contrary— enslaved women forced into sex with men they loathed; free women forced by penury into the arms of those they did not desire, forced by necessity to marry. Love had little to do with it. The sort of love we had was like the *fynbos* and *proteas* that bloomed there—peculiar beauty that could not survive outside this small place. Still, stupidly, I imagined us.

It was approaching eleven or midnight when I arrived, but the library was lit and light spilled onto the veranda; I had tied my horse and was walking toward the steps that rose to the Palladian apron when a figure stepped out from the darkness, having evidently just left the house by the servants' door.

I was startled, then shocked. It was Sanna.

I could think of only one reason that she'd be here at this hour, so late, alone. I felt as unsteady as I had years before when I'd seen the blue skirt of a woman slip behind Somerton's office door, prompting my duel with Cloete. The air felt thin, breakable. There could be no other explanation. What else would bring Sanna so far from town so late at night, unless a gentleman had sent for her, requested her presence? She'd reconciled herself to the ways of men, made her living as she could, but I was unreconciled. I felt ill at the thought that my friend, my beloved, could be among her patrons, cruel. I'd wondered if he'd known her. It hardly mattered if he hired her for himself or friends, powerful men he sought to impress by providing rare pleasures. I felt sick and sad. I felt revulsion rise, then rage. I heard men's voices from inside, spilling out into the night.

"Dr. Perry," Sanna seemed equally surprised to see me. "Are you only just arriving?"

"I might ask the same of you," I said. "I had news to deliver to the governor, but it can wait. I will see you home. These roads are not safe for a woman alone at night." I helped Sanna up into my carriage.

"How gallant," she said.

"No. How ungallant."

When Somerton inquired the next day about my failure to appear at Newlands, I said that I was sorry, that I had been detained by a patient in urgent need of care, had had no time to send on word.

"I am sorry," I said, and I was.

Lord Charles seemed unconcerned, even cheerful. "I was wrong the other day," he said, "about the letter; there is no need to alter our current arrangement. For the present, in any case."

"No," I said, "no need at all."

Because I could not explain to Somerton my urgent need to depart the Cape, I did not request a leave to travel. I simply left. Knowing it might cost me my commission, that I could be court-martialed, jailed, hanged. One of the Malay women I knew from the Rainbow Balls had family on the island of

Mauritius and spoke with admiration of the midwives and local healers there. I told her I was eager to make a study of the local techniques.

It was hard to tell on the crossing if I was sick from the sea's raging or from the child within me, but I spent the entirety of the journey to Mauritius in my cabin, grateful to Dantzen for making my excuses to the captain (whose dinner invitations I declined each night), still more grateful for the cool cloths he brought and fresh linens, and for his gentle care of Psyche. Who, like me, detested sea voyages. The creaking of the ship's timbers, the howling of the wind, the *whump* of water on the hull left me longing for land, for sunshine, for steady earth beneath my feet. So often taken for granted.

Once we arrived, I dispatched Dantzen to a house in the capital of Port Louis to care for Psyche, while I visited midwives in the countryside; I explained it was no place for man or dog, as cholera was said to be taking hold in the mountain villages in what was soon to become an epidemic. I said I might be gone six months. I depended on him to forward messages and any mail, but to reveal to no one my location. If I did not return in seven months' time, he was to voyage back to Cape Town with Psyche without me. I left ample funds at his disposal. If Dantzen was afraid for himself or for me, he had the decency not to express it.

On the solitary ride to the village, I shed my uniform for a woman's loose cotton frock. Once there, I let my hair grow long, my body plump; I no longer bound my breasts and my belly swelled like a spinnaker. As I grew heavy and stupefied with the child, my body ached. My breasts swelled so much they pained me when I turned in bed, as if sandbags lurched beneath my skin. The Mauritian midwife who attended me massaged oils infused with eucalyptus and wintergreen and rosemary (brought from the Company's Garden) into my hands and arms and thighs and belly to relieve the swelling and restore the circulation, but still I was weak. I could not keep down food, and when eventually I gave birth on the mud floor of the hut where I had lived for months, I was near delirium. Despite all my training, I was of no use. Nearly fainting with fatigue despite the painful spasms, I squatted on the floor, held up by a nurse on either arm; leaking water and piss, then shit and blood, I expelled the child and lost consciousness. When I came to, I had soaked the sheets I'd brought. Despite the fever raging in the village, the midwife was true to her reputation and vocation and did not abandon me, when reasonably she might have.

They fed me meat broth and marrow, venison and pork that I was too weak to refuse. I was delirious for a time—for what seems now like months but must have been only a few days—while I lay bathed in sweat and dazed with a fever. I heard a baby wail and had a brief bolt of memory—as if a window had been flung open on a familiar landscape—of an infant swaddled tight, skin webbed blue with veins, red with the exertion of crying, crooked in my arm, its mouth fastening finally on my breast with an ache of pleasure and pain, and then a sense of drowning and wetness at my waist, then blankness. I dreamt that Somerton came to me and held my hand; I dreamt that we were on a ship together, sailing back across some broad blue swells under a tranquil sky, sails filled, my body wet with sea spray.

By the time I recovered my senses, the child was gone. The nurse simply shook her head when I asked about the baby. I was not surprised, but I felt the news like a bludgeon blow to the chest.

"Dead," I said, laying my head back against the pillows.

"Oh, no, is a healthy boy, screaming with life."

I laughed. A boy. Dr. Perry had given birth to a son. "Bring him to me. I wish to see him."

She shook her head again.

"Where is he now?"

"It's best not to think on it."

"Where is my son?"

"He's gone to good Christian family."

"By God, I will see my child or there'll be hell to pay."

Had I had the strength then, I might have caught up with them, tracked down the adoptive parents and explained the mistake. That I wanted my child as I had not wanted anyone or anything ever except to learn, an urgency like that of the waves of contractions that had swept me like a rough tide. I sat up, pushed aside the bedclothes, stood up, and fainted to the dirt floor.

When I came to, the room was dark, the air cool, the sound of crickets or frogs, the hum of life renewing itself. Somewhere out there my son was sleeping or perhaps crying out for me, the mother he would never know. Limbs leaden. Mind numb. I felt I should never rise. Days passed. I took no care or notice of my soiled clothes, my matted hair, the sour stench of my own skin. Had the nurse not come to change my gown, to wipe my skin down with lemon and water, I'd not have washed for weeks. I saw no point. Time hung still as a noonday sun on the equator. Still as the air over a becalmed sea. Heavy and threatening.

I let myself drift dangerously into reverie, fantasy. Like

the women in the new Waverly novels, I allowed myself
to imagine our future: Somerton's relief at my return, my
confession, our reconciliation, private vows. It would be odd
to have Georgiana for my daughter but not impossible. I
imagined that I might yet find my son, our son, that I would
tell Somerton I had changed my mind and we would marry.
Ambition no longer seemed my anchor, but affection. It
seemed possible, in the sunny delirious days that followed my
confinement, that I might have other children, might be the
mother of lords.

As days passed, my breasts ached with milk, grew heavy,
then hard with what felt like pebbles shoved beneath my
tender skin until I wept, grew feverish, vomited, dazzled with
pain: the midwife pressed warm cloths to my breasts until the
ache passed and the fever broke. When it did, my heart was
dead, dried up, hard. As the milk in my breasts.

When I was reunited with Dantzen in the capital three weeks
later—nearly seven months after I'd left him and Psyche in
Port Louis—he seemed startled by my transformation, although I had resumed my uniform and boots. He remarked
on my loss of a full stone's weight, expressed concern that I'd
been ill with fever. I was glad to find him and Psyche in fine
form, robust and relaxed after their half-year sojourn. But I
was unsettled by Dantzen's report that he'd had no replies to
my letters to Lord Somerton. I knew Lord Charles must be
angry—at my refusal of his proposal, at my disappearance—
but to have replied to none of my letters since our arrival
alarmed me. I had expected a reprimand, perhaps a threat.
But there had been no word at all.

The journey back was rough—the Indian Ocean unruly

that time of year—and my imagination unruly as well. I became convinced that Lord Somerton had fallen ill again in my absence, which would explain the lack of correspondence. I grew panicked by anxiety for my friend's health. As soon as I stepped up onto the dock at Table Bay, I hired a carriage and went directly to the Government House, only to find him gone. I feared the worst. But Cloete clarified the matter quickly: the governor had sailed for England the month after I'd left for Mauritius; there was nothing to fear; he would be returning shortly with a wife. Lady Poulett.

When the invitation came months later, I could not refuse it; I agreed to join Cloete and Lord Somerton's son Henry to row out and greet the returning couple.

The day of Somerton's return, we met at the docks at dawn and rowed out in grim silence; the oars pulled through the light chop toward the ship anchored in the bay. The splash and draw and patter of water on the gunnels the only sound beside the water breaking on the bow. I was silent, watching the waves and the ship ahead of us.

"Are you unwell, Doctor?" Cloete asked.

"Should I be?" I said.

"I have been waiting all morning for you to make a witticism about the governor's new wife."

"Is matrimony a matter of levity?" I asked.

"Well, no," Cloete said. "Perhaps not."

"Never stopped you before, Dr. Perry," said Somerton's son.

"And what is this obvious witticism that I have evidently overlooked?" I asked.

Cloete colored, evidently embarrassed to be drawn into making fun of His Lordship in front of his son.

Henry put him at his ease, smiling, clearly comfortable with the boat's rocking, as if the sea were a cradle, and I realized for the first time that he was a young man made for ocean voyages and likely would make many, as I hoped fervently not to do.

"It's obvious, is it not?" Lord Somerton's son said. "Given my father's well-known affection for animals, is it surprising that he chose a pullet for a wife?"

Cloete laughed, delighted.

But I was in no mood for levity. My heart was sick, dark as the sea that late-November day.

When we pulled alongside the ship, the ladder was let down and we climbed it, arriving on deck to find the couple awaiting us. The fifty-year-old lord and his thirty-five-year-old bride. Somerton smiled, embraced his son, greeted Cloete, then looked to me; coolly, eyes dispassionate as a falcon's as they met mine, he said, "Dr. Perry, may I present my wife."

CHAPTER EIGHT

HEAVEN AND EARTH

Was it cruelty or kindness that prompted Lord Somerton to include me in their party after the arrival of his wife? I do not know, even now. The dead know what happens, not why. I had been prepared, on hearing of his marriage, to be mustered out of my apartments at Newlands to make room for Lady Poulett—that Great Hen—who, I was sure, would wish to make arrangements for companions of her own. But no such order came. To the contrary, every effort was made to maintain our previous intimacy, as if no interruption had taken place, as if they had always been the happy family and I a welcome friend and guest.

Perhaps Lord Charles feared a sudden change in our domestic arrangements might fuel the rumors that we each still heard, of an unnatural attachment between us. Perhaps his marriage had silenced such talk, or soon would. Was that why he'd married? To quell gossip? I couldn't ask. We behaved as if nothing had changed. Of course, everything had changed; Lord Somerton and I no longer met after dinner to discuss politics and gossip and retire to bed or a convenient desk. He did not quietly enter my rooms by darkness, as he had. No one spoke of love.

A week after the couple's return, a lavish dinner was held to celebrate. Lord Charles told the assembled guests his usual stories of horses and hunts, his eyes never meeting mine, passing over me as if my chair were empty, a slight only I would notice. In manner he was perfectly correct toward me, but appeared utterly indifferent. I felt the change like a drop in barometric pressure, the sudden downdraft of cold, presaging rough weather.

I recall a piece of parsley rode up and down at the corner of his lip as we dined that night with four dozen of their closest friends to celebrate the couple's safe return; I watched it as I might a fly. When he smiled, it rose to his cheek. There was a clatter of plates and silver as we sipped soup, tore apart the delicate carcasses of birds shot that same day, chewed.

I was seated to Lady Somerton's right, as if I were an honored guest, but I suspected it was perhaps to keep me from being seated nearer to her husband. She need not have worried: physical proximity did nothing to warm him toward me, to counter his implacable *froideur*. I had stood beside him in the drawing room before dinner and found him distant and chilly as the icebergs of the newly discovered Antarctic.

It pained me to hear her referred to as *Lady Somerton*, as if she had become a part of him, shared his skin. I shrank from their company as I might have from a pox, a plague that I knew would leave me scarred. Before dinner I had avoided the happy couple, moved to the far side of the drawing room, to a knot of portly men and women, among whom Georgiana stood like a gazelle among Cape buffalo.

A hideous epergne stood in the middle of the table, a monstrous trinket that Lady Poulett had brought from London,

along with her monstrous entourage; I amused myself by leaning this way and that in such a way as to remove a mouth or
an eye from my tablemates, visually beheading the guests; all
the while carrying on the required conversation with the lady
to my left.

Gone was the diverting talk of politics, gossip, and pets; now
we spoke of the weather.

"The weather has been strange," someone was saying.

"It is not *English* weather," Lady Somerton observed with a
small frown of dismay. As if weather were a personal affront.

"It is not England," I said, more curtly than I intended. "But
it has its compensations."

"And what might they be, Doctor? Do illuminate us." Some
member of her coterie spoke out of the gloom of faces.

"The beauty of morning fog on Table Mountain," I began,
selecting a small green apple from the bowl in front of me
and commencing to pare it with a knife as I spoke. "Covers
the mountaintop modestly by morning, like a lady wrapped
in her shawl, but as the day progresses and grows warm, she
drops it"—I let the peel collapse onto my plate—"to reveal
her lovely décolletage."

There was a grunt of disapproval from somewhere down the
table. Lord Somerton signaled for more wine. Georgiana did
not meet my eyes.

Was I trying to shock? Perhaps. Increasingly I was not sure
why I acted as I did, compelled by some obscure desire to
disrupt the placid surface, the suffocating complacency, the
provincial spell that seemed to have been cast since the Lady
Hen's arrival the prior week. I, who had been so careful with
my words, so strategic, now sought any ardent response. Even
outrage. Provocative for the sake of provoking.

If she was shocked, Lady Somerton did not reveal it. She reached for my hand and pressed it gently beneath her own, as if offering comfort for a loss. A gesture of solicitude more stinging than any rebuke. Her fingers almost perfectly covered my own. She looked down at our hands.

"You have uncommonly delicate hands, Dr. Perry."

"A surgeon's hands, Your Ladyship."

"They have almost a woman's grace."

I wondered whether this was flirtation or accusation; I could not know. Miss Georgiana had said much the same thing years ago; I wondered what she might have told the new Lady Somerton.

"That's most curious," I said, more loudly than our proximity required, "as they haven't touched a woman outside a surgery in years." I meant this as a joke, but it sounded like regret.

She raised her eyebrows. "Indeed, sir? Is there no remedy?"

"Beautiful women are always tonic," I replied. "But in my experience, love's the one disease without a hope of cure. In my professional opinion, Lord Somerton is quite beyond the reach of medical assistance."

Encouraging laughter from a few of our dining companions relaxed me.

"And you?" Lady Somerton inquired.

"I am working on a vaccine," I said. "Physician, heal thyself."

"I'd not have thought you were a *man*"—Bishop Burnett paused long over the word—"to quote scripture, Dr. Perry."

I ignored the remark, keeping my eyes on the new Lady Somerton. But I wondered what the bishop knew, what he guessed. I was relieved when a servant's arm came between us, lifting my plate and breaking the spell.

"You'd be surprised the things men will do when inspired by the presence of a beautiful woman." I smiled at Lady Somerton.

"Ignore Dr. Perry, darling," Lord Charles called down the table to his wife, for all to hear. "He's a most remarkable physician, but in everything else he is perfectly absurd."

I hoped the heat in my face was not obvious to others.

I had seen this side of Somerton before—superior, dismissive. But I had not had to suffer it. Now I would. It's curious that in contrast to war, in society the direct assault is harder to parry than the indirect; blunt insult left me no recourse but to leave or to laugh. I could not afford to leave.

Bishop Burnett rose and touched his glass with a knife to propose a toast to the couple's happiness and good health. I wished them misery.

At dinner that night, I was struck that Lord Somerton's good cheer seemed forced, fragile, and I was surprised and gratified. Throughout the evening, I observed the couple; Lord Somerton was courteous to a fault, smiling, deferential, admiring of his wife's good taste, but they betrayed no hint of intimacy, neither with teasing nor with pet names, their relations utterly absent of the easy, sporting affection that had defined our own and those with his children, His Lordship's intimate relations. I tried to take comfort in this, but I knew that I'd not seen him with the first Lady Somerton—that this alteration might simply be the man in love.

At dinner, talk was of a new sonata by Beethoven. The death of Napoleon, the scandal of the waltz—though by now it could hardly be considered scandalous anywhere but in the colonies, where change came slowly, where conventions were honored as cant.

Lady Charles had brought with her an entourage of maids and servants, relatives and friends. Among them was her niece, a pretty, slight thing with a fixed compressed smile and the heart of a general. In another century, another sex, she might have arranged battle plans rather than dinner parties or written laws or commanded a steamship to cross the Atlantic. She seemed hard in the way of those for whom the material world is all. As if she were indulging us in our airy talk about art and morality and books, baffled by complexities she didn't recognize or acknowledge.

I could not help noting the dull companions the new Lady Somerton attracted—but the Somerton girls seemed to adore her, asking her about fashion and dances at Almack's; they admired that she had a standing invitation there—where, we learned, she had first met their father one evening last March.

But it was her niece's fiancé who most fascinated me; he was almost fashionable, his clothes of a modish cut but oddly disarrayed—his cravat tied more like a noose, his buttons misaligned by one, one cuff displayed, the other tucked up a sleeve. He seemed oblivious of all but his good fortune in being engaged to the delicate general beside him. She was, it seems, a distant cousin, whom he claimed to have known and loved for a dozen years—*nearly his whole lifetime!*—a fact he stated as if it were fate, as if it had the power to amaze him, his great good luck. (She claimed to have known him only three years, a fact she repeated with equal persistence.)

He was that breed of young man who is a tame pet for powerful women—quick with tasteful gossip and to confirm the prejudices that passed for opinions among the matrons he attended—kept around to fetch things and to marry their younger relations. A perfect specimen.

The most interesting bit of news came from him, that unlikeliest source. He claimed to have met an American sailor in port, who had told him of a bachelor tax in the new American state of Missouri.

"Would it were enough to induce *you* to take a wife, Dr. Perry," Lady Somerton said. "I understand you are a confirmed bachelor."

I wondered what she'd heard of me.

"One hears you have broken many hearts," said the niece.

I glanced at Georgiana, who thankfully was absorbed by her own young man, Captain Glover, whom I recognized from the ball the previous year. A lifetime ago. A dull but harmless fellow, from what I'd gathered since.

"I fear that I'm the one who is brokenhearted," I said. Lord Somerton did not appear to hear the remark, but Bishop Burnett watched me openly.

I was saved from further discussion of heartbreak by Lady Somerton's niece, who was now holding forth on novels and plays being entirely unsuitable for young ladies, filling their heads with notions of romantic tragedy, which could only do them harm when life itself is not romantic in the least. When I suggested that Shakespeare's plays might perhaps be granted an exemption from her censure, she compressed her lips into a smile of frank condescension.

"They're so uneven, and coarse," she said. "A queen falls in love with an ass."

"Bottom."

"My point exactly," she said.

"And does not the beauty of the language redeem it?"

"It's far worse that the language is appealing, disguising a thousand sins against good sense. I consider them entirely unsuitable for young ladies."

"They were suitable for a queen," I could not help noting.

"A queen is a general in skirts," she said, making an observation I'd often heard Lord Somerton make. She surprised me.

She was an odd-looking girl, almost pretty but not quite; her features too soft; she had qualities one wanted to call *pretty* but somehow weren't; it was as if they were only partly formed, slightly blurred like an infant's. She had an unfinished look, which might have been becoming were she not so dull, her opinions ugly. I tried to discern in her some of Lady Somerton's qualities, but whatever Lady Somerton thought of all this, she did not say.

Only as dinner concluded did Lady Somerton lean near me and whisper, "I hope my niece did not distress you unduly, Dr. Perry. You do seem a person of uncommon sensibility. I had a cousin once who claimed that hearing bad poetry made her physically ill. I hope you are quite well."

I came close to liking her then.

As the ladies excused themselves from the dining room that night, I risked indiscretion by detaining Miss Georgiana as she passed and inviting her for a walk in the Company's Garden. *Meet me in an hour among the lemon trees*, I whispered. She frowned as she moved on. I did not know if she had heard me, if she would come. I longed to slip away from the crowded room to have a thoroughly sensible talk with her in fresh air; I longed to know what she thought of her father's bride.

I had tried to engage her in private conversation in the

drawing room before dinner but failed. I was not sure if she was observing form or rebuffing me when she'd smiled politely and moved off to greet another guest. I had hoped to be seated next to her at dinner, as had been our custom in the past, but Georgiana was paired with Captain Glover that night, which—to judge by Lord Somerton's expression as we assembled before coming in to dine—seemed to surprise and displease him as much as it did me.

She had been chilly since my return from Mauritius. I suspected it was Dantzen who had inadvertently turned her against me, meaning no harm. I was grateful for the rumor he had spread that I'd gone to Mauritius in pursuit of a lady, only to return brokenhearted, pretending to reveal more than he'd intended to a few inveterate gossips such as Mrs. Saunders and Cloete. I'd read about it in the local papers. Of my mysterious travel and mysterious return. Now, when I told people that I had traveled to Mauritius for reasons of health, they nodded knowingly. Because mine was a forthright answer, of course no one believed me.

Talk among colonial Englishmen in December 1821 was of the discovery of electromagnetism and the collapse of the Spanish colonies in the Americas; "a contagion of independence," Somerton called it, as we took our glasses and drew nearer the fire, and of the dangerous and untoward influence of the radical Simón Bolívar. I didn't mention that I'd known him when I was a child.

"There will be chaos," one man said.

"They are not fit for self-rule," said another.

"Do men learn to rule themselves by being ruled by others?" I asked.

Only the publisher Tom Pringle agreed with me, but he

said nothing, merely raised his eyebrows from across the room as he drew on his cigar. I was surprised to see Pringle there— a hopeful rapprochement. Although perhaps Lord Somerton was simply wishing to win over the local press for the sake of his new bride.

No one spoke of the hangings in Constantinople. Our eyes were trained on the American steamship that had crossed the Atlantic two years earlier, the *Savannah*. And on the first sighting of the new continent at the end of the world, Antarctica. And on the growing unrest in the Americas—the battles for independence and to abolish slavery. Some spoke with fear of the Cape economy's decline since Napoleon's recent death, which was proving catastrophic for the price of port and claret and Cape wine.

I became—as I do when threatened—argumentative.

I brought up the importance of a free press, to which Lord Somerton quoted—as he often did—the American Franklin:

"Even the Americans understand this, Doctor. It's not democracy one wants but the *semblance* of democracy, as Dr. Franklin has said."

"Perhaps had the Americans had more than a semblance of democracy theirs would not be fraying now," Tom Pringle said. "It looks like war."

"One might say the same of the Massacre at Peterloo," I replied.

"Restraining a fractious mob is hardly a massacre, Doctor," Lord Somerton said. He didn't look at me.

"They say hundreds were injured, some dozen killed."

"I can admire a soft heart, Dr. Perry, but a soft head—"

A few men laughed.

"It's not softness that drives sixty thousand men into a

field to demand representation in Parliament, Lord Charles. And it won't be by soft petitions that they'll seek justice, I assure you."

"Oh, *justice*. The French have given the word a bad name, wouldn't you say?"

"It's said, Dr. Perry, that you were a friend of Napoleon's minister?"

"He was my patient, sir."

"Your sympathies are republican?"

"My sympathies are with what is right, whatever the name."

"Hear! Hear!" said Captain Glover, not realizing that standing up for rights was wrong in this company. He coughed into his hand. Perhaps he was right to worry. Perhaps I should have worried more.

"You are an abolitionist, sir?" said one of Lady Somerton's circle.

"I am an advocate for the rights of all men."

"*And* women," Lord Somerton said, as if it were a joke.

"Lord Charles tells me you were acquainted with Mrs. Wollstonecraft," the fiancé said.

I was surprised he knew the name, the work.

"Not acquainted, I'm afraid. But I am a great admirer of her writings."

"You're an advocate for the rights of women, then?"

"I am," I said.

"More like the wrongs," Lord Somerton said.

"Are they so different?" I asked.

"Right and wrong?" Somerton said.

"Men and women, Lord Somerton."

"Surely in your profession, you've noticed a few differences."

There was a general ripple of laughter.

"Fewer than are generally claimed," I said.

"Your powers of discrimination appear to have been impaired by our tropical sun."

"Perhaps my sight's grown keener. Do you not observe that in *some* persons there's hardly *any* difference at all? The hermaphrodite's existence suggests the differences are fewer than meet the eye."

A quiet fell as I raised the indelicate subject. Sanna.

"Surely you don't mistake the exception for the rule, Dr. Perry?"

"The exception *proves* the rule: tests and *affirms* it."

Lord Somerton dismissed me with a turn of his head as he began to converse with Captain Glover on his left, ending the general conversation. I felt the rebuke, resented it.

I looked directly at the governor, speaking of what we'd never spoken, my voice loud over the general murmur of polite conversation: "The manumitted Malay slave Sanna, for example—." I was straying into dangerous terrain, but I waited for him to stop me, to change our course. "Surely you are acquainted with her, Your Lordship? She is said to be a favorite—how shall we say—*topic* among Cape gentlemen."

It was an open secret: the pleasure Cape gentlemen took in sex with Sanna, when it suited them, forced or paid. I'd never spoken of the night that I had found her outside Newlands. The night I'd gone to tell him I was pregnant, a year ago, the night I'd made my choice to leave instead, to go to Mauritius. I suspected he knew her well.

Now he looked at me as if I were a stranger, coldly, as if wondering how I'd come to be in this room. I braced for outrage. I had not anticipated the practiced indifference of the men present.

The men laughed, considered it a joke. Only Somerton, Pringle, and I did not.

It must have been clear that Lord Somerton and I were arguing about something more than politics, our private battle increasingly a public affair. A risk to us both.

I was relieved when the evening drew to a close, to be free to hurry out into the night. I stepped into the garden and found my way along the gravel paths to the lemon grove where Georgiana and I had often met in the past to sit on a bench and talk; I sat down to wait for her. The air was thick with the sharp floral fug of ripening fruit. Perhaps half an hour passed beneath the field of stars before I accepted that she would not come. I was rising to leave when I heard footfalls, looked up and saw Lord Somerton walking slowly past the rosebushes beyond the trees. I nearly called out to my friend, when I saw him pause, cut a flower, trim its stem, and turn around to give it to his lady, who emerged from the dark to stand beside him. They turned together and began walking back the way they'd come, her head gently resting on his shoulder. An unhurried, tender pace.

I stood stock-still, hoping—as I rarely did—to go unseen. They passed on and I stepped out alone into the dark.

After that celebratory dinner, I saw little of my former friend.

I waited for his card to arrive, half hoping none would, so painful had our reunion been. It was customary here as in London for a newly married man to send out calling cards to those friends respectable enough to be retained now that his bachelorhood was at an end. None came. I was not surprised.

We would continue to meet on official business, but it was

clear I did not rank among his intimates. I missed him keenly. Worse than lonely, I felt erased. I seemed a ghost, unseen, without a mirror in which to recognize myself. Except in work. Work my mirror.

But as often is the case, the poison proved the cure: what I dreaded most—separation—revived me. Thrown back onto my work, my few friends (the journalist, the pharmacist), I returned to meaningful pursuits, to the steady effort to understand, to efforts whose outcome might matter and last, unlike dinner banter.

I wondered at all the time I'd wasted in idleness.

It was late December, approaching Christmas, when I arrived home from the hospital one evening to see in the bowl on the table in the hall a calling card—Lord Somerton's. I was surprised at the relief I felt—no, the *joy*—until I lifted it and found beneath it, like a matched glove, another from his wife. I tore them up and tossed them on the fire.

After I received his card, I again joined Lord Somerton's family for the theater or a lecture on occasion; we dined together once more; these were invitations I could not refuse. But our meetings were strained. Lady Somerton's subtle wit seemed at times to betray an understanding of my true identity. I thought sometimes—by the irritated flutter of her fan, the frequency of sighs and coughs—that she was displeased by my presence in their box at the theater or at table, but if she was, she did not prevent it.

Our evenings were diluted now by other visitors in any case, as if I were part of society, not family as I had been. I didn't need to wonder if this was Lady Somerton's doing. But I wondered what she knew of our relationship. What she guessed.

My conversations with her were a careful pas de deux, as I parried inquiries about my family and my origins. In the past Lord Somerton would have protected me, deflected imprudent questions, ended such talk with a glance, but now he hardly seemed to notice I was there. I sensed in my private conversations with Lady Somerton that she guessed that her husband and I were—or had been—intimates. But she said nothing. The unacknowledged hung over us. We dined under Damocles's sword.

The strain of countering Lady Somerton's inquiries grew daily more wearisome. And by the following January, without having made the decision, I found myself in their company less and less, more and more frequently engaged in overseeing vaccinations in Simon's Town and Rondebosch, checking on private patients in Caledon, experimenting with botanicals at Mr. Poleman's lab, writing reports, and battling the poisoners who passed themselves off as apothecaries.

My work absorbed and consoled me.

Increasingly I contrived to spend my time away from Newlands and Government House, to linger in the Heerengracht over my bowl of coffee and the sugar buns that Psyche admired; it was not only Lady Somerton's presence that inclined me to more solitary pursuits but the rumors that found their way to me through Cloete. (Even Dantzen acknowledged, when pressed, that he still heard them.) The whispers of an unnatural attachment between the governor and me circulated still, even now when we were no more than distant acquaintances. I suspected that Bishop Burnett or the pharmacists (who had become my enemies) were behind the rumors, but I had no proof. It became yet another reason to leave town, throw myself into my work, shun society as increasingly it shunned me. I kept my apartment at Newlands, but I was rarely there.

Although Lord Somerton and I rarely met privately, our public collaboration grew stronger as our personal bond ebbed. I sent reports and requests but rarely did I confer with him in person, as I had. My list of private patients increased, thanks to his endorsement of my skill, keeping me away from town to see to their care. I grew wealthy and busy. I wondered if his enthusiastic promotion of my expertise was apology or if it was an attempt to keep me away from Cape Town, inspecting medical conditions far afield. It hardly mattered the reason. My work consumed me. To my relief. Days apart became weeks, then a month.

I returned to my apartment at Newlands one summer night in late February, too weary to continue on to town, expecting to find myself alone; I was surprised to find the house lit, a carriage out front. The new family enjoying a quiet evening together in the country; if I had not been so tired, I might have ridden on. As it was, I hoped I might retreat quietly to my rooms, but I met Miss Georgiana in the foyer. "Do join us, Doctor," she said. I could not decline.

We were seated in the library at Newlands that evening, Psyche in my lap, the women at their needlepoint, as I read. Our first evening alone since their return, three months before.

"Does it have a name, your dog?" Lady Somerton inquired as she pulled her needle through its frame.

"Psyche, Your Ladyship."

"Peculiar name for a dog," Lord Somerton said, as if the

name had not been his idea. I wondered if he could have forgotten.

"You know the story, darling," his wife said. "Psyche was the most beautiful of mortal women, even the gods were envious; so Venus sent her son, Cupid, to poison her. But Cupid fell in love instead. They married..." She rested a hand on her husband's arm.

"All love should end in marriage," said Georgiana.

I wondered where Captain Glover was these days.

"Of course," I said, "the story doesn't end there."

"No, it doesn't," Lady Somerton looked at me.

"How does it end?" Georgiana asked.

"Well, because Cupid was a god and Psyche mortal, it was agreed among the gods that she must never look on him," I said. "Lest his identity be revealed and all lost. The pair lived happily enough, until envious women convinced Psyche that the man she loved was a monster. So one night as Cupid slept beside her, she lit a candle, saw his true form, and lost him forever."

"How sad," Georgiana said.

"Psyche became a goddess," I said. "And immortal for her trouble."

"But she was alone," said Lady Somerton.

"Is that such a terrible price?" I asked.

"Perhaps we should consult Psyche," Lord Charles said, looking to the dog in my arms, then me.

"I fear she won't answer you, my Lord. She's *most* discreet."

"A virtue in a dog, as in a man," Lord Somerton said. It was the first time he'd met my eyes since their return, the faintest warming.

"Indeed," I said.

Outside the windows, night had settled over the bay, the breeze fragrant with gardenia, gone the day's lazy hum of flies and bees and birdcalls, the wind in the trees like the sound of the beautiful dangerous surf.

When a few days later we entered the African Theater together for a performance of *Much Ado About Nothing*, I sensed that whatever Lady Somerton might have imagined or guessed, she had come to a decision. It was settled. As we three ascended the theater stairs, she took Lord Charles's arm in hers and then my own, a gesture I understood perfectly. She had won and she knew it; whatever she knew about me, she would accept me in their house—perhaps recognizing, as I did now, that whatever our past, I had no claim on her husband's affections.

When the letter arrived from Governor Somerton several weeks later, on March 18, 1822, announcing my appointment to the post of Colonial Medical Inspector—the highest rank a physician could attain in the colony—I knew that I had been forgiven, even if I did not know what I'd been forgiven for, what there was to forgive. I was grateful for the authority it granted, the faith in me it betokened. The chance to save lives.

Increasingly I focused on the patent-medicine merchants, whose profitable poisoning of the public they passed off as medical help.

Reading the local paper had become a trial. More advert than news, the Cape *Courant* and the new, independent *South African Commercial Advertiser* advertised "remedies" sold by local shops even as they reported the untimely deaths of those I suspected had been poisoned by the very remedies they took as cure. The papers made no mention of the recent riot at the leper colony; the papers hardly qualified as news at all, but it was a civilizing sign—a sure mark of progress—to have a free press in which citizens could exchange ideas and views, unencumbered, un-harassed by government.

I was sitting in Mrs. Saunders's coffee shop, taking in the morning papers and the companionable bustle of the street outside that April morning, when I read about the death of a young mother; the month before, it had been a child. I threw the paper down onto the table, enraged, then stood and gathered up Psyche. "Everything all right, Dr. Perry?" Mrs. Saunders called across the room. I shoved in my chair and pushed through the crowded café toward the door. "No," I shouted back, as I set out for Tunhuys. "It is *not* right."

The reforms I had in mind will strike any reasonable person as common sense; I sought only to ensure that those who presented themselves in the garb of medical men were what they claimed. Which is to say, I proposed—in my new role as Colonial Medical Inspector—to license only those who could *demonstrate* that they had in fact *been trained* in the medical arts. (One would not think this an undue standard.) But where there is profit there will be outrage at being asked to prove oneself worthy of payment.

As is common amongst those driven primarily by greed, bullying and insults were their principal weapons; where reason failed to argue their case, threat of violence would.

Cloete showed me into the governor's office. I waited in the once-familiar room, noticing once-familiar things—the desk on which we'd entwined our limbs; the window against which I'd braced my hands, the Governor behind me; a marvelously firm, striped settee that accommodated two bodies perfectly. The room and its furnishings loud with the past.

When the governor entered, I was startled, stood, glad that I'd worn my highest red-heeled boots; my best coat. I rested one hand on the hilt of my sword, the other on the chairback. If Lord Somerton was unsettled to see me, he hid it well.

I got straight to the point. As Medical Inspector, I wished to license only those who could prove they had been trained in medicine.

"Demonstrate by what means?" the governor asked, settling into his chair behind his desk.

"The usual standard—a diploma or other writ from a European institution will suffice. It's hardly extravagant to require—"

"Is it really necessary, Doctor?" He'd no doubt heard from the pharmacists on the matter. "It is a *business*."

"It is an *outrage*," I said.

"Men must be free to make a living—"

"At the cost of others' lives? If mountebanks, scoundrels, and all manner of quack are free to practice their pretense of medicine in the Cape, I might as well toss out my own degree."

"Dr. Perry—" His conciliatory tone enraged me, a tone one takes with a child.

"The weight of learning may well hold little weight here, but I caution you that the cost of countenancing such ignorance is high—as you well know, having paid the price yourself."

I saw instantly that I'd said too much. I'd not meant to be cruel in reminding him of his first wife's death, only convincing, but I saw my friend flinch, if evident only in the slight lift of his chin, then the sudden interest he took in a brass button on his cuff.

"You need not tutor me in costs or Cape governance, Doctor," he said.

"I meant only—"

He did not allow me to finish, holding up his hand, palm forward. He did not meet my eye. "I know what you meant," he said. "I know that you mean well, but there are other interests to balance. It is my job to balance them." He lifted his eyes from his cuff. "Will that be all, Doctor?"

"Yes, thank you," I said. It would have to be.

I imagined myself acting on principle, but there was vanity in my proposal too. Personal interest. When he had ratified my plans in the past, his approval had seemed to betoken an allegiance between us akin to the love we shared, but better in that it was public, not private—no possible occasion for shame. I hoped that such public collaboration might continue, despite our estrangement, bear fruit, grow into some good enduring thing. As love had not.

I left uncertain if my recommendation would carry, whether I'd made my case. What I'd proposed seemed so sensible a solution, but I knew that good sense did not always win out— or even weigh heavily in the balance where there was profit to be made.

The following day, I sent the governor a formal proposal for patent-medicine reform and awaited his reply, knowing the measures would have weight only with his support. The proposal was simple—a matter of common sense: the Cape colony's medical code should be amended to require all those who wished to practice as a Physician, Surgeon, or Apothecary first to present the necessary professional documents from the established universities or colleges in Europe. Those suitably qualified would be licensed. The rest would not, and could not practice medicine, poisoning patients for profit. As Medical Inspector, I would review the applications myself.

I waited to hear from him.

I was not surprised when I did not.

You can judge a culture by its medicine, by how it treats its most vulnerable — the ill. In Cape Town there were the leprotic slaves and indentured servants, freed of their obligations only when they could no longer work. There was rampant venereal disease, riots at the leper colony, cholera that was really poverty by another name. There was the slave accused of stealing sugar and tried by the local police by means of a drunken game of Russian roulette, shot dead as punishment without even the pretense of a trial.

We treat the body in isolation; that is our first mistake. From its entry into the world, a body is not alone — singular, but decisively linked, forged by the body that encloses and expels it. Only in death. Only then. Is the body alone. Health depends on treating not simply the body but the bodies that surround it: a system, you might say, a congregation of a sort. The only faith I had.

In the years following Lord Somerton's marriage I had ample reason to wish myself free of Cape Town, away from the chill civility of the governor's house, free of the whole Somerton family, which once had seemed my own. Given my duties as Colonial Medical Inspector and Inspector of Vaccines, and despite being the Governor's Physician, I had ample occasion to leave; I took it.

So I was not displeased to swing up into the saddle that autumn morning in March 1823 to commence my two-day journey to Hemel-en-Aarde, to inspect the leper colony that the governor had established at my recommendation six years before, when we'd first discussed the matter on our journey east, when my concerns had been his own, when the impress of my words was like a seal set in soft wax, which Lord Somerton took up readily, made his own; my cause, ours, as it seemed would also be so.

I knew better now.

Dantzen handed up a parcel tied with twine, overstuffed and straining with its own weight; I tried in vain to decline.

"What is this?" The paper was oily and heavy in my hands.

"Provisions for the journey."

I planned to stop in Caledon, spend the night, then travel on from there. I would not need more than the water I'd brought, the bread, hard cheese. I didn't want to be slowed down, I said. Truth was, I didn't want to appear weak; I didn't want to consider what I might need. I never liked to consider that.

"Doctor hungers same as any man," Dantzen said, bored by my vanity. He stroked the neck of my pony. "I'm the one has to tend you if you come back sick, so don't."

If he was afraid that I might return contagious from my contact with the ill, the lepers, he disguised it well. We were men accustomed to disguise.

He handed up my parasol, red as his own. Psyche barked at a passing horse.

"Fine," I said, irritated, as I opened the saddlebag to add the package.

I could hear Psyche's high yipping behind me as I rode off.

It was approaching noon, the sun heavy overhead and baking the land and my horse's glistening withers, when I stopped to water him and rest beneath a copse of silver trees. When I dismounted to sit in the sort of shade, I was glad to have the goat's-milk cheese, the skin of cool well water, the packet of dried fruit (apples, peaches), the two sugar buns from Mrs. Saunders, and the fat sack of cellar-chilled carrots, sweet and fresh from the Company's Garden. I was grateful for his foresight.

I should have grown accustomed to the beauty of the place, given my frequent visits to the valley in those years, but each time I crested the hill that offered a view of the land below—its vineyards and wheat fields fanned out like hammered brass and malachite—I was struck again by the perfection of the place. Hemel-en-Aarde, *Heaven and Earth*.

No one seemed to know who had named it, though I'd heard a German missionary praise its aptness, given that "the hills are so high, which embrace the valley all around, they seem to touch the sky and you cannot see anything but Heaven and Earth." Dantzen said the name came from a Dutch surveyor, who claimed to have measured heaven and earth there while an angel dragged the measuring chain. (His assistant was named Engel.)

But what I had seen at the leper colony the previous October—after riots had broken out there—recalled not heaven but its opposite. The leper colony had been created by the governor at my recommendation, in a beautiful garden spot in view of the sea but sufficiently remote from town to satisfy the superstition of those who feared contagion. For a time it seemed an ideal solution, despite the lack of medical supervision. I was hopeful when the new hospital had opened there three years before, but then last October a number of patients had run away, complaining of abuse and starvation. I had traveled there immediately to investigate. My first visit I had been appalled to find patients confined to small rooms, supine on filthy stretchers, too feeble to rise. Forced to work for food, which was then cruelly withheld. I'd had the staff fired, the rations increased, exercise and medical attention ordered. That had been six months ago. Now I was returning to see how matters stood.

The entire establishment was much improved when I returned that March, under the guidance of Mr. and Mrs. Leitner, the Moravian missionaries who were now its superintendents. I was met by Mr. Leitner at the gate, and after taking some refreshment at their home we set out to tour the grounds together. We visited the communal gardens, the kitchen. I was impressed and said so.

"You've done well, Mr. Leitner," I said. "I commend you. Only imagine how much better your patients will fare with a few improvements. In respect to diet, for example—"

"Their diet is ample," Brother Leitner said. Perhaps a touch defensively. "Mrs. Leitner makes sure our charges are well provided for; they have dried peaches for digestion, when available."

"A few peaches are not of the least use," I said, waving a hand as if to clear a foul smell. "Forgive me for being frank. But proper diet is of the utmost importance in these cases."

As we walked the grounds, inspecting the out buildings and hospital, I advised that vegetables should constitute the chief part of his patients' diet. Until vegetables could be procured on a regular basis, beef might be supplied.

"All should have milk, rice, sugar, and coffee daily," I said. "A soldier's rations should suffice." Given the many women, children, and invalids present, soup should be served. Two or three persons should be appointed to cook; Mr. and Mrs. Leitner should serve the food daily to ensure adequate proportions and quality. By no means should raw meat or flour be distributed as rations. A baker should be appointed (well paid, of course), and two persons hired as nurses to see to patients and ensure that medicines were taken as required.

I concluded my recommendations there, not wishing to interfere or overstep.

"You must write to me every week as to your progress, yes?"

Mr. Leitner's face had grown flushed as we walked— from the heat, I supposed—but he declined my proposal to move inside where sun might be avoided. We continued on our walk.

"Forgive me, Doctor," he said, "but you sound more like a hostess outfitting a pantry for a party than a physician."

"More like a general mustering provisions for a war," I said.

As we passed among the houses where the patients lived, I was pleased to observe a marked improvement since my visit six months ago: the patients all looked far better and cleaner, none having the least disposition to mutiny, nor to escape. But I noted nonetheless a disturbing consistency of condition— an unsettling uniformity of illness, unusual in sickness as in health.

Men and women sat in the shade of the houses or lay quietly on cots, eyes dull, too still. Children—even those unaffected by illness—were as lethargic as the elderly, without lessons or games. I paused to squat before a young woman, a mother; I extended my hand in greeting, was surprised to find her own limp in mine and chilled. I stood.

"Are all here in such dire condition?" I asked.

"We turn no one away because of the extremity of the case," Mr. Leitner replied.

"Of course. But I mean has no one come to you more fit than these present?"

"All are welcome here."

"Welcome to die," I said.

"They have a proper Christian burial, Doctor; proper Christian rites."

"I'm sure that's a great comfort," I said.

"Their souls are comforted."

"I would benefit more than their souls," I said, impatient. "Even Christ *cured* the lepers, didn't he? He did not settle for merely harvesting their souls."

I could see that I had shocked him.

"Please," I said. "Tell me about your patients."

His report unsettled me: Of the 156 patients resident there that year, many were very weak and declining. The previous year, he said, "twelve baptized and fourteen unbaptized departed this life," a shocking mortality for any hospital, even a Cape hospital. I couldn't see why 15 percent should die each year from a treatable disease.

"But matters have improved," Brother Leitner said.

"They could hardly have gotten worse."

"Beg your pardon?"

"Continue, please," I said.

"This year," he said, "twenty-five adults and five children have been baptized and eight admitted to the Lord's Supper; ten have passed on."

"*Died*, you mean," I said.

"Yes, but to all glad tidings of great joy were proclaimed," he said. "All are instructed in the blessed truths of the Gospel. Our people are remarkably attentive and devout at all their meetings." He fairly beamed.

"Given the high mortality, one can see why they are inclined to pray."

Leitner praised the Christian goodness of the landowners who'd brought the lepers here, releasing them from their labors.

And that was when I realized what unsettled me. What was wrong. Like a picture hung at a tilt.

Not a single person present was in an early stage of the disease; all were extreme late cases, well developed, save for the few children there with their parents but themselves unafflicted. It should have been obvious what was happening. Of course.

"Might I interview the patients?" I asked.

Leitner looked alarmed. "I beg your pardon?"

"Speak with them," I said. "I should like to hear from them directly about their circumstances, how they came to be here; I should like to interview the children in particular."

Leitner said nothing; I feared he might refuse.

"I wish only to ascertain something of their history," I said, "to better understand their condition, their needs. So we can assist you in meeting them." At last he agreed.

So I spent the morning talking with patients, squatted down beside a woman on a cot, a man leaning against a building, a child, and learned what suspicion had suggested: there was not a single slave among them; all were freedmen, indentured servants, or Khoikhoi. The audacity of it shocked me, even when I thought I was beyond shock now.

When I told Brother Leitner what I'd discovered, he seemed

unconcerned; perhaps he did not understand the import of the evidence before us. So I explained.

"These are all *free* men and women, Mr. Leitner; laborers. Does that not seem peculiar to you? That only free men and women should arrive here requiring your help? Slaves fall ill, the same as any man."

"Are you suggesting that the health of slaves is superior...?"

"I am suggesting nothing of the kind," I said. "I observe that free men are simply freer to die than are the enslaved."

"I don't follow you, Doctor."

"They might have been *saved*, these people, your patients, a cure might have been effected had any care at all been taken with their health early on at the first signs of infection. But no such care *was* taken. Because they are not valuable *property*, their health was of no concern to those who sent them here only after they became too ill to work. They were sent here not to recover their health, but to die."

To his credit, Leitner seemed as shocked as I. He looked out over his charges with the horror of one viewing bodies on a battlefield. He was noticeably pale when I left soon after.

Leitner seemed a good man, well meaning, but his vocation had taken its toll. He was of that breed of dull do-gooders, ostentatious in their self-effacement, who seem to prefer not to trouble themselves over justice in this life, expecting it in the next. In his black frock and white-knotted tie, he appeared a model of Christian modesty; soft-spoken in a manner that was loud, meant to force his listeners to lean close and attend to him—an arrogant modesty. I've found it best not to trust a man who denies his appetites, knowing that such self-control can be a kind of fury, gentleness disguising its opposite.

So I endeavored to be gentle when I sent my recommendations and provisions two months after my visit, when I had
delivered to the leper colony at Hemel-en-Aarde a requisition
of medicines with a set of handwritten directions for the
Leitners' use.

The measures seemed perfectly obvious, but I have learned
that the obvious is often overlooked. Like my own sex—it is
hidden in plain sight.

Rules for the General Treatment of the Lepers, Which It Is Requested Mr. and Mrs. Leitner Attend To:

*1st. The strictest attention must be paid to the personal
cleanliness of the Lepers; their bedding and clothing must
be frequently changed, and they must bathe twice a week
at the least. The children should be bathed daily…*

*2nd. The diet is of great consequence, nothing salted,
such as fish…should be permitted. Milk, rice, vegetables,
and fruit should be used as much as possible; fresh mutton
and soup daily, unless otherwise ordered.*

*3rd. The sores must be washed twice daily with Tar
water and dressed with Tar plaster; the old plasters must
be thrown away.*

*4th. The state of the bowels must be attended to…The
venereal cases must be kept apart from the other, and
treated as ordered.*

*5th. The very bad cases of Leprosy must be separated
from the others, and a sufficient quantity of Wine given to
the sick (from 2 glasses to a pint, daily).*

*6th. The food must be clean and well cooked…the meals
should be almost daily inspected by Mr. and Mrs. Leitner.*

Good order must be preserved, but no cruelty or deprivation of food must ever be resorted to. The parties must be considered not as Convicts, but as Unfortunate. The School and Church should be encouraged, as so should industry as much as possible.

As my visits to this Institution will be frequent I shall from time to time point out any necessary changes…

I concluded with the request that Mr. Leitner *write me every week as to the changes, success, difficulties, &c.*

I hoped they would find them helpful.

I was not altogether surprised when Lord Somerton summoned me to Government House to tell me there had been a complaint; given my efforts to reform the sale of patent medicines, resistance to regulation was to be expected. In truth, I welcomed the occasion to meet with the governor, my former friend, even as we were no longer friendly.

"Let me guess," I said, when I saw the letter on his desk. "The pharmacists have lodged a complaint," I said. "The quacks." I dropped into a chair before his desk.

"It's Hemel-en-Aarde," Lord Somerton said. "Brother Leitner believes that you have exceeded your authority. He wrote to Reverend Halbeck to confirm that you have none over him."

"My God," I said. "What sort of man worries about rank when lives are at stake?"

"That's precisely when men worry about rank, is it not?"

"A soldier doesn't care about the rank of the man who saves him."

"Perhaps not. But Mr. Leitner cares a great deal about this. He is your enemy now."

"No," I said, "leprosy is."

He read aloud to me from the complaint, as if to clarify the matter: Brother Leitner had rejected my recommendations to allow patients to bathe regularly in the sea. He said that he preferred "to hold *services* rather than bathing parades."

"Funeral services," I replied. I was glib, but I understood how serious the charges were. Reverend Halbeck had forwarded the letter to Colonel Bird, who had sent it on to Lord Somerton as a courtesy, as it was a courtesy to tell me of it. It was a warning.

Lord Somerton did not smile, but nor did he reprimand me. I thought he sympathized, as he had sided with sound reason in the past, but all he said was, "You must be careful, Doctor. You're making enemies."

"Disease is my only enemy," I said. *"Honi soit qui mal y pense,"* quoting the Anglo-Norman motto like an incantation. *Shamed be he who thinks evil.*

"I'm afraid it doesn't work that way." His voice was uncommonly subdued. He seemed sad, or perhaps worried. But he said no more about the matter.

"I don't mind making enemies in a good cause," I said, as I stood. "A man is judged by his enemies. All principled men make enemies."

I pretended not to care, to be indifferent to personal criticism. How could I explain that I could not descend to the personal? I had observed how vitally important it was in the affairs of men and in the practice of medicine to be guided by reason, to rise above one's feelings—as I had two years before when Lord Somerton returned with his new wife, as I had done in regard to the child I'd carried. It was necessary in medicine, as in war, to remain objective. I was impersonal in my practice of medicine, as one must be. To see clearly and judge rightly of symptoms, one must observe dispassionately, disinterestedly. My uncle had squandered great gifts on the altar of the personal, picking fights even with his good friend Joshua Reynolds, the famed painter. I would not make the same mistake.

"Thank you," I said. "For letting me know."

Lord Charles was not quick to act on the matter of patent medicines and licensure, but when he did, he was decisive.

Perhaps he grasped the necessity of reform, perhaps he had grown tired of my harangues. Whatever the case, on September 26, 1823 the governor's office issued a proclamation that revised the Cape medical code to ensure that no one could practice medicine without the skill to do so, that all who wished to serve as physician, surgeon, or apothecary must first be licensed and provide documents to attest to their training, whether "a regular Diploma from a University or College, in Europe, or in the case of Surgeons, Apothecaries, etc., of such Certificate as is usually required."

The proclamation controlled the traffic in drugs as well, ensuring that no merchant, trader, or dealer could peddle so-called medicines without first having those drugs reviewed by the Colonial Medical Inspector. Which was to say, me.

The mob that swarmed Government House the next day was impressive, as a cloud of locusts is; almost as soon as the proclamation was made, a deputation of medical-men manqué arrived at Lord Somerton's office, demanding an explanation, outraged that their profits might be curtailed for the public good. Fools though they were, they would not be easily parted from their money.

They did not take kindly to regulation, that enemy of self-serving charlatans everywhere. Their principal complaint contained nothing of principle, mere avarice disguised as right: they had invested heavily to make a profit, and profit they would.

"We've paid to import medicine," one merchant shouted from the crowd. "On the faith of being allowed to sell what's been sanctioned by His Majesty's Letters Patent and by custom and immemorial usage."

It did not help when I pointed out that theirs was *not* an "immemorial usage" but a very *recent* right, granted after British assumption of the colony less than two decades before.

"If my memory serves, gentlemen," I said, "poisoning patients for profit has been a privilege afforded you by the Crown for just eighteen years. Poor as your memories may be, that's hardly time immemorial."

It was a frightening mob, slow to be dispersed, but I was gratified to be united with Lord Charles again. At the time, for a time, we seemed victorious, invincible.

CHAPTER NINE

CAPE OF STORMS

The morning of June 1, 1824, dawned like any other misty winter morning on the Cape. It was a Tuesday, that most undistinguished day of the week, neither a starting point nor a conclusion, unremarkable in every way. Only later would we understand how our lives would be changed.

I was still asleep when Captain John Findlay of the *Alacrity* rose early, as was his custom, to check on ships approaching the port in hopes of claiming a bounty on illegal slavers. Dressed in his gown and stockings, he pushed open the window and looked out over the quiet street, where two boys— one black, one yellow, he said—stood before a placard posted there. Captain Findlay called out to them but they slipped into the morning fog, so he dressed and walked to the sign himself to read the news there and saw the scurrilous placard, claiming to have been penned by a member of the Newlands staff and accusing Lord Somerton and me of unnatural acts. Some say the captain tore it down and tossed it in the street. Others that a cloaked horseman carried it off.

By the time he reported it, the placard was gone.

By the time I reached Mrs. Saunders's café that morning with Psyche tucked under my arm, it was already a scandal.

* * *

The placard was never found. No copy survived. Perhaps it never existed.

But the story did, and it grew.

In the official investigation conducted later that year, Captain Findlay would recall the placard's wording thus (words I try but fail to forget):

A person living at Newlands makes it known...to the Public authorities of this Colony that on the 5th instant he detected Lord Charles buggering Dr. Perry; Lady Charles...had her suspicions...which had caused a general quarrel and which was the reason of the Marchioness's going home—the person is ready to come and make oath to the above.

Had I not known that Lord Charles and I never met alone at Newlands now, that we rarely spoke in private (and only then to discuss matters related to the medical affairs of the Cape), that our relations had become purely professional in the three years since he and Lady Somerton returned from England, I might have credited the account myself. As others did. It had the tang of truth, which pained me. I had often wondered what Lady Somerton knew of our past relations; now I wondered who else knew.

I wondered briefly if Lady Somerton was behind it, hoping to separate us, but it was clear she could not have wished for this. To destroy the man she loved. As the placard threatened to do. I wondered if Bishop Burnett was behind it, or the patent-medicine peddlers.

Despite our estrangement, I went directly to his offices

at Government House when I heard the news, hoping to strategize and to be reassured. Years before, Lord Somerton had said he was not a man to fear a scandal, that his family motto was his own: *Mutare vel timere sperno. I scorn to change or fear.* I reminded him of it when we met that morning to discuss the placard.

"This is not a scandal, Dr. Perry," he said. "It is a death sentence."

Sodomy between men was a capital crime, we both knew. The obvious solution was to reveal myself, my sex, to make it known that I was a woman. Putting an end to the scandal, replacing it with a new one, which any rogue knows is the way to stop a story you don't like.

Neither of us mentioned it. I was grateful he did not ask it of me.

We had made our choices. I would live and die a man. We would fight this libel as men together. Or hang for it.

I did not witness the court proceedings, where the charges against us were aired; I did not need to: they were spoken of everywhere in the dusty streets, in the chill Castle, in the too-bright Company's Garden, the Burgher Senate, the prison, and of course in The Sun, a disreputable public house near the barracks. Not even Mrs. Saunders's shop was safe from talk of it. Kind Mr. Saunders, husband of the baker of sugar buns, commiserated when I stepped into the café: "Why, Dr. Perry," he began, "it's a most diabolical accusation." There was no escaping it, the slander. So many years had passed since we were intimates, it seemed fantastic to suggest we ever were.

Dantzen kept me up-to-date on the Fiscal's inquiry, so I might remain informed without having to suffer through the depositions: he told me of the poor clerk who fumbled while recording the repetitive statements, asking the speaker to stop in order to accurately record the charge against us, confused about the correct spelling of "buggery."

"Not 'buggeruery,'" he was told, "B-U-G-G-E-R-Y." It drew a laugh, I was told.

Over and over witnesses were brought forward to repeat the slander made against us, the placard's accusation, until, lie that it was, it took on a life of its own.

Some witnesses—friends or citizens wary of speaking ill of powerful men—made strenuous efforts to avoid repeating the charge, asking if they might "suggest the particulars delicately"; others tried to cloak it in ambiguity, speaking of our "unnatural practices."

A clerk named Thwaite was mortified to be brought forward to testify against the governor: "I cannot exactly say the identical words," he demurred, "but it conveyed to my mind, that it represented His Excellency and Dr. Perry as being caught in that situation as was unnatural. It had that impression on my mind."

"It is an outrage," I told His Lordship.

"Outrage only fuels the fire," said Lord Charles. "Bishop Burnett claims it is evidence of guilt."

But I knew he felt it keenly. Warmth drained from him, as did color; he left the door to his office open when we met. Calm as he appeared, he was not indifferent to the slander. He found other ways to punish his critics, stop their tongues: he ordered sealed the presses of publisher George Greig, whose *South African Commercial Advertiser* was the first independent newspaper in the colony; then he threatened to have Greig jailed. When Bishop Burnett suggested Lord Somerton might have arranged the placard himself to gain public sympathy for his campaign to crush a nascent free press, he threatened to arrest the bishop, too.

I was hesitant to visit with the governor after the scandal broke, afraid to feed the gossip that engulfed us, but I was more fearful of what my friend might do to suppress such talk. So I went each day to see him, as if nothing had happened.

"We are greatly wronged," I said, speaking loudly in case we should be overheard, in case servants were listening, spies for Burnett or Greig. "But it is a greater wrong to stifle the press."

"Slander does not deserve protection," he said.

"Free speech does."

"Mockery is not meaningful speech, Doctor."

"If men lack peaceful means of expressing their concerns, they will find other means less peaceful."

"Is that a threat?"

"It is an observation merely, Your Lordship."

"I will not have the Crown ridiculed nor its representative; it sows the seeds of chaos and revolution."

If Lord Somerton knew who in his household at Newlands had observed us years ago, who had spied on our intimacy or claimed to have done, he did not reveal it to me, he did not speak of it. We did not speak of it. It had been so long ago.

He punished the powerful who mocked him, but he took no steps to uncover the servant who was said to have observed us. Perhaps there was none. Perhaps he considered it beneath his dignity to punish the weak. His enemies did not recognize the virtue in this, but I did.

A kind of integrity.

There was much to admire in him; I tried to ignore what I did not.

It was Lady Somerton who proposed that we carry on as if nothing had happened, nothing changed, she who insisted we enter the African Theater that night after the scandal broke, attending together as we had planned, Lady Somerton, Lord Somerton, and I. When the audience looked up and saw us enter the governor's box I could hear their collective gasp, their intake of breath abrupt as my own, and my eyes moved to hers. She looked at me and then looked away. She stood at the front of the box as if to make an announcement. *What did she know? What had she seen?* A fixed smile on her slender lips. If she wished to expose me, this would be the moment, the stage on which to do it. I waited for her to speak, to expose us. She inclined her head graciously to the hall. And took her seat. Before the curtain rose and the drama began.

The eccentricities of a powerful man become peculiarities in the weak. A passion for expensive racehorses can seem romantic in a man who can afford to own them; the same penchant appears frivolous, absurd, even corrupt in one who cannot. That, at least, was how Lord Charles's enemies would soon portray it in the London press, his importation of breeding horses, the great mares and stallions, his habit of scheduling meetings around hunts, his plans to build a racetrack. What once had seemed insouciant now seemed irresponsible. And it pained me. I did not want to see him this way, diminished. I did not want to feel I must protect him, to know he could not protect me.

Now when I came to speak of medical reforms, Lord

Somerton spoke of his plans to make improvements to the ball-room; his whims seemed a distraction, delusional, no longer charming. His refusal to see things as they were enraged me. His high-handedness with the press was the act of a desperate man, not a decisive one. But his wounded pride made him sensitive to any slight; any advice I offered was dismissed, debated, or met with silence.

In public we battled the scandal together, the news of which had quickly spread to London. Somerton set to finding the author of the placard and to shutting down the local press, as if speech itself were the culprit, the cause of our trouble. When George Greig was found to have an insulting cartoon of Lord Somerton in his possession—depicting His Lordship as "the Devil flying away with the Fiscal"—the governor had him arrested and ordered out of the Cape colony posthaste.

For my part, I focused on battling a known enemy: the apothecaries with their faux cures, who—despite the governor's proclamation the year before—were daily killing my patients on the Cape, peddling poison for profit. The killers had turned to the courts for relief from regulation. Strength had been my salvation in the past. Challenged, I went on the offensive. But I tried to avoid the battle brewing between my friend and free-press advocates, of which I was one.

"How you can you be loyal to a man disloyal to the principles you hold dear?" Tom Pringle asked me one evening at The Sun, the awful pub in the port that I frequented now to avoid meeting those I knew, a place to hide.

"I am loyal to reason," I said.

"You are loyal to Lord Somerton."

"I am a man of science," I said. "I have no politics."

Neither of us believed me.

But as my friend's actions daily grew less reasonable, I began to have doubts.

In his fury over the ongoing scandal, Somerton sought to punish those he could. He banished Georgiana's suitor, Captain Glover, from the house. He threatened to have the Cape newspapers permanently closed. In the guise of principle. And all of that I might have withstood, accepted, almost forgiven, had he not failed me when I needed him most. In my battle with the faux pharmacists. It was a lucrative business—poisoning patients with false remedies—so naturally we had ended up in court.

"What is it you want, Dr. Perry?" the apothecary Friedrich Liesching demanded when we met before Chief Justice Truter to adjudicate the complaint.

I had begun to wonder myself.

"I would save lives," I said. Aware that daily I was thwarted in the effort. Every day it seemed increasingly unlikely that I would manage to save my own.

"The doctor would deprive us of our livelihood!" another of them shouted.

"Surely that's better than allow you to deprive men of their lives," I said.

"You have no right to interfere with our business, Doctor."

"And you've no right to kill a man for profit, though I grant it's done all the time."

Justice Truter sided with the poisoners, claiming I'd overstepped my authority. But the matter did not end there. When the colonial office overturned Truter's decision, my critics were enraged. They held a grudge. When I refused to license

Liesching's untrained son as an apothecary, he complained to the governor. When I reported the unconscionable sadism of prison guards, my confidential report to Lord Somerton was leaked and I was hauled before another judge, as if reporting the crime were the criminal act. I refused the summons, was threatened with jail. I should not have been surprised when I was notified that I was to be removed from my post as Colonial Medical Inspector for having interfered unduly with the business of the Cape, stripped of my offices and salaries, a mere Assistant Surgeon once more. I turned to Lord Somerton for help.

"The commission found your official correspondence intemperate," Lord Somerton said.

"Had I been temperate," I replied, "nothing would have been accomplished, nothing changed."

"It was a unanimous decision, Doctor," he said, as if that settled the matter.

"That doesn't make it right," I said.

"And who's to determine what is right? *You?*"

It was useless to petition him. Lord Somerton was not a man to concern himself with right or wrong, unless he was the one wronged.

If there was any good to come out of the dreadful placard affair, which dragged on in different form for years, it was that our common enemy served to remind us that we once were friends. We were infamous from the Cape to Coventry; word of our unnatural relations had been debated on the floor of Parliament, published in the *Times*. Wounded as I was by Lord Somerton's refusal to protect me from the Fiscal's wrongful judgment, I was glad to be in daily conversation again with my friend. When society abandoned us, we retreated into the familiar company of one another.

The summer after the placard appeared—in December 1825—Lord Somerton made plans to leave for England to face the charges against him—to face the accusations before Parliament, which had grown from the sodomy scandal to encompass questions about his management of the Cape colony's finances, profligacy, and fiscal irresponsibility—and to retire from public life. I was gratified to be invited to join him, to return to London as the family physician, where we might all of us begin again. I had not finished my investigations into the efficacy of local botanicals; I had only just begun to make the reforms necessary to improve health on the Cape, but I knew that my days here would be hollow without my friend and that my enemies here were now too numerous to ignore.

So on December 23, 1825, three months before Lord Somerton and his family were to set sail for London, I placed a small ad in the Cape *Courant* for the sale of all my "furniture and effects."

I was 30. I would begin again.

I was ready at last to go home.

As we prepared to return to London, I noted how plain the lines of strain had become in my friend's face. He'd aged a decade in two years' time and I worried for him. His unhappiness was stark—too obvious to ignore. He continued to ride and to hunt, but even these pursuits could only temporarily raise his spirits. He returned from his trips to Newlands and Roundhouse weary.

One February night a few weeks before we were to sail for England, we shared a quiet dinner alone at Newlands, he and I; we could allow ourselves this now. There was nothing more anyone could say against us that had not already been said.

I almost never think of it, that night. Our last together in Cape Town.

We were reminiscing about the past, talking of people we'd known, when he mentioned Sanna. "You remember her—" he said.

"The hermaphrodite," I said. "Of course." I'd not seen her in years.

"Georgiana adopted her right before you left us, insisted that we hire her on here as a maid. I had the mad idea she'd driven you away from us. As if by spell." He laughed.

"She works here, Sanna?" I asked, sickened by sudden understanding of that night seven years ago. Before I'd sailed for Mauritius.

He shook his head. "Went back to her people in Port Louis, or a village outside."

"I know it," I said.

"I suppose you do," he said.

For a moment we sat in silence. Almost peaceful, although my heart pounded as if it might burst, as if I had run a great distance.

"Why *did* you leave?" he asked.

"I never left you," I said. "I never would have."

"But you did. That summer you went to Mauritius. Without so much as a note. I could have had you court-martialed for abandoning your post. I could have brought you back in chains."

"Why didn't you?" I asked.

"Would it have mattered?"

I didn't know what to say. "I had good reason to go."

"A woman in trouble, you said."

"That's right."

"Did I know her?"

"You knew her well."

He frowned, as if I might mean Georgiana.

"I couldn't bear to give Burnett the satisfaction—"

"Of what?"

"Being right."

"There's always a first time," he said.

"He'd have ruined you if he'd known the governor's physician was carrying the governor's child." I hadn't meant to say it.

Lord Somerton seemed not to hear me; at least he made no response, staring into the fire.

"You were pregnant," he said. "With my child."

"Yes."

"And where, pray, is my child now?" He did not look at me.

"I do not know."

Was it to repay the hurt I'd felt, that I told him that night? Was it simply too hard to bear the secret alone? Or was it that I hoped somehow that by telling him then, before we left Africa, we might find a way, if not to stay, then at least to find the child and bring him with us? Mad hope. I see that now.

"You do not know." His voice was very quiet.

I knew he would not ask me more.

"A son," I said. "Adopted by a provincial officer, presumably…"

"You didn't bother to find out." He looked at me but didn't seem to see me. "What sort of unnatural monster…"

"I tried to get him back," I said, "but I was ill, far too ill, there was cholera; I thought we might manage it together, once I returned to the Cape, find him, but of course when you returned with Lady Somerton, it seemed—. Well. The subject did not come up."

For a long time we sat by the fire silently looking into the embers, each in his own thoughts, listening to the sap snap as the logs turned to charcoal, then ash.

"My son," he said.

"Our son," I said.

I who had calculated so much and so well miscalculated this. There was one thing more valuable than name, honor, wealth, horseflesh to my friend—family. How had I overlooked so obvious a fact? But I had. Until now. His pallor alarmed me.

"You must take care for your health," I began.

He raised a hand to silence me.

For a long time he was quiet, before he said gently, "Please leave."

I wasn't sure if he meant for me to quit his presence or Newlands or the Cape itself; I felt sure I'd know soon enough. I rose.

"I'm so sorry," I said. I was. I am. Even as I could have made no other choice.

We like to think that there is nothing that cannot be forgiven, no act that cannot be redeemed by love and contrition—that is what religion would teach us—that love and understanding, reason and remorse can be a kind of cure. But we are wrong. There are irredeemable choices. There are unforgivable acts.

The next morning we spoke little. Only this:

"I would have married you."

"I know."

"Then why? Was your name so much more important?"

How could I admit that my name was all I was, all I'd ever had, since my mother's death? There was no one else.

"Words are all we have," I said.

"No," he said. "You're wrong. They're just the echo."

It's ironic, really. My name: *Perry. Parry.* The unintended pun of it. All that would be destroyed in my attempt to parry harm, evade it, so I might live: my past, my sex, my mother, my child, love itself. *Parry,* indeed. From the French *parer,* "to guard, ward off," from the Italian *parare,* "to shield." From the Latin *parare,* meaning "to prepare." Nothing, of course, could have prepared me for this. All that I would lose.

It was impossible, of course, another choice. I would have lost everything if I had kept the child: my work, my reputation, my very name. Everything I was. Everything I am. But I understood in that moment that I *had* lost everything there, in Mauritius, when I gave away the child.

Giving birth, I had felt the thing I'd never felt in all of my labors, all of my years, from Cork to London, Edinburgh to the Cape: I had felt joy settle on me like sunlight through the open windows. I was stunned by the pure pleasure in its aftermath, the honeyed lethargy, drenched in the sweetness; its milky breath, its deep and trustful sleep, how good it was to have it cry and know I could provide all it needed. I had known the deep expansive pleasure of intellectual pursuits, absorption in thought and study, the warmth of friendship, the urgent release of sex, but this was different from all of them. I could spend the rest of my life with my nose buried in the soft dark down of his head, my lips on his tiny ear, his mouth on my nipple, sleeping in my arms, I'd have been content.

It was not for my good name, my reputation, that I sacrificed the child, not for vanity or pride or professional ambition, not even for fear of what Lord Somerton might do if presented with a son he had not known he'd sired, no. I did not choose renown or rank over my child, my son; delirious as I was with fever in those postpartum days, I knew, clear as I know it now, that it would have been a lie had I tried to claim after everything and all those years that I was Margaret Brackley, not Dr. Jonathan Mirandus Perry; that to do so would *not* have been a revelation; it would have been a murder. A suicide.

What are we after all: the accumulation of our works? Our name? The sum of our actions? I am what I have made myself, what I have done, no more, no less.

I should not have been surprised to receive notice that the Somertons would be departing for London without me; the ship, *The Atlas*—I was informed by runner—was unexpectedly filled to capacity by the governor's own cargo. Surely I would understand.

I understood.

It was awkward, of course, to have sold off all my furnishings months before, to be left like the less-good horses or extra baggage on the dock. I explained away the sale of my possessions by saying that we were no longer in need of such luxury, now that elegance itself had departed the Cape.

It was a story; it would serve.

Despite thick mist that pressed against the windows of Government House that morning of March 5, 1826, the gravel drive out front was filled with cloaked men on horseback trotting past and slow carriages, visitors eager to bid Lord and Lady Somerton farewell before they set sail for England. Inside all was surprisingly calm, subdued, the bags packed, the carriages being loaded; we were somber as we took breakfast for the last time together in the dining room.

As dawn came on we mounted our horses, Lord Somerton and I together in front, as we had been when we had set out for the East years before, flanked by officials, a dozen supporters behind us—the ladies following in carriages—and we rode through the thoroughfares of town, the streets lined with the governor's admirers cheering as we passed.

I was grateful to be included in the first boat with Lord Somerton and his family, where I stood in silence in the prow beside my friend. Behind us, two boats carried those who had hounded him from his post. We boarded the ship, stood at the rail together, looking back at the town.

"We will see you in London, I trust," said Lady Somerton.

"I will never return to England," I said. "My home is here."

We lingered as long as we could on board ship, until the captain announced the ship was under weigh, and we departed from it.

The shore thronged with spectators; the light bright on the bay through the clouds. At a quarter past eleven, just as Lord Charles set sail on the *Atlas*, the sun that had been obscured for much of the morning shone forth, as one observer would later report, "with more than usual brightness like the fame of an upright man which the floating breath of calumny may dim but cannot tarnish."

I did not weep that day. But a chill took hold of me that no measure of tropical sun could warm. It would last for years.

It possesses me even now. Two years later, on September 26, 1828, I would leave the Cape as well, with Dantzen and Psyche, to join the garrison at Mauritius as Staff Surgeon. Never to return, I hoped.

What lasts? A plank of sunlight on a wood floor. The taste of ginger in my morning coffee. The crunch of sugar. The shock of a cold wave against my calves. My beloved's skin against mine. Waking to watch my son's tiny face, his eyes opening to mine with an inhuman gaze, as if he saw what was to come, unforgiven. The incomparable sweetness of his tiny fists at my breast, mouth at my nipple, to live, to live. What lasts? What is honor compared to this: the capacity to create life itself. If men had that faculty they'd consider themselves gods. As it is, most do. Perhaps this is why they disparage women's bodies that work such magic, possess such power.

Strange what we remember, what we forget. What's worth re-calling? What will be recalled of me? If I am remembered in future it will be, I imagine, for saving a single life. When I ar-rived that night, it seemed I'd been called to certify a death.

There are so many ways to leave this life. Few ways to enter it. There is little to say of those final years in Cape Town, but there is this. Not long after Lord Somerton's departure from the Cape, I was summoned in the middle of a July night to attend the labor of a wealthy tobacco merchant's wife, who was dying in childbirth.

I rode through the winter rain till I reached the stucco house, illuminated as if for a party by candlelight and oil lamps. I did not bother to knock; I followed the sound of screams to a bed-room where Mrs. Wilhemena Munnick lay moaning, pale, near to death on the bloodied bedding. The room was crowded and close, reeking of mud and cigars, shit, wet wool and fear, as packed as a country dance with female family, friends, and household staff. I cleared the room of all but the midwife and Munnick himself, who—despite propriety and custom— admirably insisted on remaining by his wife's side.

I rinsed my hands at the water stand on the bureau using the bleach that I always carried then, impatient as the midwife recounted the progress of the labor that had begun well at dawn, gone awry by sundown. I asked questions about the position of the foetus, her treatment; I could guess what had happened, had seen it before. I told her to hold the lamp close as I lifted the sheet that tented Mrs. Munnick's legs. I gently prised apart her knees, which were clenched together in evident pain, her condition worse than I'd imagined. When I slipped my hand into the vaginal canal to see if the child might be extracted with my help, I felt a tiny foot, a leg, only one, the other tucked up in the womb. It was instantly clear: breach, half born. Her water long ago broken, her energy spent on hours of fruitless labor, worsened by the tonics applied to ease her pain. I pressed the leg back inside the uterus, then retracted my arm.

I ordered the strongest liquor in the house, which proved to be good Jamaican rum, and boiling water. Told the maidservant to scrub down the kitchen table with the water and bleach and to give Mr. Munnick a shot of rum.

"Get her to the kitchen," I said.

"Should she be moved, Doctor?" Munnick asked.

"No," I said. "But she will surely die if she is not."

He nodded, not understanding what risks he took or I did.

"She may die in any case, Munnick," I said. "You must

understand that. She likely will. And the child. There is a chance of saving one of them, by surgery. A slim chance, but a chance."

Later I would be asked if I hadn't worried that I put my reputation at risk by attempting the lethal operation; it didn't occur to me. I could not let a woman die to protect my name.

As a dresser at St. Thomas' Hospital, I had observed the caesarean operation performed with success, the belly slit down the midline, along the linea alba, then opened to reveal the protuberant uterine wall, which—once split— allowed for removal of the amnion sac and child. But at St. Thomas' there had been no risk, as mother and child were already dead.

The caesarean was rare for good reason: it almost always failed, or rather it almost always succeeded in killing both mother and child. I could count on a single hand the successful performance of the procedure in the last thousand years. A Swiss sow gelder had reportedly saved his wife by such means in 1500. Two surgeons—one in France and one in Holland— had claimed success in the last century, as had a single midwife in 1738 in England. But there was no proof, and such tales were held to be little better than fantasy. This much I knew: no one had successfully performed it in Africa.

More common was to kill the child to save the mother, extracting the foetus by forceps, piecemeal, so the mother might live; if she were too far gone, one waited for her to die, then cut her open to save the child. But I could not let either die while I stood by.

Mrs. Munnick was delirious with pain and beyond comprehending as we lay her on the kitchen table, which the midwife had scrubbed with hot water and bleach; her pelvis raised on cushions, her legs held wide by maids, her husband—abashed but compliant—grasped her arms and chest in his strong farmer's embrace to prevent her from wrenching away as I cut. I had nothing to give her save for a vial of laudanum—hardly enough to quell a toothache. But it stilled her some and proved tonic for her husband, who could believe she did not feel great pain. I told him to hold her firm as I put the blade to her belly to begin the long midline incision. At the first cut, as the knife split her skin, Mrs. Munnick screamed and tried to rise, but her husband held her down. She collapsed onto the table.

"Is she dead?" he asked.

"Not yet," I said. "Keep her still and she might not be."

He turned away, but the midwife held a lantern close to where I worked. I moved quickly, with an assurance I did not feel. My cutting kit set on a chair beside the table. I proceeded through the geologic layers of the body: each layer like a page in the textbooks I had studied a dozen years before now reappeared before my eyes. It was like moving through a country I had lived in long ago.

I worked quickly, drawing down the knife, cutting from xiphoid to pubis, avoiding the rectus muscles, then down through fasciae and muscle, grateful the gravid uterus had displaced the abdominal viscera, so I could see clearly the rose-pink glossy sack of the uterine wall and make a small incision there, through which I slipped a finger to guide the knife as I cut along the surface, making another vertical incision, until the uterus split open and the fetus was revealed. Sacrum posterior, as I'd feared—head up toward the mother's heart, face forward. I slipped a hand inside until my fingers found the infant's legs, then working my way by feel, I located its feet to ensure they were free of the vaginal canal, then took both legs into my hand; I attempted to lift the infant's body from the flesh cavern, but it was stuck, held firm. I tried to turn its body but to no avail; it was too large, too closely fitted to the space. I feared cutting further, feared the damage I might do—that she might bleed out and die before the child had been birthed. There on the table, my hands inside her, the child there too, delivering her unto death. The infant was stuck fast. Blood seepèd around the cuts I'd made; my pulse pounded in my ears.

"You may feel some pressure," I said to the unconscious woman on the table. "Hold her firm!" I shouted to her husband. I stepped up onto a chair and braced the heel of my hand against her sternum, and with my other hand I grasped again the infant's legs and lifted them up and pulled for all I had.

Mrs. Munnick groaned and her body rose from the table before I relented.

I braced my bootheel against the table's edge, and placed a palm once more against her sternum, the infant's legs clasped firm in my other hand, and with all my strength hauled back. I felt the mother's body rise again, felt a shift inside her bowels as if I were disemboweling her, which I feared I might just do. A line from the *Iliad* came into my mind: *planted a heel / against his chest, wrenched the spear from his wound / and the midriff came with it—*

Her face was grey-blue in the candlelight; she was dying; what choice was there but to continue? My palm against her sternum, I pulled again and felt the child shift. I reached inside the fundus, my free hand seeking the cranium now, the infant's feet cupped firm in my right. Then I lifted the baby's legs, somersaulting them toward the mother's chest, and felt the cradled head at last slip free as I raised the infant into the air, bloody and purple-blue, slicked with amniotic fluid, the umbilicus hanging like glistening rope or ribbon.

We stood amazed.

I slapped the child and it screamed, then I cut the umbilicus and knotted it before I held the infant out to Munnick—his, face pale with strain, glassy-eyed, sweat-glazed—and said, "You have a son."

I stitched up Mrs. Munnick and saw her settled into her now-clean room, before I left strict instructions for the care of the patient and the wound, ensuring the most sanitary conditions for her convalescence. Then I accepted a glass of brandy in the parlor. I sank into a chair by the fire.

"How can I thank you, Doctor?" Munnick said. His face glistened with tears and sweat.

"Take care of your wife and son," I said.

"Please," he said. "Accept our thanks." He pushed into my hand a wad of notes—a fat packet of rix-dollars—money I badly needed since my demotion the prior year.

But I declined. "You'll need it for your family, more than I, who have none."

"Is there nothing we can offer you?"

"Invite me to the christening."

"Surely there is something you desire?"

There was so much that I wanted, hoped for, wished: to have my friend back, my good name restored, above all a wish too dear even to name or think.

"There is one thing," I said, "that would mean a very great deal to me."

"Name it, and it's done," Munnick said incautiously.

"I would be honored if the boy might take my middle name as his own. As I have no children."

I could not know if the child I bore still lived, or if he did what name he bore; I could be sure only that it was not my own. I had had no right to name him or even to know what name was his, or even if he lived; I had given up that right when I had given him up. I had been so habituated to loss that it came more easily than love, than fighting to keep those I loved.

"I'll do better than that," Munnick said. "We'll name him after you."

On 20 August 1826, Jonathan Perry Munnick—my godson, my namesake, my almost consolation—was baptized at the Evangelical Lutheran Church.

I did not know, would not know for years, what I'd helped to birth that day.

CHAPTER TEN

THE END OF THE AFFAIR

For those in Cape Town, my transfer to Mauritius must have seemed an exile, a punishment like Dante's when the Black Guelphs cast him out of Florence. In truth I had put in the request for transfer as soon as Lord Somerton's plans became clear. As soon as it was clear that I was no longer welcome to join them in England. In September 1828—two and a half years after he left the Cape—I did.

I requested the posting to Mauritius for reasons of my own; I did not dare to say it, even to myself; I didn't dare to hope, to let myself want what I wanted so very badly: to find our son. I thought that I might recognize him in the street or among my patients' children—a boy of ten, his features familiar as my own or those of the man I loved—I held out hope that I might recognize his voice, his face, might hear word of him, of a boy adopted into an officer's family a decade before. Every call to every house I hoped would bring him to me. I prayed it would. Not to God exactly but to whatever principle kindles life, to whatever helped me save lives in the past. I prayed to skill, I suppose, or to the something beyond skill that seemed to overtake me when I worked well.

I told no one of this. Not even Dantzen, who of everyone

might have understood, Dantzen whose entire family had been taken from him, his arms prised open, his pregnant wife pulled from his chest along with their two-year-old son. He never saw them again. I knew of it only because he had been close to death a few months after he came into my service; he had fallen ill, delirious with fever, and had relived in terrible hallucinatory dreams the whole ordeal, which I witnessed by his side. I knew it must be true—those nightmares— when I asked about them later, after he'd recovered, and he seemed startled, shocked, then looked away, and said he never spoke of the past and never spoke of it again. I understood.

For a year in Mauritius I worked hard and well and effectively, charged with the singular hope that *this day* I would find my son. But as the months passed, I began to lose that hope.

By the time the appeal to return to London came that late August day in 1829, I had all but given up hope.

It might have been a breeze through the open window that made the letter tremble in my hand, but I knew better. Outside the day was already ablaze despite the early hour. Sounds of surf and cowbells through the open window as animals moved through the streets of Port Louis and children called out. Wind still cool.

I set my hand on the table to steady it.

"Everything all right, sir?" Dantzen asked. He was standing by the kitchen table, tearing up sugar buns for Psyche's breakfast. The greedy dog sat on a wooden chair and shivered in anticipation, snorting.

"Lord Somerton is gravely ill." I did not dare say more. I did not need to. I folded the page back inside the envelope and slipped it inside my coat.

I was grateful for Dantzen's discretion; he did not say that he was sorry; he did not express condolence of any kind. Mawkish sympathy would have been a curse.

There was no time for me to apply for a leave of absence. The letter had taken months to arrive; my friend was dying, might already be dead; I must go to him. Dantzen understood the risks as well as I. To go absent without leave, without making any official application for leave, was a grave military offense; I could lose my commission as a soldier, lose my license to practice medicine, lose the reputation that I had sacrificed so much to restore; face court-martial, jail; I could lose everything, again. Dantzen understood as I did that there was no choice. I've never known a more reasonable man.

The ship that had brought the letter, the brig *Rifleman*, would sail for England in two days' time; I would be on it.

Since coming to Mauritius the year prior, I'd hardly thought of the past; I thought of my patients, my work, each day a new oblivion, absorbed in delicious necessity—sutures, surgery, battling the daily insults that wear a body down, not illness but indifference, inattention to the body's needs.

Now it all came back to me, as I beheld the letter that bore a handwriting familiar as they once were, the Somertons. I'd recognized the hand instantly as Georgiana's; I would have recognized her hand anywhere, its gentle loops, its reticent, skeptical, backward slant. She had written for her stepmother, as I had written for my own mother more than twenty years before when she could not hold a pen, her hand unsteady with emotion, as mine was now. The letter was not sealed in black wax; I was grateful for that.

It was a small matter to pack; most of my belongings had been sold off in Cape Town, when I'd thought that I would be accompanying Lord Somerton to London. When instead he had abandoned me there, I'd not replaced them.

There are men who go to sea to escape trouble on land and feel freed by the voyage; I'm not one of them. I like trouble, if it's worth being troubled about. And I loathe the sea, or rather voyaging upon it. It is the worst of all possible modes of transport: little privacy, no solitude, restricted movement, unstable ground. Joachim du Bellay, the French poet, once wrote, *Heureux qui, comme Ulysse, a fait un beau voyage. Happy the man who, like Ulysses, has made a good voyage.* I never have. I braced myself for misery.

As we rowed out to the brig that evening, I could not help recalling Pliny the Elder, rowing toward Vesuvius as it heaved lava into the sea; his captain proposed they turn back, but Pliny insisted, *Fortes fortuna jurat! Fortune favors the brave!* He died, of course, on that little boat, singing fortune's praises. I prayed we would not. Despite the warm evening air, the spray off the bow as we broke through the chop sent a chill through me. My heart sank a little with each stroke of the oars. Psyche shivered in my lap.

From that first fateful journey to London to meet my uncle decades ago, I have detested sea voyages—without respite. I did not expect this would be any different. If I lived to see my friend, if he lived to see me, I would tell him, *It is a great love that travels by sea.*

* * *

It used to be my ambition, among my chief ambitions, that wellborn strangers should know my name. Napoleon knew my name by virtue of my reputation as a surgeon and called for me from his exile on St. Helena. My fame for performing the first successful caesarean is widely known as well. Was it too much to imagine then that my shipmates on the journey to London might be acquainted with my reputation as a surgeon rather than as a scandal? It was.

The first day aboard ship began well. I woke at break of day to the sound of a fiddle and fife. I dressed quickly and went on deck to watch the proceedings, Psyche bundled beneath my arm. It was not a joyful sound, the music, but it served to unify the sailors in their actions, and that cheered me, even if the prospect of a sea voyage did not.

I lingered on deck to watch the men haul anchor; I watched Mauritius as we left it behind. Each moment presented a different view of the island as we sailed out to sea; the motion soon became a very rocking one. The person at the helm cried out *Steady*, which word was echoed by another in a lower key, which signified the wind was fair and the ship going as it ought to do.

I did not know if I would ever return to Mauritius. More than a thousand miles off the eastern coast of Africa, ringed by reefs, Mauritius might have been the image of paradise before the fall. The water near shore clear as glass, the beaches beyond it white as bleached cuffs, beyond which rose mountains, sudden and startling as joy, rising two thousand feet into the air, the emerald green of Ireland.

I had battled the local colonial administrators there, seen those I cared for die, but I'd been happy, or at least hopeful; each day I rose charged with a sense of anticipation, an inchoate expectation that today I might meet my fate, change my life. Find him.

Now I scanned the familiar shore and the small figures on the dock come to see the ship off; I scrutinized the crowd as if I might recognize a face there. I was surprised by the ache the departure occasioned. I took it for dread of the sea.

I felt as if I were leaving hope itself behind.

It was at our first dinner together that evening that trouble arose; we had gathered in the captain's quarters for a celebratory meal—turtle soup, roast pig, cold beef, hot potatoes, a little gin and brandy—when one of our company, a provincial officer, mentioned Lord Somerton and his family, though not the scandal—"You must have known him at the Cape colony, Dr. Perry," the officer said. The man had been in India for some years, so it was possible, I suppose, that he had not heard of us, of the scandal. But from the hush that settled over the table, it was clear that if so he was the only one who hadn't.

"Does any man truly know another?" I replied, returning to my soup.

Lady Barnard insisted that I was indeed well acquainted with His Lordship. "Dr. Perry knew him very well, did you not?" she said, evidently affronted by the man's ignorance; she believed, as too many do, that the measure of a man is gauged by the fame of his acquaintance.

It might have been an innocent assertion. But I felt accused.

"I knew both Lord and Lady Somerton, yes," I said, quieting

any insinuation with a cold stare. But I felt the falseness of the claim as I uttered it; despite the letter in my coat, it felt a lie.

"What sort of man is he?" asked Captain Brine.

I knew what they wanted to know, just as I knew they wouldn't dream of asking. For once I was grateful for the curse of English propriety.

"Lord Somerton is a most remarkable man," I said, as I pushed back from the table. "Now, you must excuse me. I have some correspondence to attend to."

After dinner I walked on deck, needing air, the night uncommonly mild, the sky smeared with stars, the very heavens rearranged here, as if rewriting our fates. The stars recalled those we'd seen on the long trek east from Cape Town. It seemed I had not noticed stars in years.

When the quartermaster greeted me, I inquired about our position, learned that we were 1,200 miles off the African coast, two weeks sailing to Cape Town, then another twelve, if we were lucky, to reach London. Eight-thousand nautical miles at five knots: we'd arrive in four months' time, if the weather held, by mid-December.

I hoped my friend would live so long.

I stared west into the darkness, as if I might make out the coastline there, the edge of Africa. I could picture it in the dark, a terrain as familiar as my own body or a lover's, a beloved body. But I knew the dangers as well. The treacherous currents and unpredictable winds, especially at this time of year. I recalled the seasonal storms known as *die Kaapse dokter*, as I once had been.

We had come through just such a storm when I first arrived in the Cape colony a dozen years before. On that ship, Lord

Somerton had been the subject of conversation as well, although it was others who spoke of him then; the captain had
described him as a vain and petty man, arrogant and officious,
who cared more for his horses and dogs, for his hunting than
for the people he governed. I'd wondered then what sort of
man he was.

I declined to disembark in Cape Town when we arrived
there, claiming urgent reports to complete. I could not face it.
Dantzen went in my stead, our emissary, leaving Psyche and
me to rest aboard the anchored ship, rocked as in a cradle. I
could not bear to return to Cape Town only to leave again, that
place that had once seemed my true home. Dantzen retrieved
the newspapers—no word of Lord Somerton's death. There
was a grim report of another kind, of the hanging and public
dissection in Edinburgh of William Burke. My old teacher
Doctor Monro had presided, cutting open Burke's corpse after
he was executed for having murdered men, women, even a
child to sell their bodies to anatomists. It was said Monro
had dipped his pen in the hanged man's blood to sign the
death certificate. It was Machiavelli's trick: to decry what one
practiced as a means to evade blame. As if we'd never bought
a body dug from a Christian grave. The hypocrites. We'd
not *killed* for corpses, of course, but neither had we asked
questions. Still, I'd not be the surgeon I was without the dead.
The theft. The lie.

After we left Cape Town I stayed in my cabin, avoiding
conversation and company. If my companions did not know
of our scandal before, surely they knew now, after our stop
in Cape Town. Here where it began. I should have seen it
coming, I suppose, but I was battling other storms then. Did

not imagine there could be any storm worse than to see the person I loved married to someone else, indifferent to me.

The sea was high, but the wind blew well; I was cheered by the prospect of fast progress, at least. *London by Christmas*, Captain Brine said.

The oppressive chill of an English winter met us at the London docks. As familiar as it was unwelcome. I hired a coach and set off immediately for the Somertons' home, through the city shrouded in coal soot and fog; I arrived at their townhouse in Piccadilly as evening was coming on—the streets glossy with mist, the air thick and cold, an aching damp seeping through my heavy greatcoat, the sounds of horses and smell of coal ash as far from the clear African air as could be found; in an instant I was a student again, a dresser, 21, with life before me like a banquet. I knocked at the black enamel door, a servant showed me in; I found Lady Somerton grown thin and grave; a lemon-yellow satin dress made her skin glow pink; despite her grief, she seemed to have flourished here as my friend had not.

"Thank you for coming, Dr. Perry."

She welcomed me and led me into the first-floor drawing room that had been converted to a bedroom, so my friend needn't mount the stairs and might look out over the street at the world he loved. The dim lights, the high fire, the heaps of blankets and the faint sweet reek of laudanum left no doubt that he was here to die; they were in waiting merely. I had been summoned not as a physician, to heal, but to grieve as a family friend.

I was filled with fury, a rage to throw them out, call for light, fresh air, hot wine for my friend, my skin vibrating with rage, but I had learned in the intervening years to temper impulse. Still, I was impatient with their gloom, the city being gloomy enough on its own that bleak winter night in mid-December 1829. It seemed a luxury to give in to grief, to absolve oneself of the responsibility to cure, or try. "The man's not dead yet," I wanted to say, "though this sepulchre of a room could kill anyone." But I was silent.

Calm but grieving, clearly preparing herself for her husband's imminent death, Lady Somerton had developed the habit of sleeping on a couch beside his bed, so she could wake with him in the night, should he need her. Georgiana, who had arrived only the week before, kept vigil in that room as well. She rose from her father's bedside when I entered. She did not speak when she crossed to me, merely took my hand in hers and brought me to her father.

I heard in his labored breathing evidence of a failing heart, lips tinged blue, cyanic; his limp right hand betrayed scars from a lancet—bloodletting that had no doubt weakened him, compounded whatever ailed him. I had never seen him so ill, save when I'd treated him for typhus a dozen years before.

I had little hope of cure, but I chose hope. Hope is a choice.

I bent over my friend, his face ashen, immobile in sleep. He seemed already to have left this world. Seemed glad of it. I pulled up a chair close by the bed, only to think better of it; I sat down on the bed instead, beside my friend, taking his hand in mine, feeling for the faint pulse, unable to ignore the signs—his pallor, his gaunt features—aged beyond the toll of years, fearing he might fail to recognize me, even if he were to wake. I try to remember the moment now. Bring his face close to mine again.

"Dr. Perry—"

I startled to hear the rasping voice from a body that seemed beyond speech.

"Dr. Perry," he said again, "good of you to come," repeating the words he'd said to me a dozen years before, when we'd first met at Tunhuys under the radiant Cape sun. "The case must be truly dire to bring *you* back to England."

I had sworn never to return.

"Not dire," I lied. "I was homesick."

"As am I," he said. "Home, sick."

"Evidently."

"I have missed my home from the moment I left it." Did he recall that he had once called me *home?* I could not know; I could not ask.

"What ails you?" I asked, as if he might have the answer.

"Nothing, now that you are here."

Although I could make no certain diagnosis in the days and weeks that followed, his fast and erratic pulse, the terrible cough that often left him speechless, his pallor and cyanic lips inclined me to treat him as I would a pregnant woman suffering from anxious torpor—I sought to strengthen the heart and circulation. (I know now that it was congestive heart failure that he suffered from, but such belated knowledge is useless knowledge.) I tossed out the poisonous sedatives he'd been given, prescribed diuretics and mild stimulants instead to regulate the heart—vinegar, digitalis, warm wine, hot and hearty foods, beef, broth, garlic, warming spices. As he strengthened, I counseled fresh air, mild exercise, even if it was only to walk to his library or to the garden and back inside. To my amazement, his condition improved. As if my presence were itself tonic.

* * *

After a month of treatment, the initial crisis had passed; after two, he recovered his health enough to host a lavish dinner in my honor, like the ones he used to preside over in Cape Town; the following months in London passed quickly, happily. Together.

I thought it might be gratitude for having saved her husband's life that prompted Lady Somerton to countenance our late evenings and long solitary afternoons together, our rides and dinners at his club, from which she and the children were excluded.

The first night that he proposed we visit Almack's, I was alarmed. For myself and for my friend. It was proof of his improving health, which I could only celebrate, but I had no wish, no desire to appear in public. The scandal was just five years behind us, and still discussed in the London press; I had no desire to test society's memory or generosity. I hoped that Lady Somerton would object to the proposal. Instead she merely declined to join us, saying she preferred a quiet evening at home by the fire. I would have preferred it as well. But I could not refuse my friend's request or decline to accompany him. We all behaved as if it were the most ordinary thing, two friends reunited, spending an evening at the club, as if there were nothing extraordinary in my presence there among them.

I dressed with trepidation, annoyed by Dantzen, whose opinion of my waistcoat I solicited, only to reject; he advised me against wearing my out-of-fashion inexpressibles, the form-fitted leggings I favored; I fretted over the polish on my boots.

It was to be our first time in fashionable London society together since the scandal. He had been welcomed back into society on his return from Cape Town; *we* were another matter. Our names had been joined only in calumny. I had never been to Almack's, would never have received a coveted invitation to that club. I had reason to fear the subtle or overt humiliation that I might endure. But I could find no means to decline the invitation. And in truth, I was curious. Almack's was famous—and famously exclusive. The matrons who governed its guest list were known to stop arrivals at the door and turn them back. I dreaded the coming evening, even as I was curious to see the place that General Mirandus had frequented and I never had.

When Lady Somerton urged us to go and enjoy ourselves, saying we deserved some diversion, I wondered if she sensed my dismay, delighted in it. Georgiana said nothing at all.

Lord Somerton was weary, as we went out that evening, and I feared, as we stepped down from the coach outside Almack's, that the outing was already too much. Unsteady still from illness, he took my arm, leaning on it as we entered.

I heard the hush as we stepped inside the club. I felt the seasick dread of humiliation as we were announced on entering the ballroom; a silence fell—like that aboard ship that first night at dinner months ago—hundreds of faces staring at us before the crowd broke into applause. They applauded His Lordship's return to health, of course, not the two of us, but then he stood aside, palm open to indicate that I was the one to be congratulated for the return of his good health. He nodded to me; I bowed with a flourish to the crowd, like the actor I was. The remarkable Doctor Perry.

* * *

After that evening we frequented the club often, and Lord Charles hosted dinners in their home in Piccadilly. Through it all, I wondered what Lady Somerton knew of our past; then one evening at dinner—as he told a raucous story from the Cape Town days—she placed her hand on mine and said quietly, "My husband is transformed by your presence, Doctor; he is a different man entirely with you. Not my husband at all." And I knew that she knew. I did not know if she knew my secret, but she knew ours.

Lady Somerton had never been beautiful, but with age she had grown handsome, impressive, lovely; she possessed the calm of certain successful men who no longer need to prove their mettle. Like certain features of the landscape—the cliffs of Cornwall, the waves at Ballycotton—she had endured. And with time she seemed to have grown stronger, as my friend had not.

So many people remain children their whole lives—I'd seen men die who had never become men, who remained the boys they'd been, bewildered as death came over them, as if refusing to mature might be some inoculation against mortality. Women, too, still cleaving to their youth, coquettes at 65. Lady Somerton, it was clear, in the midst of her small family, had become herself. It was hard not to wonder what I'd have been now, become, had I kept my child. Ours.

Those fourteen months together were the happiest of my life, I see now. At home again in London, among those I best loved. We rode in Hyde Park, went to lectures and the theater and balls and hosted dinners. Visited his family's estate in Badminton. We dined together weekly at Brook's, as if no scandal had ever touched our names.

One late night, after an evening spent singing and drinking, when we'd opted to walk home from the club under a springtime moon, he pulled me suddenly into a doorway, so abruptly that for a moment I thought we had been set upon by thieves, a risk in London in those days at night. "What is it?" I asked, but he didn't answer, only put his lips gently to mine and for a moment we were back in Africa. Young again. If I wept, it was from happiness.

We live like kings. That's how it seemed as I popped another fat, fragrant raspberry into my mouth, as we sat on the terrace of his family estate at Badminton, having breakfast that morning in May 1830. Lord Charles had told me how his father, the Fifth Duke of Beaufort, had hosted hundreds of guests each weekend there. He seemed nostalgic for those days. But I preferred these quiet family times. Lazy, warm days together, alone. Plump bumblebees in their furry jackets clambered over the blooming lavender. *There will be rain.*

To see my friend each morning at breakfast was an incomparable pleasure. Like looking in the mirror on a good day, he returned me to myself, kinder, wiser, wittier than anyone else mistook me for. I was beyond grateful that we had remained friends, after everything, friendship being the greater part of love; we had each been unsteadied by the break we'd had. Like carts with three wheels we had wobbled along, missing an essential part. Whole now. Again.

Somerton's younger brother, Lord FitzRoy, had arranged a post for me in Jamaica to justify having left my own in Mauritius, but I delayed my departure, putting off from month to month the prospect of separation from my friend. The proposed post had the dual virtue of keeping me within three months' distance of my friend and providing an excuse to cover my blatant breach of duty, which might now be construed as responding to an order to report to London en route to a new post in the West Indies. But I rebuffed every attempt to draw me away.

It was late December 1830, approaching the winter solstice, as we sat together by the fire when the rest of the house had gone to bed, that Lord Charles raised the subject of his will. Perhaps it was the anniversary of his illness, or the foreshortened days, that made him withdraw into himself that winter, almost exactly a year after I'd arrived back in London. Though our habits continued unchanged, he spoke less of the future.

"When I am gone, I would be grateful if you might see to certain things."

"If you like," I said. "But as your physician, I must warn you that I've begun to suspect that you will live forever."

"It's odd," he said. "Our days are always numbered, but the prospect has a different weight when you know the date, within six months or so."

"Rubbish. You never know. You have many years yet."

"I will die soon," he said.

His tone unsettled me, but I put it down to the grim weather, the bleak time of year, recollection of the prior year's illness; I hoped his mood might lift if I agreed to his wishes, so we discussed the funeral, the will, the execution of his estate. I agreed to look after Georgiana. I went to bed that night heavy of heart.

But for all his dire prognostications, he flourished, as I did in his company.

It's such a small thing, death. You see people stumble across its threshold all the time, as if startled to find it there in their bedroom or on a battlefield or an infirmary cot, its door held open, almost welcoming. Some rage and die, some welcome it, some beg for death, some weep, others shout loved ones away ("Let me *go!*"). I recall one wealthy young woman, down with fever, who seemed simply baffled: "I thought there would be more."

Lord Somerton wanted me to help him plan for his. I would. I did.

When death comes for me, I asked only that my body be spared undignified inspection. The unexamined life may not be worth living, but I would have an unexamined death. That small dignity. Dantzen had promised me this: that I would be spared postmortem examination. Some insist their papers be burned, letters of a personal or private nature destroyed. My body was my diary, my only private text. For all my daily official correspondence and voluminous notes on the medical practice, I'd written only a handful of personal letters, almost all before the age of thirteen. I'd made my private inscriptions of my life here, on my body, the sole place I recorded a private life. I'd not have it read by strangers.

I had loved fashion and fancy dress, a dandy peacock in my silk and broadcloth, my high-polished boots, but in death I wanted the simplicity of birth, to be wrapped in the bed linens in which I die, buried in Kensal Green Cemetery. (Though sometimes I thought I should like to be buried with my broadsword and a lock of Psyche's hair, with my red military coat and Hessian boots polished to a high shine, accompanied by them as I've been in life.)

The body is a record of our lives—the most intimate accounting. If a man eats to excess or drinks, it is recorded there in the joints, in the belly. If a woman has had children or none, has suffered a pox or leaned an arm against a heated pot, it is written in the body's ledger. Only death clears the account, and sometimes not even death. If you disinter a body, you can read in its bones the death blow to a skull or a shattered sternum and read the life—or at least its end—there.

I would remain unread, an obscure volume, a palimpsest, a secret among friends.

Perhaps it was gratitude that made Lady Somerton acquiesce to the proposal of a holiday in Brighton the following February, just the two of us at the Bedford Hotel. Lord Charles wanted to ride along the shore beneath the chalk cliffs and on the Downs overlooking the sea, where he'd ridden with the Prince of Wales when young; he claimed the ocean air would do him good, be tonic. "Sea air's the best cure a man can have—even better than you, Doctor."

I hoped Lady Somerton might dissuade him, but to my surprise she raised no objection at all when he raised the subject at breakfast.

"A trip would do you good, Charles," she said.

When he proposed that he and I go alone on the holiday, she did not protest. He claimed he did not wish to take her away from London at the height of the social season.

There seemed no alternative but to accompany my friend, despite my fears for him and for us.

* * *

The Bedford Hotel on the Brighton seafront was a great layer cake—pale stone and glass, a pastry of a place—over which the Union Jack snapped in the breeze in every sort of weather. The most distinguished building in town, after the Prince Regent's extravagant Royal Pavilion. Ionic porticoes facing south and west flanked the entrances of the grand five-story structure. The interior was no less grand, with its massive Grecian hall and Ionic columns and a glazed dome overhead. As our carriage pulled up in front that February morning, I admired the shimmering salt-bright stone and the colonnade that rose three stories in the air, fringed by awnings, over which rose another two stories; I felt we were entering a wedding cake.

Even in grim February, when we arrived, the sky was promisingly blue, pale, high, threaded with thin banners of clouds that festooned the air. It was hard to be uncheerful there, easy to overlook the danger.

We arrived on a Monday, St. Valentine's Day, 1831. The lengthening of the days almost imperceptible. Although Lord Charles denied it, dismissing my concern as meddling fit for a wife, my friend was clearly fatigued. He stumbled slightly, nearly fell, when descending from the carriage and required my assistance to mount the hotel stairs. He refused dinner that evening, would not take wine or even tea to warm him and went straight to bed, alone.

He had insisted on making the sixty-mile journey from London in a single trip, refused to rest on our journey south from London, despite my cautions. ("If I must die, Doctor, please God don't let it be in Lewes.") That night in the sitting room of our suite I imagined the worst, listening to his labored breathing through the door that joined our rooms; by the time the clock chimed midnight I was exhausted, queasy with fear. Panicked by memory. But by the following dawn he banged on my door, waking me, having emerged rested, bright, eager to ride out on the Downs, if uncustomarily cautious. He joked that he should like to ride a pony like the one Georgiana had brought to me at the Cape stables years ago.

To my relief, that first afternoon proved too rainy to ride, so we returned early from the stables and strolled through town, past the Royal Pavilion, that hallucination of a palace of minarets and domes, where he'd spent many happy evenings in his youth with his friend, the Prince Regent; he described its design to me, its grand banquet hall like a peacock turned inside out—teal-green leaves painted on the domed ceiling, red and indigo walls, set off by gold gilding and crystal chandeliers— the strike of our bootheels the only noise in the quiet streets, like horse hooves striking stones. A lonely but somehow comforting sound. We seemed to be alone in the world. The only survivors of a shipwreck, stranded here in beauty.

"Do you know the story of this place?" he asked.

"I feel sure that you will tell me," I replied. He did.

He told me how some forty years earlier, the Prince of Wales had been in disgrace when he first came here in 1786. He had a taste for horses and games, had acquired massive debts, become a scandal, needed to leave town. Brighton was little known then, far from London, out of the way, so he bought a modest farmhouse here, "fixed it up" (it seemed a vast understatement), so that he might meet with the woman he loved but could not marry.

"She was a commoner?" I asked.

"Worse—Catholic." We both knew the Act of Settlement had banned marriage between faiths.

"What became of her?" I was reluctant to ask. Was not sure I wanted to know.

"She became his wife," he said. "In secret."

"Love conquers all."

"Sometimes, it does," he said.

We had returned to the hotel and sat looking out over the promenade as the waters grew rough. Outside a rain began to fall, a steady thrum like a finger tapping on the glass, building as the storm grew to a susurrus like a rushing river over falls. A comforting, blanketing sound. The sky a muffled grey, undifferentiated. We seemed wrapped, protected, far from any harm. He set a hand on my arm.

"Thank you for coming back."

"I never left you," I said.

"I wish we..." he began.

"No." I did not want to hear his regrets, I didn't believe in regret, as if it were a religion, which for some it is, melancholy held close as a mistress. I couldn't afford regret. I lived in a world of facts and what I could do about them. Sitting beside the man I loved near that extravagant pavilion built to house another hidden love, I wondered if we might have made another choice, if I might have, if we might have made a space large enough to shelter us as well. If we might yet.

Although the days were short and brisk—five hours of sun at best and cold—they were not without charm.

Each morning we took our breakfast in the terrace room overlooking the parade and beyond it the waterfront, the seascape soft and blurred with silvery mist, catching the morning light, the air so bright it seemed itself the source of light. Each morning I pressed food on my friend, urging on him hot tea, ham, scotch eggs, buttered toast and marmalade, a draught of rum, as if to weight him to the world. As soon as the hour allowed, we were out of doors at his insistence, up and moving, walking the parade or traveling to the stables to get our mounts and ride on the high green cliffs of the Downs. In the afternoon, even before the light began to fade, my friend napped while I read the papers or caught up on correspondence.

He seemed revived by the ocean breeze, the sea air; as we took our breakfast in the terrace sunroom overlooking the promenade, he admired the winter light and shimmering sea, like poured silver in the sunlight, the scream of ravenous gulls.

"How can that not cure a man?" he asked as we stepped outside to walk along the water. I pulled my greatcoat tight, raised its collar to my ears, but he turned his face to the wind off the sea. Pleased to be in the open air, despite the cold. At his insistence we arranged to ride out on each of three successive mornings that first week — Wednesday, Thursday, Friday. And we did. I began to think that he might indeed be well, might be improving, my caution misplaced. He mounted his horse and as usual I accompanied him.

On Saturday he visited the King and Queen, who were staying at the Royal Pavilion, and that night we stayed out late as had become our habit in London, reaching our rooms at the Bedford well past midnight, drunken and content, singing and laughing like schoolboys, hushing each other, then bursting into song or laughter again, whenever one or the other of us mentioned the donkey's tooth (a prank I'd played on Bishop

Burnett), telling stories of the past, talking of a future in which we would never again be separated, apart.

"I shall speak to my brother," he said, his words blurry at the edges, as he dropped into a chair, "about a transfer. You should be in London, not some godforsaken island in the middle of all fuck-all, the West Indies or Indian Ocean."

"That's debatable," I said.

"You can't prefer it, surely."

"It has its compensations."

He raised himself drunkenly on one elbow. Stared at me, or perhaps several of me, given how much he'd had to drink.

"Who?" he asked. Absurd jealousy. Then, dropping back into the chair, "Oh."

For a while we said nothing; there was nothing to say. Outside the surf whispered against the sand. Inside a fire crackled in the grate. I went in to change out of my clothes and pulled on a dressing gown he'd given me and joined him, resuming my place beside the fire, beside him.

"I tried to find him," I said, "that last year. Sometimes I thought I had."

"I would like to have met him," he said.

"Yes." I did not say that it had been my first thought on waking every day for the last twelve years. *I would like to meet him today.* It still is.

"And what have you found?" he asked.

"Nothing yet," I said. "But hope is something. One can live on less, I've found."

He placed his hand on mine.

"He'd be twelve now, almost thirteen," I said.

"If he lived."

"Yes, if he lived."

"Dying is not such a bad thing. But there is so much I will miss."

"You're not dying."

"Fog," he said. "A good fire. A good horse between my legs. The last cigar after a successful ball. A clean shot. Bathing with you at Camps Bay."

"You hated bathing at Camps Bay," I said.

"Buttered toast," he continued. "Cold plums. Morning. I will miss you."

We had passed the point of passion but not of love. When he asked me to stay with him that night, I didn't hesitate, even as I knew that if we touched, it would not be from desire but from sorrow.

It was not that desire was dead, but it had become tinctured with the foretaste of loss. We did not speak. We undressed, I unbound my chest, and went to bed. Afterward he turned me gently away from him in bed, wrapped his arms around me, his hands cupping my breasts, then snored.

I felt him loosen his embrace in the night and fall away from me; I woke in the early hours of the morning beside him, taut with dread, and knew, before I touched him, that he was gone. *Don't leave me here*, I thought, my first prayer in years. *Don't leave me now.*

When he turned in his sleep and farted, I laughed and woke him. He was annoyed to be awakened so early. I was delighted.

We trick out our ambitions in better clothes, making of professionalism a point of pride, as if the personal were a minor player, a trifle, a matter for lesser men, those whose fate it is merely to fuck and feed like animals, as if we weren't all animals, when really what honor do we gain by striving to emulate machine-like efficiency, dishonoring our most human quality: sentiment, feeling, appetite, sympathy, empathy, that which distinguishes us from the machines we were just beginning to love? I loved him, was glad to own it.

That Sunday morning rose pink and pale grey, like the nacreous belly of a mussel shell. I'd hoped for rain to keep us inside, but Lord Somerton was eager to ride, despite his evident exhaustion. The sun was a yellow burr in the mist. By noon, he insisted, the sky overhead would be robin's-egg blue; as if to oblige him, the sky cleared early, the sea mist burning off by 9 a.m.

It was February 20, the last day of his life; he insisted on riding out onto the Downs, those high chalk cliffs overlooking the sea, despite the mist and chill in the air. He was flushed as we rode and excitable, stronger than he had seemed in years; when we returned to the hotel, it appeared the air had indeed done him good. His face was ruddy with what looked like a return of health. But by evening, he was feverish. I didn't worry overmuch when he said he was tired, asked to rest. He deserved to rest. He was sixty-three.

We played cards, spoke of the dinner we would host in London and of the hunt, of the past and of the future, of spending the spring in Rome; when he lay down to nap, I read in a chair by the window. I had thought mistakenly that he could not die if I remained with him, as I had failed to stay with my mother. But death doesn't mind company. Death loves a crowd. Look at any battlefield. I didn't notice his last breath.

When I went to rouse him for dinner, I found him unbreathing, still warm. I fell to my knees beside the bed,

pressed my lips to my friend's warm hand, and sobbed. I had
lost more than a father. I had lost my almost only friend.

The funeral at St. Andrew's Church, Hove, was intimate
and quiet and small, attended only by his closest relations,
of which I was honored to be numbered. The only person
there who was not blood kin. His brother, the Sixth Duke of
Beaufort, his nephew the Marquis of Worcester among them.
He had requested that he be buried without pomp or expense,
that only family and close friends be in attendance to see him
from the world he'd loved. "My funeral may on no account
be attended with any parade"—he'd insisted that I record the
wish two months prior; I had. Lady Somerton did me the
honor of asking me to take her arm as we entered the church,
calling me over ("Where is Dr. Perry?") so that I might sit
beside her, in the family pew, among the grieving women.

The coffin bore a simple plate on which was inscribed a single
laconic phrase, words I had dictated at Somerton's request: *General the Rt. Honourable Lord Charles Somerton, died February
20th, 1831.* It was not nearly enough to say about the man.

After the funeral at St. Andrew's, we returned to the Bedford
Hotel for the night. Georgiana and I found ourselves alone in
the hotel parlor late that night, after the others had retired.

"You will miss him," she said.

"We will," I said.

"I wonder," Georgiana said. "Sometimes I think that I have
waited all my life for him to die, for his life to end, so I might
begin my own."

"You don't mean that," I said.

"Don't I?" she crossed the room to stand before a picture.

"What will you do now, Doctor?" she asked. "Will you stay in London?"

"Return to my work. Your uncle, Lord FitzRoy, has generously arranged for me take up a post in Jamaica," I said. "And you? Will you marry now?" I had known of her father's opposition to Captain Glover.

"Is that a proposal, Dr. Perry?" she asked.

"I wish with all my heart that I were in a position to make you one, but—"

"But you are not," her voice was bitter.

I was startled by how bitter, how harsh her tone was. And I was saddened to realize all at once and fully how thwarted longing had ruined her, made her vivacity into something fragile, hard, turned her delicacy into cold strength. As if yearning had calcified, become a carapace—

"Do you know, I used to admire your frankness," Georgiana said. "Almost no one was, save for you. It was such a relief, so delightfully shocking. To hear somebody say what they meant."

I smiled.

"But you're not, are you, Doctor? *Honest*. Not at all. It's always the most dishonest who make a show of their honesty. Politicians. Thieves. They're the ones who offer assurances that you can trust them. You've been lying to us all along, perhaps to yourself most of all."

"I'm sure I don't know what you mean," I said.

"I think you do."

It had not occurred to me before that the placard with its revelation of our secret life might have been Georgiana's work. It hardly mattered now.

"You're tired, Georgiana," I said. "You've suffered a terrible loss. We can talk in the morning."

"I have suffered," she said. "We have. And I am tired. But we'll talk now."

I might have left then, I suppose, walked out—perhaps I should have done. But I was a guest here, and after Lord Somerton, Georgiana had been the person I was fondest of in the world. I could not bear to lose another person I loved. There were so few.

"All right," I said. I took a seat.

"Did you know the word *passion* comes from the Greek word meaning *to suffer*? Of course you do. That is the word I would have applied to you in the past. *Passionate*. Such a passionate man, Dr. Perry; it seemed so odd that he never married, never took a wife. I used to imagine you had a woman somewhere—someone lowborn, perhaps, someone you'd met at the Rainbow Balls, someone inconvenient if you were to keep your good name; that perhaps *that* was why you'd left for Mauritius so abruptly. To marry or to dispense with an inconvenient child."

If I paled at the suggestion, she did not appear to notice.

"It was years later, not until the scandal broke, that awful business with the placard at the Heerengracht bridge, that I realized the truth," she said.

My expression must have betrayed my distaste, my shock.

"Oh, I don't mean that I believed the scandal," she said. "You were too cautious of your good name for that, as was my father." She turned to look out the window. "I used to think you were the only person alive who loved my father as much as I did," she said. "I wondered sometimes if I loved *you* simply to be loved *by him*, who loved you more than anyone. I blamed *him* that you kept your distance from me, imagining *he* kept you away, as he did Colonel Glover. My father had many virtues, but among his vices was his need to be loved above all others. It withers the heart, that sort of love. But then you know that, don't you? It's like a scorching African sun. It kills everything it does not sustain."

"It's very late," I said.

But she continued as if I'd not spoken: "I used to imagine that *he* was what stood between us; that if it weren't for his opposition, you'd propose. How silly. It wasn't me you loved at all. Was it?" She turned, looked directly at me.

"Really, Georgiana," I rose and began to pace as her father might have done. I caught myself and stopped.

"It wasn't even him. It was yourself, your good name. Above everything." She paused as if waiting for my reply. I had none.

"And now my father is dead, and I have waited all this time for someone who's not really there, who doesn't really exist at all. Dr. Perry is a ghost. Not really a person at all. Just a part you've played. The dashing doctor. Is there anyone there beneath your red coat, Doctor? Is there anyone there at all? What would you be if you ceased to be the esteemed Dr. Perry? Did you ever wonder that?"

"All the time."

"And the answer?"

I found it hard to speak. The answer was so simple, obvious.

"Nothing," I said. "I would be nothing."

She turned away, toward the window again, as if disgusted, unsatisfied. She touched a vase on the table beside her, absently.

"Don't you regret not having a family, a home?"

"Regret? No," I said. Then, because we had once been friends: "Of course I do."

"My father was not as clever as you, but he lived his life; he was alive while he lived. Can you say the same?" She turned toward me, the vase in her hands, and for a moment I thought she might throw it at my head. "I can't. I have waited half my life for someone who doesn't even exist. How is that possible?"

"I'm sorry," I said.

"That's not enough."

"I know." She turned her face aside; her shoulders shook. I crossed to her and took her in my arms, not as lovers do but as siblings might, children frightened by a storm, bereft. Each of us grieving for the man we'd loved and lost. "I know," I said. "I know."

Two weeks later, when I left London to sail for Jamaica — having been cleared of charges of abandoning my post, thanks to Lord FitzRoy's intercession — Georgiana did not come to see me off. Lady Somerton made excuses on her behalf (the constraints of mourning, etcetera), but I understood. I was not surprised to read a few months later in the London press of her marriage to Colonel Glover at Christ Church, Marylebone.

I hoped they would be happy. Together. I hoped they might have a child. Love each other well. What could possibly matter more than that?

I looked forward to my new post in Jamaica, if not to sailing there. The place had the unfortunate distinction of having the highest mortality rate in the military service. I would battle it, as I had battled death my whole life. I looked forward to the fight. Even as I knew now that battling death is different from life, from living.

I wonder what will be remembered? What I will recall, what

others will say of us? Is that the measure, or is it something simpler, closer to the bone, to the body? I had held another life inside me once, whatever happened to that child; for a time we had shared a skin, were one and the same, under the tent of flesh, under the same sky—he and I. Strange to think I sacrificed everything for the sake of a name that was not even mine.

Was it worth it? Do we ever know? What I know is what remains constant. That old brag of the heart, *I am I am I am*, until one day we're not, until one day it stops. Until then there is the pleasure of solving the puzzle, the possibility of understanding. Like holding the missing piece in your hand, looking for the connection, where it fits. The pleasure of solving the riddle remains—the body's, the heart's.

Dantzen had settled my things into the quarters below. The room with its wooden walls, footsteps overhead, seemed too like a coffin, so I lingered on deck to watch the well-wishers on the dock wish others well. The Somertons had not come to see me off. Lord FitzRoy sent a note. Only Dantzen stood on the dock, holding up Psyche for me to see; she barked, again and again. I raised a hand, held it there. I could not bear to make either of them journey with me. I would make this journey alone.

I heard the boys on deck raising the sails, unleashing them, the hiss of ropes and the great clanging of irons as the anchor was hauled free, then the flap of the sail sheets in the wind like some enormous bird beating its wings nearby overhead and then one felt it, the catch in the sails and the lurch into the waves, the pull and the pitch and the rock as we pulled free of the dock, of shore and the waves gathered beneath us and dispersed, gathered and dispersed, taking us once more out to sea. I wiped the moisture from my cheeks—sea spray, nothing more.

EPILOGUE

I know how the story ends now—mine, ours, our child's. Though this last remains too painful to relate. Some things are unspeakable, like the forced separation of a parent and child.

I will live another thirty years after Lord Charles Somerton's death, exercising that great gift that the living too often overlook: the power to change things. I will find a cure for syphilis, decocted from the Plat Doom plant, which I'd collected on the Cape; I will save thousands by containing cholera in Jamaica; while there I will be reunited with my friend Josias de Cloete. I will rise to prominence again, make enemies again, be posted to Canada, where I will obtain the highest rank a military surgeon can, equivalent of a general: Inspector General for Military Hospitals.

I will dye my short curls red again, as in my youth, and ride through the wintry streets of Montreal in a red horse-drawn sleigh, burrowed under beaver pelts, bear skins, and heavy Hudson blankets, Psyche at my side (my third poodle so named). I will live to see the coronation of Queen Victoria, the return of corsets, the first openly female graduate of medical school, the death of Goethe and the birth of Freud, the publication of *On the Origin of Species*, the American nation torn asunder by war and made whole again, miraculous as the body's own healing.

The child who bore my name—my godson, Jonathan Perry Munnick—will be my loyal correspondent for years, until he confides that he's heard I much resemble a woman; I will never write to him again. He will grow up to have children of his own, who will have children of their own, who will have children too, one of whom will become an architect of apartheid—that abomination, that outrage against justice and every principle I held dear, that Lord Somerton did. How do we measure a life? By how it's lived or by what we leave behind for those to come?

What makes a life a failure or success? What makes a hero or a heroine? Is it good works or great deeds, riches or respect, renown or liberty of mind, acclaim in one's own time or centuries later? Does a life matter more for being recalled than those whose names are not? Does it make a bad king good to be remembered a thousand years after he died? Ethelred remains unready for eternity, after all. I honored history, lived for it. Was I wrong? Was I betrayed? Did I betray myself?

If sacrifice is the measure of a life, mine was great. For I sacrificed greatly. I sacrificed everyone I loved.

I will die in London, at 14 Margaret Street, my body buried at Kensal Green Cemetery. My restless spirit traveling still.

How do I know how the story ends? How mine did? The body is a story we tell ourselves, as love is; mine continues, it seems, as long as there are those who care to hear it, who listen.

Death is always a revelation; mine was no exception: although history will demote her to a chambermaid, as history is inclined to diminish women's stature, the woman who attended me after my death from dysentery on July 25, 1865 was in fact a nurse; she is the one who discovered my secret, made public what so many had overlooked for years.

What she discovered that day was simply this, what should have been obvious all along: The hero was a woman. The heroic life—all along—was hers.

ACKNOWLEDGMENTS

This is a work of fiction: while the principal events described are inspired by actual events and persons, my descriptions are, of course, inventions. Margaret Bulkely's origins and the occasion for her transformation into James Barry in order to gain an education unavailable to women at the time, the place and time of Barry's schooling and the faculty/curriculum of the period, the friendship with Jobson, the doctor's work in Cape Town and remarkable achievements there, the close bond with Lord Somerset, the journey to the Xhosa, the duel, the sodomy scandal, a pregnancy, and Barry's subsequent return to Mauritius and later England to save Lord Somerset's life— these are historical facts. As novelist Lily King has written: "I have borrowed from the lives and experiences of these persons, but I have told a different story."

On occasion, I have tampered with the timeline for the sake of dramatic economy. For example, I have detained General Miranda in London so as to involve him more deeply in James's early education, when in fact the general sailed for Venezuela on February 2, 1806, twenty days before the death of Margaret's uncle. I have conflated certain figures: Dantzen is a composite of a man who bore that name and a longstanding companion/manservant whom Dickens dubbed "Black John." First person is an unreliable point of view; I chose it for that reason.

In token of my understanding of sex as socially scripted, my novel tips the pen to other novels of female education. In several places I allude to passages from books by Jane Austen and Elena Ferrante about female heroism and education so as to put my book in conversation with those others and to remind us that the novel—like sex, gender, race—is a narrative construction, to some extent, and that, to some extent, we may choose to follow or defy or rewrite these scripts. Specifically, the opening of *Northanger Abbey* informs my passage "No one who had ever seen…"; *The Story of a New Name* informs two descriptions of Barry in Edinburgh: "I arrived at the university…" and "I was not yet eighteen…."

When I first drafted the book in 2012–2016, I was unaware of Jeremy Dronfield and Michael du Preez's impressive research that found Dr. Barry's mother *alive*, if not exactly well, years after they parted in Edinburgh, so in my novel she is *not*. There is debate among biographers about when Margaret was pregnant, whether as an adult or a child; I side with biographer Rachel Holmes in representing this as likely having occurred in 1819, when Barry left Cape Town for Mauritius for an unexplained absence.

I have relied upon the admirably thorough research of scholars and biographers whose books have helped me immeasurably; I owe a particular debt to Rachel Holmes's *The Secret Life of Dr. James Barry: Victorian England's Most Eminent Surgeon* for countless details. Her descriptions of Barry's attire ("emerald-striped jacket…") and the road to the Xhosa ("more rock than road") echo in my own. Late in the writing process, I had the good fortune to consult *Dr. James Barry: A Woman Ahead of Her Time*, a masterly biography by Michael du Preez and Jeremy Dronfield, which clarified many matters large and small; I am grateful to its authors and highly recommend it. Other works consulted include *Jane Austen's England: Daily Life in the Georgian and Regency Periods* by Roy and Lesley Adkins; *Bolívar: American Liberator* by Marie Arana; *The Cape Journals of Lady Anne Barnard, 1797–1798*; *The Political Ideas of the English Romanticists* by Crane Brinton; *Digging Up the Dead: Uncovering the Life and Times of an Extraordinary Surgeon* by Druin Burch; *Getting Medieval: Sexualities and Communities, Pre- and Postmodern* by Carol Dinshaw; *Founding Feminisms in Medieval Studies: Essays in Honor of E. Jane Burns*, edited by Laine E. Doggett and Daniel E. O'Sullivan; *Our Tempestuous Day: A History of Regency England* by Carolly Erickson; *Sexing the Body* by Anne Fausto-Sterling; Alexander Hamilton's *Outlines of the Theory and Practice of Midwifery*; *A Manual of Military Surgery: Or, Hints on the Emergencies of Field, Camp and Hospital* by Samuel David Gross; William Harvey's *On the Motion of the Heart and Blood in Animals*, translated by Robert Willis, revised and edited by Alexander Bowie; *Neo-/Victorian Biographilia and James Miranda Barry: A Study in Transgender and Transgenre* by Ann Heilmann; *Making Sex: Body and Gender from the Greeks to Freud* by Thomas Laqueur; "The Vanished Source: Gossip and Absence in the Cape of Good Hope 'Placard Scandal' of 1824" by Kirsten McKenzie, History, University of Sydney, *ANZLH E-Journal, Refereed Paper No. 6*; *Plantagenet in South Africa: Lord Charles Somerset* by Anthony Kendal Millar; *The Science of Woman: Gynaecology and Gender in England, 1800–1929* by Ornella Moscucci;

An *Elegant Madness: High Society in Regency England* by Venetia Murray; "No. 36 Castle Street East: A Reconstruction of James Barry's House, painting and printmaking studio, and the making of 'The Birth of Pandora'" by Michael Phillips, *The British Art Journal* 9.1 (Spring 2008); *What Jane Austen Ate and Charles Dickens Knew: From Fox Hunting to Whist—the Facts of Daily Life in 19th-Century England* by Daniel Pool (whose description of London docks is echoed in my own: "Cart and carriage wheels…"); *English Society in the 18th Century* by Roy Porter; *Francisco de Miranda: A Transatlantic Life in the Age of Revolution* by Karen Racine; "Slave Orchestras and Rainbow Balls: Colonial Culture and Creolisation at the Cape of Good Hope, 1750–1838" by Anne Marieke van der Wal, in *Identity, Intertextuality, and Performance in Early Modern Song Culture* by D. E. van der Poel, Louis P. Grijp, and Wim van Anrooij; *The Castle of Otranto* by Horace Walpole; *Letters Written During a Short Residence in Sweden, Norway, and Denmark* by Mary Wollstonecraft.

I was moved to write historical fiction by the brilliant novelist Ellis Avery—and her book *The Last Nude*—whose example on and off the page continues to inspire; you are missed. Other novels influenced me as I wrote as well: Lily King's *Euphoria*; Graham Greene's *The End of the Affair*; Kazuo Ishiguro's *The Remains of the Day*; Monique Truong's *The Book of Salt*, and Jeanette Winterson's *Written on the Body*.

This book would not have been written without the generous support of many individuals and institutions: I am grateful for a 2016 F.C. Wood Institute Travel Grant from the College of Physicians of Philadelphia and for time in the Historical Medical Library and Mütter Museum; for a 2014 Faculty Development Fund Award from Colorado State University

(CSU) for time to research and revise; for an invaluable 2012–2013 Professional Development Program Grant from CSU, which enabled crucial travel and early research; Aspen Summer Words Fellowship; Sewanee's Walter E. Dakin Fellowship; my deep thanks to wonderful Chair Louann Reid and my inspiring colleagues and students at Colorado State University; I am especially grateful to Dr. Lynn Shutters for articles on medieval sexuality and gender, and to Liz van Hoose, who told me of the reliquary and whose wonderful advice I tried but failed to take. I am deeply grateful.

My profound thanks go to my brilliant agent, the calm and calming Maria Massie, who introduced me (and Dr. Barry) to my dream editor, Judith Clain. I am incredibly grateful to be working with an editor whose books I have read and admired for years as I wrote my own. This book is markedly better for the keen insights and hard work of Anna de la Rosa and Miya Kumangai and the wonderful team at Little, Brown, especially the sainted Michael Noon, Pamela Marshall, and Sabrina Callahan; and the witty Allan Fallow. Thanks, too, to Kimberly Burns and Aileen Boyle.

I owe a debt to the Writers of the Purple Loins, whom I was trying to charm when I began this, hoping with each chapter to woo you; for crucial medical advice in a time of pandemic, my deep gratitude to Dr. Cris Munoz; to Capetonian Sherry Stanton for her kind rigor and helpful corrections; to Aspen Summer Words and Sewanee friends, who continue to inspire; to all who rallied on behalf of this book—heartfelt thanks; thanks to the *Kenyon Review* crew, both students and colleagues; my thanks to Frank Culbertson, Ted and Kate Kronmiller, Amy and Chris Shank, Céline Leroy, and Nathalie Zberro for your faith and ongoing support; thanks to Nicholas Delbanco, who long ago bet on the horse, and to the immortal Lee K. Abbott and Nancy Zafris; thanks also to Glenda Morgan, who first told me unforgettable stories of the Cape.

My deepest thanks to the family and friends who sustain me in perilous times and celebrate the good ones: my parents, Seymour Levy and Virginia Mae Riggs Levy (who was a heroine all along); Howard Levy, Sawnie Morris and Brian Shields, Lisa Schamess, Dr. Amy Weil, Susan Rosen, Steven Schwartz, Emily Hammond, Stephanie G'Schwind, and above all Maureen Stanton, brilliant writer, best friend, who inspires me daily both as a writer and a person, who has kept the faith and always takes my calls at the help line; neither this book nor I would be here without you; to my beloved partner, Bill, for whom I'm grateful daily, even as we make a most unlikely pair; and to our beloved daughter, Sophia, who—like William Harvey—has changed my understanding of the workings of the human heart.

QUESTIONS AND TOPICS FOR DISCUSSION

1. Set amid the dazzling coast and rugged mountains around Cape Town in the 1810s and 1820s, on the lush island of Mauritius, in glittering Georgian London, and in sodden Edinburgh (when it was an international intellectual hub, the "seat of Scottish genius"), the novel reflects the itinerant life of an army surgeon and colonial officers of the time. How does setting affect Jonathan's development as a student, surgeon, and dandy in the first decades of the nineteenth century? Do the different settings reflect different emotional states?

2. When Margaret is born in Cork, Ireland, in 1795, the rights of women and Catholics (like her family) are severely limited by the state and by common law. In the novel (as in life), Margaret takes on the identity of a young man in 1809 in order to enter Edinburgh's famed medical school, from which women were excluded. What lessons does she need to learn before she can successfully live as a young man? What are some of the crucial steps she takes to master her "role" and live as Jonathan? Does clothing make the man, or is more required? Has such performance of gender ever applied in your life? How so?

3. Education plays a major role in the novel—not only the study of literature and practical medical training, but also social education, including learning gender. Do the rewards and risks of education differ for girls and boys, for men and women? How are they similar? How do they differ? Are such differences a thing of the past, or do they still apply?

4. Throughout the novel, the rights of women in the early nineteenth century—their unequal access to education, to employment, to the fruits of their labor, to the vote, and to political power—is a topic of discussion. Queen Elizabeth I is noted as an exception to the rule, having been a woman more powerful than men 250 years earlier: "She was a son in daughter's clothing" (p.164). Why was Queen Elizabeth an exception? What circumstances and choices liberated her from the usual constraints of her sex in the sixteenth century? Why could she get away with things other women could not? By foregrounding Queen Elizabeth, what point might Dr. Perry and the novel be making about the nature of sex, gender, class, coverture, and power?

5. In the course of the story, Dr. Perry achieves remarkable things—rising from obscure origins to become one of the most renowned surgeons of the day (the first to have performed a successful caesarian section in Africa)—but the doctor also suffers many losses, financial and personal. While a student, Jonathan Perry claims that "knowledge is the only lasting treasure" (125–126). Do you think this is

true? What, if anything, might be more lasting than knowledge? How do you think this view affects his choices?

6. Once he arrives in the Cape Colony in 1816, Dr. Perry becomes an avid collector of native plants, in search of medicinal uses; he is eager to learn the names of plants from local people, but he recognizes there are risks that attend naming—whether categorizing plants, animals, places, or people (166–167). What power do names have in the book? How accurately do people's names reflect their true identities in the novel? Are names a disguise here, or do they tell a deeper truth of these lives?

7. Late in the novel, Dr. Perry says of a friend's marriage, "I hoped they would be happy. Together. I hoped then they might have a child. Love each other well. What could possibly matter more than that?" (325). Given all that Dr. Perry achieved, and given Perry's own sacrifices, do you think this observation is accurate or ironic? Is love what matters most, the measure of a life? Do you think Dr. Perry made the right choice?

8. Throughout much of the novel, Jonathan Perry believes he is lying to everyone but himself. However, at the end of the story, Georgiana confronts him and claims in anger that he is the biggest fraud of them all and has lied to himself the most. Do you agree or disagree? Why or why not? Discuss.

ABOUT THE AUTHOR

E. J. Levy has been featured in *The Paris Review*, *The New York Times*, and *Best American Essays*, among other publications, and has received a Pushcart Prize. Her debut story collection—*Love, in Theory*—won the 2012 Flannery O'Connor Award and the 2014 Great Lakes Colleges Association's New Writers Award. Her anthology, *Tasting Life Twice: Literary Lesbian Fiction by New American Writers*, won a Lambda Literary Award. She holds a degree in History from Yale and an MFA from Ohio State University, where she was the first creative writer to receive a Presidential Fellowship.